NO REASON TO TRUST

NEW YORK TIMES BESTSELLING AUTHOR
TESS GERRITSEN

Previously published as *Never Say Die*
and *Witness Protection*

Recycling programs
for this product may
not exist in your area.

ISBN-13: 978-1-335-40645-3

No Reason to Trust
First published as Never Say Die in 1992.
This edition published in 2021.
Copyright © 1992 by Terry Gerritsen

Witness Protection
First published in 2014. This edition published in 2021.
Copyright © 2014 by Barb Han

This edition published by arrangement with Harlequin Books S.A.

For questions and comments about the quality of this book, please contact us at CustomerService@Harlequin.com.

Harlequin Enterprises ULC
22 Adelaide St. West, 40th Floor
Toronto, Ontario M5H 4E3, Canada
www.Harlequin.com

Printed in U.S.A.

CONTENTS

Internationally bestselling author **Tess Gerritsen** is a graduate of Stanford University and went on to medical school at the University of California, San Francisco, where she was awarded her MD. Since 1987, her books have been translated into thirty-seven languages, and more than twenty-five million copies have been sold around the world. She has received the Nero Award and the RITA® Award, and she was a finalist for the Edgar Award. Now retired from medicine, she writes full-time. She lives in Maine.

Books by Tess Gerritsen

Visit the Author Profile page at Harlequin.com for more titles.

NEVER SAY DIE

Tess Gerritsen

Prologue

1970
Laos–North Vietnam border

Thirty miles out of Muong Sam, they saw the first tracers slash the sky.

Pilot William "Wild Bill" Maitland felt the DeHavilland Twin Otter buck like a filly as they took a hit somewhere back in the fuselage. He pulled into a climb, instinctively opting for the safety of altitude. As the misty mountains dropped away beneath them, a new round of tracers streaked past, splattering the cockpit with flak.

"Damn it, Kozy. You're bad luck," Maitland muttered to his copilot. "Seems like every time we go up together, I taste lead."

Kozlowski went right on chomping his wad of bubble gum. "What's to worry?" he drawled, nodding at the shattered windshield. "Missed ya by at least two inches."

"Try one inch."

"Big difference."

"One extra inch can make a *hell* of a lot of difference."

Kozy laughed and looked out the window. "Yeah, that's what my wife tells me."

The door to the cockpit swung open. Valdez, the cargo kicker, his shoulders bulky with a parachute pack, stuck his head in. "What the hell's goin' on any—" He froze as another tracer spiraled past.

"Got us some mighty big mosquitoes out there," Kozlowski said and blew a huge pink bubble.

"What was that?" asked Valdez. "AK-47?"

"Looks more like .57-millimeter," said Maitland.

"They didn't say nothin' about no .57s. What kind of briefing did we get, anyway?"

Kozlowski shrugged. "Only the best your tax dollars can buy."

"How's our 'cargo' holding up?" Maitland asked. "Pants still dry?"

Valdez leaned forward and confided, "Man, we got us one weird passenger back there."

"So what's new?" Kozlowski said.

"I mean, this one's *really* strange. Got flak flyin' all 'round and he doesn't bat an eye. Just sits there like he's floatin' on some lily pond. You should see the medallion he's got 'round his neck. Gotta weigh at least a kilo."

"Come on," said Kozlowski.

"I'm tellin' you, Kozy, he's got a kilo of gold hangin' around that fat little neck of his. Who is he?"

"Some Lao VIP," said Maitland.

"That all they told you?"

"I'm just the delivery boy. Don't need to know any more than that." Maitland leveled the DeHavilland off at eight thousand feet. Glancing back through the open cockpit doorway, he caught sight of their lone passenger sitting placidly among the jumble of supply crates. In the dim cabin, the Lao's face gleamed like burnished mahogany. His eyes were closed, and his lips were moving silently. In prayer? wondered Maitland. Yes, the man was definitely one of their more interesting cargoes.

Not that Maitland hadn't carried strange passengers before. In his ten years with Air America, he'd transported German shepherds and generals, gibbons and girlfriends. And he'd fly them anywhere they had to go. If hell had a landing strip, he liked to say, he'd take them there—as long as they had a ticket. Anything, anytime, anywhere, was the rule at Air America.

"Song Ma River," said Kozlowski, glancing down through the fingers of mist at the lush jungle floor. "Lot of cover. If they got any more .57s in place, we're gonna have us a hard landing."

"Gonna be a hard landing anyhow," said Maitland, taking stock of the velvety green ridges on either side of them. The valley was narrow; he'd have to swoop in fast and low. It was a hellishly short landing strip, nothing but a pin scratch in the jungle, and there was always the chance of an unreported gun emplacement. But the orders were to drop the Lao VIP, whoever he was, just inside North Vietnamese territory. No return pickup had been scheduled; it sounded to Maitland like a one-way trip to oblivion.

"Heading down in a minute," he called over his

shoulder to Valdez. "Get the passenger ready. He's gonna have to hit the ground running."

"He says that crate goes with him."

"What? I didn't hear anything about a crate."

"They loaded it on at the last minute. Right after we took on supplies for Nam Tha. Pretty heavy sucker. I might need some help."

Kozlowski resignedly unbuckled his seatbelt. "Okay," he said with a sigh. "But remember, I don't get paid for kickin' crates."

Maitland laughed. "What the hell *do* you get paid for?"

"Oh, lots of things," Kozlowski said lazily, ducking past Valdez and through the cockpit door. "Eatin'. Sleepin'. Tellin' dirty jokes—"

His last words were cut off by a deafening blast that shattered Maitland's eardrums. The explosion sent Kozlowski—or what was left of Kozlowski—flying backward into the cockpit. Blood spattered the control panel, obscuring the altimeter dial. But Maitland didn't need the altimeter to tell him they were going down fast.

"Kozy!" screamed Valdez, staring down at the remains of the copilot. *"Kozy!"*

His words were almost lost in the howling maelstrom of wind. The DeHavilland shuddered, a wounded bird fighting to stay aloft. Maitland, wrestling with the controls, knew immediately that he'd lost hydraulics. The best he could hope for was a belly flop on the jungle canopy.

He glanced back to survey the damage and saw, through a swirling cloud of debris, the bloodied body of the Lao passenger, thrown against the crates. He also saw sunlight shining through oddly twisted steel, glimpsed blue sky and clouds where the cargo door should have been. What the hell? Had the blast come from *inside* the plane?

He screamed to Valdez, "Bail out!"

The cargo kicker didn't respond; he was still staring in horror at Kozlowski.

Maitland gave him a shove. "Get the hell *out* of here!"

Valdez at last reacted. He stumbled out of the cockpit and into the morass of broken crates and rent metal. At the gaping cargo door he paused. "Maitland?" he yelled over the wind's shriek.

Their gazes met, and in that split second, they knew. They both knew. It was the last time they'd see each other alive.

"I'll be out!" Maitland shouted. *"Go!"*

Valdez backed up a few steps. Then he launched himself out the cargo door.

Maitland didn't glance back to see if Valdez's parachute had opened; he had other things to worry about.

The plane was sputtering into a dive.

Even as he reached for his harness release, he knew his luck had run out. He had neither the time nor the altitude to struggle into his parachute. He'd never believed in wearing one anyway. Strapping it on was like admitting you didn't trust your skill as a pilot, and Maitland knew—everyone knew—that he was the best.

Calmly he refastened his harness and grasped the controls. Through the shattered cockpit window he watched the jungle floor, lush and green and heart-wrenchingly beautiful, swoop up to meet him. Somehow he'd always known it would end this way: the wind whistling through his crippled plane, the ground rushing toward him, his hands gripping the controls. This time he wouldn't be walking away....

It was startling, this sudden recognition of his own mortality. An astonishing thought. *I'm going to die.*

And astonishment was exactly what he felt as the DeHavilland sliced into the treetops.

Vientiane, Laos

At 1900 hours the report came in that Air America Flight 5078 had vanished.

In the Operations Room of the U.S. Army Liaison, Colonel Joseph Kistner and his colleagues from Central and Defense Intelligence greeted the news with shocked silence. Had their operation, so carefully conceived, so vital to U.S. interests, met with disaster?

Colonel Kistner immediately demanded confirmation.

The command at Air America provided the details. Flight 5078, due in Nam Tha at 1500 hours, had never arrived. A search of the presumed flight path—carried on until darkness intervened—had revealed no sign of wreckage. But flak had been reported heavy near the border, and .57-millimeter gun emplacements were noted just out of Muong Sam. To make things worse, the terrain was mountainous, the weather unpredictable and the number of alternative nonhostile landing strips limited.

It was a reasonable assumption that Flight 5078 had been shot down.

Grim acceptance settled on the faces of the men gathered around the table. Their brightest hope had just perished aboard a doomed plane. They looked at Kistner and awaited his decision.

"Resume the search at daybreak," he said.

"That'd be throwing away live men after dead," said the CIA officer. "Come on, gentlemen. We all know that crew's gone."

Cold-blooded bastard, thought Kistner. But as always, he was right. The colonel gathered together his papers and rose to his feet. "It's not the men we're searching for," he said. "It's the wreckage. I want it located."

"And then what?"

Kistner snapped his briefcase shut. "We melt it."

The CIA officer nodded in agreement. No one argued the point. The operation had met with disaster. There was nothing more to be done.

Except destroy the evidence.

Chapter 1

Present
Bangkok, Thailand

General Joe Kistner did not sweat, a fact that utterly amazed Willy Jane Maitland, since she herself seemed to be sweating through her sensible cotton underwear, through her sleeveless chambray blouse, all the way through her wrinkled twill skirt. Kistner looked like the sort of man who ought to be sweating rivers in this heat. He had a fiercely ruddy complexion, bulldog jowls, a nose marbled with spidery red veins, and a neck so thick, it strained to burst free of his crisp military collar. *Every inch the blunt, straight-talking, tough old soldier,* she thought. *Except for the eyes. They're uneasy. Evasive.*

Those eyes, a pale, chilling blue, were now gazing across the veranda. In the distance the lush Thai hills seemed to steam in the afternoon heat. "You're on a fool's errand, Miss Maitland," he said. "It's been twenty years. Surely you agree your father is dead."

"My mother's never accepted it. She needs a body to bury, General."

Kistner sighed. "Of course. The wives. It's always the wives. There were so many widows, one tends to forget—"

"*She* hasn't forgotten."

"I'm not sure what I can tell you. What I ought to tell you." He turned to her, his pale eyes targeting her face. "And really, Miss Maitland, what purpose does this serve? Except to satisfy your curiosity?"

That irritated her. It made her mission seem trivial, and there were few things Willy resented more than being made to feel insignificant. Especially by a puffed up, flat-topped warmonger. Rank didn't impress her, certainly not after all the military stuffed shirts she'd met in the past few months. They'd all expressed their sympathy, told her they couldn't help her and proceeded to brush off her questions. But Willy wasn't a woman to be stonewalled. She'd chip away at their silence until they'd either answer her or kick her out.

Lately, it seemed, she'd been kicked out of quite a few offices.

"This matter is for the Casualty Resolution Committee," said Kistner. "They're the proper channel to go—"

"They say they can't help me."

"Neither can I."

"We both know you can."

There was a pause. Softly, he asked, "Do we?"

She leaned forward, intent on claiming the advantage. "I've done my homework, General. I've written letters, talked to dozens of people—everyone who had anything to do with that last mission. And whenever I mention Laos or Air America or Flight 5078, your name keeps popping up."

He gave her a faint smile. "How nice to be remembered."

"I heard you were the military attaché in Vientiane. That your office commissioned my father's last flight. And that you personally ordered that final mission."

"Where did you hear *that* rumor?"

"My contacts at Air America. Dad's old buddies. I'd call them a reliable source."

Kistner didn't respond at first. He was studying her as carefully as he would a battle plan. "I may have issued such an order," he conceded.

"Meaning you don't remember?"

"Meaning it's something I'm not at liberty to discuss. This is classified information. What happened in Laos is an extremely sensitive topic."

"We're not discussing military secrets here. The war's been over for fifteen years!"

Kistner fell silent, surprised by her vehemence. Given her unassuming size, it was especially startling. Obviously Willy Maitland, who stood five-two, tops, in her bare feet, could be as scrappy as any six-foot marine, and she wasn't afraid to fight. From the minute she'd walked onto his veranda, her shoulders squared, her jaw angled stubbornly, he'd known this was not a woman to be ignored. She reminded him of that old Eisenhower chestnut, "It's not the size of the dog in the fight but the size of the fight in the dog." Three wars, fought in Japan, Korea and Nam, had taught Kistner never to underestimate the enemy.

He wasn't about to underestimate Wild Bill Maitland's daughter, either.

He shifted his gaze across the wide veranda to the brilliant green mountains. In a wrought-iron birdcage, a macaw screeched out a defiant protest.

At last Kistner began to speak. "Flight 5078 took off from Vientiane with a crew of three—your father, a cargo kicker and a copilot. Sometime during the flight, they diverted across North Vietnamese territory, where we assume they were shot down by enemy fire. Only the cargo kicker, Luis Valdez, managed to bail out. He was immediately captured by the North Vietnamese. Your father was never found."

"That doesn't mean he's dead. Valdez survived—"

"I'd hardly call the man's outcome 'survival.'"

They paused, a momentary silence for the man who'd endured five years as a POW, only to be shattered by his return to civilization. Luis Valdez had returned home on a Saturday and shot himself on Sunday.

"You left something out, General," said Willy. "I've heard there was a passenger...."

"Oh. Yes," said Kistner, not missing a beat. "I'd forgotten."

"Who was he?"

Kistner shrugged. "A Lao. His name's not important."

"Was he with Intelligence?"

"That information, Miss Maitland, is classified." He looked away, a gesture that told her the subject of the Lao was definitely off-limits. "After the plane went down," he continued, "we mounted a search. But the ground fire was hot. And it became clear that if anyone *had* survived, they'd be in enemy hands."

"So you left them there."

"We don't believe in throwing lives away, Miss Maitland. That's what a rescue operation would've been. Throwing live men after dead."

Yes, she could see his reasoning. He was a military tactician, not given to sentimentality. Even now, he sat ramrod straight in his chair, his eyes calmly surveying the verdant hills surrounding his villa, as though eternally in search of some enemy.

"We never found the crash site," he continued. "But that jungle could swallow up anything. All that mist and smoke hanging over the valleys. The trees so thick, the ground never sees the light of day. But you'll get a feeling for it yourself soon enough. When are you leaving for Saigon?"

"Tomorrow morning."

"And the Vietnamese have agreed to discuss this matter?"

"I didn't tell them my reason for coming. I was afraid I might not get the visa."

"A wise move. They aren't fond of controversy. What *did* you tell them?"

"That I'm a plain old tourist." She shook her head and laughed. "I'm on the deluxe private tour. Six cities in two weeks."

"That's what one has to do in Asia. You don't confront the issues. You dance around them." He looked at his watch, a clear signal that the interview had come to an end.

They rose to their feet. As they shook hands, she felt him give her one last, appraising look. His grip was brisk and matter-of-fact, exactly what she expected from an old war dog.

"Good luck, Miss Maitland," he said with a nod of dismissal. "I hope you find what you're looking for."

He turned to look off at the mountains. That's when she noticed for the first time that tiny beads of sweat were glistening like diamonds on his forehead.

General Kistner watched as the woman, escorted by a servant, walked back toward the house. He was uneasy. He remembered Wild Bill Maitland only too clearly, and the daughter was very much like him. There would be trouble.

He went to the tea table and rang a silver bell. The tinkling drifted across the expanse of veranda, and seconds later, Kistner's secretary appeared.

"Has Mr. Barnard arrived?" Kistner asked.

"He has been waiting for half an hour," the man replied.

"And Ms. Maitland's driver?"

"I sent him away, as you directed."

"Good." Kistner nodded. "Good."

"Shall I bring Mr. Barnard in to see you?"

"No. Tell him I'm canceling my appointments. Tomorrow's, as well."

The secretary frowned. "He will be quite annoyed."

"Yes, I imagine he will be," said Kistner as he turned and headed toward his office. "But that's his problem."

A Thai servant in a crisp white jacket escorted Willy through an echoing, cathedral-like hall to the reception room. There he stopped and gave her a politely questioning look. "You wish me to call a car?" he asked.

"No, thank you. My driver will take me back."

The servant looked puzzled. "But your driver left some time ago."

"He couldn't have!" She glanced out the window in annoyance. "He was supposed to wait for—"

"Perhaps he is parked in the shade beyond the trees. I will go and look."

Through the French windows, Willy watched as the servant skipped gracefully down the steps to the road. The estate was vast and lushly planted; a car could very well be hidden in that jungle. Just beyond the driveway, a gardener clipped a hedge of jasmine. A neatly graveled path traced a route across the lawn to a tree-shaded garden of flowers and stone benches. And in the far distance, a fairy blue haze seemed to hang over the city of Bangkok.

The sound of a masculine throat being cleared caught her attention. She turned and for the first time noticed the man standing in a far corner of the reception room. He cocked his head in a casual acknowledgment of her presence. She caught a glimpse of a crooked grin, a stray lock of brown hair drooping over a tanned forehead. Then he turned his attention back to the antique tapestry on the wall.

Strange. He didn't look like the sort of man who'd be interested in moth-eaten embroidery. A patch of sweat had soaked through the back of his khaki shirt, and his sleeves were shoved up carelessly to his elbows. His trousers looked as if they'd been slept in for a week. A briefcase, stamped U.S. Army ID Lab, sat on the floor beside him, but he didn't strike her as the military type. There was certainly nothing disciplined about his posture. He'd seem more at home slouching at a bar somewhere instead of cooling his heels in General Kistner's marble reception room.

"Miss Maitland?"

The servant was back, shaking his head apologetically. "There must have been a misunderstanding. The gardener says your driver returned to the city."

"Oh, no." She looked out the window in frustration. "How do I get back to Bangkok?"

"Perhaps General Kistner's driver can take you back? He has gone up the road to make a delivery, but he should return very soon. If you wish, you can see the garden in the meantime."

"Yes. Yes, I suppose that'd be nice."

The servant, smiling proudly, opened the door. "It is a very famous garden. General Kistner is known for his collection of dendrobiums. You will find them at the end of the path, near the carp pond."

She stepped out into the steam bath of late afternoon and started down the gravel path. Except for the *clack-clack* of the gardener's hedge clippers, the day was absolutely still. She headed toward a stand of trees. But halfway across the lawn she suddenly stopped and looked back at the house.

At first all she saw was sunlight glaring off the marble facade. Then she focused on the first floor and saw the figure of a man standing at one of the windows. The servant, perhaps?

Turning, she continued along the path. But every step of the way, she was acutely aware that someone was watching her.

Guy Barnard stood at the French windows and observed the woman cross the lawn to the garden. He liked the way the sunlight seemed to dance in her clipped, honey-colored hair. He also liked the way she moved, the coltish swing of her walk. Methodically, his gaze slid down, over the sleeveless blouse and the skirt with its regrettably sensible hemline, taking in the essentials. Trim waist. Sweet hips. Nice calves. Nice ankles. Nice...

He reluctantly cut off that disturbing train of thought. This was not a good time to be distracted. Still, he couldn't help one last appreciative glance at the diminutive figure. Okay, so she was a touch on the scrawny side. But she had great legs. Definitely great legs.

Footsteps clipped across the marble floor. Guy turned and saw Kistner's secretary, an unsmiling Thai with a beardless face.

"Mr. Barnard?" said the secretary. "Our apologies for the delay. But an urgent matter has come up."

"Will he see me now?"

The secretary shifted uneasily. "I am afraid—"

"I've been waiting since three."

"Yes, I understand. But there is a problem. It seems General Kistner cannot meet with you as planned."

"May I remind you that I didn't request this meeting. General Kistner did."

"Yes, but—"

"I've taken time out of *my* busy schedule—" he took the liberty of exaggeration "—to drive all the way out here, and—"

"I understand, but—"

"At least tell me why he insisted on this appointment."

"You will have to ask him."

Guy, who up till now had kept his irritation in check,

drew himself up straight. Though he wasn't a particularly tall man, he stood a full head taller than the secretary. "Is this how the general normally conducts business?"

The secretary merely shrugged. "I am sorry, Mr. Barnard. The change was entirely unexpected...." His gaze shifted momentarily and focused on something beyond the French windows.

Guy followed the man's gaze. Through the glass, he saw what the man was looking at: the woman with the honey-colored hair.

The secretary shuffled his feet, a signal that he had other duties to attend to. "I assure you, Mr. Barnard," he said, "if you call in a few days, we will arrange another appointment."

Guy snatched up his briefcase and headed for the door. "In a few days," he said, "I'll be in Saigon."

A whole afternoon wasted, he thought in disgust as he walked down the front steps. He swore again as he reached the empty driveway. His car was parked a good hundred yards away, in the shade of a poinciana tree. The driver was nowhere to be seen. Knowing Puapong, the man was probably off flirting with the gardener's daughter.

Resignedly Guy trudged toward the car. The sun was like a broiler, and waves of heat radiated from the gravel road. Halfway to the car, he happened to glance at the garden, and he spotted the honey-haired woman, sitting on a stone bench. She looked dejected. No wonder; it was a long drive back to town, and Lord only knew when her ride would turn up.

What the hell, he thought, starting toward her. He could use some company.

She seemed to be deep in thought; she didn't look up until he was standing right beside her.

"Hi there," he said.

She squinted up at him. "Hello." Her greeting was neutral, neither friendly nor unfriendly.

"Did I hear you needed a lift back to town?"

"I have one, thank you."

"It could be a long wait. And I'm heading there anyway." She didn't respond, so he added, "It's really no trouble."

She gave him a speculative look. She had silver-gray eyes, direct, unflinching; they seemed to stare right through him. No shrinking violet, this one. Glancing back at the house, she said, "Kistner's driver was going to take me...."

"I'm here. He isn't."

Again she gave him that look, a silent third degree. She must have decided he was okay, because she finally rose to her feet. "Thanks. I'd appreciate it."

Together they walked the graveled road to his car. As they approached, Guy noticed a back door was wide open and a pair of dirty brown feet poked out. His driver was sprawled across the seat like a corpse.

The woman halted, staring at the lifeless form. "Oh, my God. He's not—"

A blissful snore rumbled from the car.

"He's not," said Guy. "Hey. Puapong!" He banged on the car roof.

The man's answering rumble could have drowned out thunder.

"Hello, Sleeping Beauty!" Guy banged the car again. "You gonna wake up, or do I have to kiss you first?"

"What? What?" groaned a voice. Puapong stirred

and opened one bloodshot eye. "Hey, boss. You back so soon?"

"Have a nice nap?" Guy asked pleasantly.

"Not bad."

Guy graciously gestured for Puapong to vacate the back seat. "Look, I hate to be a pest, but do you mind? I've offered this lady a ride."

Puapong crawled out, stumbled around sleepily to the driver's seat and sank behind the wheel. He shook his head a few times, then fished around on the floor for the car keys.

The woman was looking more and more dubious. "Are you sure he can drive?" she muttered under her breath.

"This man," said Guy, "has the reflexes of a cat. When he's sober."

"*Is* he sober?"

"Puapong! Are you sober?"

With injured pride, the driver asked, "Don't I look sober?"

"There's your answer," said Guy.

The woman sighed. "That makes me feel *so* much better." She glanced back longingly at the house. The Thai servant had appeared on the steps and was waving goodbye.

Guy motioned for the woman to climb in. "It's a long drive back to town."

She was silent as they drove down the winding mountain road. Though they both sat in the back seat, two feet apart at the most, she seemed a million miles away. She kept her gaze focused on the scenery.

"You were in with the general quite a while," he noted.

She nodded. "I had a lot of questions."

"You a reporter?"

"What?" She looked at him. "Oh, no. It was just... some old family business."

He waited for her to elaborate, but she turned back to the window.

"Must've been some pretty important family business," he said.

"Why do you say that?"

"Right after you left, he canceled all his appointments. Mine included."

"You didn't get in to see him?"

"Never got past the secretary. And Kistner's the one who asked to see *me*."

She frowned for a moment, obviously puzzled. Then she shrugged. "I'm sure I had nothing to do with it."

And I'm just as sure you did, he thought in sudden irritation. Lord, why was the woman making him so antsy? She was sitting perfectly still, but he got the distinct feeling a hurricane was churning in that pretty head. He'd decided that she *was* pretty after all, in a no-nonsense sort of way. She was smart not to use any makeup; it would only cheapen that girl-next-door face. He'd never before had any interest in the girl-next-door type. Maybe the girl down the street or across the tracks. But this one was different. She had eyes the color of smoke, a square jaw and a little boxer's nose, lightly dusted with freckles. She also had a mouth that, given the right situation, could be quite kissable.

Automatically he asked, "So how long will you be in Bangkok?"

"I've been here two days already. I'm leaving tomorrow."

Damn, he thought.

"For Saigon."

His chin snapped up in surprise. "Saigon?"

"Or Ho Chi Minh City. Whatever they call it these days."

"Now that's a coincidence," he said softly.

"What is?"

"In two days, *I'm* leaving for Saigon."

"Are you?" She glanced at the briefcase, stenciled with U.S. Army ID Lab, lying on the seat. "Government affairs?"

He nodded. "What about you?"

She looked straight ahead. "Family business."

"Right," he said, wondering what the hell business her family was in. "You ever been to Saigon?"

"Once. But I was only ten years old."

"Dad in the service?"

"Sort of." Her gaze stayed fixed on some faraway point ahead. "I don't remember too much of the city. Lot of dust and heat and cars. One big traffic jam. And the beautiful women…"

"It's changed a lot since then. Most of the cars are gone."

"And the beautiful women?"

He laughed. "Oh, they're still around. Along with the heat and dust. But everything else has changed." He was silent a moment. Then, almost as an afterthought, he added, "If you get stuck, I might be able to show you around."

She hesitated, obviously tempted by his invitation. *Come on, come on, take me up on it,* he thought. Then he caught a glimpse of Puapong, grinning and winking wickedly at him in the rearview mirror.

He only hoped the woman hadn't noticed.

But Willy most certainly *had* seen Puapong's winks and grins and had instantly comprehended the meaning. *Here we go again,* she thought wearily. *Now he'll ask me if I want to have dinner and I'll say no I can't, and then he'll say, what about a drink? and I'll break down and say yes because he's such a damnably good-looking man....*

"Look, I happen to be free tonight," he said. "Would you like to have dinner?"

"I can't," she said, wondering who had written this tired script and how one ever broke out of it.

"Then how about a drink?" He shot her a half smile and she felt herself teetering at the edge of a very high cliff. The crazy part was, he really *wasn't* a handsome man at all. His nose was crooked, as if, after managing to get it broken, he hadn't bothered to set it back in place. His hair was in need of a barber or at least a comb. She guessed he was somewhere in his late thirties, though the years scarcely showed except around his eyes, where deep laugh lines creased the corners. No, she'd seen far better-looking men. Men who offered more than a sweaty one-night grope in a foreign hotel.

So why is this guy getting to me?

"Just a drink?" he offered again.

"Thanks," she said. "But no thanks."

To her relief, he didn't press the issue. He nodded, sat back and looked out the window. His fingers drummed the briefcase. The mindless rhythm drove her crazy. She tried to ignore him, just as he was trying to ignore her, but it was hopeless. He was too imposing a presence.

By the time they pulled up at the Oriental Hotel, she was ready to leap out of the car. She practically did.

"Thanks for the ride," she said, and slammed the door shut.

"Hey, wait!" called the man through the open window. "I never caught your name!"

"Willy."

"You have a last name?"

She turned and started up the hotel steps. "Maitland," she said over her shoulder.

"See you around, Willy Maitland!" the man yelled.

Not likely, she thought. But as she reached the lobby doors, she couldn't help glancing back and watching the car disappear around the corner. That's when she realized she didn't even know the man's name.

Guy sat on his bed in the Liberty Hotel and wondered what had compelled him to check into this dump. Nostalgia, maybe. Plus cheap government rates. He'd always stayed here on his trips to Bangkok, ever since the war, and he'd never seen the need for a change until now. Certainly the place held a lot of memories. He'd never forget those hot, lusty nights of 1973. He'd been a twenty-year-old private on R and R; she'd been a thirty-year-old army nurse. Darlene. Yeah, that was her name. The last he'd seen of her, she was a chain-smoking mother of three and about fifty pounds overweight. What a shame. The woman, like the hotel, had definitely gone downhill.

Maybe I have, too, he thought wearily as he stared out the dirty window at the streets of Bangkok. How he used to love this city, loved the days of wandering through the markets, where the colors were so bright they hurt the eyes; loved the nights of prowling the back streets of Pat Pong, where the music and the girls never quit. Nothing bothered him in those days—not the noise or the heat or the smells.

Not even the bullets. He'd felt immune, immortal. It was always the *other* guy who caught the bullet, the other guy who got shipped home in a box. And if you thought otherwise, if you worried too long and hard about your own mortality, you made a lousy soldier.

Eventually, he'd become a lousy soldier.

He was still astonished that he'd survived. It was something he'd never fully understand: the simple fact that he'd made it back alive.

Especially when he thought of all the other men on that transport plane out of Da Nang. Their ticket home, the magic bird that was supposed to deliver them from all the madness.

He still had the scars from the crash. He still harbored a mortal dread of flying.

He refused to think about that upcoming flight to Saigon. Air travel, unfortunately, was part of his job, and this was just one more plane he couldn't avoid.

He opened his briefcase, took out a stack of folders and lay down on the bed to read. The file he opened first was one of dozens he'd brought with him from Honolulu. Each contained a name, rank, serial number, photograph and a detailed history—as detailed as possible—of the circumstances of disappearance. This one was a naval airman, Lieutenant Commander Eugene Stoddard, last seen ejecting from his disabled bomber forty miles west of Hanoi. Included was a dental chart and an old X-ray report of an arm fracture sustained as a teenager. What the file left out were the nonessentials: the wife he'd left behind, the children, the questions.

There were always questions when a soldier was missing in action.

Guy skimmed the pages, made a few mental notes and reached for another file. These were the most likely cases, the men whose stories best matched the newest collection of remains. The Vietnamese government was turning over three sets, and Guy's job was to confirm the skeletons were non-Vietnamese and to give each one a name, rank and serial number. It wasn't a particularly pleasant job, but one that had to be done.

He set aside the second file and reached for the next.

This one didn't contain a photograph; it was a supplementary file, one he'd reluctantly added to his briefcase at the last minute. The cover was stamped Confidential, then, a year ago, restamped Declassified. He opened the file and frowned at the first page.

Code Name: Friar Tuck
Status: Open (Current as of 10/85)
File Contains:
1. Summary of Witness Reports
2. Possible Identities
3. Search Status

Friar Tuck. A legend known to every soldier who'd fought in Nam. During the war, Guy had assumed those tales of a rogue American pilot flying for the enemy were mere fantasy.

Then, a few weeks ago, he'd learned otherwise.

He'd been at his desk at the Army Lab when two men, representatives of an organization called the Ariel Group, had appeared in his office. "We have a proposition," they'd said. "We know you're visiting Nam soon, and we want you to look for a war criminal." The man they were seeking was Friar Tuck.

"You've got to be kidding." Guy had laughed. "I'm not a military cop. And there's no such man. He's a fairy tale."

In answer, they'd handed him a twenty-thousand-dollar check—"for expenses," they'd said. There'd be more to come if he brought the traitor back to justice.

"And if I don't want the job?" he'd asked.

"You can hardly refuse," was their answer. Then they'd told Guy exactly what they knew about him, about his past, the thing he'd done in the war. A brutal secret that could destroy him, a secret he'd kept hidden away behind a wall of fear and self-loathing. They told him exactly what he could expect if it came to light. The hard glare of publicity. The trial. The jail cell.

They had him cornered. He took the check and awaited the next contact.

The day before he left Honolulu, this file had arrived special delivery from Washington. Without looking at it, he'd slipped it into his briefcase.

Now he read it for the first time, pausing at the page listing possible identities. Several names he recognized from his stack of MIA files, and it struck him as unfair, this list. These men were missing in action and probably dead; to brand them as possible traitors was an insult to their memories.

One by one, he went over the names of those voiceless pilots suspected of treason. Halfway down the list, he stopped, focusing on the entry "William T. Maitland, pilot, Air America." Beside it was an asterisk and, below, the footnote: "Refer to File #M-70-4163, Defense Intelligence. (Classified.)"

William T. Maitland, he thought, trying to remember where he'd heard the name. Maitland, Maitland.

Then he thought of the woman at Kistner's villa, the little blonde with the magnificent legs. I'm here on family business, she'd said. For that she'd consulted General Joe Kistner, a man whose connections to Defense Intelligence were indisputable.

See you around, Willy Maitland.

It was too much of a coincidence. And yet...

He went back to the first page and reread the file on Friar Tuck, beginning to end. The section on Search Status he read twice. Then he rose from the bed and began to pace the room, considering his options. Not liking any of them.

He didn't believe in using people. But the stakes were sky-high, and they were deeply, intensely personal. *How many men have their own little secrets from the war?* he wondered. *Secrets we can't talk about? Secrets that could destroy us?*

He closed the file. The information in this folder wasn't enough; he needed the woman's help.

But am I cold-blooded enough to use her?

Can I afford not to? whispered the voice of necessity.

It was an awful decision to make. But he had no choice.

It was 5:00 p.m., and the Bong Bong Club was not yet in full swing. Up onstage, three women, bodies oiled and gleaming, writhed together like a trio of snakes. Music blared from an old stereo speaker, a relentlessly primitive beat that made the very darkness shudder.

From his favorite corner table, Siang watched the action, the men sipping drinks, the waitresses dangling after tips. Then he focused on the stage, on the girl in the middle. She was special. Lush hips, meaty thighs, a pink, carnivorous tongue. He couldn't define what it was about her eyes, but she had *that look*. The numeral 7 was pinned on her G-string. He would have to inquire later about number seven.

"Good afternoon, Mr. Siang."

Siang looked up to see the man standing in the shadows. It never failed to impress him, the size of that man. Even now, twenty years after their first meeting, Siang could not help feeling he was a child in the presence of this giant.

The man ordered a beer and sat down at the table. He watched the stage for a moment. "A new act?" he asked.

"The one in the middle is new."

"Ah, yes, very nice. Your type, is she?"

"I will have to find out." Siang took a sip of whiskey, his gaze never leaving the stage. "You said you had a job for me."

"A small matter."

"I hope that does not mean a small reward."

The man laughed softly. "No, no. Have I ever been less than generous?"

"What is the name?"

"A woman." The man slid a photograph onto the table. "Her name is Willy Maitland. Thirty-two years old. Five foot two, dark blond hair cut short, gray eyes. Staying at the Oriental Hotel."

"American?"

"Yes."

Siang paused. "An unusual request."

"There is some…urgency."

Ah. The price goes up, thought Siang. "Why?" he asked.

"She departs for Saigon tomorrow morning. That leaves you only tonight."

Siang nodded and looked back at the stage. He was pleased to see that the girl in the middle, number seven, was looking straight at him. "That should be time enough," he said.

Willy Maitland was standing at the river's edge, staring down at the swirling water.

From across the dining terrace, Guy spotted her, a tiny figure leaning at the railing, her short hair fluffing in the wind. From the hunch of her shoulders, the determined focus of her gaze, he got the impression she wanted to be left alone. Stopping at the bar, he picked up a beer—Oranjeboom, a good Dutch brand he hadn't tasted in years. He stood there a moment, watching her, savoring the touch of the frosty bottle against his cheek.

She still hadn't moved. She just kept gazing down at the river, as though hypnotized by something she saw in the muddy depths. He moved across the terrace toward her, weaving past empty tables and chairs, and eased up beside her at the railing. He marveled at the way her hair seemed to reflect the red and gold sparks of sunset.

"Nice view," he said.

She glanced at him. One look, utterly uninterested, was all she gave him. Then she turned away.

He set his beer on the railing. "Thought I'd check back with you. See if you'd changed your mind about that drink."

She stared stubbornly at the water.

"I know how it is in a foreign city. No one to share

your frustrations. I thought you might be feeling a little—"

"Give me a break," she said, and walked away.

He must be losing his touch, he thought. He snatched up his beer and followed her. Pointedly ignoring him, she strolled along the edge of the terrace, every so often flicking her hair off her face. She had a cute swing to her walk, just a little too frisky to be considered graceful.

"I think we should have dinner," he said, keeping pace. "And maybe a little conversation."

"About what?"

"Oh, we could start off with the weather. Move on to politics. Religion. My family, your family."

"I assume this is all leading up to something?"

"Well, yeah."

"Let me guess. An invitation to your room?"

"Is that what you think I'm trying to do?" he asked in a hurt voice. "Pick you up?"

"Aren't you?" she said. Then she turned and once again walked away.

This time he didn't follow her. He didn't see the point. Leaning back against the rail, he sipped his beer and watched her climb the steps to the dining terrace. There, she sat down at a table and retreated behind a menu. It was too late for tea and too early for supper. Except for a dozen boisterous Italians sitting at a nearby table, the terrace was empty. He lingered there a while, finishing off the beer, wondering what his next approach should be. Wondering if anything would work. She was a tough nut to crack, surprisingly fierce for a dame who barely came up to his shoulder. A mouse with teeth.

He needed another beer. And a new strategy. He'd think of it in a minute.

He headed up the steps, back to the bar. As he crossed the dining terrace, he couldn't help a backward glance at the woman. Those few seconds of inattention almost caused him to collide with a well-dressed Thai man moving in the opposite direction. Guy murmured an automatic apology. The other man didn't answer; he walked right on past, his gaze fixed on something ahead.

Guy took about two steps before some inner alarm went off in his head. It was pure instinct, the soldier's premonition of disaster. It had to do with the eyes of the man who'd just passed by.

He'd seen that look of deadly calm once before, in the eyes of a Vietnamese. They had brushed shoulders as Guy was leaving a popular Da Nang nightclub. For a split second their gazes had locked. Even now, years later, Guy still remembered the chill he'd felt looking into that man's eyes. Two minutes later, as Guy had stood waiting in the street for his buddies, a bomb ripped apart the building. Seventeen Americans had been killed.

Now, with a growing sense of alarm, he watched the Thai stop and survey his surroundings. The man seemed to spot what he was looking for and headed toward the dining terrace. Only two of the tables were occupied. The Italians sat at one, Willy Maitland at the other. At the edge of the terrace, the Thai paused and reached into his jacket.

Reflexively, Guy took a few steps forward. Even before his eyes registered the danger, his body was already reacting. Something glittered in the man's hand, an object that caught the bloodred glare of sunset. Only then could Guy rationally acknowledge what his instincts had warned him was about to happen.

He screamed, "Willy! Watch out!"

Then he launched himself at the assassin.

Chapter 2

At the sound of the man's shout, Willy lowered her menu and turned. To her amazement, she saw it was the crazy American, toppling chairs as he barreled across the cocktail lounge. What was that lunatic up to now?

In disbelief, she watched him shove past a waiter and fling himself at another man, a well-dressed Thai. The two bodies collided. At the same instant, she heard something hiss through the air, felt an unexpected flick of pain in her arm. She leapt up from her chair as the two men slammed to the ground near her feet.

At the next table, the Italians were also out of their chairs, pointing and shouting. The bodies on the ground rolled over and over, toppling tables, sending sugar bowls crashing to the stone terrace. Willy was lost in utter confusion. What was happening? Why was that idiot fighting with a Thai businessman?

Both men staggered to their feet. The Thai kicked high, his heel thudding squarely into the other man's belly. The American doubled over, groaned and landed with his back propped up against the terrace wall.

The Thai vanished.

By now the Italians were hysterical.

Willy scrambled through the fallen chairs and shattered crockery and crouched at the man's side. Already a bruise the size of a golf ball had swollen his cheek. Blood trickled alarmingly from his torn lip. "Are you all right?" she cried.

He touched his cheek and winced. "I've probably looked worse."

She glanced around at the toppled furniture. "Look at this mess! I hope you have a good explanation for— What are you doing?" she demanded as he suddenly gripped her arm. "Get your hands off me!"

"You're bleeding!"

"What?" She followed the direction of his gaze and saw that a shocking blotch of red soaked her sleeve. Droplets splattered to the flagstones.

Her reaction was immediate and visceral. She swayed dizzily and sat down smack on the ground, right beside him. Through a cottony haze, she felt her head being shoved down to her knees, heard her sleeve being ripped open. Hands probed gently at her arm.

"Easy," he murmured. "It's not bad. You'll need a few stitches, that's all. Just breathe slowly."

"Get your hands off me," she mumbled. But the instant she raised her head, the whole terrace seemed to swim. She caught a watery view of mass confusion. The Italians chattering and shaking their heads. The waiters staring openmouthed in horror. And the American watching her with a look of worry. She focused on his eyes. Dazed as she was, she registered the fact that those eyes were warm and steady.

By now the hotel manager, an effete Englishman wearing an immaculate suit and an appalled expression, had appeared. The waiters pointed accusingly at Guy. The manager kept clucking and shaking his head as he surveyed the damage.

"This is dreadful," he murmured. "This sort of behavior is simply not tolerated. Not on *my* terrace. Are you a guest? You're not?" He turned to one of the waiters. "Call the police. I want this man arrested."

"Are you all blind?" yelled Guy. "Didn't any of you see he was trying to kill her?"

"What? What? Who?"

Guy poked around in the broken crockery and fished out the knife. "Not your usual cutlery," he said, holding up the deadly looking weapon. The handle was ebony, inlaid with mother of pearl. The blade was razor sharp. "This one's designed to be thrown."

"Oh, rubbish," sputtered the Englishman.

"Take a look at her arm!"

The manager turned his gaze to Willy's blood-soaked sleeve. Horrified, he took a stumbling step back. "Good God. I'll—I'll call a doctor."

"Never mind," said Guy, sweeping Willy off the ground. "It'll be faster if I take her straight to the hospital."

Willy let herself be gathered into Guy's arms. She found his scent strangely reassuring, a distinctly male mingling of sweat and aftershave. As he carried her across the terrace, she caught a swirling view of shocked waiters and curious hotel guests.

"This is embarrassing," she complained. "I'm all right. Put me down."

"You'll faint."

"I've never fainted in my life!"

"It's not a good time to start." He got her into a waiting taxi, where she curled up in the back seat like a wounded animal.

The emergency-room doctor didn't believe in anesthesia. Willy didn't believe in screaming. As the curved suture needle stabbed again and again into her arm, she clenched her teeth and longed to have the lunatic American hold her hand. If only she hadn't played tough and sent him out to the waiting area. Even now, as she fought back tears of pain, she refused to admit, even to herself, that she needed any man to hold her hand. Still, it would have been nice. It would have been wonderful.

And I still don't know his name.

The doctor, whom she suspected of harboring sadistic tendencies, took the final stitch, tied it off and snipped the silk thread. "You see?" he said cheerfully. "That wasn't so bad."

She felt like slugging him in the mouth and saying, *You see? That wasn't so bad, either.*

He dressed the wound with gauze and tape, then gave her a cheerful slap—on her wounded arm, of course— and sent her out into the waiting room.

He was still there, loitering by the reception desk. With all his bruises and cuts, he looked like a bum who'd wandered in off the street. But the look he gave her was warm and concerned. "How's the arm?" he asked.

Gingerly she touched her shoulder. "Doesn't this country believe in Novocaine?"

"Only for wimps," he observed. "Which you obviously aren't."

Outside, the night was steaming. There were no taxis available, so they hired a *tuk-tuk,* a motorcycle-powered rickshaw, driven by a toothless Thai.

"You never told me your name," she said over the roar of the engine.

"I didn't think you were interested."

"Is that my cue to get down on my knees and beg for an introduction?"

Grinning, he held out his hand. "Guy Barnard. Now do I get to hear what the Willy's short for?"

She shook his hand. "Wilone."

"Unusual. Nice."

"Short of Wilhelmina, it's as close as a daughter can get to being William Maitland, Jr."

He didn't comment, but she saw an odd flicker in his eyes, a look of sudden interest. She wondered why. The *tuk-tuk* puttered past a *klong,* its stagnant waters shimmering under the streetlights.

"Maitland," he said casually. "Now that's a name I seem to remember from the war. There was a pilot, a guy named Wild Bill Maitland. Flew for Air America. Any relation?"

She looked away. "Just my father."

"No kidding! You're Wild Bill Maitland's kid?"

"You've heard the stories about him, have you?"

"Who hasn't? He was a living legend. Right up there with Earthquake Magoon."

"That's about what he was to me, too," she muttered. "Nothing but a legend."

There was a pause in their exchange, and she wondered if Guy Barnard was shocked by the bitterness in her last statement. If so, he didn't show it.

"I never actually met your old man," he said. "But I saw him once, on the Da Nang airstrip. I was working ground crew."

"With Air America?"

"No. Army Air Cav." He sketched a careless salute. "Private First Class Barnard. You know, the real scum of the earth."

"I see you've come up in the world."

"Yeah." He laughed. "Anyway, your old man brought in a C-46, engine smoking, fuel zilch, fuselage so shot up you could almost see right through her. He sets her down on the tarmac, pretty as you please. Then he climbs out and checks out all the bullet holes. Any other pilot would've been down on his knees kissing the ground. But your dad, he just shrugs, goes over to a tree and takes a nap." Guy shook his head. "Your old man was something else."

"So everyone tells me." Willy shoved a hank of wind-blown hair off her face and wished he'd stop talking about her father. That's how it'd been, as far back as she could remember. When she was a child in Vientiane, at every dinner party, every cocktail gathering, the pilots would invariably trot out another Wild Bill story. They'd raise toasts to his nerves, his daring, his crazy humor, until she was ready to scream. All those stories only emphasized how unimportant she and her mother were in the scheme of her father's life.

Maybe that's why Guy Barnard was starting to annoy her.

But it was more than just his talk about Bill Maitland. In some odd, indefinable way, Guy reminded her too much of her father.

The *tuk-tuk* suddenly hit a bump in the road, throwing her against Guy's shoulder. Pain sliced through her arm and her whole body seemed to clench in a spasm.

He glanced at her, alarmed. "Are you all right?"

"I'm—" She bit her lip, fighting back tears. "It's really starting to hurt."

He yelled at the driver to slow down. Then he took Willy's hand and held it tightly. "Just a little while longer. We're almost there...."

It was a long ride to the hotel.

Up in her room, Guy sat her down on the bed and gently stroked the hair off her face. "Do you have any pain killers?"

"There's—there's some aspirin in the bathroom." She started to rise to her feet. "I can get it."

"No. You stay right where you are." He went into the bathroom, came back out with a glass of water and the bottle of aspirin. Even through her cloud of pain, she was intensely aware of him watching her, studying her as she swallowed the tablets. Yet she found his nearness strangely reassuring. When he turned and crossed the room, the sudden distance between them left her feeling abandoned.

She watched him rummage around in the tiny refrigerator. "What are you looking for?"

"Found it." He came back with a cocktail bottle of whiskey, which he uncapped and handed to her. "Liquid anesthesia. It's an old-fashioned remedy, but it works."

"I don't like whiskey."

"You don't have to like it. By definition, medicine's not supposed to taste good."

She managed a gulp. It burned all the way down her throat. "Thanks," she muttered. "I think."

He began to walk a slow circle, surveying the plush furnishings, the expansive view. Sliding glass doors opened onto a balcony. From the Chaophya River flowing just below came the growl of motorboats plying the waters. He wandered over to the nightstand, picked up a rambutan from the complimentary fruit basket and peeled off the prickly shell. "Nice room," he said, thoughtfully chewing the fruit. "Sure beats my dive—the Liberty Hotel. What do you do for a living, anyway?"

She took another sip of whiskey and coughed. "I'm a pilot."

"Just like your old man?"

"Not exactly. I fly for the paycheck, not the excitement. Not that the pay's great. No money in flying cargo."

"Can't be too bad if you're staying here."

"I'm not paying for this."

His eyebrows shot up. "Who is?"

"My mother."

"Generous of her."

His note of cynicism irritated her. What right did he have to insult her? Here he was, this battered vagabond, eating *her* fruit, enjoying *her* view. The *tuk-tuk* ride had tossed his hair in all directions, and his bruised eye was swollen practically shut. Why was she even putting up with this jerk?

He was watching her with curiosity. "So what else is Mama paying for?" he asked.

She looked him hard in the eye. "Her own funeral

arrangements," she said, and was satisfied to see his smirk instantly vanish.

"What do you mean? Is your mother dead?"

"No, but she's dying." Willy gazed out the window at the lantern lights along the river's edge. For a moment they seemed to dance like fireflies in a watery haze. She swallowed; the lights came back into focus. "God," she sighed, wearily running her fingers through her hair. "What the hell am I doing here?"

"I take it this isn't a vacation."

"You got that right."

"What is it, then?"

"A wild-goose chase." She swallowed the rest of the whiskey and set the tiny bottle down on the nightstand. "But it's Mom's last wish. And you're always supposed to grant people their dying wish." She looked at Guy. "Aren't you?"

He sank into a chair, his gaze locked on her face. "You told me before that you were here on family business. Does it have to do with your father?"

She nodded.

"And that's why you saw Kistner today?"

"We were hoping—I was hoping—that he'd be able to fill us in about what happened to Dad."

"Why go to Kistner? Casualty resolution isn't his job."

"But Military Intelligence is. In 1970, Kistner was stationed in Laos. He was the one who commissioned my father's last flight. And after the plane went down, he directed the search. What there was of a search."

"And did Kistner tell you anything new?"

"Only what I expected to hear. That after twenty

years, there's no point pursuing the matter. That my father's dead. And there's no way to recover his remains."

"It must've been tough hearing that. Knowing you've
come all this way for nothing."

"It'll be hard on my mother."

"And not on you?"

"Not really." She rose from the bed and wandered out
onto the balcony, where she stared down at the water.
"You see, I don't give a damn about my father."

The night was heavy with the smells of the river. She
knew Guy was watching her; she could feel his gaze on
her back, could imagine the shocked expression on his
face. Of course, he would be shocked; it was appalling,
what she'd just said. But it was also the truth.

She sensed, more than heard, his approach. He came
up beside her and leaned against the railing. The glow
of the river lanterns threw his face into shadow.

She stared down at the shimmering water. "You don't
know what it's like to be the daughter of a legend. All
my life, people have told me how brave he was, what a
hero he was. God, he must have loved the glory."

"A lot of men do."

"And a lot of women suffer for it."

"Did your mother suffer?"

She looked up at the sky. "My mother..." She shook
her head and laughed. "Let me tell you about my mother.
She was a nightclub singer. All the best New York clubs.
I went through her scrapbook, and I remember some re-
viewer wrote, 'Her voice spins a web that will trap any
audience in its magic.' She was headed for the moon.
Then she got married. She went from star billing to a—a
footnote in some man's life. We lived in Vientiane for
a few years. I remember what a trouper she was. She

wanted so badly to go home, but there she was, scrap-ing the store shelves for decent groceries. Laughing off the hand grenades. Dad got the glory. But she's the one who raised me." Willy looked at Guy. "That's how the world works. Isn't it?"

He didn't answer.

She turned her gaze back to the river. "After Dad's contract ended with Air America, we tried it for a while in San Francisco. He worked for a commuter air-line. And Mom and I, well, we just enjoyed living in a town without mortars and grenades going off. But…" She sighed. "It didn't last. Dad got bored. I guess he missed the old adrenaline high. And the glory. So he went back."

"They got divorced?"

"He never asked for one. And Mom wouldn't hear of it anyway. She loved him." Willy's voice dropped. "She still loves him."

"He went back to Laos alone, huh?"

"Signed up for another two years. Guess he preferred the company of danger junkies. They were all like that, those A.A. pilots—all volunteers, not draftees—all of 'em laughing death in the face. I think flying was the only thing that gave them a rush, made them feel alive. Must've been the ultimate high for Dad. Dying."

"And here you are, over twenty years later."

"That's right. Here I am."

"Looking for a man you don't give a damn about. Why?"

"It's not me asking the questions. It's my mother. She's never wanted much. Not from me, not from any-one. But this was something she had to know."

"A dying wish."

Willy nodded. "That's the one nice thing about cancer. You get some time to tie up the loose ends. And my father is one hell of a big loose end."

"Kistner gave you the official verdict—your father's dead. Doesn't that tie things up?"

"Not after all the lies we've been told."

"Who's lied to you?"

She laughed. "Who hasn't? Believe me, we've made the rounds. We've talked to the Joint Casualty Resolution Committee. Defense Intelligence. The CIA. They all had the same advice—drop it."

"Maybe they have a point."

"Maybe they're hiding the truth."

"Which is?"

"That Dad survived the crash."

"What's your evidence?"

She studied Guy for a moment, wondering how much to tell him. Wondering why she'd already told him as much as she had. She knew nothing about him except that he had fast reflexes and a sense of humor. That his eyes were brown, and his grin distinctly crooked. And that, in his own rumpled way, he was the most attractive man she'd ever met.

That last thought was as jolting as a bolt of lightning on a clear summer's day. But he *was* attractive. There was nothing she could specifically point to that made him that way. Maybe it was his self-assurance, the confident way he carried himself. *Or maybe it's the damn whiskey,* she thought. That's why she was feeling so warm inside, why her knees felt as if they were about to buckle.

She gripped the steel railing. "My mother and I, we've had, well, *hints* that secrets have been kept from us."

"Anything concrete?"

"Would you call an eyewitness concrete?"

"Depends on the eyewitness."

"A Lao villager."

"He saw your father?"

"No, that's the whole point—he didn't."

"I'm confused."

"Right after the plane went down," she explained, "Dad's buddies printed up leaflets advertising a reward of two kilos of gold to anyone who brought in proof of the crash. The leaflets were dropped along the border and all over Pathet Lao territory. A few weeks later a villager came out of the jungle to claim the reward. He said he'd found the wreckage of a plane, that it had crashed just inside the Vietnam border. He described it right down to the number on the tail. And he swore there were only two bodies on board, one in the cargo hold, another in the cockpit. The plane had a crew of *three*."

"What did the investigators say about that?"

"We didn't hear this from them. We learned about it only after the classified report got stuffed into our mailbox, with a note scribbled 'From a friend.' I think one of Dad's old Air America buddies got wind of a cover-up and decided to let the family know about it."

Guy was standing absolutely still, like a cat in the shadows. When he spoke, she could tell by his voice that he was very, very interested.

"What did your mother do then?" he asked.

"She pursued it, of course. She wouldn't give up. She hounded the CIA. Air America. She got nothing out of them. But she did get a few anonymous phone calls telling her to shut up."

"Or?"

"Or she'd learn things about Dad she didn't want to know. Embarrassing things."

"Other women? What?"

This was the part that made Willy angry. She could barely bring herself to talk about it. "They implied—" She let out a breath. "They implied he was working for the other side. That he was a traitor."

There was a pause. "And you don't believe it," he said softly.

Her chin shot up. "Hell, no, I don't believe it! Not a word. It was just their way to scare us off. To keep us from digging up the truth. It wasn't the only stunt they pulled. When we kept asking questions, they stopped release of Dad's back pay, which by then was somewhere in the tens of thousands. Anyway, we floundered around for a while, trying to get information. Then the war ended, and we thought we'd finally hear the answers. We watched the POWs come back. It was tough on Mom, seeing all those reunions on TV. Hearing Nixon talk about our brave men finally coming home. Because hers didn't. But we were surprised to hear of one man who did make it home—one of the crew members on Dad's plane."

Guy straightened in surprise. "Then there *was* a survivor?"

"Luis Valdez, the cargo kicker. He bailed out as the plane was going down. He was captured almost as soon as he hit the ground. Spent the next five years in a North Vietnamese prison camp."

"Doesn't that explain the missing body? If Valdez bailed out—"

"There's more. The very day Valdez flew back to the States, he called us. I answered the phone. I could hear he was scared. He'd been warned by Intelligence not to talk to anyone. But he thought he owed it to Dad to let us know what had happened. He told us there was a passenger on that flight, a Lao who was already dead when the plane went down. And that the body in the cockpit was probably Kozlowski, the copilot. That still leaves a missing body."

"Your father."

She nodded. "We went back to the CIA with this information. And you know what? They denied there was any passenger on that plane, Lao or otherwise. They said it carried only a shipment of aircraft parts."

"What did Air America say?"

"They claim there's no record of any passenger."

"But you had Valdez's testimony."

She shook her head. "The day after he called, the day he was supposed to come see us, he shot himself in the head. Suicide. Or so the police report said."

She could tell by his long silence that Guy was shocked. "How convenient," he murmured.

"For the first time in my life, I saw my mother scared. Not for herself, but for me. She was afraid of what might happen, what they might do. So she let the matter drop. Until..." Willy paused.

"There was something else?"

She nodded. "About a year after Valdez died—I guess it was around '76—a funny thing happened to my mother's bank account. It picked up an extra fifteen thousand dollars. All the bank could tell her was that the deposit had been made in Bangkok. A year later, it happened again, this time, around ten thousand."

"All that money, and she never found out where it came from?"

"No. All these years she's been trying to figure it out. Wondering if one of Dad's buddies, or maybe Dad himself—" Willy shook her head and sighed. "Anyway, a few months ago, she found out she had cancer. And suddenly it seemed very important to learn the truth. She's too sick to make this trip herself, so she asked me to come. And I'm hitting the same brick wall she hit twenty years ago."

"Maybe you haven't gone to the right people."

"Who *are* the right people?"

Quietly, Guy shifted toward her. "I have connections," he said softly. "I could find out for you."

Their hands brushed on the railing; Willy felt a delicious shock race through her whole arm. She pulled her hand away.

"What sort of connections?"

"Friends in the business."

"Exactly what *is* your business?"

"Body counts. Dog tags. I'm with the Army ID Lab."

"I see. You're in the military."

He laughed and leaned sideways against the railing. "No way. I bailed out after Nam. Went back to college, got a master's in stones and bones. That's physical anthropology, emphasis on Southeast Asia. Anyway, I worked a while in a museum, then found out the army paid better. So I hired on as a civilian contractor. I'm still sorting bones, only these have names, ranks and serial numbers."

"And that's why you're going to Vietnam?"

He nodded. "There are new sets of remains to pick up in Saigon and Hanoi."

Remains. Such a clinical word for what was once a human being.

"I know a few people," he said. "I might be able to help you."

"Why?"

"You've made me curious."

"Is that all it is? Curiosity?"

His next move startled her. He reached out and brushed back her short, tumbled hair. The brief contact of his fingers seemed to leave her whole neck sizzling. She froze, unable to react to this unexpectedly intimate contact.

"Maybe I'm just a nice guy," he whispered.

Oh, hell, he's going to kiss me, she thought. *He's going to kiss me and I'm going to let him, and what happens next is anyone's guess....*

She batted his hand away and took a panicked step back. "I don't believe in nice guys."

"Afraid of men?"

"I'm not afraid of men. But I don't trust them, either."

"Still," he said with an obvious note of laughter in his voice, "you let me into your room."

"Maybe it's time to let you out." She stalked across the room and yanked open the door. "Or are you going to be difficult?"

"Me?" To her surprise, he followed her to the door. "I'm never difficult."

"I'll bet."

"Besides, I can't hang around tonight. I've got more important business."

"Really."

"Really." He glanced at the lock on her door. "I see you've got a heavy-duty dead bolt. Use it. And take my advice—don't go out on the town tonight."

"Darn! That was next on my agenda."

"Oh, and in case you need me—" he turned and grinned at her from the doorway "—I'm staying at the Liberty Hotel. Call anytime."

She started to snap, *Don't hold your breath*. But before she could get out the words, he'd left.

She was staring at a closed door.

Chapter 3

Tobias Wolff swiveled his wheelchair around from the liquor cabinet and faced his old friend. "If I were you, Guy, I'd stay the hell out of it."

It had been five years since they'd last seen each other. Toby still looked as muscular as ever—at least from the waist up. Fifteen years' confinement to a wheelchair had bulked out those shoulders and arms. Still, the years had taken their inevitable toll. Toby was close to fifty now, and he looked it. His bushy hair, cut Beethoven style, was almost entirely gray. His face was puffy and sweating in the tropical heat. But the dark eyes were as sharp as ever.

"Take some advice from an old Company man," he said, handing Guy a glass of Scotch. "There's no such thing as a coincidental meeting. There are only planned encounters."

"Coincidence or not," said Guy, "Willy Maitland could be the break I've been waiting for."

"Or she could be nothing but trouble."

"What've I got to lose?"

"Your life?"

"Come on, Toby! You're the only one I can trust to give me a straight answer."

"It was a long time ago. I wasn't directly connected to the case."

"But you were in Vientiane when it happened. You must remember something about the Maitland file."

"Only what I heard in passing, none of it confirmed. Hell, it was like the Wild West out there. Rumors flying thicker'n the mosquitoes."

"But not as thick as you covert-action boys."

Toby shrugged. "We had a job to do. We did it."

"You remember who handled the Maitland case?"

"Had to be Mike Micklewait. I know he was the case officer who debriefed that villager—the one who came in for the reward."

"Did Micklewait think the man was on the level?"

"Probably not. I know the villager never got the reward."

"Why wasn't Maitland's family told about all this?"

"Hey, Maitland wasn't some poor dumb draftee. He was working for Air America. In other words, CIA. That's a job you don't talk about. Maitland knew the risks."

"The family deserved to hear about any new evidence." Guy thought about the surreptitious way Willy and her mother *had* learned of it.

Toby laughed. "There was a secret war going on, remember? We weren't even supposed to be in Laos.

Keeping families informed was at the bottom of any-one's priority list."

"Was there some other reason it was hushed up? Something to do with the passenger?"

Toby's eyebrows shot up. "Where did you hear that rumor?"

"Willy Maitland. She heard there was a Lao on board. Everyone's denying his existence, so my guess is he was a very important person. Who was he?"

"I don't know." Toby wheeled around and looked out the open window of his apartment. From the darkness came the sounds and smells of the Bangkok streets. Meat sizzling on an open-air grill. Women laughing. The rumble of a *tuk-tuk*. "There was a hell of a lot going on back then. Things we never talked about. Things we were even ashamed to talk about. What with all the agents and counteragents and generals and soldiers of fortune, you could never really be sure who was run-ning the place. Everyone was pulling strings, trying to get rich quick. I couldn't wait to get the hell out." He slapped the wheelchair in anger. "And this is where I end up. Great retirement." Sighing, he leaned back and stared out at the night. "Let it be, Guy," he said softly. "If you're right—if someone's out to hit Mait-land's kid—then this is too hot to handle."

"Toby, that's the point! *Why* is the case so hot? Why, after all these years, would Maitland's brat be making them nervous? What do they think she'll find out?"

"Does she know what she's getting into?"

"I doubt it. Anyway, nothing'll stop this dame. She's a chip off the old block."

"Meaning she's trouble. How're you going to get her to work with you?"

"That's the part I haven't figured out yet."

"There's always the Romeo approach."

Guy grinned. "I'll keep it in mind."

In fact, that was precisely the tactic he'd been considering all evening. Not because he was so sure it would work, but because she was an attractive woman and he couldn't help wondering what she was really like under that tough-gal facade.

"Alternatively," Toby said, "you could try telling her the truth. That you're not after her. You're after the three million bounty."

"Two million."

"Two million, three million, what's the difference? It's a lot of dough."

"And I could use a lot of help," Guy said with quiet significance.

Toby sighed. "Okay," he said, at last wheeling around to look at him. "You want a name, I'll give you one. May or may not help you. Try Alain Gerard, a Frenchman, living these days in Saigon. He used to have close ties with the Company, knew all the crap going on in Vientiane."

"Ex-Company and living in Saigon? Why haven't the Vietnamese kicked him out?"

"He's useful to them. During the war he made his money exporting, shall we say, raw pharmaceuticals. Now he's turned humanitarian in his old age. U.S. trade embargoes cut the Viets off from Western markets. Gerard brings in medical supplies from France, antibiotics, X-ray film. In return, they let him stay in the country."

"Can I trust him?"

"He's ex-Company."

"Then I can't trust him."

Toby grunted. "You seem to trust me."

"You're different."

"That's only because I owe you, Barnard. Though I often think you should've left me to burn in that plane." Toby kneaded his senseless thighs. "No one has much use for half a man."

"Doesn't take legs to make a man, Toby."

"Ha. Tell that to Uncle Sam." Using his powerful arms, Toby shifted his weight in the chair. "When're you leaving for Saigon?"

"Tomorrow morning. I moved my flight up a few days." Guy's palms were already sweating at the thought of boarding that Air France plane. He tossed back a mind-numbing gulp of Scotch. "Wish I could take a boat instead."

Toby laughed. "You'd be the first boat person going *back* to Vietnam. Still scared to fly, huh?"

"White knuckles and all." He set his glass down and headed for the door. "Thanks for the drink. And the tip."

"I'll see what else I can do for you," Toby called after him. "I still might have a few contacts in-country. Maybe I can get 'em to watch over you. And the woman. By the way, is anyone keeping an eye on her tonight?"

"Some buddies of Puapong's. They won't let anyone near her. She should get to the airport in one piece."

"And what happens then?"

Guy paused in the doorway. "We'll be in Saigon. Things'll be safer there."

"In Saigon?" Toby shook his head. "Don't count on it."

The crowd at the Bong Bong Club had turned wild, the men drunkenly shouting and groping at the stage as the girls, dead-eyed, danced on. No one took notice of the two men huddled at a dark corner table.

"I am disappointed, Mr. Siang. You're a professional, or so I thought. I fully expected you to deliver. Yet the woman is still alive."

Stung by the insult, Siang felt his face tighten. He was not accustomed to failure—or to criticism. He was glad the darkness hid his burning cheeks as he set his glass of vodka down on the table. "I tell you, this could not be predicted. There was interference—a man—"

"Yes, an American, so I've been told. A Mr. Barnard."

Siang was startled. "You've learned his name?"

"I make it a point to know everything."

Siang touched his bruised face and winced. This Mr. Barnard certainly had a savage punch. If they ever crossed paths again, Siang would make him pay for this humiliation.

"The woman leaves for Saigon tomorrow," said the man.

"Tomorrow?" Siang shook his head. "That does not leave me enough time."

"You have tonight."

"Tonight? Impossible." Siang had, in fact, already spent the past four hours trying to get near the woman. But the desk clerk at the Oriental had stood watch like a guard dog over the passkeys, the hotel security officer refused to leave his post near the elevators, and a bell-boy kept strolling up and down the hall. The woman had been untouchable. Siang had briefly considered climbing up the balcony, but his approach was hampered by two vagrants camped on the riverbank beneath her window. Though hostile-looking, the tramps had posed no real threat to a man like Siang, but he hadn't wanted to risk a foolish, potentially messy scene.

And now his professional reputation was at stake.

"The matter grows more urgent," said the man. "This must be done soon."

"But she leaves Bangkok tomorrow. I can make no guarantees."

"Then do it in Saigon. Whether you finish it here or there, *it has to be done*."

Siang was stunned. "Saigon? I cannot return—"

"We'll send you under Thai diplomatic cover. A cultural attaché, perhaps. I'll decide and arrange the entry papers accordingly."

"Vietnamese security is tight. I will not be able to bring in any—"

"The diplomatic pouch goes out twice a week. Next drop is in three days. I'll see what weapons I can slip through. Until then, you'll have to improvise."

Siang fell silent, wondering how it would feel to once again walk the streets of Saigon. And he wondered about Chantal. How many years had it been since he'd seen her? Did she still hate him for leaving her behind? Of course, she would; she never forgot a grudge. Somehow, he'd have to work his way back into her affections. He didn't think that would be too difficult. Life in the new Vietnam must be hard these days, especially for a woman. Chantal liked her comforts; for a few precious luxuries, she might do anything. Even sell her soul.

She was a woman he could understand.

He looked across the table. "There will be expenses."

The man nodded. "I can be generous. As you well know."

Already Siang was making a mental list of what he'd

need. Old clothes—frayed shirts and faded trousers—so he wouldn't stand out in a crowd. Cigarettes, soap and razor blades for bartering favors on the streets. And then he'd need a few special gifts for Chantal....

He nodded. The bargain was struck.

"One more thing," said the man as he rose to leave.

"Yes?"

"Other...parties seem to be involved. The Company, for instance. I wouldn't want to pull that particular tiger's tail. So keep bloodshed to a minimum. Only the woman dies. No one else."

"I understand."

After the man had left, Siang sat alone at the corner table, thinking. Remembering Saigon. Had it really been fifteen years? His last memories of the city were of panicked faces, of hands clawing frantically at a helicopter door, of the roar of chopper blades and the swirl of dust as the rooftops fell away.

Siang took a deep swallow of vodka and stood to leave. Just then, whistles and applause rose from the crowd gathered around the dance stage. A lone girl stood brown and naked in the spotlight. Around her waist was wrapped an eight-foot boa constrictor. The girl seemed to shudder as the snake slithered down between her thighs. The men shouted their approval.

Siang grinned. Ah, the Bong Bong Club. Always something new.

Saigon

From the rooftop garden of the Rex Hotel, Willy watched the bicycles thronging the intersection of Le Loi and Nguyen Hue. A collision seemed inevitable, only a matter of time. Riders whisked through at breakneck speed, blithely ignoring the single foolhardy pedestrian inching fearfully across the street. Willy was so intent on silently cheering the man on that she scarcely registered the monotonous voice of her government escort.

"And tomorrow, we will take you by car to see the National Palace, where the puppet government ruled in luxury, then on to the Museum of History, where you will learn about our struggles against the Chinese and the French imperialists. The next day, you will see our lacquer factory, where you can buy many beautiful gifts to bring home. And then—"

"Mr. Ainh," Willy said with a sigh, turning at last to her guide. "It all sounds very fascinating, this tour you've planned. But have you looked into my other business?"

Ainh blinked. Though his frame was chopstick thin, he had a cherubic face made owlish by his thick glasses. "Miss Maitland," he said in a hurt voice, "I have arranged a private car! And many wonderful meals."

"Yes, I appreciate that, but—"

"You are unhappy with your itinerary?"

"To be perfectly honest, I don't really care about a tour. I want to find out about my father."

"But you have paid for a tour! We must provide one."

"I paid for the tour to get a visa. Now that I'm here, I need to talk to the right people. You can arrange that for me, can't you?"

Ainh shifted nervously. "This is a…a complication. I do not know if I can…that is, it is not what I…" He drifted into helpless silence.

"Some months ago, I wrote to your foreign ministry

about my father. They never wrote back. If you could arrange an appointment…"

"How many months ago did you write?"

"Six, at least."

"You are impatient. You cannot expect instant results."

She sighed. "Obviously not."

"Besides, you wrote the Foreign Ministry. I have nothing to do with them. I am with the Ministry of Tourism."

"And you folks don't communicate with each other, is that it?"

"They are in a different building."

"Then maybe—if it's not too much trouble—you could take me to their building?"

He looked at her bleakly. "But then who will take the tour?"

"Mr. Ainh," she said with gritted teeth, "*cancel* the tour."

Ainh looked like a man with a terrible headache. Willy almost felt sorry for him as she watched him retreat across the rooftop garden. She could imagine the bureaucratic quicksand he would have to wade through to honor her request. She'd already seen how the system operated—or, rather, how it didn't operate. That afternoon, at Ton Son Nhut Airport, it had taken three hours in the suffocating heat just to run the gauntlet of immigration officials.

A breeze swept the terrace, the first she'd felt all afternoon. Though she'd showered only an hour ago, her clothes were already soaked with sweat. Sinking into a chair, she gazed off at the skyline of Saigon, now painted a dusty gold in the sunset. Once, this must have been a glorious town of tree-lined boulevards and out-door cafés where one could while away the afternoons sipping coffee.

But after its fall to the North, Saigon slid from the dizzy impudence of wealth to the resignation of poverty. The signs of decay were everywhere, from the chipped paint on the old French colonials to the skeletons of buildings left permanently unfinished. Even the Rex Hotel, luxurious by local standards, seemed to be fraying at the edges. The terrace stones were cracked. In the fish pond, three listless carp drifted like dead leaves. The rooftop swimming pool had bloomed an unhealthy shade of green. A lone Russian tourist sat on the side and dangled his legs in the murky water, as though weighing the risks of a swim.

It occurred to Willy that her immediate situation was every bit as murky as that water. The Vietnamese obviously believed in a proper channel for everything, and without Ainh's help, there was no way she could navigate *any* channel, proper or otherwise.

What then? she thought wearily. *I can't do this alone. I need help. I need a guide. I need—*

"Now *there's* a lady who looks down on her luck," said a voice.

She looked up to see Guy Barnard's tanned face framed against the sunset. Her instant delight at seeing someone familiar—even *him*—only confirmed the utter depths of despair to which she'd sunk.

He flashed her a smile that could have charmed the habit off a nun. "Welcome to Saigon, capital of fallen dreams. How's it goin', kid?"

She sighed. "You need to ask?"

"Nope. I've been through it before, running around

like a headless chicken, scrounging up seals of approval for every piddly scrap of paper. This country has got bureaucracy down to an art."

"I could live without the pep talk, thank you."

"Can I buy you a beer?"

She studied that smile of his, wondering what lay behind it. Suspecting the worst.

Seeing her weaken, he called for two beers, then dropped into a chair and regarded her with rumpled cheerfulness.

"I thought you weren't due in Saigon till Wednesday," she said.

"Change of plans."

"Pretty sudden, wasn't it?"

"Flexibility happens to be one of my virtues." He added, ruefully, "Maybe my only virtue."

The bartender brought over two frosty Heinekens. Guy waited until the man left before he spoke again.

"They brought in some new remains from Dak To," he said.

"MIAs?"

"That's what I have to find out. I knew I'd need a few extra days to examine the bones. Besides—" he took a gulp of beer "—I was getting bored in Bangkok."

"Sure."

"No, I mean it. I was ready for a change of scenery."

"You left the fleshpot of the East to come here and check out a few dead soldiers?"

"Believe it or not, I take my job seriously." He set the bottle down on the table. "Anyway, since I happen to be in town, maybe I could help you out. Since you probably need it."

Something about the way he looked at her, head

cocked, teeth agleam in utter self-assurance, irritated her. "I'm doing okay," she said.

"Are you, now? So when's your first official meeting?"

"Things are being arranged."

"What sorts of things?"

"I don't know. Mr. Ainh's handling the details, and—"

"Mr. Ainh? You don't mean your *tour guide?*" He burst out laughing.

"Just why is that so funny?" she demanded.

"You're right," Guy said, swallowing his laughter. "It's not funny. It's pathetic. Do you want an advance look in my crystal ball? Because I can tell you exactly what's going to happen. First thing in the morning, your guide will show up with an apologetic look on his face."

"Why apologetic?"

"Because he'll tell you the ministry is closed for the day. After all, it's the grand and glorious holiday of July 18."

"Holiday? What holiday?"

"Never mind. He'll make something up. Then he'll ask if you wouldn't rather see the lacquer factory, where you can buy many beautiful gifts to bring home…."

Now she was laughing. Those were, in fact, Mr. Ainh's exact words.

"Then, the following day, he'll come up with some other reason you can't visit the ministry. Say, they're all sick with the swine flu or there's a critical shortage of pencil erasers. *But*—you can visit the National Palace!"

She stopped laughing. "I think I'm beginning to get your point."

"It's not that the man's deliberately sabotaging your

plans. He simply knows how hopeless it is to untangle this bureaucracy. All he wants is to do his own little job, which is to be a tour guide and file innocuous reports about the nice lady tourist. Don't expect more from him. The poor guy isn't paid enough for what he already does."

"I'm not helpless. I can always start knocking on a few doors myself."

"Yeah, but *which* doors? And where are they hidden? And do you know the secret password?"

"Guy, you're making this country sound like a carnival funhouse."

"*Fun* is not the operative word here."

"What *is* the operative word?"

"*Chaos.*" He pointed down at the street, where pedestrians and bicycles swarmed in mass anarchy. "See that? That's how this government works. It's every man for himself. Ministries competing with ministries, provinces with provinces. Every minor official protecting his own turf. Everyone scared to move an inch without a nod from the powers that be." He shook his head. "Not a system for the faint of heart."

"That's one thing I've never been."

"Wait till you've been sitting in some sweatbox of a 'reception' area for five hours. And your belly hurts from the bad water. And the closest bathroom is a hole in the—"

"I get the picture."

"Do you?"

"What are you suggesting I do?"

Smiling, he sat back. "Hang around with me. I have a contact here and there. Not in the Foreign Ministry, I admit, but they might be able to help you."

He wants something, she thought. *What is it?* Though his gaze was unflinching, she sensed a new tension in his posture, saw in his eyes the anticipation rippling beneath the surface.

"You're being awfully helpful. Why?"

He shrugged. "Why not?"

"That's hardly an answer."

"Maybe at heart I'm still the Boy Scout helping old ladies cross the street. Maybe I'm a nice guy."

"Maybe you could tell me the truth."

"Have you always had this problem trusting men?"

"Yes, and don't change the subject."

For a moment, he didn't speak. He sat drumming his fingers against the beer bottle. "Okay," he admitted. "So I fibbed a little. I was never a Boy Scout. But I meant it about helping you out. The offer stands."

She didn't say a thing. For Guy, that silence, that look of skepticism, said it all. The woman didn't trust him. But why not, when he'd sounded his most sincere? He wondered what had made her so mistrustful. Too many hard knocks in life? Too many men who'd lied to her?

Well, watch out, baby, 'cause this one's no different, he thought with a twinge of self-disgust.

He just as quickly shook off the feeling. The stakes were too high to be developing a conscience. Especially at his age.

Now he'd have to tell another lie. He'd been lying a lot lately. It didn't get any easier.

"You're right," he said. "I'm not doing this out of the kindness of my heart."

She didn't look surprised. That annoyed him. "What do you expect in return?" she asked, her eyes hard on his. "Money?" She paused. "Sex?"

That last word, flung out so matter-of-factly, made his belly do a tiny loop-the-loop. Not that he hadn't already thought about that particular subject. He'd thought about it a lot ever since he'd met her. And now that she was sitting only a few feet away, watching him with those unyielding eyes, he was having trouble keeping certain images out of his head. Briefly he considered the possibility of throwing a little sex into the deal, but he just as quickly discarded the idea. He felt low enough as it was.

He calmly reached for the Heineken. The frostiness had gone out of the bottle. "No," he said. "Sex isn't part of the bargain."

"I see." She bit her lip. "Then it's money."

He gave a nod.

"I think you should know that I don't have any. Not for you, anyway."

"It's not *your* money I'm after."

"Then whose?"

He paused, willing his expression to remain bland. His voice dropped to a murmur. "Have you ever heard of the Ariel Group?"

"Never."

"Neither had I. Until two weeks ago, when I was contacted by two of their representatives. They're a veterans' organization, dedicated to bringing our MIAs home—alive. Even if it means launching a Rambo operation."

"I see," she said, her lips tightening. "We're talking about paramilitary kooks."

"That's what I thought—at first. I was about to kick 'em out of my office when they pulled out a check—a very generous one, I might add. Twenty thousand. For expenses, they said."

"Expenses? What are they asking you to do?"

"A little moonlighting. They knew I was scheduled to fly in-country. They wanted me to conduct a small, private search for MIAs. But they aren't interested in skeletons and dog tags. They're after flesh and blood."

"Live ones? You don't really think there are any, do you?"

"They do. And they only have to produce one. A single living MIA to back up their claims. With the publicity that'd generate, Washington would be forced to take action."

He fell silent as the waiter came by to collect the empty beer bottles. Only when the man had left did Willy ask softly, "And where do I come in?"

"It's not you. It's your father. From what you've told me, there's a chance—a small one, to be sure—that he's still alive. If he is, I can help you find him. I can help you bring him home."

His words, uttered so quietly, so confidently, made Willy fall still. Guy could tell she was trying to read his face, trying to figure out what he wasn't telling her. And he wasn't telling her a lot.

"What do you get out of this?" she asked.

"You mean besides the pleasure of your company?"

"You said there was money involved. Since I'm not paying you, I assume someone else is. The Ariel Group? Are they offering you more than just expenses?"

"Move to the head of the class."

"How much?"

"For an honest to God live one? Two million."

"Two million *dollars?*"

He squeezed her hand, hard. "Keep it down, will you? This isn't exactly public information."

She dropped her voice to a whisper. "You're serious? Two million?"

"That's their offer. Now you think about *my* offer. Work with me, and we could both come out ahead. You'd get your father back. I'd pick up a nice little retirement fund. A win-win situation." He grinned, knowing he had her now. She'd be stupid to refuse. And Willy Maitland was definitely not stupid. "I think you'll agree," he said. "It's a match made in heaven."

"Or hell," she muttered darkly. She sat back and gave him a look of pure cast iron. "You're nothing but a bounty hunter."

"If that's what you want to call me."

"I could call you quite a few things. None of them flattering."

"Before you start calling me names, maybe you should think about your options. Which happen to be pretty limited. The way I see it, you can go it alone, which so far hasn't gotten you a helluva lot of mileage. Or—" he leaned forward and beamed her his most convincing smile "—you could work with me."

Her mouth tightened. "I don't work with mercenaries."

"What've you got against mercenaries?"

"Just a minor matter—principle."

"It's the money that bothers you, isn't it? The fact that I'm doing it for cash and not out of the goodness of my heart."

"This isn't some big-game hunt! We're talking about *men*. Men whose families have wiped out their savings to pay worthless little Rambos like you! I know those families. Some of them are still hanging in, twisting around on that one shred of hope. And you know as well as I do that those soldiers aren't sitting around in some POW camp, waiting to be rescued. They're *dead*."

"You think *your* old man's alive."

"He's a different story."

"Right. And every one of those five hundred other MIAs could be another 'different story.'"

"*I* happen to have evidence!"

"But you don't have the smarts it takes to find him." Guy leaned forward, his gaze hard on hers. In the last light of sunset, her face seemed alight with fire, her cheeks glowing a beautiful dusky red. "If he's alive, you can't afford to screw up this chance. And you may get only one chance to find him. Because I'll tell you now, the Vietnamese won't let you back in the country for another deluxe tour. Admit it, Willy. You need me."

"No," she shot back. "You need *me*. Without my help, how are you going to cash in on your 'live one'?"

"How're *you* going to find him?"

She was the one leaning forward now, so close, he almost pulled back in surprise. "Don't underestimate me, sleazeball," she muttered.

"And don't overestimate yourself, Junior. It's not easy finding answers in this country. No one, nothing's ever what it seems here. A flicker in the eye, a break in the voice can mean all the difference in the world. You *need* a partner. And, hey, I'm not unreasonable. I'll even think about splitting the reward with you. Say, ten percent. That's money you never expected, just to let me—"

"I don't give a damn about the money!" She rose

sharply to her feet. "Go get rich off someone else's old man." She spun around and walked away.

"Won't you even think about it?" he yelled.

She just kept marching away across the rooftop garden, oblivious to the curious glances aimed her way.

"Take it from me, Willy! You need me!"

A trio of Russian tourists, their faces ruddy from a few rounds of vodka, glanced up as she passed. One of the men raised his glass in a drunken salute. "Maybe you like Russian man better?" he shouted.

She didn't even break her stride. But as she walked away, every guest on that rooftop heard her answer, which came floating back with disarming sweetness over her shoulder. "Go to hellski."

Chapter 4

Guy watched her storm away, her chambray skirt snapping smartly about those fabulous legs. Annoyed as he was, he couldn't help laughing when he heard that comeback to the Russian.

Go to hellski. He laughed harder. He was still laughing as he wandered over to the bar and called for another Heineken. The beer was so cold, it made his teeth ache.

"For a fellow who's just gotten the royal heave-ho," said a voice, obviously British, "you seem to be in high spirits."

Guy glanced at the portly gentleman hunched next to him at the bar. With those two tufts of hair on his bald head, he looked like a horned owl. China blue eyes twinkled beneath shaggy eyebrows.

Guy shrugged. "Win some, lose some."

"Sensible attitude. Considering the state of womanhood these days." The man hoisted a glass of Scotch to his lips. "But then, I could have predicted she'd be a no go."

"Sounds like an expert talking."

"No, I sat behind her on the plane. Listened to some oily Frenchman ooze his entire repertoire all over her. Smashing lines, I have to say, but she didn't fall for it." He squinted at Guy. "Weren't *you* on that flight out of Bangkok?"

Guy nodded. He didn't remember the man, but then, he'd spent the entire flight white-knuckling his armrest and gulping down whiskey. Airplanes did that to him. Even nice big 747s with nice French stewardesses. It never failed to astonish him that the wings didn't fall off.

At the other end of the garden, the trio of Russians had started to sing. Not, unfortunately, in the same key. Maybe not even the same song. It was hard to tell.

"Never would've guessed it," the Englishman said, glancing over at the Russians. "I still remember the Yanks drinking at that very table. Never would've guessed there'd be Russians sitting there one day."

"When were you here?"

"Sixty-eight to '75." He held out a pudgy hand in greeting. "Dodge Hamilton, *London Post*."

"Guy Barnard. Ex-draftee." He shook the man's hand. "Reporter, huh? You here on a story?"

"I was." Hamilton looked mournfully at his Scotch. "But it's fallen through."

"What has? Your interviews?"

"No, the concept. I called it a sentimental journey. Visit to old friends in Saigon. Or, rather, to one friend in particular." He took a swallow of Scotch. "But she's gone."

"Oh. A woman."

"That's right, a woman. Half the human race, but they might as well be from Mars for all I understand the sex." He slapped down the glass and motioned for another refill. The bartender resignedly shoved the whole bottle of Scotch over to Hamilton. "See, the story I had in mind was the search for a lost love. You know, the sort of copy that sells papers. My editor went wild about it." He poured the Scotch, recklessly filling the glass to the brim. "Ha! Lost love! I stopped by her old house today, over on Rue Catinat. Or what used to be Rue Catinat. Found her brother still living there. But it seems my old love ran away with some new love. A sergeant. From Memphis, no less."

Guy shook his head in sympathy. "A woman has a right to change her mind."

"One day after I left the country?"

There wasn't much a man could say to that. But Guy couldn't blame the woman. He knew how it was in Saigon—the fear, the uncertainty. No one knowing if there'd be a slaughter and everyone expecting the worst. He'd seen the news photos of the city's fall, recognized the look of desperation on the faces of the Vietnamese scrambling aboard the last choppers out. No, he couldn't blame a woman for wanting to get out of the country, any way she could.

"You could still write about it," Guy pointed out. "Try a different angle. How one woman escaped the madness. The price of survival."

"My heart's not in it any longer." Hamilton gazed sadly around the rooftop. "Or in this town. I used to love it here! The noise, the smells. Even the whomp of the mortar rounds. But Saigon's changed. The spirit's flown out of it. The funny part is, this hotel looks exactly the same. I used to stand at this very bar and hear your generals whisper to each other, 'What the hell are we doing here?' I don't think they ever quite figured it out." He laughed and took another gulp of Scotch. "Memphis. Why would she want to go to Memphis?"

He was muttering to himself now, some private monologue about women causing all the world's miseries. An opinion with which Guy could almost agree. All he had to do was think about his own miserable love life and he, too, would get the sudden, blinding urge to get thoroughly soused.

Women. All the same. Yet, somehow, all different.

He thought about Willy Maitland. She talked tough, but he could tell it was an act, that there was something soft, something vulnerable beneath that hard-as-nails surface. Hell, she was just a kid trying to live up to her old man's name, pretending she didn't need a man when she did. He had to admire her for that: her pride.

She was smart to turn down his offer. He wasn't sure he had the stomach to go through with it anyway. Let the Ariel Group tighten his noose. He'd lived with his skeletons long enough; maybe it was time to let them out of the closet.

I should just do my job, he thought. *Go to Hanoi, pick up a few dead soldiers, fly them home.*

And forget about Willy Maitland.

Then again…

He ordered another beer. Drank it while the debate raged on in his head. Thought about all the ways he could help her, about how much she needed *someone's* help.

Considered doing it not because he was being forced into it, but because he wanted to. *Out of the goodness of my heart?* Now that was a new concept. No, he'd never been a Boy Scout. Something about those uniforms, about all that earnest goodliness and godliness, had struck him as faintly ridiculous. But here he was, Boy Scout Barnard, ready to offer his services, no strings attached.

Well, maybe a few strings. He couldn't help fantasizing about the possibilities. He thought of how it would be, taking her up to his room. Undressing her. Feeling her yield beneath him. He swallowed hard and reached automatically for the Heineken.

"No doubt about it," Hamilton muttered. "I tell you, it's all their fault."

"Hmm?" Guy turned. "Whose fault?"

"Women, of course. They cause more trouble than they're worth."

"You said it, pal." Guy sighed and lifted the beer to his lips. "You said it."

Men. They cause more trouble than they're worth, Willy thought as she viciously wound her alarm clock.

A bounty hunter. She should have guessed. Warning bells should have gone off in her head the minute he so generously offered his help. *Help.* What a laugh. She thought of all the solicitation letters she and her mother had received, all the mercenary groups who'd offered, for a few thousand dollars, to provide just such worthless help. There'd been the MIA Search Fund, the Men Alive Committee, Operation Chestnut—Let's Pull 'em Out Of The Fire! had been *their* revolting slogan. How many grieving families had invested their hopes and savings on such futile dreams?

She stripped down to a tank top and flopped onto the bed. A decent night's sleep, she could tell, was another futile dream. The mattress was lumpy, and the pillow seemed to be stuffed with concrete. Not that it mattered. How could she get any rest with that damned disco music vibrating through the walls? At 8:00 the first driving drumbeats had announced the opening of Dance Night at the Rex Hotel. *Lord,* she thought, *what good is communism if it can't even stamp out disco?*

It occurred to her that, at that very minute, Guy Barnard was probably loitering downstairs in that dance hall, checking out the action. Sometimes she thought that was the real reason men started wars—it was an excuse to run away from home and check out the action.

What do I care if he's down there eyeing the ladies? The man's scum. He's not worth a second thought.

Still, she had to admit he had a certain tattered charm. Nice straight teeth and a dazzling smile and eyes that were brown as a wolf's. A woman could get in trouble for the sake of those eyes. *And heaven knows, I don't need that kind of trouble.*

Someone knocked on the door. She sat up straight and called out, "Who is it?"

"Room service."

"There must be a mistake. I didn't order anything."

There was no response. Sighing, she pulled on a robe and padded over to open the door.

Guy grinned at her from the darkness. "Well?" he inquired. "Have you thought about it?"

"Thought about what?" she snapped back.

"You and me. Working together."

She laughed in disbelief. "Either you're hard of hearing or I didn't make myself clear."

"That was two hours ago. I figured you might have changed your mind."

"I will *never* change my mind. Good *night*." She slammed the door, shoved the bolt home and stepped back, seething.

There was a tapping on her window. She yanked the curtain aside and saw Guy smiling through the glass.

"Just one more question," he called.

"What?"

"Is that answer final?"

She jerked the curtain closed and stood there, waiting to see where he'd turn up next. Would he drop down from the ceiling? Pop up like a jack-in-the-box through the floor?

What was that rustling sound?

Glancing down sharply, she saw a piece of paper slide under the door. She snatched it up and read the scrawled message. "Call me if you need me."

Ha! she thought, ripping the note to pieces. "The day I need you is the day hell freezes over!" she yelled.

There was no answer. And she knew, without even looking, that he had already walked away.

Chantel gazed at the bottle of champagne, the tins of caviar and foie gras, and the box of chocolates, and she licked her lips. Then she said, "How dare you show up after all these years."

Siang merely smiled. "You have lost your taste for champagne? What a pity. It seems I shall have to drink it all myself." He reached for the bottle. Slowly, he untwisted the wire. The flight from Bangkok had jostled the contents; the cork shot out, spilling pale gold bubbles all over the earthen floor. Chantal gave a little sob.

She appeared ready to drop to her knees and lap up the precious liquid. He poured champagne into one of two fluted glasses he'd brought all the way from Bangkok. One could not, after all, drink champagne from a teacup. He took a sip and sighed happily. "Taittinger. Delightful."

"Taittinger?" she whispered.

He filled the second glass and set it on the rickety table in front of her. She kept staring at it, watching the bubbles spiral to the surface.

"I need help," he said.

She reached for the glass, put it to her trembling lips, tasted the rim, then the contents. He could almost see the bubbles sliding over her tongue, slipping down that fine, long throat. Even if the rest of her was sagging, she still had that beautiful throat, slender as a stalk of grass. A legacy from her Vietnamese mother. Her Asian half had held up over the years; the French half hadn't done so well. He could see the freckles, the fine lines tracing the corners of her greenish eyes.

She was no longer merely tasting the champagne; she was guzzling. Greedily, she drained the last drop from her glass and reached for the bottle.

He slid it out of her reach. "I said I need your help."

She wiped her chin with the back of her hand. "What kind of help?"

"Not much."

"Ha. That's what you always say."

"A pistol. Automatic. Plus several clips of ammunition."

"What if I don't have a pistol?"

"Then you will find me one."

She shook her head. "This is not the old days. You don't know what it's like here. Things are difficult."

She paused, looking down at her slightly crepey hands. "Saigon is a hell."

"Even hell can be made comfortable. I can see to that."

She was silent. He could read her mind almost as easily as if her eyes were transparent. She gazed down at the treasures he'd brought from Bangkok. She swallowed, her mouth still tingling with the taste of champagne. At last she said, "The gun. What do you want it for?"

"A job."

"Vietnamese?"

"American. A woman."

A spark flickered in Chantal's eyes. Curiosity. Maybe jealousy. Her chin came up. "Your lover?"

He shook his head.

"Then why do you want her dead?"

He shrugged. "Business. My client has offered generous compensation. I will split it with you."

"The way you did before?" she shot back.

He shook his head apologetically. "Chantal, Chantal." He sighed. "You know I had no choice. It was the last flight out of Saigon." He touched her face; it had lost its former silkiness. That French blood again: it didn't hold up well under years of harsh sunlight. "This time, I promise. You'll be paid."

She sat there looking at him, looking at the champagne. "What if it takes me time to find a gun?"

"Then I'll improvise. And I will need an assistant. Someone I can trust, someone discreet." He paused. "Your cousin, is he still in need of money?"

Their gazes met. He gave her a slow, significant smile. Then he filled her glass with champagne.

"Open the caviar," she said.

* * *

"I need your help," said Willy.

Guy, dazed and still half-asleep, stood in his doorway, blinking at the morning sunlight. He was uncombed, unshaven and wearing only a towel—a skimpy one at that. She tried to stay focused on his face, but her gaze kept dropping to his chest, to that mat of curly brown hair, to the scar knotting the upper abdomen.

He shook his head in disbelief. "You couldn't have told me this last night? You had to wait till the crack of dawn?"

"Guy, it's eight o'clock."

He yawned. "No kidding."

"Maybe you should try going to bed at a decent hour."

"Who says I didn't?" He leaned carelessly in the doorway and grinned. "Maybe sleep didn't happen to be on my agenda."

Dear God. Did he have a woman in his room? Automatically, Willy glanced past him into the darkened room. The bed was rumpled but unoccupied.

"Gotcha," he said, and laughed.

"I can see you're not going to be any help at all." She turned and walked away.

"Willy! Hey, come on." He caught her by the arm and pulled her around. "Did you mean it? About wanting my help?"

"Forget it. It was a lapse in judgment."

"Last night, hell had to freeze over before you'd come to me for help. But here you are. What made you change your mind?"

She didn't answer right off. She was too busy trying not to notice that his towel was slipping. To her relief, he snatched it together just in time and fastened it more securely around his hips.

At last she shook her head and sighed. "You were right. It's all going exactly as you said it would. No official will talk to me. No one'll answer my calls. They hear I'm coming and they all dive under their desks!"

"You could try a little patience. Wait another week."

"Next week's no good, either."

"Why?"

"Haven't you heard? It's Ho Chi Minh's birthday."

Guy looked heavenward. "How could I forget?"

"So what should I do?"

For a moment, he stood there thoughtfully rubbing his unshaven chin. Then he nodded. "Let's talk about it."

Back in his room, she sat uneasily on the edge of the bed while he dressed in the bathroom. The man was a restless sleeper, judging by the rumpled sheets. The blanket had been kicked off the bed entirely, the pillows punched into formless lumps by the headboard. Her gaze settled on the nightstand, where a stack of files lay. The top one was labeled Operation Friar Tuck. Declassified. Curious, she flipped open the cover.

"It's the way things work in this country," she heard him say through the bathroom door. "If you want to get from point A to point B, you don't go in a straight line. You walk two steps to the left, two to the right, turn and walk backward."

"So what should I do now?"

"The two-step. Sideways." He came out, dressed and freshly shaved. Spotting the open file on the nightstand, he calmly closed the cover. "Sorry. Not for public view," he said, sliding the stack of folders into his briefcase. Then he turned to her. "Now. Tell me what else is going on."

"What do you mean?"

"I get the feeling there's something more. It's eight o'clock in the morning. You can't have battled the bureaucracy this early. What really made you change your mind about me?"

"Oh, I haven't changed my mind about *you*. You're still a mercenary." Her disgust seemed to hang in the air like a bad odor.

"But now you're willing to work with me. Why?"

She looked down at her lap and sighed. Reluctantly she opened her purse and pulled out a slip of paper. "I found this under my door this morning."

He unfolded the paper. In a spidery hand was written "Die Yankee." Just seeing those two words again made her angry. A few minutes ago, when she'd shown the message to Mr. Ainh, his only reaction was to shake his head in regret. At least Guy was an American; surely *he'd* share her sense of outrage.

He handed the note back to her. "So?"

"'*So?*'" She stared at him. "I get a death threat slipped under my door. The entire Vietnamese government hides at the mention of my name. Ainh practically *commands* me to tour his stupid lacquer factory. And that's all you can say? 'So?'"

Clucking sympathetically, he sat down beside her. *Why does he have to sit so close?* she thought. She tried to ignore the tingling in her leg as it brushed against his, struggled to sit perfectly straight though his weight on the mattress was making her sag toward him.

"First of all," he explained, "this isn't necessarily

a personal death threat. It could be merely a political statement."

"Oh, is *that* all," she said blandly.

"And think of the lacquer factory as a visit to the dentist. You don't want to go, but everyone thinks you should. And as for the elusive Foreign Ministry, you wouldn't learn a thing from those bureaucrats anyway. Speaking of bureaucrats, where's your babysitter?"

"You mean Mr. Ainh?" She sighed. "Waiting for me in the lobby."

"You have to get rid of him."

"I wish."

"We can't have him around." Rising, Guy took her hand and pulled her to her feet. "Not where we're going."

"Where *are* we going?" she demanded, following him out the door.

"To see a friend. I think."

"Meaning he might not see us?"

"Meaning I can't be sure he's a friend."

She groaned as they stepped into the elevator. "Terrific."

Down in the lobby, they found Ainh by the desk, waiting to ambush her. "Miss Maitland!" he called. "Please, you must hurry. We have a very busy schedule today."

Willy glanced at Guy, who simply shrugged and looked off in another direction. Drat the man, he was leaving it up to her. "Mr. Ainh," she said, "about this little tour of the lacquer factory—"

"It will be quite fascinating! But they do not take dollars, so if you wish to exchange for dong, I can—"

"I'm afraid I don't feel up to it," she said flatly.

Ainh blinked in surprise. "You are ill?"

"Yes, I…" She suddenly noticed that Guy was shaking his head. "Uh, no, I'm not. I mean—"

"What she means," said Guy, "is that I offered to show her around. You know—" he winked at Ainh "—a little *personal* tour."

"P-personal?" Flushing, Ainh glanced at Willy. "But what about *my* tour? It is all arranged! The car, the sightseeing, a special lunch—"

"I tell you what, pal," said Guy, bending toward him conspiratorially. "Why don't *you* take the tour?"

"I have been on the tour," Ainh said glumly.

"Ah, but that was work, right? This time, why don't you take the day off, both you and the driver. Go see the sights of Saigon. And enjoy Ms. Maitland's lunch. After all, it's been paid for."

Ainh suddenly looked interested. "A free lunch?"

"And a beer." Guy slipped a few dollars into the man's breast pocket and patted the flap. "On me." He took Willy's arm and directed her across the lobby.

"But, Miss Maitland!" Ainh called out bleakly.

"Boy, what a blast you two guys're gonna have!" Guy sounded almost envious. "Air-conditioned car. Free lunch. No schedule to tie you down."

Ainh followed them outside, into a wall of morning heat so thick, it made Willy draw a breath of surprise. "Miss Maitland!" he said in desperation. "This is *not* the way it is supposed to be done!"

Guy turned and gave the man a solemn pat on the shoulder. "That, Mr. Ainh, is the whole idea."

They left the poor man standing alone on the steps, staring after them.

"What do you think he'll do?" whispered Willy.

"I think," said Guy, moving her along the crowded sidewalk, "he's going to enjoy a free lunch."

She glanced back and saw that Mr. Ainh had, indeed, disappeared into the hotel. She also noticed they were being followed. A street urchin, no more than twelve years old, caught up and danced around on the hot pavement.

"Lien-xo?" he chirped, dark eyes shining in a dirty face. They tried to ignore him, but the boy skipped along beside them, chattering all the way. His shirt hung in tatters; his feet were stained an apparently permanent brown. He pointed at Guy. *"Lien-xo?"*

"No, not Russian," said Guy. "Americanski."

The boy grinned. "Americanski? Yes?" He stuck out a smudgy hand and whooped. "Hello, Daddy!"

Resigned, Guy shook the boy's hand. "Yeah, it's nice to meet you too."

"Daddy rich?"

"Sorry. Daddy poor."

The boy laughed, obviously thinking that a grand joke. As Guy and Willy continued down the street, the boy hopped along at their side, shooing all the other urchins who had joined the procession. It was a tattered little parade marching through a sea of confusion. Bicycles whisked by, a multitude of wheels. And on the sidewalks, merchants squatted beside their meager collections of wares.

The boy tugged on Guy's arm. "Hey, Daddy. You got cigarette?"

"No," said Guy.

"Come on, Daddy. I do you favor, keep the beggars away."

"Oh, all right." Guy fished a pack of Marlboro cigarettes from his shirt pocket and handed the boy a cigarette.

"Guy, how could you?" Willy protested. "He's just a kid!"

"Oh, he's not going to smoke it," said Guy. "He'll trade it for something else. Like food. See?" He nodded at the boy, who was busy wrapping his treasure in a grimy piece of cloth. "That's why I always pack a few cartons when I come. They're handy when you need a favor." He turned and frowned up at one of the street signs. "Which, come to think of it, we do." He beckoned to the boy. "Hey, kid, what's your name?"

The boy shrugged.

"They must call you something."

"Other Americanski, he say I look like Oliver."

Guy laughed. "Probably meant Oliver Twist. Okay, Oliver. I got a deal for you. You do us a favor."

"Sure thing, Daddy."

"I'm looking for a street called Rue des Voiles. That's the old name, and it's not on the map. You know where it is?"

"Rue des Voiles? Rue des Voiles..." The boy scrunched up his face. "I think that one they call Binh Tan now. Why you want to go there? No stores, nothing to see."

Guy took out a thousand-dong note. "Just get us there."

The boy snapped up the money. "Okay, Daddy. You wait. Promise, you wait!" The boy trotted off down the street. At the corner, he glanced back and yelled again for good measure, "You wait!"

A minute later, he reappeared, trailed by a pair of

bicycle-driven cyclos. "I find you the best. Very fast," said Oliver.

Guy and Willy stared in dismay at the two drivers. One smiled back toothlessly; the other was wheezing like a freight train.

Guy shook his head. "Where on earth did he dig up these fossils?" he muttered.

Oliver pointed proudly to the two old men and grinned. "My uncles!"

A voice behind the door said, "Go away."

"Mr. Gerard?" Guy called. There was no answer, but the man was surely lurking near the door; Willy could almost feel him crouched silently on the other side. Guy reached for the knocker fashioned after some grotesque face—either a horned lion or a goat with teeth—that hung on the door like a brass wart. He banged it a few times. "Mr. Gerard!"

Still no answer.

"It's important! We have to talk to you!"

"I said, go away!"

Willy muttered, "Do you suppose it's just possible he doesn't want to talk to us?"

"Oh, he'll talk to us." Guy banged on the door again. "The name's Guy Barnard!" he yelled. "I'm a friend of Toby Wolff."

The latch slid open. One pale eye peeped out through a crack in the door. The eye flicked back and forth, squinting first at Guy, then at Willy. The voice attached to the eye hissed, "Toby Wolff is an idiot."

"Toby Wolff is also calling in his chips."

The eye blinked. The door opened a fraction of an

inch wider, the slit revealing a bald, crablike little man. "Well?" he snapped. "Are you just going to stand there?"

Inside, the house was dark as a cave, all the curtains drawn tightly over the windows. Guy and Willy followed the crustacean of a Frenchman down a narrow hallway. In the shadows, Gerard's outline was barely visible, but Willy could hear him just ahead of her, scuttling across the wood floor.

They emerged into what appeared to be a large sitting room. Slivers of light shimmered through worn curtains. In the suffocating darkness hulked vaguely discernible furniture.

"Sit, sit," ordered Gerard. Guy and Willy moved toward a couch, but Gerard snapped, "Not *there!* Can't you see that's a genuine Queen Anne?" He pointed at a pair of massive rosewood chairs. "Sit there." He settled into a brocade armchair by the window. With his arms crossed and his knobby knees jutting out at them, he looked like a disagreeable pile of bones. "So what does Toby want from me now?" he demanded.

"He said you could pass us some information."

Gerard snorted. "I am not in the business."

"You used to be."

"No longer. The stakes are too high."

Willy glanced thoughtfully around the room, noting in the shadows the soft gleam of ivory, the luster of fine old china. She suddenly realized they were surrounded by a treasure trove of antiques. Even the house was an antique, one of Saigon's lovely old French colonials, laced with climbing vines. By law it belonged to the state. She wondered what the Frenchman had done to keep such a home.

"It has been years since I had any business with the

Company," said Gerard. "I know nothing that could possibly help you now."

"Maybe you do," said Guy. "We're here about an old matter. From the war."

Gerard laughed. "These people are perpetually at war! Which enemy? The Chinese? The French? The Khmer Rouge?"

"You know which war," Guy said.

Gerard sat back. "*That* war is over."

"Not for some of us," said Willy.

The Frenchman turned to her. She felt him studying her, measuring her significance. She resented being appraised this way. Deliberately she returned his stare.

"What's the girl got to do with it?" Gerard demanded.

"She's here about her father. Missing in action since 1970."

Gerard shrugged. "My business is imports. I know nothing about missing soldiers."

"My father wasn't a soldier," said Willy. "He was a pilot for Air America."

"Wild Bill Maitland," Guy added.

The sudden silence in the room was thick enough to slice. After a long pause, Gerard said softly, "Air America."

Willy nodded. "You remember him?"

The Frenchman's knobby fingers began to tap the armrest. "I knew of them, the pilots. They carried goods for me on occasion. At a price."

"Goods?"

"Pharmaceuticals," said Guy.

Gerard slapped the armrest in irritation. "Come, Mr. Barnard, we both know what we're talking about!

Opium. I don't deny it. There was a war going on, and there was money to be made. So I made it. Air America happened to provide the most reliable delivery service. The pilots never asked questions. They were good that way. I paid them what they were worth. In gold."

Again there was a silence. It took all Willy's courage to ask the next question. "And my father? Was he one of the pilots you paid in gold?"

Alain Gerard shrugged. "Would it surprise you?"

Somehow, it wouldn't, but she tried to imagine what all those old family friends would say, the ones who'd thought her father a hero.

"He was one of the best," said Gerard.

She looked up. "The best?" She felt like laughing. "At what? Running drugs?"

"Flying. It was his calling."

"My father's calling," she said bitterly, "was to do whatever he wanted. With no thought for anyone else."

"Still," insisted Gerard, "he was one of the best."

"The day his plane went down…" said Guy. "Was he carrying something of yours?"

The Frenchman didn't answer. He fidgeted in his chair, then rose and went to the window, where he fussed prissily with the curtains.

"Gerard?" Guy prodded.

Gerard turned and looked at them. "Why are you here? What purpose do these questions serve?"

"I have to know what happened to him," said Willy.

Gerard turned to the window and peered out through a slit in the curtains. "Go home, Miss Maitland. Before you learn things you don't want to know."

"What things?"

"Unpleasant things."

"He was my father! I have a right—"

"A right?" Gerard laughed. "He was in a war zone! He knew the risks. He was just another man who did not come back alive."

"I want to know why. I want to know what he was doing in Laos."

"Since when does *anyone* know what they were really doing in Laos?" He moved around the room, covetously touching his precious treasures. "You cannot imagine the things that went on in those days. Our secret war. Laos was the country we didn't talk about. But we were all there. Russians, Chinese, Americans, French. Friends and enemies, packed into the same filthy bars of Vientiane. Good soldiers, all of us, out to make a living." He stopped and looked at Willy. "I still do not understand that war."

"But you knew more than most," said Guy. "You were working with Intelligence."

"I saw only part of the picture."

"Toby Wolff suggested you took part in the crash investigation."

"I had little to do with it."

"Then who was in charge?"

"An American colonel by the name of Kistner."

Willy looked up in surprise. "*Joseph* Kistner?"

"Since promoted to general," Guy noted softly.

Gerard nodded. "He called himself a military attaché."

"Meaning he was really CIA."

"Meaning any number of things. I was liaison for French Intelligence, and I was told only the minimum. That was the way the colonel worked, you see. For him, information was power. He shared very little of it."

"What do you know about the crash?"

Gerard shrugged. "They called it 'a routine loss.' Hostile fire. A search was called at the insistence of the other pilots, but no survivors were found. After a day, Colonel Kistner put out the order to melt any wreckage. I don't know if the order was ever executed."

Willy shook her head. "Melt?"

"That's jargon for destroy," explained Guy. "They do it whenever a plane goes down during a classified mission. To get rid of the evidence."

"But my father wasn't flying a classified mission. It was a routine supply flight."

"They were *all* listed as routine supply flights," said Gerard.

"The cargo manifest listed aircraft parts," said Guy. "Not a reason to melt the plane. What was really on that flight?"

Gerard didn't answer.

"There was a passenger," Willy said. "They were carrying a passenger."

Gerard's gaze snapped toward her. "Who told you this?"

"Luis Valdez, Dad's cargo kicker. He bailed out as the plane went down."

"You spoke to this man Valdez?"

"It was only a short phone call, right after he was released from the POW camp."

"Then…he is still alive?"

She shook her head. "He shot himself the day after he got back to the States."

Gerard began to pace around the room again, touching each piece of furniture. He reminded her of a greedy gnome fingering his treasures.

"Who was the passenger, Gerard?" asked Guy.

Gerard picked up a lacquer box, set it back down again.

"Military? Intelligence? What?"

Gerard stopped pacing. "He was a phantom, Mr. Barnard."

"Meaning you don't know his name?"

"Oh, he had many names, many faces. A rumor always does. Some said he was a general. Or a prince. Or a drug lord." Turning, he stared out the curtain slit, a shriveled silhouette against the glow of light. "Whoever he was, he represented a threat to someone in a high place."

Someone in a high place. Willy thought of the intrigue that must have swirled in Vientiane, 1970. She thought of Air America and Defense Intelligence and the CIA. Who among all those players would have felt threatened by this one unnamed Lao?

"Who do *you* think he was, Mr. Gerard?" she asked.

The silhouette at the window shrugged. "It makes no difference now. He's dead. Everyone on that plane is dead."

"Maybe not all of them. My father—"

"Your father has not been seen in twenty years. And if I were you, I would leave well enough alone."

"But if he's alive—"

"If he's alive, he may not wish to be found." Gerard turned and looked at her, his expression hidden against the backglow of the window. "A man with a price on his head has good reason to stay dead."

Chapter 5

She stared at him. "A price? I don't understand."

"You mean no one has told you about the bounty?"

"Bounty for what?"

"For the arrest of Friar Tuck."

She fell instantly still. An image took shape in her mind: words typed on a file folder. *Operation Friar Tuck. Declassified.* She turned to Guy. "You know what he's talking about, don't you. Who's Friar Tuck?"

Guy's expression was unreadable, as if a mask had fallen over his face. "It's nothing but a story."

"But you had his file in your room."

"It's just a nickname for a renegade pilot. A legend—"

"Not just a legend," insisted Gerard. "He was a real man, a traitor. Intelligence does not offer two-million-dollar bounties for mere legends."

Willy's gaze shot back to Guy. She wondered how he

had the nerve—the gall—to meet her eyes. *You knew,* she thought. *You bastard. All the time, you knew.* Rage had tightened her throat almost beyond speech.

She barely managed to force out her next question, which she directed at Alain Gerard. "You think this— this renegade pilot is my father?"

"Intelligence thought so."

"Based on what evidence? That he could fly planes? The fact that he's not here to defend himself?"

"Based on the timing, the circumstances. In July 1970, William Maitland vanished from the face of the earth. In August of the same year, we heard the first reports of a foreign pilot flying for the enemy. Running weapons and gold."

"But there were hundreds of foreign pilots in Laos! Friar Tuck could have been a Frenchman, a Russian, a—"

"This much we did know—he was American."

She raised her chin. "You're saying my father was a traitor."

"I am telling you this only because it's something you should know. If he's alive, this is the reason he may not want to be found. You think you are on some sort of rescue mission, Miss Maitland, but you may be sadly mistaken. Your father could go home to a jail cell."

In the silence that followed, she turned her gaze to Guy. He still hadn't said a word; that alone proved his guilt. *Who do you work for?* she wondered. *The CIA? The Ariel Group? Or your lying, miserable self?*

She couldn't stand the sight of him. Even being in the same room with him made her recoil in disgust.

She rose. "Thank you, Mr. Gerard. You've told me things I needed to hear. Things I didn't expect."

"Then you agree it's best you drop the matter?"

"I don't agree. You think my father's a traitor. Obviously you're not the only one who thinks so. But you're all wrong."

"And how will you prove it?" Gerard snorted. "Tell me, Miss Maitland, how will you perform this grand miracle after twenty years?"

She didn't have an answer. The truth was, she didn't know what her next move would be. All she knew was that she would have to do it alone.

Her spine was ramrod straight as she followed Gerard back down the hall. The whole time, she was intensely aware of Guy moving right behind her. *I knew I couldn't trust him,* she thought. *From the very beginning I knew it.*

No one said a word until they reached the front door. There Gerard paused. Quietly he said, "Mr. Barnard? You will relay a message to Toby Wolff?"

Guy nodded. "Certainly. What's the message?"

"Tell him he has just called in his last chip." Gerard opened the front door. Outside, the sunshine was blinding. "There will be no more from me."

She made it scarcely five steps before her rage burst through.

"You lied to me. You scum, you were *using* me!"

The look on his face was the only answer Willy needed. It was written there clearly; the acknowledgment, the guilt.

"You knew about Friar Tuck. About the bounty. You weren't after just any 'live one,' were you? You were after a particular man—my father!"

Guy gave a shrug as though, now that the truth was out, it hardly mattered.

"How was this 'deal' with me supposed to work?" she pressed on. "Tell me, I'm curious. Were you going to turn him in the instant we found him—and my part of the deal be damned? Or were you going to humor me awhile, give me a chance to get my father home, let him step off the plane and onto American soil before you had him arrested? What was the plan, Guy? What *was* it?"

"There was no plan."

"Come on. A man like you always has a plan."

He looked tired. Defeated. "There was no plan."

She stared straight up at him, her fists clenching, unclenching. "I bet you had plans for that two million dollars. I bet you knew exactly how you were going to spend it. Every penny. And all you had to do was put my father away. You bastard." She should have slugged him right then and there. Instead, she walked away.

"Sure, I could use two million bucks!" he yelled. "I could use a lot of things! But I didn't want to use *you!*"

She kept walking. It took him only a few quick strides to catch up to her.

"Willy. Dammit, will you listen?"

"To what? More of your lies?"

"No. The truth."

"The truth?" She laughed. "Since when have you bothered with the truth?"

He grabbed her arm and pulled her around to face him. "Since right now."

"Let me go."

"Not until you hear me out."

"Why should I believe anything you say?"

"Look, I admit it. I knew about Friar Tuck. About the reward. And—"

"And you knew my father was on their list."

"Yes."

"Then why didn't you tell me?"

"I would have. I was going to."

"It was all worked out from the beginning, wasn't it? Use me to track down my father."

"I thought about it. At first."

"Oh, you're low, Guy. You're really scraping bottom. Does money mean so much to you?"

"I wasn't doing it for the money. I didn't have a choice. They backed me into it."

"Who?"

"The Ariel Group. I told you—two weeks ago they showed up in my office. They knew I was headed back to Nam. What I didn't tell you was the real reason they wanted me to work for them. They weren't tracking MIAs. They were tracking an old war criminal."

"Friar Tuck."

He nodded. "I told them I wasn't interested. They offered me money. A lot of it. I got a little interested. Then they made me an offer I couldn't refuse."

"Ah," she said with disdain.

"Not money…" he protested.

"Then what's the payoff?"

He ran his hand through his hair and let out a tired breath. "Silence."

She frowned, not understanding. He didn't say a thing, but she could see in his eyes some deep, dark agony. "Then that's it," she finally whispered. "Blackmail. What do they have on you, Guy? What are you hiding?"

"It's not—" he swallowed "—something I can talk about."

"I see. It must be pretty damn shocking. Which is

no big surprise, I guess. But it still doesn't justify what you tried to do to me." She turned and walked away in disgust.

The road shimmered in the midmorning heat. Guy was right on her heels, like a stray dog that refused to be left behind. And he wasn't the only stray following her. The slap of bare feet announced the reappearance of Oliver, who skipped along beside her, chirping, "You want cyclo ride? It is very hot day! A thousand dong— I get you ride!"

She heard the squeak of wheels, the wheeze of an out-of-breath driver. Now Oliver's uncles had joined the procession.

"Go away," she said. "I don't want a ride."

"Sun very hot, very strong today. Maybe you faint. Once I see Russian lady faint." Oliver shook his head at the memory. "It was very bad sight."

"Go *away!*"

Undaunted, Oliver turned to Guy. "How about you, Daddy?"

Guy slapped a few bills into Oliver's grubby hand. "There's a thousand. Now scram."

Oliver vanished. Unfortunately, Guy wasn't so easily brushed off. He followed Willy into the town marketplace, past stands piled high with melons and mangoes, past counters where freshly butchered meat gathered flies.

"I was going to tell you about your father," Guy said. "I just wasn't sure how you'd take it."

"I'm not afraid of the truth."

"Sure you are! You're trying to protect him. That's why you keep ignoring the evidence."

"He wasn't a traitor!"

"You still love him, don't you?"

She turned sharply and walked away. Guy was right beside her. "What's wrong?" he said. "Did I hit a nerve?"

"Why should I care about him? He walked out on us."

"And you still feel guilty about it."

"Guilty?" She stopped. "Me?"

"That's right. Somewhere in that little-girl head of yours, you still blame yourself for his leaving. Maybe you had a fight, the way kids and dads always do, and you said something you shouldn't have. But before you had the chance to make up, he took off. And his plane went down. And here you are, twenty years later, still trying to make it up to him."

"Practicing psychiatry without a license now?"

"It doesn't take a shrink to know what goes on in a kid's head. I was fourteen when *my* old man walked out. I never got over being abandoned, either. Now I worry about my own kid. And it hurts."

She stared at him, astonished. "You have a child?"

"In a manner of speaking." He looked down. "The boy's mother and I, we weren't married. It's not something I'm particularly proud of."

"Oh."

"Yeah."

You walked out on them, she thought. *Your father left you. You left your son. The world never changes.*

"He wasn't a traitor," she insisted, returning to the matter at hand. "He was a lot of things—irresponsible, careless, insensitive. But he wouldn't turn against his own country."

"But he's on that list of suspects. If he's not Friar Tuck himself, he's probably connected somehow. And it's got to be a dangerous link. That's why someone's trying to stop you. That's why you're hitting brick walls wherever you turn. That's why, with every step you take, you're being followed."

"What!" In reflex, she turned to scan the crowd.

"Don't be so obvious." Guy grabbed her arm and dragged her to a pharmacy window. "Man at two o'clock," he murmured, nodding at a reflection in the glass. "Blue shirt, black trousers."

"Are you sure?"

"Absolutely. I just don't know who he's working for."

"He looks Vietnamese."

"But he could be working for the Russians. Or the Chinese. They both have a stake in this country."

Even as she stared at the reflection, the man in the blue shirt melted into the crowd. She knew he was still lingering nearby; she could feel his gaze on her back.

"What do I do, Guy?" she whispered. "How do I get rid of him?"

"You can't. Just keep in mind he's there. That you're probably under constant surveillance. In fact, we seem to be under the surveillance of a whole damn army." At least a dozen faces were now reflected there, all of them crowded close and peering curiously at the two foreigners. In the back, a familiar figure kept bouncing up and down, waving at them in the glass.

"Hello, Daddy!" came a yell.

Guy sighed. "We can't even get rid of *him*."

Willy stared hard at Guy's reflection. And she thought, *But I can get rid of you.*

Major Nathan Donnell of the Casualty Resolution team had shocking red hair, a booming voice and a cigar that stank to high heaven. Guy didn't know which was worse—the stench of that cigar or the odor of decay emanating from the four skeletons on the table. Maybe that's why Nate smoked those rotten cigars; they masked the smell of death.

The skeletons, each labeled with an ID number, were laid out on separate tarps. Also on the table were four plastic bags containing the personal effects and various other items found with the skeletons. After twenty or more years in this climate, not much remained of these bodies except dirt-encrusted bones and teeth. At least that much was left; sometimes fragments were all they had to work with.

Nate was reading aloud from the accompanying reports. In that grim setting, his resonant voice sounded somehow obscene, echoing off the walls of the Quonset hut. "Number 784-A, found in jungle, twelve klicks west of Camp Hawthorne. Army dog tag nearby—name, Elmore Stukey, Pfc."

"The tag was lying nearby?" Guy asked. "Not around the neck?"

Nate glanced at the Vietnamese liaison officer, who was standing off to the side. "Is that correct? It wasn't around the neck?"

The Vietnamese man nodded. "That is what the report said."

"Elmore Stukey," muttered Guy, opening the man's military medical record. "Six foot two, Caucasian, perfect teeth." He looked at the skeleton. Just a glance at the femur told him the man on the table couldn't have stood much taller than five-six. He shook his head. "Wrong guy."

"Cross off Stukey?"

"Cross off Stukey. But note that someone made off with his dog tag."

Nate let out a morbid laugh. "Not a good sign."

"What about these other three?"

"Oh, those." Nate flipped to another report. "Those three were found together eight klicks north of LZ Bird. Had that U.S. Army helmet lying close by. Not much else around."

Guy focused automatically on the relevant details: pelvic shape, configuration of incisors. "Those two are females, probably Asian," he noted. "But that one..." He took out a tape measure, ran it along the dirt-stained femur. "Male, five foot nine or thereabouts. Hmm. Silver fillings on numbers one and two." He nodded. "Possible."

Nate glanced at the Vietnamese liaison officer. "Number 786-A. I'll be flying him back for further examination."

"And the others?"

"What do you think, Guy?"

Guy shrugged. "We'll take 784-A, as well. Just to be safe. But the two females are yours."

The Vietnamese nodded. "We will make the arrangements," he said, and quietly withdrew.

There was a silence as Nate lit up another cigar, shook out the match. "Well, you sure made quick work of it. I wasn't expecting you here till tomorrow."

"Something came up."

"Yeah?" Nate's expression was thoughtful through the stinking cloud of smoke. "Anything I can help you with?"

"Maybe."

Nate nodded toward the door. "Come on. Let's get out of here. This place gives me the creeps."

They walked outside and stood in the dusty courtyard of the old military compound. Barbed wire curled on the wall above them. A rattling air conditioner dripped water from a window of the Quonset hut.

"So," said Nate, contentedly puffing on his cigar. "Is this business or personal?"

"Both. I need some information."

"Not classified, I hope."

"You tell me."

Nate laughed and squinted up at the barbed wire. "I may not tell you anything. But ask anyway."

"You were on the repatriation team back in '73, right?"

"Seventy-three through '75. But my job didn't amount to much. Just smiled a lot and passed out razors and toothbrushes. You know, a welcome-home handshake for returning POWs."

"Did you happen to shake hands with any POWs from Tuyen Quan?"

"Not many. Half a dozen. That was a pretty miserable camp. Had an outbreak of typhoid near the end. A lot of 'em died in captivity."

"But not all of them. One of the POWs was a guy named Luis Valdez. Remember him?"

"Just the name. And only because I heard he shot himself the day after he got home. I thought it was a crying shame."

"Then you never met him?"

"No, he went through closed debriefing. Totally separate channel. No outside contact."

Guy frowned, wondering about that closed debriefing. Why had Intelligence shut Valdez off from the others?

"What about the other POWs from Tuyen Quan?"

asked Guy. "Did anyone talk about Valdez? Mention why he was kept apart?"

"Not really. Hey, they were a pretty delirious bunch. All they could talk about was going home. Seeing their families. Anyway, I don't think any of them knew Valdez. The camp held its prisoners two to a cell, and Valdez's cellmate wasn't in the group."

"Dead?"

"No. Refused to get on the plane. If you can believe it."

"Didn't want to fly?"

"Didn't want to go home, period."

"You remember his name?"

"Hell, yes. I had to file a ten-page report on the guy. Lassiter. Sam Lassiter. Incident got me a reprimand."

"What happened?"

"We tried to drag him aboard. He kept yelling that he wanted to stay in Nam. And he was this big blond Viking, you know? Six foot four, kicking and screaming like a two-year-old. Should've seen the Vietnamese, laughing at it all. Anyway, the guy got loose and tore off into the crowd. At that point, we figured, what the hell. Let the jerk stay if he wants to."

"Then he never went home?"

Nate blew out a cloud of cigar smoke. "Never did. For a while, we tried to keep tabs on him. Last we heard, he was sighted over in Cantho, but that was a few years ago. Since then he could've moved on. Or died." Nate glanced around at the barren compound. "Nuts—that's my diagnosis. Gotta be nuts to stay in this godforsaken country."

Maybe not, thought Guy. *Maybe he didn't have a choice.*

"What happened to the other guys from Tuyen?" Guy asked. "After they got home?"

"They had the usual problems. Post-traumatic-stress reaction, you know. But they adjusted okay. Or as well as could be expected."

"All except Valdez."

"Yeah. All except Valdez." Nate flicked off a cigar ash. "Couldn't do a thing for him, or for wackos like Lassiter. When they're gone, they're gone. All those kids— they were too young for that war. Didn't have their heads together to begin with. Whenever I think of Lassiter and Valdez, it makes me feel pretty damn useless."

"You did what you could."

Nate nodded. "Well, I guess we're good for something." Nate sighed and looked over at the Quonset hut. "At least 786-A's finally going home."

The Russians were singing again. Otherwise it was a pleasant enough evening. The beer was cold, the bartender discreetly attentive. From his perch at the rooftop bar, Guy watched the Russkies slosh another round of Stolichnaya into their glasses. They, at least, seemed to be having a good time; it was more than he could say for himself.

He had to come up with a plan, and fast. Everything he'd learned, from Alain Gerard that morning and from Nate Donnell that afternoon, had backed up what he'd already suspected: that Willy Maitland was in over her pretty head. He was convinced that the attack in Bangkok hadn't been a robbery attempt. Someone was out to stop her. Someone who didn't want her rooting around in Bill Maitland's past. The CIA? The Vietnamese? Wild Bill himself?

That last thought he discarded as impossible. No man, no matter how desperate, would send someone to attack his own daughter.

But what if it had been meant only as a warning? A scare tactic?

All the possibilities, all the permutations, were giving Guy a headache. Was Maitland alive? What was his connection to Friar Tuck? Were they one and the same man?

Why was the Ariel Group involved?

That was the other part of the puzzle—the Ariel Group. Guy mentally replayed that visit they'd paid him two weeks ago. The two men who'd appeared in his office had been unremarkable: clean shaven, dark suits, nondescript ties, the sort of faces you'd forget the instant they walked out your door. Only when they'd presented the check for twenty thousand dollars did he sit up and take notice. Whoever they were, they had cash to burn. And there was more money waiting—a lot more—if only he'd do them one small favor: locate a certain pilot known as Friar Tuck. "Your patriotic duty," they'd called it. The man was a traitor, a red-blooded American who'd gone over to the other side. Still, Guy had hesitated. It wasn't his kind of job. He wasn't a bounty hunter.

That's when they'd played their trump card.

Ariel, Ariel. He kept mulling over the name. Something Biblical. Lionlike men. Odd name for a vets organization. If that's what they were.

Ariel wasn't the only group hunting the elusive Friar Tuck. The CIA had a bounty on the man. For all Guy knew, the Vietnamese, the French and the men from Mars were after the pilot, as well.

And at the very eye of the hurricane was naive, stubborn, impossible Willy Maitland.

That she was so damnably attractive only made things worse. She was a maddening combination of toughness and vulnerability, and he'd been torn between using her and protecting her. Did any of that make sense?

The rhythmic thud of disco music drifted up from a lower floor. He considered heading downstairs to find some willing dance partner and trample a few toes. As he took another swallow of beer, a familiar figure passed through his peripheral vision. Turning, he saw Willy head for a table near the railing. He wondered if she'd consider joining him for a drink.

Obviously not, he decided, seeing how determinedly she was ignoring him. She stared off at the night, her back rigid, her gaze fixed somewhere in the distance. A strand of tawny hair slid over her cheek, and she tucked it behind her ear, a tight little gesture that made him think of a schoolmarm.

He decided to ignore her, too. But the more fiercely he tried to shove all thought of her from his mind, the more her image seemed to burn into his brain. Even as he focused his gaze on the bartender's dwindling bottle of Stolichnaya, he felt her presence, like a crackling fire radiating somewhere behind him.

What the hell. He'd give it one more try.

He shoved to his feet and strode across the rooftop.

Willy sensed his approach but didn't bother to look up, even when he grabbed a chair, sat down and leaned across the table.

"I still think we can work together," he said.

She sniffed. "I doubt it."

"Can't we at least talk about it?"

"I don't have a thing to say to you, Mr. Barnard."

"So it's back to Mr. Barnard."

Her frigid gaze met his across the table. "I could call you something else. I could call you a—"

"Can we skip the sweet talk? Look, I've been to see a friend of mine—"

"You have friends? Amazing."

"Nate was part of the welcome-home team back in '75. Met a lot of returning POWs. Including the men from Tuyen Quan."

Suddenly she looked interested. "He knew Luis Valdez?"

"No. Valdez was routed through classified debriefing. No one got near him. But Valdez had a cellmate in Tuyen Quan, a man named Sam Lassiter. Nate says Lassiter didn't go home."

"He died?"

"He never left the country."

She leaned forward, her whole body suddenly rigid with excitement. "He's still here in Nam?"

"Was a few years ago anyway. In Cantho. It's a river town in the Delta, about a hundred and fifty kilometers southwest of here."

"Not very far," she said, her mind obviously racing. "I could leave tomorrow morning…get there by afternoon…"

"And just how are you going to get there?"

"What do you mean, how? By car, of course."

"You think Mr. Ainh's going to let you waltz off on your own?"

"That's what bribes are for. Some people will do anything for a buck. Won't they?"

He met her hard gaze with one equally unflinching. "Forget the damn money. Don't you see someone's trying to use *both* of us? I want to know why." He leaned forward, his voice soft, coaxing. "I've made arrangements for a driver to Cantho first thing in the morning. We can tell Ainh I've invited you along for the ride. You know, just another tourist visiting the—"

She laughed. "You must think I have the IQ of a turnip. Why should I trust you? Bounty hunter. Opportunist. *Jerk.*"

"Lovely evening, isn't it?" cut in a cheery voice.

Dodge Hamilton, drink in hand, beamed down at them. He was greeted with dead silence.

"Oh, dear. Am I intruding?"

"Not at all," Willy said with a sigh, pulling a chair out for the ubiquitous Englishman. No doubt he wanted company for his misery, and she would do fine. They could commiserate a little more about his lost story and her lost father.

"No, really, I wouldn't dream of—"

"I insist." Willy tossed a lethal glance at Guy. "Mr. Barnard was just leaving."

Hamilton's gaze shifted from Guy to the offered chair. "Well, if you insist." He settled uneasily into the chair, set his glass down on the table and looked at Willy. "What I wanted to ask you, Miss Maitland, is whether you'd consent to an interview."

"Me? Why on earth?"

"I decided on a new focus for my Saigon story—a daughter's search for her father. Such a touching angle. A sentimental journey into—"

"Bad idea," Guy said, cutting in.

"Why?" asked Hamilton.

"It…has no passion," he improvised. "No romance. No excitement."

"Of course, there's excitement. A missing father—"

"Hamilton." Guy leaned forward. "No."

"He's asking *me,*" Willy said. "After all, it's about my father."

Guy's gaze swung around to her. "Willy," he said quietly, "think."

"I'm thinking a little publicity might open a few doors."

"More likely it'd close doors. The Vietnamese hate to hang out their dirty laundry. What if they know what happened to your father, and it wasn't a nice ending? They're not going to want the details all over the London papers. It'd be much easier to throw you out of the country."

"Believe me," said Hamilton, "I can be discreet."

"A discreet reporter. Right," Guy muttered.

"Not a word would be printed till she's left the country."

"The Vietnamese aren't dumb. They'd find out what you were working on."

"Then I'll give them a cover story. Something to throw them off the track."

"Excuse me…" Willy said politely.

"The matter's touchier than you realize, Hamilton," Guy said.

"I've covered delicate matters before. When I say something's off the record, I keep it off the record."

Willy rose to her feet. "I give up. I'm going to bed."

Guy looked up. "You can't go to bed. We haven't finished talking."

"You and I have definitely finished talking."

"What about tomorrow?"

"What about my story?"

"Hamilton," she said, "if it's dirty laundry you're looking for, why don't you interview *him?*" She pointed to Guy. Then she turned and walked away.

Hamilton looked at Guy. "What dirty laundry do you have?"

Guy merely smiled.

He was still smiling as he crumpled his beer can in his bare hands.

Lord, deliver me from the jerks of the world, Willy thought wearily as she stepped into the elevator. The doors slid closed. *Above all, deliver me from Guy Barnard.*

Leaning back, she closed her eyes and waited for the elevator to creep down to the fourth floor. It moved at a snail's pace, like everything else in this country. The stale air was rank with the smell of liquor and sweat. Through the creak of the cables she could hear a faint squeaking, high in the elevator shaft. Bats. She'd seen them the night before, flapping over the courtyard. Wonderful. Bats and Guy Barnard. Could a girl ask for anything more?

If only there was some way she could have the benefit of his insider's knowledge without having to put up with *him.* The man was clever and streetwise, and he had those shadowy but all-important connections. Too bad he couldn't be trusted. Still, she couldn't help wondering what it would be like to take him up on his offer. Just the thought of working cheek to cheek with the man made her stomach dance a little pirouette of excitement. An ominous sign. The man was getting to her.

Oh, she'd been in love before; she knew how unreasonable hormones could be, how much havoc they could wreak, cavorting in a deprived female body.

I just won't think about him. It's the wrong time, the wrong place, the wrong situation.

And definitely the wrong man.

The elevator groaned to a halt, and the doors slid open to the deserted outdoor walkway. The night trembled to the distant beat of disco music as she headed through the shadows to her room. The entire fourth floor seemed abandoned this evening, all the windows unlit, the curtains drawn. She whirled around in fright as a chorus of shrieks echoed off the building and spiraled up into the darkness. Beyond the walkway railing, the shadows of bats rose and fluttered like phantoms over the courtyard.

Her hands were still shaking when she reached her door, and it took a moment to find the key. As she rummaged in her purse, a figure glided into her peripheral vision. Some sixth sense—a premonition of danger—made her turn.

At the end of the walkway, a man emerged from the shadows. As he passed beneath the glow of an outdoor lamp, she saw slick black hair and a face so immobile it seemed cast in wax. Then something else drew her gaze. Something in his hand. He was holding a knife.

She dropped her purse and ran.

Just ahead, the walkway turned a corner, past a huge air-conditioning vent. If she kept moving, she would reach the safety of the stairwell.

The man was yards behind. Surely the purse was what he wanted. But as she tore around the corner, she heard his footsteps thudding in pursuit. Oh, God, he wasn't after her money.

He was after her.

The stairwell lay ahead at the far end of the walkway. Just one flight down was the dance hall. She'd find people there. Safety…

With a desperate burst of speed, she sprinted forward. Then, through a fog of panic, she saw that her escape route was cut off.

Another man had appeared. He stood in the shadows at the far end of the walkway. She couldn't see his expression; all she saw was the faint gleam of his face.

She halted, spun around. As she did, something whistled past her cheek and clattered onto the walkway. A knife. Automatically, she snatched it up and wielded it in front of her.

Her gaze shifted first to one man, then the other. They were closing in.

She screamed. Her cry mingled with the dance music, echoed off the buildings and funneled up into the night. A wave of startled bats fluttered up through the darkness. *Can't anyone hear me?* she thought in desperation.

She cast another frantic look around, searching for a way out. In front of her, beyond the railing, lay a four-story drop to the courtyard. Just behind her, sunk into a square expanse of graveled roof, was the enormous air-conditioning vent. Through the rusted grating she saw its giant fan blades spinning like a plane's propeller. The blast of warm air was so powerful it made her skirt billow.

The men moved in for the kill.

Chapter 6

She had no choice. She scrambled over the railing and dropped onto the grating. It sagged under her weight, lowering her heart-stoppingly close to the deadly blades. A rusted fragment crumbled off into the fan; the clatter of metal was deafening.

She inched her way over the grate, heading for a safe island of rooftop. It was only a few steps across, but it felt like miles of tightrope suspended over oblivion. Her legs were trembling as she finally stepped off the grate. It was a dead end; beyond lay a sheer drop. And a crumbling expanse of grating was all that separated her from the killers.

The two men glanced around in frustration, searching for a safe way to reach her. There was no other route; they would have to cross the vent. But the grating had barely supported her weight; these men were far heavier. She looked at the deadly whirl of the blades. They wouldn't risk it, she thought.

But to her disbelief, one of the men climbed over the railing and eased himself onto the vent. The mesh sagged but held. He stared at her over the spinning blades, and she saw in his eyes the impassive gaze of a man who'd simply come to do his job.

Trapped, she thought. *Dear God, I'm trapped!*

She screamed again, but her cry of terror was lost in the fan's roar.

He was halfway across, his knife poised. She clutched her knife and backed away to the very edge of the roof. She had two choices: a four-story drop to the pavement below, or hand-to-hand combat with an experienced assassin. Both prospects seemed equally hopeless.

She crouched, knife in trembling hand, to slash, to claw—anything to stay alive. The man took another step. The blade moved closer.

Then gunfire ripped the night.

Willy stared in bewilderment as the killer clutched his belly and looked down at his bloody hand, his face a mask of astonishment. Then, like a puppet whose strings have been cut, he crumpled. As dead weight hit the weakened grating, Willy closed her eyes and cringed.

She never saw his body fall through. But she heard the squeal of metal, felt the wild shuddering of the fan blades. She collapsed to her knees, retching into the darkness below.

When the heaving finally stopped, she forced her head up.

Her other attacker had vanished.

Across the courtyard, on the opposite walkway, something gleamed. The barrel of a gun being lowered. A small face peering at her over the railing. She struggled to make sense of why the boy was there, why he had just saved her life. Stumbling to her feet, she whispered, "Oliver?"

The boy merely put a finger to his lips. Then, like a ghost, he slipped away into the darkness.

Dazed, she heard shouts and the thud of approaching footsteps.

"Willy! Are you all right?"

She turned and saw Guy. And she heard the panic in his voice.

"Don't move! I'll come get you."

"No!" she cried. "The grate—it's broken—"

For a moment, he studied the spinning blades. Then, glancing around, he spotted a workman's ladder propped beneath a broken window. He dragged it to the railing, hoisted it over and slid it horizontally across the broken grate. Then he eased himself over the railing, carefully stepped onto a rung and extended his arm to Willy. "I'm right here," he said. "Put your left foot on the ladder and grab my hand. I won't let you fall, I swear it. Come on, sweetheart. Just reach for my hand."

She couldn't look down at the fan blades. She looked across them at Guy's face, tense and gleaming with sweat. At his hand, reaching for her. And in that instant she knew, without a shred of doubt, that he would catch her. That she could trust him with her life.

She took a breath for courage, then took the step forward, over the whirling blades.

Instantly his hand locked over hers. For a split second she teetered. Guy's rigid grasp steadied her. Slowly, jerkily, she lunged forward onto the rung where he balanced.

"I've got you!" he yelled as he swept her into his arms, away from the yawning vent. He swung her easily over the railing onto the walkway, then dropped down beside her. He pulled her into the safety of his arms.

"It's all right," he murmured over and over into her hair. "Everything's all right...."

Only then, as she felt his heart pounding against hers, did she realize how terrified he'd been for her.

She was shaking so hard she could barely stand on her own two legs. It didn't matter. She knew the arms now wrapped around her would never let her fall.

They both stiffened as a harsh command was issued in Vietnamese. The people gathered about them quickly stepped aside to let a policeman through. Willy squinted as a blinding light shone in her eyes. The flashlight's beam shifted and froze on the air-conditioning vent. From the spectators came a collective gasp of horror.

"Dear God," she heard Dodge Hamilton whisper. "What a bloody mess."

Mr. Ainh was sweating. He was also hungry and tired, and he needed badly to use the toilet. But all these concerns would have to wait. He had learned that much from the war: patience. *Victory comes to those who endure.* This was what he kept saying to himself as he sat in his hard chair and stared down at the wooden table.

"We have been careless, Comrade." The minister's voice was soft, no more than a whisper; but then, the voice of power had no need to shout.

Slowly Ainh raised his head. The man sitting across from him had eyes like smooth, sparkling river stones.

Though the face was wrinkled and the hair hung in silver wisps as delicate as cobwebs, the eyes were those of a young man—bold and black and brilliant. Ainh felt their gaze slice through him.

"The death of an American tourist would be most embarrassing," said the minister.

Ainh could only nod in meek agreement.

"You are certain Miss Maitland is uninjured?"

Ainh cleared his throat. Nodded again.

The minister's voice, so soft just a moment before, took on a razor's edge. "This Barnard fellow—he prevented an international incident, something our own people seem incapable of."

"But we had no warning, no reason to think this would happen."

"The attack in Bangkok—was that not a warning?"

"A robbery attempt! That's what the report—"

"And reports are never wrong, are they?" The minister's smile was disconcertingly bland. "First Bangkok. Then tonight. I wonder what our little American tourist has gotten herself into."

"The two attacks may not be connected."

"Everything, Comrade, is connected." The minister sat very still, thinking. "And what about Mr. Barnard? Are he and Miss Maitland—" the minister paused delicately "—involved?"

"I think not. She called him a…what is that American expression? A *jerk*."

The minister laughed. "Ah. Mr. Barnard has trouble with the ladies!"

There was a knock on the door. An official entered, handed a report to the minister and respectfully withdrew.

"There is progress in the case?" inquired Ainh.

The minister looked up. "Of a sort. They were able to piece together fragments of the dead man's identity card. It seems he was already well-known to the police."

"Then that explains it!" said Ainh. "Some of these thugs will do anything for a few thousand dong."

"This was no robbery." The minister handed the report to Ainh. "He has connections to the old regime."

Ainh scanned the page. "I see mention only of a woman cousin—a factory worker." He paused, then looked up in surprise. "A mixed blood."

The minister nodded. "She is being questioned now. Shall we look in on her?"

Chantel was slouched on a wooden bench, aiming lethal glares at the policeman in charge of questioning.

"I have done nothing!" she spat out. "Why should I want anyone dead? An American bitch, you say? What, do you think I am crazy? I have been home all night! Talk to the old man who lives above me! Ask him who's been playing my radio all night! Ask him why he's been beating on my ceiling, the old crank! Oh, but I could tell you stories about *him*."

"You accuse an old man?" said the policeman. "*You* are the counterrevolutionary! You and your cousin!"

"I hardly know my cousin."

"You were working together."

Chantal snorted. "I work in a factory. I have nothing to do with him."

The policeman swung a bag onto the table. He took out the items, placed them in front of her. "Caviar. Champagne. Pâté. We found these in your cupboards. How does a factory worker afford these things?"

Chantal's lips tightened, but she said nothing.

The policeman smiled. He gestured to a guard and Chantal, rigidly silent, was led from the room.

The policeman then turned respectfully to the minister, who, along with Ainh, was watching the proceedings. "As you can see, Minister Tranh, she is uncooperative. But give us time. We will think of a way to—"

"Let her go," said the minister.

The policeman looked startled. "I assure you, she can be made to talk."

Minister Tranh smiled. "There are other ways to get information. Release her. Then wait for the fly to drift back to the honeypot."

The policeman left, shaking his head. But, of course, he would do as ordered. After all, Minister Tranh had far more experience in such matters. Hadn't the old fox honed his skills on years of wartime espionage?

For a long time, the minister sat thinking. Then he picked up the champagne bottle and squinted at the label. "Ah. Taittinger." He sighed. "A favorite from my days in Paris." Gently he set the bottle back down and looked at Ainh. "I sense that Miss Maitland has blundered into something dangerous. Perhaps she is asking too many questions. Stirring up dragons from the past."

"You mean her father?" Ainh shook his head. "That is a very old dragon."

To which the minister said softly, "But perhaps not a vanquished one."

A large black cockroach crawled across the table. One of the guards slapped it with a newspaper, brushed the corpse onto the floor and calmly went on writing.

Above him, a ceiling fan whirred in the heat, fluttering papers on the desk.

"Once again, Miss Maitland," said the officer in charge. "Tell me what happened."

"I've told you everything."

"I think you have left something out."

"Nothing. I've left nothing out."

"Yes, you have. There was a gunman."

"I saw no gunman."

"We have witnesses. They heard a shot. Who fired the gun?"

"I told you, I didn't see anyone. The grating was weak—he fell through."

"Why are you lying?"

Her chin shot up. "Why do you insist I'm lying?"

"Because we both know you are."

"Lay off her!" Guy cut in. "She's told you everything she knows."

The officer turned, looked at Guy. "You will kindly remain silent, Mr. Barnard."

"And you'll cut out the Gestapo act! You've been questioning her for two hours now. Can't you see she's exhausted?"

"Perhaps it is time you left."

Guy wasn't about to back down. "She's an American. You can't hold her indefinitely!"

The officer looked at Willy, then at Guy. He gave a nonchalant shrug. "She will be released."

"When?"

"When she tells the truth." Turning, he walked out.

"Hang in," Guy muttered. "We'll get you out of here yet." He followed the officer into the next room, slamming the door behind him.

The arguing went on for ten minutes. She could hear them shouting behind the door. At least Guy still had the strength to shout; she could barely hold her head up.

When Guy returned at last, she could see from his look of disgust that he'd gotten nowhere. He dropped wearily onto the bench beside her and rubbed his eyes.

"What do they want from me?" she asked. "Why can't they just leave me alone?"

"I get the feeling they're waiting for something. Some sort of approval...."

"Whose?"

"Hell if I know."

A rolled up newspaper whacked the table. Willy looked over and saw the guard flick away another dead roach. She shuddered.

It was midnight.

At 1:00 a.m., Mr. Ainh appeared, looking as sallow as an old bed sheet. Willy was too numb to move from the bench. She simply sat there, propped against Guy's shoulder, and let the two men do the talking.

"We are very sorry for the inconvenience," said Ainh, sounding genuinely contrite. "But you must understand—"

"Inconvenience?" Guy snapped. "Ms. Maitland was nearly killed earlier tonight, and she's been kept here for three hours now. What the hell's going on?"

"The situation is...unusual. A robbery attempt—on a foreigner, no less—well..." He shrugged helplessly.

Guy was incredulous. "You're calling this an attempted *robbery?*"

"What would you call it?"

"A cover-up."

Ainh shuffled uneasily. Turning, he exchanged a

few words in Vietnamese with the guard. Then he gave Willy a polite bow. "The police say you are free to leave, Miss Maitland. On behalf of the Vietnamese government, I apologize for your most unfortunate experience. What happened does not in any way reflect on our high regard and warm feelings for the American people. We hope this will not spoil the remainder of your visit."

Guy couldn't help a laugh. "Why should it? It was just a little murder attempt."

"In the morning," Ainh went on quickly, "you are free to continue your tour."

"Subject to what restrictions?" Guy asked.

"No restrictions." Ainh cleared his throat and made a feeble attempt to smile. "Contrary to your government propaganda, Mr. Barnard, we are a reasonable people. We have nothing to hide."

To which Guy answered flatly, "Or so it seems."

"I don't get it. First they run you through the wringer. Then they hand you the keys to the country. It doesn't make sense."

Willy stared out the taxi window as the streets of Saigon glided past. Here and there, a lantern flickered in the darkness. A noodle vendor huddled on the sidewalk beside his steaming cart. In an open doorway, a beaded curtain shuddered, and in the dim room beyond, sleeping children could be seen, curled up like kittens on their mats.

"Nothing makes sense," she whispered. "Not this country. Or the people. Or anything that's happened...."

She was trembling. The horror of everything that had happened that night suddenly burst through the numbing dam of exhaustion. Even Guy's arm, which had magically materialized around her shoulders, couldn't keep away the unnamed terrors of the night.

He pulled her against his chest, and only when she inhaled that comfortable smell of fatigue, felt the slow and steady beat of his heart, did her trembling finally stop. He kept whispering, "It's all right, Willy. I won't let anything happen to you." She felt his kiss, gentle as rain, on her forehead.

When the driver stopped in front of the hotel, Guy had to coax her out of the car. He led her through the nightmarish glare of the lobby. He was the pillar that supported her in the elevator. And it was his arm that guided her down the shadowed walkway and past the air-conditioning vent, now ominously silent. He didn't even ask her if she wanted his company for the night; he simply opened the door to his room, led her inside and sat her down on his bed. Then he locked the door and slid a chair in front of it.

In the bathroom, he soaked a washcloth with warm water. Then he came back out, sat down beside her on the bed and gently wiped her smudged face. Her cheeks were pale. He had the insane urge to kiss her, to breathe some semblance of life back into her body. He knew she wouldn't fight him; she didn't have the strength. But it wouldn't be right, and he wasn't the kind of man who'd take advantage of the situation, of her.

"There," he murmured, brushing back her hair. "All better."

She stirred and gazed up at him with wide, stunned eyes. "Thank you," she whispered.

"For what?"

"For…" She paused, searching for the right words. "For being here."

He touched her face. "I'll be here all night. I won't leave you alone. If that's what you want."

She nodded. It hurt him to see her look so tired, so defeated. *She's getting to me,* he thought. *This isn't supposed to happen. This isn't what I expected.*

He could see, from the brightness of her eyes, that she was trying not to cry. He slid his arm around her shoulders.

"You'll be safe, Willy," he whispered into the softness of her hair. "You'll be going home in the morning. Even if I have to strap you into that plane myself, you'll be going home."

She shook her head. "I can't."

"What do you mean, you can't?"

"My father..."

"Forget him. It isn't worth it."

"I made a promise...."

"All you promised your mother was an answer. Not a body. Not some official report, stamped and certified. Just a simple answer. So give her one. Tell her he's dead, tell her he died in the crash. It's probably the truth."

"I can't lie to her."

"You have to." He took her by the shoulders, forcing her to look at him. "Willy, someone's trying to kill you. They've flubbed it twice. But what happens the third time? The fourth?"

She shook her head. "I'm not worth killing. I don't know anything!"

"Maybe it's not what you know. It's what you might find out."

Sniffling, she looked up in bewilderment. "That my father's dead? Or alive? What *difference* does it make to anyone?"

He sighed, a sound of overwhelming weariness. "I don't know. If we could talk to Oliver, find out who he works for—"

"He's just a kid!"

"Obviously not. He could be sixteen, seventeen. Old enough to be an agent."

"For the Vietnamese?"

"No. If he was one of theirs, why'd he vanish? Why did the police keep hounding you about him?"

She huddled on the bed, her confusion deepening. "He saved my life. And I don't even know why."

There it was again, that raw edge of vulnerability, shimmering in her eyes. She might be Wild Bill Maitland's brat, but she was also a woman, and Guy was having a hard time concentrating on the problem at hand. Why was someone trying to kill her?

He was too tired to think. It was late, she was so near, and there was the bed, just waiting.

He reached up and gently stroked her face. She seemed to sense immediately what was about to happen. Even though her whole body remained stiff, she didn't fight him. The instant their lips met, he felt a shock leap through her, through him, as though they'd both been hit by some glorious bolt of lightning. *My God,* he thought in surprise. *You wanted this as much as I did....*

He heard her murmur, "No," against his mouth, but he knew she didn't mean it, so he went on kissing her until he knew that if he didn't stop right then and there, he'd do something he really didn't want to do.

Oh, yes I do, he thought with sudden abandon. *I want her more than I've wanted any other woman.*

She put her hand against his chest and murmured

another "No," this one fainter. He would have ignored it, too, had it not been for the look in her eyes. They were wide and confused, the eyes of a woman pushed to the brink by fear and exhaustion. This wasn't the way he wanted her. Maddening as she could be, he wanted the living, breathing, *real* Willy Maitland in his arms.

He released her. They sat on the bed, not speaking for a while, just looking at each other with a shared sense of quiet astonishment.

"Why—why did you do that?" she asked weakly.

"You looked like you needed a kiss."

"Not from you."

"From someone, then. It's been a while since you've been kissed. Hasn't it?"

She didn't answer, and he knew he'd guessed the truth. *Hell, what a waste,* he thought, his gaze dropping briefly to that perfect little mouth. He managed a disinterested laugh. "That's what I thought."

Willy stared at his grinning face and wondered, *Is it so obvious?* Not only hadn't she been kissed in a long time, she hadn't *ever* been kissed like *that.* He knew exactly how to do it; he'd probably had years of practice with other women. For some insane reason, she found herself wondering how she compared, found herself hating every woman he'd ever kissed before her, hating even more every woman he'd kiss after her.

She flung herself down on the bed and turned her back on him. "Oh, leave me alone!" she cried. "I can't deal with this! I can't deal with you. I'm tired. I just want to sleep."

He didn't say anything. She felt him smooth her hair. It was nothing more than a brush of his fingers, but somehow, that one touch told her that he wouldn't leave, that he'd be there all night, watching over her. He rose from the bed and switched off the lamp. She lay very still in the darkness, listening to him move around the room. She heard him check the windows, then the door, testing how firmly the chair was wedged against it. Then, apparently satisfied, he went into the bathroom, and she heard water running in the sink.

She was still awake when he came back to bed and stretched out beside her. She lay there, worrying that he'd kiss her again and hoping desperately that he would.

"Guy?" she whispered.

"Yes?"

"I'm scared."

He reached for her through the darkness. Willingly, she let him pull her against his bare chest. He smelled of soap and safety. Yes, that's what it was. Safety.

"It's okay to be scared," he whispered. "Even if you are Wild Bill Maitland's kid."

As if she had a choice, she thought as she lay in his arms. The sad part was, she'd never wanted to be the daughter of a legend. What she'd wanted from Wild Bill wasn't valor or daring or the reflected glory of a hero.

What she'd wanted most of all was a father.

Siang crouched motionless in a stinking mud puddle and stared up the road at Chantal's building. Two hours had passed and the man was still there by the curb. Siang could see his vague form huddled in the darkness. A police agent, no doubt, and not a very good one. Was that a snore rumbling in the night? Yes, Siang thought, definitely a snore. How fortunate that surveillance was always relegated to those least able to withstand its monotony.

Siang decided to make his move.

He withdrew his knife. Noiselessly he edged out of the alley and circled around, slipping from shadow to shadow along the row of hootches. Barely five yards from his goal, he froze as the man's snores shuddered and stopped. The shadow's head lifted, shaking off sleep.

Siang closed in, yanked the man's head up by the hair and slit the throat.

There was no cry, only a gurgle, and then the hiss of a last breath escaping the dead man's lungs. Siang dragged the body around to the back of the building and rolled it into a drainage ditch. Then he slipped through an open window into Chantal's flat.

He found her asleep. She awakened instantly as he clapped his hand over her mouth.

"You!" she ground out through his fingers. "Damn you, you got me in trouble!"

"What did you tell the police?"

"Get away from me!"

"What did you tell them?"

She batted away his hand. "I didn't tell them anything!"

"You're lying."

"You think I'm stupid? You think I'd tell them I have friends in the CIA?"

He released her. As she sat up, the silky heat of her breast brushed against his arm. So the old whore still slept naked, he thought with an automatic stirring of desire.

She rose from the bed and pulled on a robe.

"Don't turn on the lights," he said.

"There was a man outside—a police agent. What did you do with him?"

"I took care of him."

"And the body?"

"In the ditch out back."

"Oh, nice, Siang. Very nice. Now they'll blame me for that, too." She struck a match and lit a cigarette. By the flame's brief glow, he could see her face framed by a tangle of black hair. In the semidarkness she still looked tempting, young and soft and succulent.

The match went out. He asked, "What happened at the police station?"

She let out a slow breath. The smell of exhaled smoke filled the darkness. "They asked about my cousin. They say he's dead. Is that true?"

"What do they know about me?"

"Is Winn really dead?"

Siang paused. "It couldn't be helped."

Chantal laughed. Softly at first, then with wild abandon. "*She* did that, did she? The American bitch? You cannot finish off even a woman? Oh, Siang, you must be slipping!"

He felt like hitting her, but he controlled the urge. Chantal was right. He must be slipping.

She began to pace the room, her movements as sure as a cat's in the darkness. "The police are interested. Very interested. And I saw others there—Party members, I think—watching the interrogation. What have you gotten me into, Siang?"

He shrugged. "Give me a cigarette."

She whirled on him in rage. "Get your own cigarettes! You think I have money to waste on *you?*"

"You'll get the money. All you want."

"You don't know how much I want."

"I still need a gun. You promised me you'd get one. Plus twenty rounds, minimum."

She let out a harsh breath of smoke. "Ammunition is hard to come by."

"I can't wait any longer. This has to be—"

They both froze as the door creaked open. *The police,* thought Siang, automatically reaching for his knife.

"You're so right, Mr. Siang," said a voice in the darkness. Perfect English. "It has to be done. But not quite yet."

The intruder moved lazily into the room, struck a match and calmly lit a kerosene lamp on the table.

Chantal's eyes were wide with astonishment. And fear. "It's you," she whispered. "You've come back...."

The intruder smiled. He laid a pistol and a box of .38-caliber ammunition on the table. Then he looked at Siang. "There's been a slight change of plans."

Chapter 7

She was flying. High, high above the clouds, where the sky was so cold and clear, it felt as if her plane were floating in a crystalline sea. She could hear the wings cut the air like knives through silk. Someone said, "Higher, baby. You have to climb higher if you want to reach the stars."

She turned. It was her father sitting in the copilot's seat, quicksilver smoke dancing around him. He looked the way she'd always remembered him, his cap tilted at a jaunty angle, his eyes twinkling. Just the way he used to look when she'd loved him. When he'd been the biggest, boldest Daddy in the world.

She said, "But I don't want to climb higher."

"Yes, you do. You want to reach the stars."

"I'm afraid, Daddy. Don't make me...."

But he took the joystick. He sent the plane upward,

upward, into the blue bowl of sky. He kept saying, "This is what it's all about. Yessir, baby, this is what it's all about." Only his voice had changed. She saw that it was no longer her father sitting in the copilot's seat; it was Guy Barnard, pushing them into oblivion. "I'll take us to the stars!"

Then it was her father again, gleefully gripping the joystick. She tried to wrench the plane out of the climb, but the joystick broke off in her hand.

The sky turned upside down, righted. She looked at the copilot's seat. Guy was sitting there, laughing. They went higher. Her father laughed.

"Who *are* you?" she screamed.

The phantom smiled. "Don't you know me?"

She woke up, still reaching desperately for that stump of a joystick.

"It's me," the voice said.

She stared up wildly. "Daddy!"

The man looking down at her smiled, a kind smile. "Not quite."

She blinked, focused on Guy's face, his rumpled hair, unshaven jaw. Sweat gleamed on his bare shoulders. Through the curtains behind him, daylight shimmered.

"Nightmare?" he asked.

Groaning, she sat up and shoved back a handful of tangled hair. "I don't usually have them. Nightmares."

"After last night, I'd be surprised if you didn't have one."

Last night. She looked down and saw she was still wearing the same blood-spattered dress, now damp and clinging to her back.

"Power's out," said Guy, giving the silent air conditioner a slap. He padded over to the window and nudged open the curtain. Sunlight blazed in, so piercing, it hurt Willy's eyes. "Gonna be a hell of a scorcher."

"Already is."

"Are you feeling okay?" He stood silhouetted against the window, his unbelted trousers slung low over his hips. Once again she saw the scar, noticed how it rippled its way down his abdomen before vanishing beneath the waistband.

"I'm hot," she said. "And filthy. And I probably don't smell so good."

"I hadn't noticed." He paused and added ruefully, "Probably because I smell even worse."

They laughed, a short, uneasy laugh that was instantly cut off when someone knocked on the door. Guy called out, "Who's there?"

"Mr. Barnard? It is eight o'clock. The car is ready."

"It's my driver," Guy said, and he unbolted the door.

A smiling Vietnamese man stood outside. "Good morning! Do you still wish to go to Cantho this morning?"

"I don't think so," said Guy, discreetly stepping outside to talk in private. Willy heard him murmur, "I want to get Ms. Maitland to the airport this afternoon. Maybe we can…"

Cantho. Willy sat on the bed, listening to the buzz of conversation, trying to remember why that name was so important. Oh, yes. There was a man there, someone she needed to talk to. A man who might have the answers. She closed her eyes against the window's glare, and the dream came back to her, the grinning face of her father, the sickening climb of a doomed plane. She thought of her mother, lying near death at home. Heard her mother ask, "Are you sure, Willy? Do you know for certain he's dead?" Heard herself tell another lie, all the time hating herself, hating her own cowardice, hating the fact that she could never live up to her father's name. Or his courage.

"So stick around the hotel," Guy said to the driver. "Her plane takes off at four, so we should leave around—"

"I'm going to Cantho," said Willy.

Guy glanced around at her. "What?"

"I said I'm going to Cantho. You said you'd take me."

He shook his head. "Things have changed."

"Nothing's changed."

"The stakes have."

"But not the questions. They haven't gone away. They'll never go away."

Guy turned to the driver. "Excuse me while I talk some sense into the lady...."

But Willy had already risen to her feet. "Don't bother. You can't talk sense into me." She went into the bathroom and shut the door. "I'm Wild Bill Maitland's kid, remember?" she yelled.

The driver looked sympathetically at Guy. "I will get the car."

The road out of Saigon was jammed with trucks, most of them ancient and spewing clouds of black exhaust. Through the open windows of their car came the smells of smoke and sun-baked pavement and rotting fruit. Laborers trudged along the roadside, a bobbing column of conical hats against the bright green of the rice paddies.

Five hours and two ferry crossings later, Guy and Willy stood on a Cantho pier and watched a multitude of boats glide across the muddy Mekong. River women dipped and swayed as they rowed, a strange and graceful dance at the oars. And on the riverbank swirled the noise and confusion of a thriving market town. Schoolgirls, braided hair gleaming in the sunshine, whisked past on bicycles. Stevedores heaved sacks of rice and crates of melons and pineapples onto sampans.

Overwhelmed by the chaos, Willy asked bleakly, "How are we ever going to find him?"

Guy's answer didn't inspire much confidence. He simply shrugged and said, "How hard can it be?"

Very hard, it turned out. All their inquiries brought the same response. "A tall man?" people would say. "And blond?" Invariably their answer would be a shake of the head.

It was Guy's inspired hunch that finally sent them into a series of tailor shops. "Maybe Lassiter's no longer blond," he said. "He could have dyed his hair or gone bald. But there's one feature a man can't disguise—his height. And in this country, a six-foot-four man is going to need specially tailored clothes."

The first three tailors they visited turned up nothing. It was with a growing sense of futility that they entered the fourth shop, wedged in an alley of tin-roofed hootches. In the cavelike gloom within, an elderly seamstress sat hunched over a mound of imitation silk. She didn't seem to understand Guy's questions. In frustration, Guy took out a pen and jotted a few words in Vietnamese on a scrap of newspaper. Then, to illustrate his point, he sketched in the figure of a tall man.

The woman squinted down at the drawing. For a long time, she sat there, her fingers knotted tightly around the shimmering fabric. Then she looked up at Guy. No words were exchanged, just that silent, mournful gaze.

Guy gave a nod that he understood. He reached into his pocket and lay a twenty-dollar bill on the table in front of her. She stared at it in wonder. American dollars. For her, it was a fortune.

At last she took up Guy's pen and, with painful precision, began to write. The instant she'd finished, Guy swept up the scrap of paper and jammed it into his pocket. "Let's go," he whispered to Willy.

"What does it say?" Willy whispered as they headed back along the row of hootches.

Guy didn't answer; he only quickened his pace. In the silence of the alley, Willy suddenly became aware of eyes, everywhere, watching them from the windows and doorways.

Willy tugged on Guy's arm. "Guy…"

"It's an address. Near the marketplace."

"Lassiter's?"

"Don't talk. Just keep moving. We're being followed."

"What?"

He grabbed her arm before she could turn to look. "Come on, keep your head. Pretend he's not there."

She fought to keep her eyes focused straight ahead, but the sense of being stalked made every muscle in her body strain to run. *How does he stay so calm?* she wondered, glancing at Guy. He was actually whistling now, a tuneless song that scraped her nerves raw. They reached the end of the alley, and a maze of streets lay before them. To her surprise, Guy stopped and struck up a cheerful conversation with a boy selling cigarettes at the corner. Their chatter seemed to go on forever.

"What are you doing?" Willy ground out. "Can't we get out of here?"

"Trust me." Guy bought a pack of Winstons, for which he paid two American dollars. The boy beamed and sketched a childish salute.

Guy took Willy's hand. "Get ready."

"Ready for what?"

The words were barely out of her mouth when Guy wrenched her around the corner and up another alley. They made a sharp left, then a right, past a row of tin-roofed shacks, and ducked into an open doorway.

Inside, it was too murky to make sense of their surroundings. For an eternity they huddled together, listening for footsteps. They could hear, in the distance, children laughing and a car horn honking incessantly. But just outside, in the alley, there was silence.

"Looks like the kid did his job," whispered Guy.

"You mean that cigarette boy?"

Guy sidled over to the doorway and peered out. "Looks clear. Come on, let's get out of here."

They slipped into the alley and doubled back. Even before they saw the marketplace, they could hear it: the shouts of merchants, the frantic squeals of pigs. Hurrying along the outskirts, they scanned the street names and finally turned into what was scarcely more than an alley jammed between crumbling apartment buildings. The address numbers were barely decipherable.

At last, at a faded green building, they stopped. Guy squinted at the number over the doorway and nodded. "This is it." He knocked.

The door opened. A single eye, iris so black the pupil was invisible, peered at them through the crack. That was all they saw, that one glimpse of a woman's face,

but it was enough to tell them she was afraid. Guy spoke
to her in Vietnamese. The woman shook her head and
tried to close the door. He put his hand out to stop it
and spoke again, this time saying the man's name, "Sam
Lassiter."

Panicking, the woman turned and screamed something in Vietnamese.

Somewhere in the house, footsteps thudded away,
followed by the shattering of glass.

"Lassiter!" Guy yelled. Shoving past the woman,
he raced through the apartment, Willy at his heels. In
a back room, they found a broken window. Outside in
the alley, a man was sprinting away. Guy scrambled
out, dropped down among the glass shards and took
off after the fugitive.

Willy was about to follow him out the window when
the Vietnamese woman, frantic, grasped her arm.

"Please! No hurt him!" she cried. "Please!"

Willy, trying to pull free, found her fingers linked for
an instant with the other woman's. Their eyes met. "We
won't hurt him," Willy said, gently disengaging her arm.

Then she pulled herself up onto the windowsill and
dropped into the alley.

Guy was pulling closer. He could see his quarry
loping toward the marketplace. It had to be Lassiter.
Though his hair was a lank, dirty brown, there was no
disguising his height; he towered above the crowd. He
ducked beneath the marketplace canopy and vanished
into shadow.

Damn, thought Guy, struggling to move through the
crowd. *I'm going to lose him.*

He shoved into the central market tent. The sun's

glare abruptly gave way to a close, hot gloom. He stumbled blindly, his eyes adjusting slowly to the change in light. He made out the cramped aisles, the counters overflowing with fruit and vegetables, the gay sparkle of pinwheels spinning on a toy vendor's cart. A tall silhouette suddenly bobbed off to the side. Guy spun around and saw Lassiter duck behind a gleaming stack of cookware.

Guy scrambled after him. The man leapt up and sprinted away. Pots and pans went flying, a dozen cymbals crashing together.

Guy's quarry darted into the produce section. Guy made a sharp left, leapt over a crate of mangoes and dashed up a parallel aisle. "Lassiter!" he yelled. "I want to talk! That's all, just talk!"

The man spun right, shoved over a fruit stand and stumbled away. Watermelons slammed to the ground, exploding in a brilliant rain of flesh. Guy almost slipped in the muck. "Lassiter!" he shouted.

They headed into the meat section. Lassiter, desperate, shoved a crate of ducks into Guy's path, sending up a cloud of feathers as the birds, freed from their prison, flapped loose. Guy dodged the crate, leapt over a fugitive duck and kept running. Ahead lay the butcher counters, stacked high with slabs of meat. A vendor was hosing down the concrete floor, sending a stream of bloody water into the gutter. Lassiter, moving full tilt, suddenly slid and fell to his knees in the offal. At once he tried to scramble back to his feet, but by then Guy had snagged his shirt collar.

"Just—just talk," Guy managed to gasp between breaths. "That's all—talk—"

Lassiter thrashed, struggling to pull free.

"Gimme a chance!" Guy yelled, dragging him back down.

Lassiter rammed his shoulders at Guy's knees, sending Guy sprawling. In an instant, Lassiter had leapt to his feet. But as he turned to flee, Guy grabbed his ankle, and Lassiter toppled forward and splashed, headfirst, into a vat of squirming eels.

The water seemed to boil with slippery bodies, writhing in panic. Guy dragged the man's head out of the vat. They both collapsed, gasping on the slick concrete.

"Don't!" Lassiter sobbed. "Please…"

"I told you, I just—just want to talk—"

"I won't say anything! I swear it. You tell 'em that for me. Tell 'em I forgot everything…."

"Who?" Guy took the other man by the shoulders. "Who are *they?* Who are you afraid of?"

Lassiter took a shaky breath and looked at him, seemed to make a decision. "The Company."

"Why does the CIA want you dead?" Willy asked.

They were sitting at a wooden table on the deck of an old river barge. Neutral territory, Lassiter had said of this floating café. During the war, by some unspoken agreement, V.C. and South Vietnamese soldiers would sit together on this very deck, enjoying a small patch of peace. A few hundred yards away, the war might rage on, but here no guns were drawn, no bullets fired.

Lassiter, gaunt and nervous, took a deep swallow of beer. Behind him, beyond the railing, flowed the Mekong, alive with the sounds of river men, the putter of boats. In the last light of sunset, the water rippled with gold. Lassiter said, "They want me out of the way for the same reason they wanted Luis Valdez out of the way. I know too much."

"About what?"

"Laos. The bombings, the gun drops. The war your average soldier didn't know about." He looked at Guy. "Did you?"

Guy shook his head. "We were so busy staying alive, we didn't care what was going on across the border."

"Valdez knew. Anyone who went down in Laos was in for an education. If they survived. And that was a big *if.* Say you did manage to eject. Say you lived through the G force of shooting out of your cockpit. If the enemy didn't find you, the animals would." He stared down at his beer. "Valdez was lucky to be alive."

"You met him at Tuyen Quan?" asked Guy.

"Yeah. Summer camp." He laughed. "For three years we were stuck in the same cell." His gaze turned to the river. "I was with the 101st when I was captured. Got separated during a firefight. You know how it is in those valleys, the jungle's so thick you can't be sure which way's up. I was going in circles, and all the time I could hear those damn Hueys flying overhead, *right overhead,* picking guys up. Everyone but me. I figured I'd been left to die. Or maybe I was already dead, just some corpse walking around in the trees…." He swallowed; the hand clutching the beer bottle was unsteady. "When they finally boxed me in, I just threw my rifle down and put up my hands. I got force marched north, into NVA territory. That's how I ended up at Tuyen Quan."

"Where you met Valdez," said Willy.

"He was brought in a year later, transferred in from some camp in Laos. By then I was an old-timer. Knew the ropes, worked my own vegetable patch. I was hanging in okay. Valdez, though, was holding on by the skin of his teeth. Yellow from hepatitis, a broken arm that wouldn't heal right. It took him months to get strong enough even to work in the garden. Yeah, it was just him and me in that cell. Three years. We did a lot of talking. I heard all his stories. He said a lot of things I didn't want to believe, things about Laos, about what we were doing there...."

Willy leaned forward and asked softly, "Did he ever talk about my father?"

Lassiter turned to her, his eyes dark against the glow of sunset. "When Valdez last saw him, your father was still alive. Trying to fly the plane."

"And then what happened?"

"Luis bailed out right after she blew up. So he couldn't be sure—"

"Wait," cut in Guy. "What do you mean, 'blew up'?"

"That's what he said. Something went off in the hold."

"But the plane was shot down."

"It wasn't enemy fire that brought her down. Valdez was positive about that. They might have been going through flak at the time, but this was something else, something that blew the fuselage door clean off. He kept going over and over what they had in the cargo, but all he remembered listed on the manifest were aircraft parts."

"And a passenger," said Willy.

Lassiter nodded. "Valdez mentioned him. Said he was a weird little guy, quiet, almost, well, *holy*. They could tell he was a VIP, just by what he was wearing around his neck."

"You mean gold? Chains?" asked Guy.

"Some sort of medallion. Maybe a religious symbol."

"Where was this passenger supposed to be dropped off?"

"Behind lines. VC territory. It was billed as an in-and-out job, strictly under wraps."

"Valdez told *you* about it," said Willy.

"And I wish to hell he never had." Lassiter took another gulp of beer. His hand was shaking again. Sunset flecked the river with bloodred ripples. "It's funny. At the time we felt almost, well, *protected* in that camp. Maybe it was just a lot of brainwashing, but the guards kept telling Valdez he was lucky to be a prisoner. That he knew things that'd get him into trouble. That the CIA would kill him."

"Sounds like propaganda."

"That's what I figured it was—Commie lies designed to break him down. But they got Valdez scared. He kept waking up at night, screaming about the plane going down...."

Lassiter stared out at the water. "Anyway, after the war, they released us. Valdez and the other guys headed home. He wrote me from Bangkok, sent the letter by way of a Red Cross nurse we'd met in Hanoi right after our release. An English gal, a little anti-American but real nice. When I read that letter, I thought, now the poor bastard's really gone over the edge. He was saying crazy things, said he wasn't allowed to go out, that all his phone calls were monitored. I figured he'd be all right once he got home. Then I got a call from Nora Walker, that Red Cross nurse. She said he was dead. That he'd shot himself in the head."

Willy asked, "Do you think it was suicide?"

"I think he was a liability. And the Company doesn't

like liabilities." He turned his troubled gaze to the water. "When we were at Tuyen, all he could talk about was going home, you know? Seeing his old hangouts, his old buddies. Me, I had nothing to go home to, just a sister I never much cared for. Here, at least, I had my girl, someone I loved. That's why I stayed. I'm not the only one. There are other guys like me around, hiding in villages, jungles. Guys who've gone bamboo, gone native." He shook his head. "Too bad Valdez didn't. He'd still be alive."

"But isn't it hard living here?" asked Willy. "Always the outsider, the old enemy? Don't you ever feel threatened by the authorities?"

Lassiter responded with a laugh and cocked his head at a far table where four men were sitting. "Have you said hello to our local police? They've probably been tailing you since you hit town."

"So we noticed," said Guy.

"My guess is they're assigned to protect me, their resident lunatic American. Just the fact that I'm alive and well is proof this isn't the evil empire." He raised his bottle of beer in a toast to the four policemen. They stared back sheepishly.

"So here you are," said Guy, "cut off from the rest of the world. Why would the CIA bother to come after you?"

"It's something Nora told me."

"The nurse?"

Lassiter nodded. "After the war, she stayed on in Hanoi. Still works at the local hospital. About a year ago, some guy—an American—dropped in to see her. Asked if she knew how to get hold of me. He said he had an urgent message from my uncle. But Nora's a sharp gal, thinks fast on her feet. She told him I'd left the country, that I was living in Thailand. A good thing she did."

"Why?"

"Because I don't have an uncle."

There was a silence. Softly Guy said, "You think that was a Company man."

"I keep wondering if he was. Wondering if he'll find me. I don't want to end up like Luis Valdez. With a bullet in my head."

On the river, boats glided like ghosts through the shadows. A café worker silently circled the deck, lighting a string of paper lanterns.

"I've kept a low profile," said Lassiter. "Never make noise. Never draw attention. See, I changed my hair." He grinned faintly and tugged on his lank brown ponytail. "Got this shade from the local herbalist. Extract of cuttlefish and God knows what else. Smells like hell, but I'm not blond anymore." He let the ponytail flop loose, and his smile faded. "I kept hoping the Company would lose interest in me. Then you showed up at my door, and I—I guess I freaked out."

The bartender put a record on the turntable, and the needle scratched out a Vietnamese love song, a haunting melody that drifted like mist over the river. Wind swayed the paper lanterns, and shadows danced across the deck. Lassiter stared at the five beer bottles lined up in front of him on the table. He ordered a sixth.

"It takes time, but you get used to it here," he said. "The rhythm of life. The people, the way they think. There's not a lot of whining and flailing at misfortune. They accept life as it is. I like that. And after a while, I got to feeling this was the only place I've ever belonged, the only place I ever felt safe." He looked at Willy. "It could be the only place *you're* safe."

"But I'm not like you," said Willy. "I can't stay here the rest of my life."

"I want to put her on the next plane to Bangkok," said Guy.

"Bangkok?" Lassiter snorted. "Easiest place in the world to get yourself killed. And going home'd be no safer. Look what happened to Valdez."

"But *why?*" Willy said in frustration. "Why would they kill Valdez? Or me? I don't know anything!"

"You're Bill Maitland's daughter. You're a direct link—"

"To *what?* A dead man?"

The love song ended, fading to the *scritch-scritch* of the needle.

Lassiter set his beer down. "I don't know," he said. "I don't know why you're such a threat to them. All I know is, something went wrong on that flight. And the Company's still trying to cover it up...." He stared at the line of empty beer bottles gleaming in the lantern light. "If it takes a bullet to buy silence, then a bullet's what they'll use."

"Do you think he's right?" Willy whispered.

From the back seat of the car, they watched the rice paddies, silvered by moonlight, slip past their windows. For an hour they'd driven without speaking, lulled into silence by the rhythm of the road under their wheels. But now Willy couldn't help voicing the question she was afraid to ask. "Will I be any safer at home?"

Guy looked out at the night. "I wish I knew. I wish I could tell you what to do. Where to go..."

She thought of her mother's house in San Francisco,

thought of how warm and safe it had always seemed, that blue Victorian on Third Avenue. Surely no one would touch her there.

Then she thought of Valdez, shot to death in his Houston rooming house. For him, even a POW camp had been safer.

The driver slid a tape into the car's cassette player. A Vietnamese song twanged out, sung by a woman with a sorrowful voice. Outside, the rice paddies swayed like waves on a silver ocean. Nothing about this moment seemed real, not the melody or the moonlit country-side or the danger. Only Guy was real—real enough to touch, to hold.

She let her head rest against his shoulder, and the darkness, the warmth, made sleep impossible to re-sist. Guy's arm came around her, cradled her against his chest. She felt his breath in her hair, the brush of his lips on her forehead. A kiss, she thought drowsily. It felt so nice to be kissed....

The hum of the wheels over the road seemed to take on a new rhythm, the whisper of the ocean, the soothing hiss of waves. Now he was kissing her all over, and they were no longer in the back seat of the car; they were on a ship, swaying on a black sea. The wind moaned in the rigging, a soulful song in Vietnamese. She was lying on her back, and somehow, all her clothes had vanished. He was on top of her, his hands trapping her arms against the deck, his lips exploring her throat, her breasts, with a conqueror's triumph. How she wanted him to make love to her, wanted it so badly that her body arched up to meet his, straining for some blessed release from this ache within her. But his lips melted away, and then she heard, "Wake up. Willy, wake up...."

She opened her eyes. She was lying in the back seat of the car, her head in Guy's lap. Through the window came the faint glow of city lights.

"We're back in Saigon," he whispered, stroking her face. The touch of his hand, so new yet so familiar, made her tremble in the night heat. "You must have been tired."

Still shaken by the dream, she pulled away and sat up. Outside, the streets were deserted. "What time is it?"

"After midnight. Guess we forgot about supper. Are you hungry?"

"Not really."

"Neither am I. Maybe we should just call it a—" He paused. She felt his arm stiffen against hers. "Now what?" he muttered, staring straight ahead.

Willy followed his gaze to the hotel, which had just swung into view. A surreal scene lay ahead: the midnight glare of streetlights, the army of policemen blocking the lobby doors, the gleam of AK-47s held at the ready.

Their driver muttered in Vietnamese. Willy could see his face in the rearview mirror. He was sweating.

The instant they pulled to a stop at the curb, their car was surrounded. A policeman yanked the passenger door open.

"Stay inside," Guy said. "I'll take care of this."

But as he stepped out of the car, a uniformed arm reached inside and dragged her out as well. Groggy with sleep, bewildered by the confusion, she clung to Guy's arm as voices shouted and men shoved against her.

"Barnard!" It was Dodge Hamilton, struggling down the hotel steps toward them. "What the hell's going on?"

"Don't ask me! We just got back to town!"

"Blast, where's that man Ainh?" said Hamilton, glancing around. "He was here a minute ago…."

"I am here," came the answer in a shaky voice. Ainh, glasses askew and blinking nervously, stood at the top of the lobby steps. He was swiftly escorted by a policeman through the crowd. Gesturing to a limousine, he said to Guy, "Please. You and Miss Maitland will come with me."

"Why are we under arrest?" Guy demanded.

"You are not under arrest."

Guy pulled his arm free of a policeman's grasp. "Could've fooled me."

"They are here only as a precaution," said Ainh, ushering them into the car. "Please get in. Quickly."

It was the ripple of urgency in his voice that told Willy something terrible had happened. "What is it?" she asked Ainh. "What's wrong?"

Ainh nervously adjusted his glasses. "About two hours ago, we received a call from the police in Cantho."

"We were just there."

"So they told us. They also said they'd found a body. Floating in the river…"

Willy stared at him, afraid to ask, yet already knowing. Only when she felt Guy's hand tighten around her arm did she realize she'd sagged against him.

"Sam Lassiter?" Guy asked flatly.

Ainh nodded. "His throat was cut."

Chapter 8

The old man who sat in the carved rosewood chair appeared frail enough to be toppled by a stiff wind. His arms were like two twigs crossed on his lap. His white wisp of a beard trembled in the breath of the ceiling fan. But his eyes were as bright as quicksilver. Through the open windows came the whine of the cicadas in the walled garden. Overhead, the fan spun slowly in the midnight heat.

The old man's gaze focused on Willy. "Wherever you walk, Miss Maitland," he said, "it seems you leave a trail of blood."

"We had nothing to do with Lassiter's death," said Guy. "When we left Cantho, he was alive."

"I think you misunderstand, Mr. Barnard." The man turned to Guy. "I do not accuse you of anything."

"Who *are* you accusing?"

"That detail I leave to our people in Cantho."

"You mean those police agents you had following us?"

Minister Tranh smiled. "You made it a difficult assignment. That boy on the corner—an ingenious move. No, we're aware that Mr. Lassiter was alive when you left him."

"And after we left?"

"We know that he sat in the river café for another twenty minutes. That he drank a total of eight beers. And then he left. Unfortunately, he never arrived home."

"Weren't your people keeping tabs on him?"

"Tabs?"

"Surveillance."

"Mr. Lassiter was a friend. We don't keep…tabs—is that the word?—on our friends."

"But you followed *us,*" said Willy.

Minister Tranh's placid gaze shifted to her. "Are you our friend, Miss Maitland?"

"What do you think?"

"I think it is not easy to tell. I think even you cannot tell your friends from your enemies. It is a dangerous state of affairs. Already it has led to three murders."

Willy shook her head, puzzled. "Three? Lassiter's the only one I've heard about."

"Who else has been killed?" Guy asked.

"A Saigon policeman," said the minister. "Murdered last night on routine surveillance duty."

"I don't see the connection."

"Also last night, another man dead. Again, the throat cut."

"You can't blame us for every murder in Saigon!" said Willy. "We don't even know those other victims—"

"But yesterday you paid one of them a visit. Or have you forgotten?"

Guy stared across the table. "Gerard."

In the darkness outside, the cicadas' shrill music rose to a scream. Then, in an instant, the night fell absolutely silent.

Minister Tranh gazed ahead at the far wall, as though divining some message from the mildewed wallpaper. "Are you familiar with the Vietnamese calendar, Miss Maitland?" he asked quietly.

"Your calendar?" She frowned, puzzled by the new twist of conversation. "It—it's the same as the Chinese, isn't it?"

"Last year was the year of the dragon. A lucky year, or so they say. A fine year for babies and marriages. But this year…" He shook his head.

"The snake," said Guy.

Minister Tranh nodded. "The snake. A dangerous symbol. An omen of disaster. Famine and death. A year of misfortune…." He sighed and his head drooped, as though his fragile neck was suddenly too weak to support it. For a long time he sat in silence, his white hair fluttering in the fan's breath. Then, slowly, he raised his head. "Go home, Miss Maitland," he said. "This is not a year for you, a place for you. Go home."

Willy thought about how easy it would be to climb onto that plane to Bangkok, thought longingly of the simple luxuries that were only a flight away. Perfumed soap and clean water and soft pillows. But then another image blotted out everything else: Sam Lassiter's face, tired and haunted, against the sky of sunset. And his Vietnamese woman, pleading for his life. All these years Sam Lassiter had lived safe and hidden in a peaceful river town. Now he was dead. Like Valdez. Like Gerard.

It was true, she thought. Wherever she walked, she left a trail of blood. And she didn't even know why.

"I can't go home," she said.

The minister raised an eyebrow. "Cannot? Or will not?"

"They tried to kill me in Bangkok."

"You're no safer here. Miss Maitland, we have no wish to forcibly deport you. But you must understand that you put us in a difficult position. You are a guest in our country. We Vietnamese honor our guests. It is a custom we hold sacred. If you, a guest, were to be found murdered, it would seem…" He paused and added with a quietly whimsical lilt, "Inhospitable."

"My visa's still good. I want to stay. I *have* to stay. I was planning to go on to Hanoi."

"We cannot guarantee your safety."

"I don't expect you to." She added wearily, "No one can guarantee my safety. Anywhere."

The minister looked at Guy, saw his troubled look. "Mr. Barnard? Surely you will convince her?"

"But she's right," said Guy.

Willy looked up and saw in Guy's eyes the worry, the uncertainty. It frightened her to realize that even he didn't have the answers.

"If I thought she'd be safer at home, I'd put her on that plane myself," he said. "But I don't think she will be safe. Not until she knows what she's running from."

"Surely she has friends to turn to."

"But you yourself said it, Minister Tranh. She can't tell her friends from her enemies. It's a dangerous state to be in."

The minister looked at Willy. "What is it you seek in the North?"

"It's where my father's plane went down," she said. "He could still be alive, in some village. Maybe he's lost his memory or he's afraid to come out of the jungle or—"

"Or he is dead."

She swallowed. "Then that's where I'll find his body. In the North."

Minister Tranh shook his head. "The jungles are full of skeletons. Americans. Vietnamese. You forget, we have our MIAs too, Miss Maitland. Our widows, our orphans. Among all those bones, to find the remains of one particular man..." He let out a heavy breath.

"But I have to try. I have to go to Hanoi."

Minister Tranh gazed at her, his eyes glowing with a strange black fire. She stared straight back at him. Slowly, a benign smile formed on his lips and she knew that she had won.

"Does nothing frighten you, Miss Maitland?" he asked.

"Many things frighten me."

"And well they should." He was still smiling, but his eyes were unfathomable. "I only hope you have the good sense to be frightened now."

Long after the two Americans had left, Minister Tranh and Mr. Ainh sat smoking cigarettes and listening to the screech of the cicadas in the night.

"You will inform our people in Hanoi," said the minister.

"But wouldn't it be easier to cancel her visa?" said Ainh. "Force her to leave the country?"

"Easier, perhaps, but not wiser." The minister lit another cigarette and inhaled a warm and satisfying breath of smoke. A good American brand. His one weakness.

He knew it would only hasten his death, that the cancer now growing in his right lung would feed ravenously on each lethal molecule of smoke. How ironic that the very enemy that had worked so hard to kill him during the war would now claim victory, and all because of his fondness for their cigarettes.

"What if she comes to harm?" Ainh asked. "We would have an international incident."

"That is why she must be protected." The minister rose from his chair. The old body, once so spry, had grown stiff with the years. To think this dried-up carcass had fought two savage jungle wars. Now it could barely shuffle around the house.

"We could scare her into going home—arrange an incident to frighten her," suggested Ainh.

"Like your Die Yankee note?" Minister Tranh laughed as he headed for the door. "No, I do not think she frightens easily, that one. Better to see where she leads us. Perhaps we, too, will learn a few secrets. Or have you lost your curiosity, Comrade?"

Ainh looked miserable. "I think curiosity is a dangerous thing."

"So we let her make the moves, take the risks." The minister glanced back, smiling, from the doorway. "After all," he said. "It is *her* destiny."

"You don't have to go to Hanoi," said Guy, watching Willy pack her suitcase. "You could stay in Saigon. Wait for me."

"While you do what?"

"While I do the legwork up north. See what I can find." He glanced out the window at the two police agents loitering in the walkway. "Ainh's got you covered from all directions. You'll be safe here."

"I'll also go nuts." She snapped the suitcase shut. "Thanks for offering to stick your neck out for me, but I don't need a hero."

"I'm not trying to be a hero."

"Then why're you playing the part?"

He shrugged, unable to produce an answer.

"It's the money, isn't it? The bounty for Friar Tuck."

"It's not the money."

"Then it's that skeleton dancing around in your closet." He didn't answer. "What are you trying to hide? What's the Ariel Group got on you, anyway?" He remained silent. She locked her suitcase. "Never mind. I don't really want to know."

He sat down on the bed. Looking utterly weary, he propped his head in his hands. "I killed a man," he said.

She stared at him. Head in his hands, he looked ragged, spent, a man who'd used up his last reserves of strength. She had the unexpected impulse to sit beside him, to take him in her arms and hold him, but she couldn't seem to move her feet. She was too stunned by his revelation.

"It happened here. In Nam. In 1972." His laugh was muffled against his hands. "The Fourth of July."

"There was a war going on. Lots of people got killed."

"This was different. This wasn't an act of war, where you shoot a few men and get a medal for your trouble." He raised his head and looked at her. "The man I killed was American."

Slowly she went over and sank down beside him on the bed. "Was it…a mistake?"

He shook his head. "No, not a mistake. It was something I did without thinking. Call it reflexes. It just happened."

She said nothing, waiting for him to go on. She knew he *would* go on; there was no turning back now.

"I was in Da Nang for the day, to pick up supplies," he said. "Got a little turned around and wound up on some side street. Just an alley, really, a dirt lane, few old hootches. I got out of the jeep to ask for directions, and I heard this—this screaming...."

He paused, looked down at his hands. "She was just a kid. Fifteen, maybe sixteen. A small girl, not more than ninety pounds. There was no way she could've fought him off. I—I just reacted. I didn't really think about what I was doing, what I was going to do. I dragged him off her, shoved him on the ground. He got up and swung at me. I didn't have a choice but to fight back. By the time I stopped hitting him, he wasn't moving. I turned and saw what he'd done to the girl. All the blood..."

Guy rubbed his forehead, as though trying to erase the image. "By then there were other people there. I looked around, saw all these eyes watching me. Vietnamese. One of the women came up, whispered that I should leave, that they'd get rid of the body for me. That's when I realized the man was dead."

For a long time they sat side by side, not touching, not speaking. He'd just confessed to killing a man. Yet she couldn't condemn him; she felt only a sense of sadness about the girl, about all the silent, nameless casualties of war.

"What happened then?" she asked gently.

He shrugged. "I left. I never said a word to anyone. I guess I was scared to. A few days later I heard they'd found a soldier's body on the other side of town. His death was listed as an assault by unknown locals. And that was the end of it. I thought."

"How did the Ariel Group find out?"

"I don't know." Restless, he rose and went to the window where he looked out at the dimly lit walkway. "There were half a dozen witnesses, all of them Vietnamese. Word must've gotten around. And somehow the Ariel Group got wind of it. What I don't understand is why they waited this long."

"Maybe they only just heard about it."

"Or maybe they were waiting for the right chance to use it." He turned to look at her. "Doesn't it bother you, how we got thrown together? That we *happened* to meet in Kistner's villa? That you *happened* to need a ride into town?"

"And that the man you've been asked to find just happens to be my father."

He nodded.

"They're using us," she said. Then, with rising anger she added, "They're using *me*."

"Welcome to the club."

She looked up. "What do we do about it?"

"In the morning I'll fly to Hanoi, start asking questions."

"What about me?"

"You stay where Ainh can watch you."

"Sounds like a lousy plan."

"Have you got a better one?"

"Yes. I come with you."

"You'll only complicate things. If your father's alive, I'll find him."

"And what happens when you do? Are you going to turn him in? Trade him for silence?"

"I've given up on silence," Guy said quietly. "I'll settle for answers now."

She hauled her packed suitcase off the bed and set it down by the door. "Why am I arguing with you? I don't need your permission. I don't need any man's permission. He's *my* father. I know his face. His voice. After twenty years, *I'm* the one who'll recognize him."

"You're also the one who could get killed. Or is that part of the fun, Junior, going for thrills? Hell." He laughed. "It's probably written in your genes. You're as loony as your old man. He loved getting shot at, didn't he? He was a thrill junkie, and you are, too. Admit it. You're having the time of your life!"

"Look who's talking."

"I'm not in this for thrills. I'm in it because I had to be. Because I didn't have a choice."

"Neither of us has a choice!" She turned away, but he grabbed her arm and pulled her around to face him. He was standing so close it made her neck ache to look up at him.

"Stay in Saigon," he said.

"You must really want me out of the way."

"I want you safe."

"Why?"

"Because I— You—" He stopped. They were staring at each other, both of them breathing so hard neither of them could speak. Without another word he hauled her into his arms.

It was just a kiss, but it hit her with such hurricane force that her legs seemed to wobble away into oblivion. He was all rough edges—stubbled jaw and callused hands and frayed shirt. Automatically, she reached up and her arms closed behind his neck, pulling him hard against her mouth. He needed no encouragement. As his body pressed into hers, those dream images reignited in her head: the swaying deck of a ship, the night sky, Guy's face hovering above hers. If she let it, it would happen here, now. Already he was nudging her toward the bed, and she knew that if they fell across that mattress, he'd take her and she'd let him, and that was that. Never mind what made sense, what was good for her. She wanted him.

Even if it's the worst mistake I'll ever make in my life?

The thump of her legs against the side of the bed jarred her back to reality. She twisted away, pushed him to arm's length.

"That wasn't supposed to happen!" she said.

"I think it was."

"We got our wires crossed and—"

"No," he said softly. "I'd say our wires connected just fine."

She crossed to the door and yanked it open. "I think you should get out."

"I'm not going."

"You're not staying."

But his stance, feet planted like tree roots, told her he most certainly *was* staying. "Have you forgotten? Someone wants you dead."

"But *you're* the one who's threatening me."

"It was just a kiss. Has it been *that* long, Willy? Does it shake you up that much, just being kissed?"

Yes it does! she wanted to scream. *It shakes me up because I've never been kissed that way before!*

"I'm staying tonight," he said quietly. "You need me. And, I admit it, I need you. You're my link to Bill Maitland. I won't touch you, if that's what you want. But I won't leave, either."

She had to concede defeat. Nothing she could do or say would make him budge. She let the door swing shut. Then she went to the bed and sat down. "God, I'm tired," she said. "Too tired to fight you. I'm even too tired to be afraid."

"And that's when things get dangerous. When all the adrenaline's used up. When you're too exhausted to think straight."

"I give up." She collapsed onto the bed, feeling as if every bone in her body had suddenly dissolved. "I don't care what happens anymore. I just want to go to sleep."

He didn't have to say anything; they both knew the debate was over and she'd lost. The truth was, she was glad he was there. It felt so good to close her eyes, to have someone watching over her. She realized how muddled her thinking had become, that she now considered a man like Guy Barnard *safe*.

But safe was what she felt.

Standing by the bed, Guy watched her fall asleep. She looked so fragile, stretched out on the bedcovers like a paper doll.

She hadn't felt like paper in his arms. She'd been real flesh and blood, warm and soft, all the woman he could ever want. He wasn't sure just what he felt toward her. Some of it was good old-fashioned lust. But there was something more, a primitive male instinct that made him want to carry her off to a place where no one could hurt her.

He turned and looked out the window. The two police agents were still loitering near the stairwell; he could see their cigarettes glowing in the darkness. He only hoped they did their job tonight, because he had already crossed his threshold of exhaustion.

He sat down in a chair and tried to sleep.

Twenty minutes later, his whole body crying out

for rest, he gave up and went to the bed. Willy didn't stir. What the hell, he thought, She'll never notice. He stretched out beside her. The shifting mattress seemed to rouse her; she moaned and turned toward him, curling up like a kitten against his chest. The sweet scent of her hair made him feel like a drunken man. Dangerous, dangerous.

He'd been better off in the chair.

But he couldn't pull away now. So he lay there holding her, thinking about what came next.

They now had a name, a tentative contact, up north: Nora Walker, the British Red Cross nurse. Lassiter had said she worked in the local hospital. Guy only hoped she'd talk to them, that she wouldn't think this was just another Company trick and clam up. Having Willy along might make all the difference. After all, Bill Maitland's daughter had a right to be asking questions. Nora Walker just might decide to provide the answers.

Willy sighed and nestled closer to his chest. That brought a smile to his face. *You crazy dame,* he thought, and kissed the top of her head. *You crazy, crazy dame.* He buried his face in her hair.

So it was decided. For better or worse, he was stuck with her.

Chapter 9

The flight attendant walked up the aisle of the twin-engine Ilyushin and waved halfheartedly at the flies swarming around her head. Puffs of cold mist rose from the air-conditioning vents and swirled in the cabin; the woman seemed to be floating in clouds. Through the fog, Willy could barely read the emergency sign posted over the exit: Escape Rope. Now *there* was a safety feature to write home about. She had visions of the plane soaring through blue sky, trailing passengers on a ten thousand-foot rope.

A bundle of taffy landed in her lap, courtesy of the jaded attendant. "You will fasten your seat belt," came the no-nonsense request.

"I'm already buckled in," said Willy. Then she realized the woman was speaking to Guy. Willy nudged him. "Guy, your seat belt."

"What? Oh, yeah." He buckled the belt and managed a tight smile.

That's when she noticed he was clenching the armrest. She touched his hand. "Are you all right?"

"I'm fine."

"You don't look fine."

"It's an old problem. Nothing, really…" He stared out the window and swallowed hard.

She couldn't help herself; she burst out laughing. "Guy Barnard, don't tell me you're afraid of *flying?*"

The plane lurched forward and began bumping along the tarmac. A stream of Vietnamese crackled over the speaker system, followed by Russian and then very fractured English.

"Look," he protested, "some guys have a thing about heights or closed spaces or snakes. I happen to have a phobia about planes. Ever since the war."

"Did something happen on your tour?"

"End of my tour." He stared at the ceiling and laughed. "There's the irony. I make it through Nam alive. Then I board that big beautiful freedom bird. That's how I met Toby Wolff. He was sitting right next to me. We were both high, cracking jokes as we taxied up the runway. Going home." He shook his head. "We were two of the lucky ones. Sitting in the last row of seats. The tail broke off on impact…."

She took his hand. "You don't have to talk about it, Guy."

He looked at her in obvious admiration. "You're not in the least bit nervous, are you?"

"No. I've been in planes all my life. I've always felt at home."

"Must be something you inherited from your old man. Pilot's genes."

"Not just genes. Statistics."

The Ilyushin's engines screamed to life. The cabin shuddered as they made their take-off roll down the runway. The ground suddenly fell away, and the plane wobbled into the sky.

"I happen to know flying is a perfectly safe way to travel," she added.

"Safe?" Guy yelled over the engines' roar. "Obviously, you've never flown Air Vietnam!"

In Hanoi, they were met by a Vietnamese escort known only as Miss Hu, beautiful, unsmiling and cadre to the core. Her greeting was all business, her handshake strictly government issue. Unlike Mr. Ainh, who'd been a fountain of good-humored chatter, Miss Hu obviously believed in silence. And the Revolution. Only once on the drive into the city did the woman offer a voluntary remark. Directing their attention to the twisted remains of a bridge, she said, "You see the damage? American bombs." That was it for small talk. Willy stared at the woman's rigid shoulders and realized that, for some people on both sides, the war would never be over.

She was so annoyed by Miss Hu's comment that she didn't notice Guy's preoccupied look. Only when she saw him glance for the third time out the back window did she realize what he was focusing on: a Mercedes with darkly tinted windows was trailing right behind them. She and Guy exchanged glances.

The Mercedes followed them all the way into town. Only when they pulled up in front of the hotel did the

other car pass them. It headed around the corner, its oc-
cupants obscured behind dark glass.

Willy's door was pulled open. Heat poured in, a
knock-down, drag-out heat that left her stunned.

Miss Hu stood waiting outside, her face already
pearled with sweat. "The hotel is air-conditioned," she
said and added, with a note of disdain, "for the comfort of *foreigners*."

As it turned out, the so-called air-conditioning was
scarcely functioning. In fact, the hotel itself seemed to
be sputtering along on little more than its old French
colonial glory. The entry rug was ratty and faded, the
lobby furniture a sad mélange of battered rosewood
and threadbare cushions. While Guy checked in at the
reception desk, Willy stationed herself near their suitcases and kept watch over the lobby entrance.

She wasn't surprised when, seconds later, two Vietnamese men, both wearing dark glasses, strolled through
the door. They spotted her immediately and veered off
toward an alcove, where they loitered behind a giant potted fern. She could see the smoke from their cigarettes
curling toward the ceiling.

"We're all checked in," said Guy. "Room 308. View
of the city."

Willy touched his arm. "Two men," she whispered.
"Three o'clock…"

"I see them."

"What do we do now?"

"Ignore them."

"But—"

"Mr. Barnard?" called Miss Hu. They both turned.
The woman was waving a slip of paper. "The desk clerk
says there is a telegram for you."

Guy frowned. "I wasn't expecting any telegram."

"It arrived this morning in Saigon, but you had just left. The hotel called here with the message." She handed Guy the scribbled phone memo and watched with sharp eyes as he read it.

If the message was important, Guy didn't show it. He casually stuffed it into his pocket and, picking up the suitcases, nudged Willy into a waiting elevator.

"Not bad news?" called Miss Hu.

Guy smiled at her. "Just a note from a friend," he said, and punched the elevator button.

Willy caught a last glimpse of the two Vietnamese men peering at them from behind the fern, and then the door slid shut. Instantly, Guy gripped her hand. *Don't say a word,* she read in his eyes.

It was a silent ride to the third floor.

Up in their room, Willy watched in puzzlement as Guy circled around, discreetly running his fingers under lampshades and along drawers, opened the closet, searched the nightstands. Behind the headboard, he finally found what he was seeking: a wireless microphone, barely the size of a postage stamp. He left it where it was. Then he went to the window and stared down at the street.

"How flattering," he murmured. "We rate baby-sitting service."

She moved beside him and saw what he was looking at: the black Mercedes, parked on the street below. "What about that telegram?" she whispered.

In answer, he pulled out the slip of paper and handed it to her. She read it twice, but it made no sense.

Uncle Sy asking about you. Plans guided tour of
Nam. Happy Trails. Bobbo.

Guy let the curtain flap shut and began to pace fu-
riously around the room. By the look of him, he was
thinking up a blizzard, planning some scheme.

He suddenly halted. "Do you want something for
your stomach?" he asked.

She blinked. "Excuse me?"

"Pepto Bismol might help. And you'd better lie down
for a while. That old intestinal bug can get pretty damn
miserable."

"Intestinal bug?" She gave him a helpless look.

He stalked to the desk and rummaged in a drawer
for a piece of hotel stationery, talking all the while. "I'll
bet it's that seafood you ate last night. Are you still feeling really lousy?" He held up a sheet of paper on which
he'd scribbled, "Yes!!!"

"Yes," she said. "Definitely lousy. I—I think I should
lie down." She paused. "Shouldn't I?"

He was writing again. The sheet of paper now said,
"You want to go to the hospital!"

She nodded and went into the bathroom, where she
groaned loudly a few times and flushed the toilet. "You
know, I feel really rotten. Maybe I should see a doctor...." It struck her then, as she stood by the sink and
watched the water hiss out of the faucet, exactly what he
was up to. *The man's a genius,* she thought with sudden
admiration. Turning to look at him, she said, "Do you
think we'll find anyone who speaks English?"

She was rewarded with a thumbs-up sign.

"We could try the hospital," he said. "Maybe it won't

be a doctor, but they should have someone who'll understand you."

She went to the bed and sat down, bouncing a few times to make the springs squeak. "God, I feel awful."

He sat beside her and placed his hand on her forehead. His eyes were twinkling as he said, "Lady, you're really hot."

"I know," she said gravely.

They could barely hold back their laughter.

"She did not seem ill an hour ago," Miss Hu said as she ushered them into the limousine ten minutes later.

"The cramps came on suddenly," said Guy.

"I would say *very* suddenly," Miss Hu noted aridly.

"I think it was the seafood," Willy whimpered from the back seat.

"You Americans," Miss Hu sniffed. "Such delicate stomachs."

The hospital waiting room was hot as an oven and overflowing with patients. As Willy and Guy entered, a hush instantly fell over the crowd. The only sounds were the rhythmic clack of the ceiling fan and a baby crying in its mother's lap. Every eye was watching as the two Americans moved through the room toward the reception desk.

The Vietnamese nurse behind the desk stared in mute astonishment. Only when Miss Hu barked out a question did the nurse respond with a nervous shake of the head and a hurried answer.

"We have only Vietnamese doctors here," translated Miss Hu. "No Europeans."

"You have no one trained in the West?" Guy asked.

"Why, do you feel your Western medicine is superior?"

"Look, I'm not here to argue East versus West. Just find someone who speaks English. A nurse'll do. You have English-speaking nurses, don't you?"

Scowling, Miss Hu turned and muttered to the desk nurse, who made a few phone calls. At last Willy was led down a corridor to a private examination room. It was stocked with only the basics: an examining table, a sink, an instrument cart. Cotton balls and tongue depressors were displayed in dusty glass jars. A fly buzzed lazily around the one bare lightbulb. The nurse handed Willy a tattered gown and gestured for her to undress.

Willy had no intention of stripping while Miss Hu stood watch in the corner.

"I would appreciate some privacy," Willy said.

The other woman didn't move. "Mr. Barnard is staying," she pointed out.

"No." Willy looked at Guy. "Mr. Barnard is leaving."

"In fact, I was just on my way out," said Guy, turning toward the door. He added, for Miss Hu's benefit, "You know, Comrade, in America it's considered quite rude to watch while someone undresses."

"I was only trying to confirm what I've heard about Western women's undergarments," Miss Hu insisted as she and the nurse followed Guy out the door.

"What, exactly, have you heard?" asked Guy.

"That they are designed with the sole purpose of arousing prurient interest from the male sex."

"Comrade," said Guy with a grin, "I would be delighted to share my knowledge on the topic of ladies' undergarments...."

The door closed, leaving Willy alone in the room. She changed into the gown and sat on the table to wait.

Moments later, a tall, fortyish woman wearing a

white lab coat walked in. The name tag on her lapel confirmed that she was Nora Walker. She gave Willy a brisk nod of greeting and paused beside the table to glance through the notes on the hospital clipboard. Strands of gray streaked her mane of brown hair; her eyes were a deep green, as unfathomable as the sea.

"I'm told you're American," the woman said, her accent British. "We don't see many Americans here. What seems to be the problem?"

"My stomach's been hurting. And I've been nauseated."

"How long now?"

"A day."

"Any fever?"

"No fever. But lots of cramping."

The woman nodded. "Not unusual for Western tourists." She looked back down at the clipboard. "It's the water. Different bacterial strains than you're used to. It'll take a few days to get over it. I'll have to examine you. If you'll just lie down, Miss—" She focused on the name written on the clipboard. Instantly she fell silent.

"Maitland," said Willy softly. "My name is Willy Maitland."

Nora cleared her throat. In a flat voice she said, "Please lie down."

Obediently, Willy settled back on the table and allowed the other woman to examine her abdomen. The hands probing her belly were cold as ice.

"Sam Lassiter said you might help us," Willy whispered.

"You've spoken to Sam?"

"In Cantho. I went to see him about my father."

Nora nodded and said, suddenly businesslike, "Does that hurt when I press?"

"No."

"How about here?"

"A little tender."

Now, once again in a whisper, Nora asked, "How is Sam doing these days?"

Willy paused. "He's dead," she murmured.

The hands resting on her stomach froze. "Dear God. How—" Nora caught herself, swallowed. "I mean, how...much does it hurt?"

Willy traced her finger, knifelike, across her throat.

Nora took a breath. "I see." Her hands, still resting on Willy's abdomen, were trembling. For a moment she stood silent, her head bowed. Then she turned and went to a medicine cabinet. "I think you need some antibiotics." She took out a bottle of pills. "Are you allergic to sulfa?"

"I don't think so."

Nora took out a blank medication label and began to fill in the instructions. "May I see proof of identification, Miss Maitland?"

Willy produced a California driver's license and handed it to Nora. "Is that sufficient?"

"It will do." Nora pocketed the license. Then she taped the medication label on the pill bottle. "Take one four times a day. You should notice some results by tomorrow night." She handed the bottle to Willy. Inside were about two dozen white tablets. On the label was listed the drug name and a standard set of directions. No hidden messages, no secret instructions.

Willy looked up expectantly, but Nora had already turned to leave. Halfway to the door, she paused.

"There's a man with you, an American. Who is he? A relative?"

"A friend."

"I see." Nora gave her a long and troubled look. "I trust you're absolutely certain about your drug allergies, Miss Maitland. Because if you're wrong, that medication could be very, very dangerous." She opened the door to find Miss Hu standing right outside.

The Vietnamese woman instantly straightened. "Miss Maitland is well?" she inquired.

"She has a mild intestinal infection. I've given her some antibiotics. She should be feeling much better by tomorrow."

"I feel a little better already," said Willy, climbing off the table. "If I could just have some fresh air..."

"An excellent idea," said Nora. "Fresh air. And only light meals. No milk." She headed out the door. "Have a good stay in Hanoi, Miss Maitland."

Miss Hu turned a smug smile on Willy. "You see? Even here in Vietnam, one can find the best in medical care."

Willy nodded and reached for her clothes. "I quite agree."

Fifteen minutes later, Nora Walker left the hospital, climbed onto her bicycle and pedaled to the cloth merchants' road. At a streetside noodle stand she bought a lemonade and a bowl of *pho,* for which she paid the vendor a thousand-dong note, carefully folded at opposite corners. She ate her noodles while squatted on the sidewalk, beside all the other customers. Then, after draining the last of the peppery broth, she strolled into a tailor's shop. It appeared deserted. She slipped through a beaded curtain into a dimly lit back room. There, among the dusty bolts of silks and cottons and brocade, she waited.

The rattle of the curtain beads announced the entrance of her contact. Nora turned to face him.

"I've just seen Bill Maitland's daughter," she said in Vietnamese. She handed over Willy's driver's license.

The man studied the photograph and smiled. "I see there is a family resemblance."

"There's also a problem," said Nora. "She's traveling with a man—"

"You mean Mr. Barnard?" There was another smile. "We're well aware of him."

"Is he CIA?"

"We think not. He is, to all appearances, an independent."

"So you've been tracking them."

The man shrugged. "Hardly difficult. With so many children on the streets, they'd scarcely notice a stray boy here and there."

Nora swallowed, afraid to ask the next question. "She said Sam's dead. Is this true?"

The man's smile vanished. "We are sorry. Time, it seems, has not made things any safer."

Turning away, she tried to clear her throat, but the ache remained. She pressed her forehead against a bolt of comfortless silk. "You're right. Nothing's changed. Damn them. *Damn* them."

"What do you ask of us, Nora?"

"I don't know." She took a ragged breath and turned to face him. "I suppose—I suppose we should send a message."

"I will contact Dr. Andersen."

"I need to have an answer by tomorrow."

The man shook his head. "That leaves us little time for arrangements."

"A whole day. Surely that's enough."

"But there are..." He paused. "Complications."

Nora studied the man's face, a perfect mask of impassivity. "What do you mean?"

"The Party is now interested. And the CIA. Perhaps there are others."

Others, thought Nora. Meaning those they knew nothing about. The most dangerous faction of all.

As Nora left the tailor shop and walked into the painful glare of afternoon, she sensed a dozen pairs of eyes watching her, marking her leisurely progress up Gia Ngu Street. The brightly embroidered blouse she'd just purchased in the shop made her feel painfully conspicuous. Not that she wasn't already conspicuous. In Hanoi, all foreigners were watched with suspicion. In every shop she visited, along every street she walked, there were always those eyes.

They would be watching Willy Maitland, as well.

"We've made the first move," Guy said. "The next move is hers."

"And if we don't hear anything?"

"Then I'm afraid we've hit a dead end." Guy thrust his hands into his pockets and turned his gaze across the waters of Returned Sword Lake. Like a dozen other couples strolling the grassy banks, they'd sought this park for its solitude, for the chance to talk without being heard. Flame red blossoms drifted down from the trees. On the footpath ahead, children chattered over a game of ball and jacks.

"You never explained that telegram," she said. "Who's Bobbo?"

He laughed. "Oh, that's a nickname for Toby Wolff. After that plane crash, we wound up side by side in a military hospital. I guess we gave the nurses a lot of grief. You know, a few too many winks, too many sly comments. They got to calling us the evil Bobbsey twins. Pretty soon he was Bobbo One and I was Bobbo Two."

"Then Toby Wolff sent the telegram."

He nodded.

"And what does it mean? Who's Uncle Sy?"

Guy paused and gave their surroundings a thoughtful perusal. She knew it was more than just a casual look; he was searching. And sure enough, there they were: two Vietnamese men, stationed in the shadow of a poinciana tree. Police agents, most likely, assigned to protect them.

Or was it to isolate them?

"Uncle Sy," Guy said, "was our private name for the CIA."

She frowned, recalling the message. *Uncle Sy asking about you. Plans guided tour of Nam. Happy trails. Bobbo.*

"It was a warning," Guy said. "The Company knows about us. And they're in the country. Maybe watching us this very minute."

She glanced apprehensively around the lake. A bicycle glided past, pedaled by a serene girl in a conical hat. On the grass, two lovers huddled together, whispering secrets. It struck Willy as too perfect, this view of silver lake and flowering trees, an artist's fantasy for a picture postcard.

All except for the two police agents watching from the trees.

"If he's right," she said, "if the CIA's after us, how are we going to recognize them?"

"That's the problem." Guy turned to her, and the uneasiness she saw in his eyes frightened her. "We won't."

So close. Yet so unreachable.

Siang squatted in the shadow of a pedicab and watched the two Americans stroll along the opposite bank of the lake. They took their time, stopping like tourists to admire the flowers, to laugh at a child toddling in the path, both of them oblivious to how easily they could be captured in a rifle's crosshairs, their lives instantly extinguished.

He turned his attention to the two men trailing a short distance behind. Police agents, he assumed, on protective surveillance. They made things more difficult, but Siang could work around them. Sooner or later, an opportunity would arise.

Assassination would be so easy, as simple as a curtain left open to a well-aimed bullet. What a pity that was no longer the plan.

The Americans returned to their car. Siang rose, stamped the blood back into his legs and climbed onto his bicycle. It was a beggarly form of transportation, but it was practical and inconspicuous. Who would notice, among the thousands crowding the streets of Hanoi, one more shabbily dressed cyclist?

Siang followed the car back to the hotel. One block farther, he dismounted and discreetly observed the two Americans enter the lobby. Seconds later, a black Mercedes pulled up. The two agents climbed out and followed the Americans into the hotel.

It was time to set up shop.

Siang took a cloth-wrapped bundle from his bicycle basket, chose a shady spot on the sidewalk and spread out a meager collection of wares: cigarettes, soap and greeting cards. Then, like all the other itinerant merchants lining the road, he squatted down on his straw mat and beckoned to passersby.

Over the next two hours he managed to sell only a single bar of soap, but it scarcely mattered. He was there simply to watch. And to wait.

Like any good hunter, Siang knew how to wait.

Chapter 10

Guy and Willy slept in separate beds that night. At least, Guy slept. Willy lay awake, tossing on the sheets, thinking about her father, about the last time she had seen him alive.

He had been packing. She'd stood beside the bed, watching him toss clothes into a suitcase. She knew by the items he'd packed that he was returning to the lovely insanity of war. She saw the flak jacket, the Laotian-English dictionary, the heavy gold chains—a handy form of ransom with which a downed pilot could bargain for his life. There was also the Government-issue blood chit, printed on cloth and swiped from a U.S. Air Force pilot.

I am a citizen of the United States of America. I do not speak your language. Misfortune forces me to seek your assistance in obtaining food, shelter and protection. Please take me to someone who will provide for my safety and see that I am returned to my people.

It was written in thirteen languages.

The last item he packed was his .45, the trigger seat filed to a feather release. Willy had stood by the bed and stared at the gun, struck in that instant by its terrible significance.

"Why are you going back?" she'd asked.

"Because it's my job, baby," he'd said, slipping the pistol in among his clothes. "Because I'm good at it, and because we need the paycheck."

"We don't need the paycheck. We need you."

He closed the suitcase. "Your mom's been talking to you again, has she?"

"No, this is me talking, Daddy. *Me*."

"Sure, baby." He laughed and mussed her hair, his old way of making her feel like his little girl. He set the suitcase down on the floor and grinned at her, the same grin he always used on her mother, the same grin that always got him what he wanted. "Tell you what. How 'bout I bring back a little surprise? Something nice from Vientiane. Maybe a ruby? Or a sapphire? Bet you'd love a sapphire."

She shrugged. "Why bother?"

"What do you mean, 'why bother'? You're my baby, aren't you?"

"Your baby?" She looked at the ceiling and laughed. "When was I ever *your* baby?"

His grin vanished. "I don't care for your tone of voice, young lady."

"You don't care about anything, do you? Except flying your stupid planes in your stupid war." Before he could answer, she'd pushed past him and left the room.

As she fled down the hall she heard him yell, "You're just a kid. One of these days you'll understand! Grow up a little! Then you'll understand...."

One of these days. One of these days.

"I still don't understand," she whispered to the night.

From the street below came the whine of a passing car. She sat up in bed and, running a hand through her damp hair, gazed around the room. The curtains fluttered like gossamer in the moonlit window. In the next bed, Guy lay asleep, the covers kicked aside, his bare back gleaming in the darkness.

She rose and went to the window. On the corner below, three pedicab drivers, dressed in rags, squatted together in the dim glow of a street lamp. They didn't say a word; they simply huddled there in a midnight tableau of weariness. She wondered how many others, just as weary, just as silent, wandered in the night.

And to think they won the war.

A groan and the creak of bedsprings made her turn. Guy was lying on his back now, the covers kicked to the floor. By some strange fascination, she was drawn to his side. She stood in the shadows, studying his rumpled hair, the rise and fall of his chest. Even in his sleep he wore a half smile, as though some private joke were echoing in his dreams. She started to smooth back his hair, then thought better of it. Her hand lingered over him as she struggled against the longing to touch him, to be held by him. It had been so long since she'd felt this way about a man, and it frightened her; it was the first sign of surrender, of the offering up of her soul.

She couldn't let it happen. Not with this man.

She turned and went back to her own bed and threw herself onto the sheets. There she lay, thinking of all the ways he was wrong for her, all the ways they were wrong for each other.

The way her mother and father had been wrong for each other.

It was something Ann Maitland had never recognized, that basic incompatibility. It had been painfully obvious to her daughter. Bill Maitland was the wild card, the unpredictable joker in life's game of chance. Ann cheerfully accepted whatever surprises she was dealt because he was her husband, because she loved him.

But Willy didn't need that kind of love. She didn't need a younger version of Wild Bill Maitland.

Though, God knew, she wanted him. And he was right in the next bed.

She closed her eyes. Restless, sweating, she counted the hours until morning.

"A most curious turn of events." Minister Tranh, recently off the plane from Saigon, settled into his hard-backed chair and gazed at the tea leaves drifting in his cup. "You say they are behaving like mere tourists?"

"Typical *capitalist* tourists," said Miss Hu in disgust. She opened her notebook, in which she'd dutifully recorded every detail, and began her report. "This morning at nine-forty-five, they visited the tomb of our beloved leader but offered no comment. At 12:17, they were served lunch at the hotel, a menu which included fried fish, stewed river turtle, steamed vegetables and custard. This afternoon, they were escorted to the Museum of War, then the Museum of Revolution—"

"This is hardly the itinerary of capitalist tourists."

"And then—" she flipped the page "—they went *shopping*." Triumphantly, she snapped the notebook closed.

"But Comrade Hu, even the most dedicated Party member must, on occasion, shop."

"For antiques?"

"Ah. They value tradition."

Miss Hu bent forward. "Here is the part that raises my suspicions, Minister Tranh. It is the leopard revealing its stripes."

"Spots," corrected the minister with a smile. The fervent Comrade Hu had been studying her American idioms again. What a shame she had absorbed so little of their humor. "What, exactly, did they do?"

"This afternoon, after the antique shop, they spent two hours at the Australian embassy—the cocktail lounge, to be precise—where they conversed in private with various suspect foreigners."

Minister Tranh found it of only passing interest that the Americans would retreat to a Western embassy. Like anyone in a strange country, they probably missed the company of their own type of people. Decades ago in Paris, Tranh had felt just such a longing. Even as he'd sipped coffee in the West Bank cafés, even as he'd reveled in the joys of Bohemian life, at times, he had ached for the sight of jet black hair, for the gentle twang of his own language. Still, how he had loved Paris....

"So you see, the Americans are well monitored," said Miss Hu. "Rest assured, Minister Tranh. Nothing will go wrong."

"Assuming they continue to cooperate with us."

"Cooperate?" Miss Hu's chin came up in a gesture

of injured pride. "They are not aware we're following them."

What a shame the politically correct Miss Hu was so lacking in vision and insight. Minister Tranh hadn't the energy to contradict her. Long ago, he had learned that zealots were seldom swayed by reason.

He looked down at his tea leaves and sighed. "But, of course, you are right, Comrade," he said.

"It's been a day now. Why hasn't anyone contacted us?" Willy whispered across the oilcloth-covered table.

"Maybe they can't get close enough," Guy said. "Or maybe they're still looking us over."

The way everyone else was looking them over, Willy thought as her gaze swept the noisy café. In one glance she took in the tables cluttered with coffee cups and soup bowls, the diners veiled in a vapor of cooking grease and cigarette smoke, the waiters ferrying trays of steaming food. *They're all watching us,* she thought. In a far corner, the two police agents sat flicking ashes into a saucer. And through the dirty street windows, small faces peered in, children straining for a rare glimpse of Americans.

Their waiter, gaunt and silent, set two bowls of noodle soup on their table and vanished through a pair of swinging doors. In the kitchen, pots clanged and voices chattered over a cleaver's staccato. The swinging doors kept slapping open and shut as waiters pushed through, bent under the weight of their trays.

The police agents were staring.

Willy, by now brittle with tension, reached for her chopsticks and automatically began to eat. It was modest fare, noodles and peppery broth and paper-thin slices of what looked like beef. Water buffalo, Guy told her. Tasty but tough. Head bent, ignoring the stares, she ate in silence. Only when she inadvertently bit into a chili pepper and had to make a lunge for her glass of lemonade did she finally put her chopsticks down.

"I don't know if I can take this idle-tourist act much longer." She sighed. "Just how long are we supposed to wait?"

"As long as it takes. That's one thing you learn in this country. Patience. Waiting for the right time. The right situation."

"Twenty years is a long time to wait."

"You know," he said, frowning, "that's the part that bothers me. That it's been twenty years. Why would the Company still be mucking around in what should be a dead issue?"

"Maybe they're not interested. Maybe Toby Wolff's wrong."

"Toby's never wrong." He looked around at the crowded room, his gaze troubled. "And something else still bothers me. Has from the very beginning. Our so-called accidental meeting in Bangkok. Both of us looking for the same answers, the same man." He paused. "In addition to mild paranoia, however, I get also this sense of…"

"Coincidence?"

"Fate."

Willy shook her head. "I don't believe in fate."

"You will." He stared up at the haze of cigarette smoke swirling about the ceiling fan. "It's this country. It changes you, strips away your sense of reality, your sense of control. You begin to think that events are meant to happen, that they *will* happen, no matter how you fight it. As if our lives are all written out for us and it's impossible to revise the book."

Their gazes met across the table. "I don't believe in fate, Guy," she said softly. "I never have."

"I'm not asking you to."

"I don't believe you and I were *meant* to be together. It just happened."

"But something—luck, fate, conspiracy, whatever you want to call it—has thrown us together." He leaned forward, his gaze never leaving her face. "Of all the crazy places in the world, here we are, at the same table, in the same dirty Vietnamese café. And..." He paused, his brown eyes warm, his crooked smile a fleeting glimmer in his seriousness. "I'm beginning to think it's time we gave in and followed this crazy script. Time we followed our instincts."

They stared at each other through the veil of smoke. And she thought, *I'd like nothing better than to follow my instincts, which are to go back to our hotel and make love with you. I know I'll regret it. But that's what I want. Maybe that's what I've wanted since the day I met you.*

He reached across the table; their hands met. And as their fingers linked, it seemed as if some magical circuit had just been completed, as if this had always been meant to be, that this was where fate—good, bad or indifferent—had meant to lead them. Not apart, but together, to the same embrace, the same bed.

"Let's go back to the room," he whispered.

She nodded. A smile slid between them, one of knowing, full of promise. Already the images were drifting through her head: shirts slowly unbuttoned, belts unbuckled. Sweat glistening on backs and shoulders. Slowly she pushed her chair back from the table.

But as they rose to their feet, a voice, shockingly familiar, called to them from across the room.

Dodge Hamilton lumbered toward them through the maze of tables. Pale and sweating, he sank into a chair beside them.

"What the hell are *you* doing here?" Guy asked in astonishment.

"I'm bloody lucky to be here at all," said Hamilton, wiping a handkerchief across his brow. "One of our engines trailed smoke all the way from Da Nang. I tell you, I didn't fancy myself splattered all over some mountaintop."

"But I thought you were staying in Saigon," said Willy.

Hamilton stuffed the handkerchief back in his pocket. "Wish I had. But yesterday I got a telex from the finance minister's office. He's finally agreed to an interview—something I've been working at for months. So I squeezed onto the last flight out of Saigon." He shook his head. "Just about my last flight, period. Lord, I need a drink." He pointed to Willy's glass. "What's that you've got there?"

"Lemonade."

Hamilton turned and called to the waiter. "Hello, there! Could I have one of these—these lemon things?"

Willy took a sip, watching Hamilton thoughtfully over the rim of her glass. "How did you find us?"

"What? Oh, that was no trick. The hotel clerk directed me here."

"How did *he* know?"

Guy sighed. "Obviously we can't take a step without everyone knowing about it."

Hamilton frowned dubiously as the waiter set a napkin and another glass of lemonade on the table. "Probably carries some fatal bacteria." He lifted the glass and sighed. "Might as well live dangerously. Well, here's to the trusty Ilyushins of the sky! May they never crash. Not with me aboard, anyway."

Guy raised his glass in a wholehearted toast. "Amen. From now on, I say we all stick to boats."

"Or pedicabs," said Hamilton. "Just think, Barnard, we could be pedaled across China!"

"I think you'd be safer in a plane," Willy said, and reached for her glass. As she lifted it, she noticed a dark stain bleeding from the wet napkin onto the tablecloth. It took her a few seconds to realize what it was, that tiny trickle of blue. Ink. There was something written on the other side of her napkin....

"It all depends on the plane," said Hamilton. "After today, no more Russian rigs for me. Pardon the pun, but I've been thoroughly dis-Ilyushined."

It was Guy's burst of laughter that pulled Willy out of her feverish speculation. She looked up and found Hamilton frowning at her. Dodge Hamilton, she thought. He was always around. Always watching.

She crumpled the napkin in her fist. "If you don't mind, I think I'll go back to the hotel."

"Is something wrong?" Guy asked.

"I'm tired." She rose, still clutching the napkin. "And a little queasy."

Hamilton at once shoved aside his glass of lemonade. "I *knew* I should have stuck to whiskey. Can I fetch you anything? Bananas, maybe? That's the cure, you know."

"She'll be fine," said Guy, helping Willy to her feet. "I'll look after her."

Outside, the heat and chaos of the street were overwhelming. Willy clung to Guy's arm, afraid to talk, afraid to voice her suspicions. But he'd already sensed her agitation. He pulled her through the crowd toward the hotel.

Back in their room, Guy locked the door and drew the curtains. Willy unfolded the napkin. By the light of a bedside lamp, they struggled to decipher the smudgy message.

"0200. Alley behind hotel. Watch your back."

Willy looked at him. "What do you think?"

He didn't answer. She watched him pace the room, thinking, weighing the risks. Then he took the napkin, tore it to shreds and vanished into the bathroom. She heard the toilet flush and knew the evidence had been disposed of. When he came out of the bathroom, his expression was flat and unreadable.

"Why don't you lie down," he said. "There's nothing like a good night's sleep to settle an upset stomach." He turned off the lamp. By the glow of her watch, she saw it was just after seven-thirty. It would be a long wait.

They scarcely slept that night.

In the darkness of their room, they waited for the hours to pass. Outside, the noises of the street, the voices, the tinkle of pedicab bells faded to silence. They didn't undress; they lay tensed in their beds, not daring to exchange a word.

It must have been after midnight when Willy at last slipped into a dreamless sleep. It seemed only moments had passed when she felt herself being nudged awake.

Guy's lips brushed her forehead, then she heard him whisper, "Time to move."

She sat up, instantly alert, her heart off and racing. Carrying her shoes, she tiptoed after him to the door.

The hall was deserted. The scuffed wood floor gleamed dully beneath a bare lightbulb. They slipped out into the corridor and headed for the stairs.

From the second-floor railing, they peered down into the lobby. The hotel desk was unattended. The sound of snoring echoed like a lion's roar up the stairwell. As they moved down the steps, the hotel lounge came into view, and they spotted the lobby attendant sprawled out on a couch, mouth gaping in blissful repose.

Guy flashed Willy a grin and a thumbs-up sign. Then he led the way down the steps and through a service door. Crates lined a dark and dingy hallway; at the far end was another door. They slipped out the exit.

Outside, the darkness was so thick Willy found herself groping for some tangible clue to her surroundings. Then Guy took her hand and his touch was steadying; it was a hand she'd learned she could trust. Together they crept through the shadows, into the narrow alley behind the hotel. There they waited.

It was 2:01.

At 2:07, they sensed, more than heard, a stirring in the darkness. It was as if a breath of wind had congealed into something alive, solid. They didn't see the woman until she was right beside them.

"Come with me," she said. Willy recognized the voice: it was Nora Walker's.

They followed her up a series of streets and alleys, weaving farther and farther into the maze that was Hanoi. Nora said nothing. Every so often they caught a glimpse of her in the glow of a street lamp, her hair concealed beneath a conical hat, her dark blouse anonymously shabby.

At last, in an alley puddled with stagnant water, they came to a halt. Through the darkness, Willy could just make out three bicycles propped against a wall. A bundle was thrust into her hands. It contained a set of pajamalike pants and blouse, a conical hat smelling of fresh straw. Guy, too, was handed a change of clothes.

In silence they dressed.

On bicycles they followed Nora through miles of back streets. In that landscape of shadows, everything took on a life of its own. Tree branches reached out to snag them. The road twisted like a serpent. Willy lost all sense of direction; as far as she knew, they could be turning in circles. She pedaled automatically, following the faint outline of Nora's hat floating ahead in the darkness.

The paved streets gave way to dirt roads, the buildings to huts and vegetable plots. At last, at the outskirts of town, they dismounted. An old truck sat at the side of the road. Through the driver's window, a cigarette could be seen glowing in the darkness. The door squealed open, and a Vietnamese man hopped out of the cab. He and Nora whispered together for a moment. Then the man tossed aside the cigarette and gestured to the back of the truck.

"Get in," said Nora. "He'll take you from here."

"Where are we going?" asked Willy.

Nora flipped aside the truck's tarp and motioned for them to climb in. "No time for questions. Hurry."

"Aren't you coming with us?"

"I can't. They'll notice I'm gone."

"*Who'll* notice?"

Nora's voice, already urgent, took on a note of panic. "Please. Get in *now*."

Guy and Willy scrambled onto the rear bumper and dropped down lightly among a pile of rice sacks.

"Be patient," said Nora. "It's a long ride. There's food and water inside—enough to hold you."

"Who's the driver?" asked Guy.

"No names. It's safer."

"But can we trust him?"

Nora paused. "Can we trust anyone?" she said. Then she yanked on the tarp. The canvas fell, closing them off from the night.

It was a long bicycle ride back to her apartment. Nora pedaled swiftly, her body slicing through the night, her hat shuddering in the wind. She knew the way well; even in the darkness she could sense where the hazards, the unexpected potholes, lay.

Tonight she could also sense something else. A presence, something evil, floating in the night. The feeling was so unshakable she felt compelled to stop and look back at the road. For a full minute she held her breath and waited. Nothing moved, only the shadows of clouds hurtling before the moon. *It's my imagination,* she thought. No one was following her. No one *could* have followed her. She'd been too cautious, taking the Americans up and down so many turns that no one could possibly have kept up unnoticed.

Breathing easier, she pedaled all the way home.

She parked her bicycle in the community shed and climbed the rickety steps to her apartment. The door was unlocked. The significance of that fact didn't strike her until she'd already taken one step over the threshold. By then it was too late.

The door closed behind her. She spun around just as a light sprang on, shining full in her face. Blinded, she took a panicked step backward. "Who—what—"

From behind, hands wrenched her into a brutal embrace. A knife blade slid lightly across her neck.

"Not a word," whispered a voice in her ear.

The person holding the light came forward. He was a large man, so large, his shadow blotted out the wall. "We've been waiting for you, Miss Walker," he said. "Where did you take them?"

She swallowed. "Who?"

"You went to the hotel to meet them. Where did you go from there?"

"I didn't—" She gasped as the blade suddenly stung her flesh; she felt a drop of blood trickle warmly down her neck.

"Easy, Mr. Siang," said the man. "We have all night."

Nora began to cry. "Please. Please, I don't know anything...."

"But, of course, you do. And you'll tell us, won't you?" The man pulled up a chair and sat down. She could see his teeth gleaming like ivory in the shadows. "It's only a question of when."

From beneath the flapping canvas, Willy caught glimpses of dawn: light filtering through the trees, dust swirling in the road, the green brilliance of rice paddies. They'd been traveling for hours now, and the sacks of rice were beginning to feel like bags of concrete against their backs. At least they'd been provided with food and drink. In an open crate they'd found a bottle of water, a loaf of French bread and four hard-boiled eggs. It seemed sufficient—at first. But as the day wore on and the heat grew suffocating, that single bottle of water became more and more precious. They rationed it, one sip every half hour; it was barely enough to keep their throats moist.

At noon the truck began to climb.

"Where are we going?" she asked.

"Heading west, I think. Into the mountains. Maybe the road to Dien Bien Phu."

"Towards Laos?"

"Where your father's plane went down." In the shadows of the truck, Guy's face, dirty and unshaven, was a tired mask of resolution. She wondered if she looked as grim.

He shrugged off his sweat-soaked shirt and threw it aside, oblivious to the mosquitoes buzzing around them. The scar on his bare abdomen seemed to ripple in the gloom. In silent fascination, Willy started to reach out to him, then thought better of it.

"It's okay," he said softly, guiding her hand to the scar. "It doesn't hurt."

"It must have hurt terribly when you got it."

"I don't remember." At her puzzled look, he added, "I mean, not on any sort of conscious level. It's funny, though, how well I remember what happened just before the plane went down. Toby, sitting next to me, telling jokes. Something about the pilot looking like an old buddy of his from Alcoholics Anonymous. He'd heard in flight school that the best military pilots were always the drunks; a sober man wouldn't dream of flying the sort of junk heap we were in. I remember laughing as we taxied down the runway. Then—" He shook his head. "They say I pulled him out of the wreckage. That I unbuckled him and dragged him out just before the whole thing blew. They even called me a hero." He uncapped the water bottle, took a sip. "What a laugh."

"Sounds like you earned the label," she said.

"Sounds more like I was knocked in the head and didn't know what the hell I was doing."

"The best heroes in the world are the reluctant ones. Courage isn't fearlessness—it's acting in the face of fear."

"Yeah?" He laughed. "Then that makes me the best of the best." He stiffened as the truck suddenly slowed, halted. A voice barked orders in the distance. They stared at each other in alarm.

"What is it?" she whispered. "What're they saying?"

"Something about a roadblock…soldiers are stopping everyone. Some sort of inspection…."

"My God. What do we—"

He put a finger to his lips. "Sounds like a lot of traffic in front. Could take a while before they get to us."

"Can we back up? Turn around?"

He scrambled to the back of the truck and glanced through a slit in the canvas. "No chance. We're socked in tight. Trucks on both sides."

Willy frantically surveyed the gloom, searching for empty burlap bags, a crate, anything large enough in which to hide.

The soldiers' voices moved closer.

We have to make a run for it, thought Willy. Guy had already risen to a crouch. But a glance outside told them they were surrounded by shallow rice paddies. Without cover, their flight would be spotted immediately.

But they won't hurt us, she thought. *They wouldn't dare. We're Americans.*

As if, in this crazy world, an eagle on one's passport bought any sort of protection.

The soldiers were right outside—two men by the sound of the voices. The truck driver was trying to cajole his way out of the inspection, laughing, offering cigarettes. The man had to have nerves of steel; not a single note of apprehension slipped into his voice.

His attempts at bribery failed. Footsteps continued along the graveled roadside, heading for the back of the truck.

Guy instinctively shoved Willy against the rice sacks, shielding her behind him. He'd be the one they'd see first, the one they'd confront. He turned to face the inevitable.

A hand poked through, gripping the canvas flap....

And paused. In the distance, a car horn was blaring. Tires screeched, followed by the thud of metal, the angry shouts of drivers.

The hand gripping the canvas pulled away. The flap slid shut. There were a few terse words exchanged between the soldiers, then footsteps moved away, crunching up the gravel road.

It took only seconds for their driver to scramble back into the front seat and hit the gas. The truck lurched forward, throwing Guy off his feet. He toppled, landing right next to Willy on the rice sacks. As their truck roared full speed around the traffic and down the road, they sprawled together, too stunned by their narrow escape to say a word. Suddenly they were both laughing, rolling around on the sacks, giddy with relief.

Guy hauled her into his arms and kissed her hard on the mouth.

"What was that for?" she demanded, pulling back in surprise.

"That," he whispered, "was pure instinct."

"Do you always follow your instincts?"

"Whenever I can get away with it."

"And you really think I'll let you get away with it?"

In answer, he gripped her hair, trapping her head against the sacks, and kissed her again, longer, deeper. Pleasure leapt through her, a desire so sudden, so fierce, it left her voiceless.

"I think," he murmured, "you want it as much as I do."

With a gasp of outrage, she shoved him onto his back and climbed on top of him, pinning him beneath her. "Guy Barnard, you miserable jerk, I'm going to give you what you deserve."

He laughed. "Are you now?"

"Yes, I am."

"And what, exactly, do I deserve?"

For a moment she stared at him through the dust and gloom. Then, slowly, she lowered her face to his. "This," she said softly.

The kiss was different this time. Warmer. Hungrier. She was a full and willing partner; he knew it and he responded. She didn't need to be warned that she was playing a dangerous game, that they were both hurtling toward the point of no return. She could already feel him swelling beneath her, could feel her own body aching to accommodate that new hardness. And the whole time she was kissing him, the whole time their bodies were pressed together, she was thinking, *I'm going to regret this. As sure as I breathe, I'm going to pay for this. But it feels so right….*

She pulled away, fighting to catch her breath.

"Well!" said Guy, grinning up at her. "Miss Willy Maitland, I *am* surprised."

She sat up, nervously shoving her hair back into place. "I never meant to do that."

"Yes, you did."

"It was a stupid thing to do."

"Then why did you?"

"It was…" She looked him in the eye. "Pure instinct."

He laughed. In fact, he fell backward laughing, rolling around on the sacks of rice. The truck hit a pothole, bouncing her up and down so hard, she collapsed onto the floor beside him.

And still he was laughing.

"You're a crazy man," she said.

He threw an arm around her neck and pulled her warmly against him. "Only about you."

In a black limousine with tinted windows, Siang sat gripping the steering wheel and cursing the wretched highway—or what this country called a highway. He had never understood why communism and decent roads had to be mutually exclusive. And then there was the traffic, added to the annoyance of that government vehicle inspection. It had given him a moment's apprehension, the sight of the armed soldiers standing at the roadside. But it took only a few smooth words from the man in the back seat, the wave of a Soviet diplomatic passport, and they were allowed to move on without incident.

They continued west; a road sign confirmed it was

the highway to Dien Bien Phu. A strange omen, Siang thought, that they should be headed for the town where the French had met defeat, where East had triumphed over West. Centuries before, an Asian scribe had written a prophetic statement.

To the south lie the mountains,
The land of the Viets.
He who marches against them
Is surely doomed to failure.

Siang glanced in the rearview mirror, at the man in the back seat. *He* wouldn't be thinking in terms of East versus West. *He* cared nothing about nations or motherlands or patriotism. Real power, he'd once told Siang, lay in the hands of individuals, special people who knew how to use it, to keep it, and *he* was going to keep it.

Siang had no doubt he would.

He remembered the day they'd first met in Happy Valley, at an American base the GIs had whimsically dubbed "the Golf Course." It was 1967. Siang had a different name then. He was a slender boy of thirteen, barefoot, scratching out a hungry existence among all the other orphans. When he'd first seen the American, his initial impression was of hugeness. An enormous fleshy face, alarmingly red in the heat; boots made for a giant; hands that looked strong enough to snap a child's arm in two. The day was hot, and Siang was selling soft drinks. The man bought a Coca Cola, drank it down in a few gulps and handed the empty bottle back. As Siang took it, he felt the man's gaze studying him, measuring him. Then the man walked away.

The next day, and every day for a week, the American emerged from the GI compound to buy a Coca Cola. Though a dozen other children clamored for his business, each waving soft drinks, the man bought only from Siang.

At the end of the week, the man presented Siang with a brand-new shirt, three tins of corned beef and an astonishing amount of cash. He said he was leaving the valley early the next morning, and he asked the boy to hire the prettiest girl he could find and bring her to him for the night.

It was only a test, as Siang found out later. He passed it. In fact, the American seemed surprised when Siang appeared at the compound gate that evening with an extraordinarily beautiful girl. Obviously, the man had expected Siang to take the money and vanish.

To Siang's astonishment, the man sent the girl away without even touching her. Instead, he asked the boy to stay—not as a lover, as Siang at first feared, but as an assistant. "I need someone I can trust," the man said. "Someone I can train…."

Even now, after all these years, Siang still felt that young boy's sense of awe whenever he looked at the American. He glanced at the rearview mirror, at the face that had changed so little since that day they'd met in Happy Valley. The cheeks might be thicker and ruddier, but the eyes were the same, sharp and all-knowing. Just like the mind. Those eyes almost frightened him.

Siang turned his attention back to the road. The man in the back seat was humming a tune: "Yankee Doodle." A whimsical choice, considering the Soviet passport he was carrying. Siang smiled at the irony of it all.

Nothing about the man was ever quite what it seemed.

Chapter 11

It was late in the day when the truck at last pulled to a halt. Willy, half-asleep among the rice sacks, rolled drowsily onto her back and struggled to clear her head. The signals her body was sending gave new meaning to the word *misery*. Every muscle ached; every bone felt shattered. The truck engine cut off. In the new silence, mosquitoes buzzed in the gloom, a gloom so thick she could scarcely breathe.

"Are you awake?" came a whisper. Guy's face, gleaming with sweat, appeared above her.

"What time is it?"

"Late afternoon. Five or so. My watch stopped."

She sat up and her head swam in the heat. "Where are we?"

"Can't be sure. Near the border, I'd guess…" Guy stiffened as footsteps tramped toward them. Men's voices, speaking Vietnamese, moved closer.

The canvas flap was thrown open. Against the sudden glare of daylight, the faces of the two men staring in were black and featureless.

One of the men gestured for them to climb out. "You follow," he ordered. "Say nothing."

Willy at once scrambled out and dropped onto the spongy jungle floor. Guy followed her. They swayed for a moment, blinking dazedly, gulping in their first fresh air in hours. Chips of afternoon sunlight dappled the ground at their feet. In the branches above, an invisible bird screeched out a warning.

The Vietnamese man motioned to them to move. They had just started into the woods when an engine roared to life. Willy turned in alarm to see the truck rattle away without them. She glanced at Guy and saw in his eyes the same thought that had crossed her mind, *There's no turning back now.*

"No stop. Go, go!" said the Vietnamese.

They moved on into the forest.

The man obviously knew where he was going. Without a trail to guide him, he led them through a tangle of vines and trees to an isolated hut. A tattered U.S. Army blanket hung over the doorway. Inside, straw matting covered the earthen floor and a mosquito net, filmy as lace, draped a sleeping pallet. On a low table was set a modest meal of bananas, cracked coconuts and cold tea.

"You wait here," said the man. "Long time, maybe."

"Who are we waiting for?" asked Guy.

The man didn't answer; perhaps he didn't understand the question. He turned and, like a ghost, slipped into the forest.

For a long time, Willy and Guy lingered in the doorway, waiting, listening to the whispers of the jungle.

They heard only the clattering of palms in the wind, the lonely cry of a bird.

How long would they wait? Willy wondered. Hours? Days? She stared up through the dense canopy at the last sunlight sparkling on the wet leaves. It would be dark soon. "I'm hungry," she said, and she turned back into the gloom of the hut.

Together they devoured every banana, gnawed every sliver of coconut from its husk, drank down every drop of tea. In all her life, Willy had never tasted any meal quite so splendid! At last, their stomachs full, their legs trembling with exhaustion, they crawled under the mosquito netting and, side by side, they fell asleep.

At dusk, it began to rain. It was a glorious downpour, monsoonlike in its ferocity, but it brought no relief from the heat. Willy, awake in the darkness, lay with her clothes steeped in sweat. In the shadows above, the mosquito net billowed and fell like a hovering ghost.

She clawed her way free of the netting. If she didn't get some air, she was going to smother.

She left Guy asleep on the pallet and went to the doorway, where she gulped in breaths of rain-drenched air. The swirl of cool mist was irresistible; she stepped out into the downpour.

All around her, the jungle clattered like a thousand cymbals. She shivered in the thunderous darkness as the water streamed down her face.

"What the hell are you doing?" called a sleepy voice. She turned and saw Guy in the doorway.

She laughed. "I'm taking a shower!"

"With your clothes on?"

"It's lovely out here! Come on, before it stops!"

He hesitated, then plunged outside after her.

"Doesn't it feel wonderful?" she cried, throwing her arms out to welcome the raindrops. "I couldn't take the heat any longer. God, I couldn't even stand the smell of my own clothes."

"You think that's bad? Just wait till the mildew sets in." Turning his face to the sky, he let out a satisfied growl. "Now *this* is the way we were meant to take a shower. The way the kids do it. When I was here during the war, I used to get a kick out of seeing 'em run around without their clothes on. Nothing cuter than all those little brown bodies dancing in the rain. No shame, no embarrassment."

"The way it should be."

"That's right," he said. Softly he added, "The way it should be."

All at once, Willy felt him watching her. She turned and stared back. The palms clattered, and the rain beat its tattoo on the leaves. Without a word, he came toward her, stood so close to her, she could feel the heat rippling between them. Yet she didn't move, didn't speak. The rain streaming down her face was as warm as teardrops.

"So what are we doing with our clothes on?" he murmured.

She shook her head. "This isn't supposed to happen."

"Maybe it is."

"A one-night stand—that's all it'd be—"

"Better once than never."

"And then you'll be gone."

"You don't know that. I don't know that."

"I do know it. You'll be gone...."

She started to turn away, but he pulled her back, twisted her around to face him. At the first meeting of their lips, she knew it was over, the battle lost.

Better once than never, she thought as her last shred
of resistance fell away. *Better to have you once and lose
you than to always wonder how it might have been.*
Reaching up, she threw her arms around his neck and
met his kiss with her own, just as hungry, just as fierce.
Their bodies pressed together so tightly, their fever heat
mingled through the damp clothes.

He was already fumbling for the buttons of her
blouse. She trembled as the fabric slid away and rain
trickled down her bare shoulders. Then the warmth of
his hand closed around her breast, and she was shivering not with cold but with desire.

Together they stumbled into the darkness of the hut.
They were tugging desperately at each other's clothes
now, flinging the wet garments into oblivion. When at
last they faced each other with no barriers, no defenses,
he pulled her face up and gently pressed his lips to hers.
No kiss had ever pierced so true to her soul. The darkness swam around her; the earth gave way. She let him
lower her to the pallet and felt the mosquito net whisper down around them.

Making love in the clouds, she thought as the white-
ness billowed above. Then she closed her eyes and lost
all sense of where she was. There was only the pounding of the rain and the magical touch of Guy's hands,
his mouth. It had been so long since a man had made
love to her, so long since she'd bared herself to the pleasure. The pain. And there *would* be pain after it was
over, after he was gone from her life. With a man like
Guy, the ending was inevitable.

She ignored those whispers of warning; she had
drifted beyond all reach of salvation. She pulled him
down against her, and whispered, "Now. Please."

He was already struggling against his own needs, his own urgencies. Her quiet plea slashed away his last thread of control.

"I give up," he groaned. Seizing her hands, he pinned her arms above her head, trapping her, his willing captive, beneath him.

His hardness filled her so completely, it made her catch her breath in astonishment. But her surprise quickly melted into pleasure. She was moving against him now, and he against her, both of them driving that blessed ache to new heights of agony.

The world fell away; the night seemed to swirl with mist and magic. They brought each other to the very edge, and there they lingered, between pleasure and torment, unwilling to surrender to the inevitable. Then the jungle sounds of beating rain, of groaning trees were joined by their cries as they plummeted over the brink.

Even when she fell back to earth, she was still floating. In the darkness above, the netting billowed like parachute silk falling through the emptiness of space.

There was no need to speak; it was enough just to lie together, limbs entwined, and listen to the rhythms of the night.

Gently, Guy stroked a tangled lock of hair off her cheek. "Why did you say that?" he asked.

"Say what?"

"That I'd be gone. That I'd leave you."

She pulled away and rolled onto her back. "Because you will."

"Do you want me to?"

She didn't answer. What difference would it make, after all, to bare her soul? And did he really want to hear the truth: that after tonight, she would probably do anything to keep him, to make him love her?

"Willy?"

She turned away. "Why are we talking about this?"

"Because I want to talk about it."

"Well, I don't." She sat up and hugged her knees protectively against her chest. "It doesn't do anyone any good, all this babbling about what comes next, where do we go from here. I've been through it before."

"You really don't trust men, do you?"

She laughed. "Should I?"

"Is it all because your old man walked out on you? Or was it something else? A bad love affair? What?"

"You could say all of the above."

"I see." There was a long silence. She shivered at the touch of his hand stroking her naked back. "Who else has left you? Besides your father?"

"Just a man I loved. Someone who said he loved me."

"And he didn't."

"Oh, I suppose he did, in his way." She shrugged. "Not a very permanent way."

"If it's only temporary, it's not love."

"Now that sounds like the title of a song." She laughed.

"A lousy song."

At once, she fell silent. She pressed her forehead to her knees. "You're right. A lousy song."

"Other people manage to get over rotten love affairs...."

"Oh, I got over it." She raised her head and stared up at the netting. "Took only a month to fall in love with him. And over a year to watch him walk away. One thing I've learned is that it doesn't fall apart in a day.

Most lovers don't just get up and walk out the door. They do it by inches, step by step, and every single one hurts. First they start out with, 'Who needs to get married, it's just a piece of paper.' And then, at the end, they tell you, 'I need more space.' Then it's 'How can anyone promise forever?' Maybe it was better the way my dad did it. No excuses. He just walked out the door."

"There's no such thing as a good way to leave someone."

"You're right." She pushed aside the netting and swung her feet out. "That's why I don't let it happen to me anymore."

"How do you avoid it?"

"I don't give any man the chance to leave me."

"Meaning you walk away first?"

"Men do it all the time."

"Some men."

Including you, she thought with a distinct twinge of bitterness. "So how did you walk away from your girlfriend, Guy? Did you leave before or after you found out she was pregnant?"

"That was an unusual situation."

"It always is."

"We'd broken up months before. I didn't hear about the kid till after he was born. By then there was nothing I could do, nothing I could change. Ginny was already married to another man."

"Oh." She paused. "That made it simple."

"Simple?" For the first time she heard his anger, and she longed to take back her awful words, longed to cleanse the bitterness from his voice. "You've got some crazy notion that men are all the same," he said. "All of us trying to claw our way free of responsibility, never looking back at the people we've hurt. Let me tell you something, Willy. Having a Y chromosome doesn't make someone a lousy human being."

"I shouldn't have said that," she said, gently touching his hand. "I'm sorry."

He lay quietly in the shadows, staring up at the ceiling. "Sam's three years old now. I've seen him a grand total of twice, once on Ginny's front porch, once on the playground at his preschool. I went over there to get a look at him, to see what kind of kid he was, whether he looked happy. I guess the teachers must've reported it. Not long after, Ginny called me, screaming bloody murder. Said I was messing with her marriage. Even threatened to slap me with a restraining order. I haven't been near him since...." He paused to clear his throat. "I guess I realized I wouldn't be doing him any favors anyways, trying to shove my way into his life. Sam already has a father—a good one, from what I hear. And it would've hurt everyone if I'd tried to fight it out in court. Maybe later, when he's older, I'll find a way to tell him. To let him know how much I wanted to be part of his life."

And my life? she thought with sudden sadness. *You won't be part of it, either, will you?*

She rose to her feet and groped around in the darkness for her scattered clothes. "Here's a little advice, Guy," she said over her shoulder. "Don't ever give up on your son. Take it from a kid who's been left behind. Daddies are a precious commodity."

"I know," he said softly. He paused, then said, "You'll never get over it, will you? Your father walking out."

She shook out her wet blouse. "There are some things a kid can't ever forget."

"Or forgive."

Outside, the rain had softened to a whisper. In the thatching above, insects rustled. "Do you think I should forgive him?"

"Yes."

"I suppose I could forgive him for hurting *me*. But not for hurting my mother. Not when I remember what she went through just to—" Her voice died in midsentence.

They both heard it at the same time: the footsteps slapping through the mud outside.

Guy rolled off the pallet and sprang to his feet beside her. Shoes scraped over the threshold, and the shadow of a man filled the doorway.

The intruder held up a lantern. The flood of light caught them in freeze-frame: Willy, clutching the blouse to her naked breasts; Guy, poised in a fighter's crouch. The stranger, his face hidden in the shadow of a drab green poncho, slowly lowered the lantern and set it on the table. "I am sorry for the delay," he said. "The road is very bad tonight." He tossed a cloth-wrapped bundle down beside the lantern. "At ease, Mr. Barnard. If I'd wanted to kill you, you'd be dead now." He paused and added, "Both of you."

"Who the hell are you?" Guy asked.

Water droplets splattered onto the floor as the man shoved back the hood of his poncho. His hair was blond, almost white in the lantern light. He had pale eyes set in a moonlike face. "Dr. Gunnel Andersen," he said, nodding by way of introduction. "Nora sent word you were coming." Raindrops flew as he shook out the poncho and hung it up to dry. Then he sat down at the table. "Please, feel free to put on your clothes."

"How did Nora reach you?" Guy asked, pulling on his trousers.

"We keep a shortwave radio for medical emergencies. Not all frequencies are monitored by the government."

"Are you with the Swedish mission?"

"No, I work for the U.N." Andersen's impassive gaze wandered to Willy, who was self-consciously struggling into her damp clothes. "We provide medical care in the villages. Humanitarian aid. Malaria, typhoid, it's all here. Probably always will be." He began to unwrap the bundle he'd set on the table. "I assume you have not eaten. This isn't much but it's the best I could do. It's been a bad year for crops, and protein is scarce." Inside the bundle was a bamboo box filled with cold rice, pickled vegetables and microscopic flecks of pork congealed in gravy.

Guy at once sat down. "After bananas and coconuts, this looks like a feast to me."

Dr. Andersen glanced at Willy, who was still lingering in the corner, watching suspiciously. "Are you not hungry, Miss Maitland?"

"I'm starved."

"Then why don't you eat?"

"First I want to know who you are."

"I have told you my name."

"Your name doesn't mean a thing to me. What's your connection to Nora? To my father?"

Dr. Andersen's eyes were as transparent as water. "You've waited twenty years for an answer. You can surely wait a few minutes longer."

Guy said, "Willy, you need to eat. Come, sit down."

Hunger finally pulled her to the table. Dr. Andersen

had brought no utensils. Willy and Guy used their fingers to scoop up the rice. All the time she was eating, she felt the Swede's eyes watching her.

"I see you do not trust me," he said.

"I don't trust anyone anymore."

He nodded and smiled. "Then you have learned, in a few short days, what took me months to learn."

"Mistrust?"

"Doubt. Fear." He looked around the hut, at the shadows dancing on the walls. "What I call the creeping uneasiness. A sense that things are not right in this place. That, just under the surface, lies some…secret, something…terrible."

The lantern light flickered, almost died. He glanced up as the rain pounded the roof. A puff of wind swept through the doorway, dank with the smells of the jungle.

"You sense it, too," he said.

"All I know is, there've been too many coincidences," said Guy. "Too many tidy little acts of fate. As though paths have been laid out for us and we're just following the trail."

Andersen nodded. "We all have roads laid out for us. We usually choose the path of least resistance. It's when we wander off that path that things become dangerous." He smiled. "You know, at this very minute, I could be sitting in my house in Stockholm, sipping coffee, growing fat on cakes and cookies. But I chose to stay here."

"And has life become dangerous?" asked Willy.

"It's not my life I worry about now. It was a risk bringing you here. But Nora felt the time was right."

"Then it was her decision?"

He nodded. "She thought it might be your last chance for a reunion."

Willy froze, staring at him. "Did you—did you say *reunion?*"

Dr. Andersen met her gaze. Slowly, he nodded.

She tried to speak but found her voice was gone. The significance of that one word reduced her to numb silence.

Her father was alive.

It was Guy who finally spoke. "Where is he?"

"A village northwest of here."

"A prisoner?"

"No, no. A guest. A friend."

"He's not being held against his will?"

"Not since the war." Andersen looked at Willy, who had not yet found her voice. "It may be hard for you to accept, Miss Maitland, but there *are* Americans who find happiness in this country."

She looked at him in bewilderment. "I don't understand. All these years he's been alive…he could have come home…."

"Many men didn't return."

"*He* had the choice!"

"He also had his reasons."

"Reasons? He had every reason to come home!"

Her anguished cry seemed to hang in the room. For a moment neither man spoke. Then Andersen rose to his feet. "Your father must speak for himself…" he said, and he started for the door.

"Then why isn't he here?"

"There are arrangements that have to be made. A time, a place—"

"When will I see him?"

The doctor hesitated. "That depends."

"On what?"

He looked back from the doorway. "On whether your father wants to see *you*."

Long after Andersen had left, Willy stood in the doorway, staring out at the curtain of rain.

"Why *wouldn't* he want to see me?" she cried into the darkness.

Quietly Guy came to stand behind her. His arms came around her shoulders, pulled her into the tight circle of his embrace.

"Why wouldn't he?"

"Willy, stop."

She turned and pressed her face into his chest. "Do you think it was so terrible?" she sobbed. "Being my father?"

"Of course not."

"It must have been. I must have made him miserable."

"You were just a kid, Willy! You can't blame yourself! Sometimes men…change. Sometimes they need—"

"Why?" she cried.

"Hey, not all men walk out. Some of us, we hang around, for better or for worse."

Gently, he led her back to the sleeping pallet. Beneath the silvery mosquito net, she let him hold her, an embrace not of passion, but of comfort. The arms of a friend. It felt right, the way their making love earlier that evening had felt right. But she couldn't help wondering, even as she lay in his arms, when this, too, would change, when *he* would change.

It hurt beyond all measure, the thought that he, too, would someday leave her, that this was but a momentary mingling of limbs and warmth and souls. It was hurt she expected, but one she'd never, ever be ready for.

Outside, the leaves clattered in the downpour.

It rained all night.

At dawn the jeep appeared.

"I take only the woman," insisted the Vietnamese driver, planting himself in Guy's path. The man gestured toward the hut. "You stay, GI."

"She's not going without me," said Guy.

"They tell me only the woman."

"Then she's not going."

The two men faced each other, challenge mirrored in their eyes. The driver shrugged and turned for the jeep. "Then I don't take anybody."

"Guy, please," said Willy. "Just wait here for me. I'll be okay."

"I don't like it."

She glanced at the driver, who'd already climbed behind the wheel and started the engine. "I don't have a choice," she said, and she stepped into the jeep.

The driver released the brake and spun the jeep around. As they rolled away, Willy glanced back and saw Guy standing alone among the trees. She thought he called out something—her name, perhaps—but then the jungle swallowed him from view.

She turned her attention to the road—or what served as a road. In truth, it was scarcely more than a muddy track through the forest. Branches slashed the windshield; water flew from the leaves and splattered their faces.

"How far is it?" she asked. The driver didn't answer.

"Where are we going?" she asked. Again, no answer. She sat back and waited to see what would happen next.

A few miles into the forest the mud track petered out, and they halted before a solid wall of jungle. The driver cut the engine. A few rays of sunlight shone dimly through the canopy of leaves. Only the cry of a single bird sliced through the silence.

The driver climbed out and walked around to the rear. Willy watched as he rooted around under a camouflage tarp covering the back seat. Then she saw the blade slide out from beneath the tarp. He was holding a machete.

He turned to face her. For a few heartbeats they stared at each other, gazes meeting over the gleam of razor-sharp steel. Then she saw amusement flash in his eyes.

"We walk now," he said.

A nod was the only reply she could manage. Wordlessly, she climbed out of the jeep and followed him into the jungle.

He moved silently through the trees, the only sound of his passage the whistle and slash of the machete. Vines hung like shrouds from the branches; clouds of mosquitoes swarmed up from stagnant puddles. He moved onward without a second's pause, melting like a phantom through the brush. Willy, stumbling in the tangle of trees, barely managed to keep the back of his tattered shirt in view.

It didn't take long for her to give up slapping mosquitoes. She decided it was a lost cause. Let them suck her dry; her blood was up for grabs. She could only concentrate on moving forward, on putting one foot in front of the other. She was sliding through some timeless vacuum where distance was measured by the gaps between trees, the span between footsteps.

By the time they finally halted, she was staggering from exhaustion. Conquered, she sagged against the nearest tree and waited for his next command.

"Here," he said.

Bewildered, she looked up at him. "But what are you—"

To her astonishment, he turned and trotted off into the jungle.

"Wait!" she cried. "You're not going to leave me here!"

The man kept moving.

"Please, you have to tell me!" she screamed. He paused and glanced back. "Where am I? What is this place?"

"The same place we find *him*," was the reply. Then he slipped away, vanishing into the forest.

She whirled around, scanning the jungle, watching, waiting for some savior to appear. She saw no one. The man's last words echoed in her head.

What is this place?

The same place we find him.

"Who?" she cried.

In desperation, she stared up at the branches crisscrossing the sky. That's when she saw it, the monstrous silhouette rising like a shark's fin among the trees.

It was the tail of a plane.

Chapter 12

She moved closer. Gradually she discerned, amid the camouflage of trees and undergrowth, the remains of what was once an aircraft. Vines snaked over jagged metal. Fuselage struts reached skyward from the jungle floor, as bare and stark as the bleached ribs of a dead animal. Willy halted, her gaze drawn back to the tail above her in the branches. Years of rust and tropical decay had obscured the markings, but she could still make out the serial number: 5410.

This was Air America flight 5078. Point of origin: Vientiane, Laos. Destination: a shattered treetop in a North Vietnamese jungle.

In the silence of the forest, she bowed her head. A thin shaft of sunlight sliced through the branches and danced at her feet. And all around her the trees soared like the walls of a cathedral. How fitting that this rusted altar to war should come to rest in a place of such untarnished peace.

There were tears in her eyes when she finally forced herself to turn and study the fuselage—what was left of it. Most of the shell had burned or rotted away, leaving only a little flooring and a few crumbling struts. The wings were missing entirely—probably sheared off on impact. She moved forward to the remnants of the cockpit.

Sunlight sparkled through the shattered windshield. The navigational equipment was gutted; charred wires hung from holes in the instrument panel. Her gaze shifted to the bulkhead, riddled with bullet holes. She ran her fingers across the ravaged metal and then pulled away.

As she took a step back, she heard a voice say, "There isn't much left of her. But I guess you could say the same of me."

Willy spun around. And froze.

He came out of the forest, a man in rags, walking toward her. It was the gait she recognized, not the body, which had been worn down to its rawest elements. Nor the face.

Certainly not the face.

He had no ears, no eyebrows. What was left of his hair grew in tortured wisps. He came to within a few yards of her and stopped, as though afraid to move any closer.

They looked at each other, not speaking, perhaps not daring to speak.

"You're all grown up," he finally said.

"Yes." She cleared her throat. "I guess I am."

"You look good, Willy. Real good. Are you married yet?"

"No."

"You should be."

"I'm not."

A pause. They both looked down, looked back up, strangers groping for common ground.

Softly he asked, "How's your mother?"

Willy blinked away a new wave of tears. "She's… dying." She felt a comfortless sense of retribution at her father's shocked silence. "It's cancer," she continued. "I wanted her to see a doctor months ago, but you know how she is. Never thinking about herself. Never taking the time to…" Her voice cracked, faded.

"I had no idea," he whispered.

"How could you? You were dead." She looked up at the sky and suddenly laughed, an ugly sound in that quiet circle of trees. "It never occurred to you to write to us? One letter from the grave?"

"It only would have made things harder."

"Harder than *what?* Than it's already been?"

"With me gone, dead, Ann was free to move on," he said, "to…find someone else. Someone better for her."

"But she didn't! She never even tried! All she could think about was *you.*"

"I thought she'd forget. I thought she'd get over me."

"You thought wrong."

He bowed his head. "I'm sorry, Wilone."

After a pause, she said, "I'm sorry, too."

A bird sang in the trees, its sweet notes piercing the silence between them.

She asked, "What happened to you?"

"You mean this?" He gestured vaguely at his face.

"I mean...everything."

"Everything," he repeated. Then, laughing, he looked up at the branches. "Where the hell do I start?" He began to walk in a circle, moving among the trees like a lost man. At last he stopped beside the fuselage. Gazing at the jagged remains, he said, "It's funny. I never lost consciousness. Even when I hit the trees, when everything around me was being ripped apart, I stayed awake all the way down. I remember thinking, 'So when do I get to see heaven?' Or hell, for that matter. Then it all went up in flames. And I thought, 'There's my answer. My eternity...'"

He stopped, let out a deep sigh. "They found me a short way from here, stumbling around under the trees. Most of my face was burned away. But I don't remember feeling much of anything." He looked down at his scarred hands. "The pain came later. When they tried to clean the burns. When the nerves grew back. I'd scream at them to let me die, but they wouldn't. I guess I was too valuable."

"Because you were American?"

"Because I was a pilot. Someone to pump for information, someone to trade. Maybe someone to spread the Party line back home...."

"Did they...hurt you?"

He shook his head. "I guess they figured I'd been hurt enough. It was a quieter sort of persuasion. Endless discussions. Relentless arguments as I recovered. I swore I wasn't going to let the enemy twist my head around. But I was weak. I was far from home. And they said things—so many things—I couldn't argue with. And after a while...after a while it made...well, sense. About this country being their house, about us being the burglars in the house. And wouldn't anyone with burglars in their house fight back?"

He let out a sigh. "I don't know anymore. It sounds so feeble now, but I just got tired. Tired of arguing. Tired of trying to explain what I was doing in their country. Tired of trying to defend God only knew what. It was easier just to agree with them. And after a while, I actually started to believe it. Believe what they were telling me." He looked down. "According to some people, that makes me a traitor."

"To some people. Not to me."

He was silent.

"Why didn't you come home?" she asked.

"Look at me, Willy. Who'd want me back?"

"*We* did."

"No, you didn't. Not the man I'd become." He laughed hollowly. "Everyone would be pointing at me, whispering behind my back, talking about my face. Is that the kind of father you wanted? The kind of husband your mother wanted? Back home, people expect you to have a nose and ears and eyebrows." He shook his head. "Ann... Ann was so beautiful. I—I couldn't go back to that."

"But what do you have here? Look at you, at what you're wearing, at how skinny you are. You're starving, wasting away."

"I eat what the rest of the village eats. It's enough to live on." He picked at the rag that served as his shirt. "Clothes, I never much cared about."

"You gave up a family!"

"I—I found another family, Willy. Here."

She stared at him, stunned.

"I have a wife. Her name's Lan. And we have children. A baby girl and two boys…eight and ten. They can speak English, and a little French…." he said helplessly.

"*We* were at home!"

"But I was here. And Lan was here. She saved my life, Willy. She was the one who kept me alive through the infections, the fevers, the endless pain."

"You said you begged to die."

"Lan was the one who made me want to live again."

Willy stared at that man with half a face, the man she'd once called her father. The lashless eyes looked back at her, unblinking. Awaiting judgment.

She still had a face, a normal life, she thought. What right did she have to condemn him?

She looked away. "So. What do I tell Mom?"

"I don't know. Maybe nothing."

"She has a right to know."

"Maybe it would be kinder if she didn't."

"Kinder to whom? You or her?"

He looked down at his feet in their dirty slippers. "I suppose I deserve that. Whatever you have to say, I deserve it. But God knows, I wanted to make it up to her. And to you. I sent money—twenty, maybe thirty thousand dollars. You got it, didn't you?"

"We never knew who sent it."

"You weren't supposed to know. Nora Walker arranged it through a bank in Bangkok. It was everything I had. All that was left of the gold."

She gave him a bewildered look and saw that his gaze had shifted toward the plane's fuselage. "You were carrying gold?"

"I didn't know it at the time. It was our little rule at Air America: Never ask about the cargo. Just fly the plane. But after she went down, after I crawled out of the wreckage, I saw it. Gold bars scattered all over the ground. It was crazy. There I was, half my damn face burned off, and I remember thinking, 'I'm rich. If I live through this, son of a bitch, I'm *rich.*'" He laughed, then, at his own lunacy, at the absurdity of a dying man rejoicing among the ashes. "I buried some of the gold, threw some in the bushes. I thought—I guess I thought it would be my ticket out. That if I was captured, I could use it to bargain for my freedom."

"What happened?"

He looked off at the trees. "They found me. NVA soldiers. And they found most of the gold." He shrugged. "They kept us both."

"But not forever. You didn't have to stay—" She stopped. "Didn't you *ever* think of us?"

"I never stopped thinking of you. After the war, after all that—that insanity was over, I came back here, dug up what gold they hadn't found. I asked Nora to get it out to you." He looked at Willy. "Don't you see? I never forgot you. I just..." He stopped, and his voice dropped to a whisper. "I just couldn't go back."

In the trees above, branches rattled in the wind. Leaves drifted down in a soft rain of green.

He turned away. "I suppose you'll want to go back to Hanoi. I'll see that someone drives you...."

"Dad?"

He halted, not daring to look at her.

"Your little boys. You—say they understand English?"

He nodded.

She paused. "Then we ought to understand each other, the boys and I," she said. "I mean, assuming they want to meet me...."

Her father quickly rubbed a hand across his eyes. But when he turned to look at her, she could still see the tears glistening there. He smiled…and held out his hand to her.

She'd been gone too long.

Three hours had passed, and Guy was more than worried. He was scared out of his head. Something wasn't right. It was that old instinct of his, that sense of doom closing in, and he was helpless to do anything about it. A dozen different images kept forming in his mind, each one progressively more terrible. Willy screaming. Dying. Or already dead in the jungle. When at last he heard the rumble of the jeep, he was hovering at the edge of panic.

Dr. Andersen was at the wheel. "Good morning, Mr. Barnard!" he called cheerily as Guy stalked over to him.

"Where is she?"

"She is safe."

"Prove it."

Andersen threw open the door and gestured for him to get in. "I will take you to her."

Guy climbed in and slammed the door. "Where are we going?"

"It is a long drive." Andersen threw the jeep into gear and spun them around onto a dirt track. "Be patient."

The night's rainfall had turned the path to muck, and on either side the jungle pressed in, close and strangling. They might have gone for miles or tens of miles; on a road locked in by jungle, distance was impossible to judge. When Andersen finally pulled off to the side, Guy could see no obvious reason for stopping. Only when he'd climbed out and stood among the trees did he notice the tiny footpath leading into the bush. He couldn't see what lay beyond; the forest hid everything from view.

"From here we walk," said Andersen, foraging around for a few loose branches.

"Why the camouflage?" asked Guy, watching Andersen drape the branches over the jeep.

"Protection for the village."

"What are they afraid of?"

Andersen reached under the tarp on the back seat and pulled out an AK-47. Casually, he slung it over his shoulder. "Everything," he said, and headed off into the jungle.

The footpath led into a shadowy world of hundred-foot trees and tangled vines. Watching Andersen's back, Guy was struck by the irony of a doctor lugging an automatic rifle. He wondered what enemy he planned to use it on.

The smells of rotting vegetation, of mud simmering in the heat were only too familiar. "The whole damn jungle smells of death," the GIs used to say. Guy felt his gait change to a silent glide, felt his reflexes kick into overdrive. His five senses were painfully acute; the snap of a branch under Andersen's boot was as shocking as gunfire.

He heard the sounds of the village before he saw it. Somewhere deep in the forest, children were laughing. And then he heard water rushing and the cry of a baby.

Andersen pushed ahead, and as the last curtain of branches parted, Guy saw, beneath a towering stand of trees, the circle of huts. In the central courtyard, children batted a pebble back and forth with their feet. They froze as Guy and Andersen emerged from the forest.

One of the girls called out; instantly, a dozen adults emerged from the huts. In silence they all watched Guy.

Then, in the doorway of one hut, a familiar figure appeared. As Willy came toward Guy, he had the sudden desire to take her in his arms and kiss her right then and there, in view of the whole village, the whole world. But he couldn't seem to move. He could only stare down at her smiling face.

"I found him," Willy said.

He shook his head. "What?"

"My father. He's here."

Guy turned and saw that someone else had emerged from the hut. A man without ears, without eyebrows. The horrifying apparition held out its hand; a fingertip was missing.

William Maitland smiled. "Welcome to Na Co, Mr. Barnard."

Dr. Andersen's jeep was easy to spot, even through the camouflage. How fortunate the rains had been so heavy the night before; without all that mud, Siang would never have been able to track the jeep to this trail head.

He threw aside the branches and quickly surveyed the jeep's interior. On the back seat, beneath a green canvas tarp, was a jug of drinking water, a few old tools and a weathered notebook, obviously a journal, filled with scribbling. The name "Dr. Gunnel Andersen" was written inside the front cover.

Siang left the jeep, tramped a few paces into the jungle and peered through the shadows. It took only a moment to spot the footprints. Two men. Dr. Andersen and who else? Barnard? He followed the tracks a short way and saw that, just beyond the first few trees, the footprints led to a distinct trail, no doubt an old and established path. The village of Na Co must lie farther ahead.

He returned to the limousine where the man was waiting. "They have gone into the forest," Siang said. "There's a village trail."

"Is it the right one?"

Siang shrugged. "There are many villages in these mountains. But the jeep belongs to Dr. Andersen."

"Then it's the right village." The man sat back, satisfied. "I want our people here tonight."

"So soon?"

"It's the way I work. In and out. The men are ready."

In fact the mercenary team had been waiting two days for the signal. They'd been assembled in Thailand, fifteen men equipped with the most sophisticated in small arms. As soon as the order went through, they would be on their way, no questions asked.

"Tell them we need the dogs as well," said the man. "For mopping up. The whole village goes."

Siang paused. "The children?"

"One mustn't leave orphans."

This troubled Siang a little, but he said nothing. He knew better than to argue with the voice of necessity. Or power.

"Is there a radio in the jeep?" asked the man.

"Yes," said Siang.

"Rip it out."

"Andersen will see—"

"Andersen will see nothing."

Siang nodded in instant understanding.

The man drove off in the limousine, headed for a rendezvous spot a mile ahead. Siang waited until the car had disappeared, then he trotted back to the jeep, ripped out the wires connecting the radio and smashed the panel for good measure. He found a cool spot beneath a tree and sat down. Closing his eyes, he summoned forth the strength needed for his task.

Soon he would have assistance. By tonight, the well paid team of mercenaries would stand assembled on this road. He wouldn't allow himself to think of the victims—the women, the children. It was a consequence of war. In every skirmish, there were the innocent casualties. He'd learned to accept it, to shrug it off as inevitable. The act of pulling a trigger required a clear head swept free of emotions. It was, after all, the way of battle.

It was the way of success.

"Does she understand the danger?" asked Maitland.

"I don't know." Guy stood in the doorway and gazed out at the leaf-strewn courtyard where the village kids were mobbing Willy, singing out questions. The wonderful bedlam of children, he thought wistfully. He turned and looked at the mass of scars that was Bill Maitland's face. "I'm not sure *I* understand the danger."

"She said things have been happening."

"Things? More like dead bodies falling left and right of us. We've been followed every—"

"Who's been following you?"

"The local police. Maybe others."

"The Company?"

"I don't know. They didn't come and introduce themselves."

Maitland, suddenly agitated, began to pace the hut. "If they've traced you here…"

"Who're you hiding from? The Company? The local police?"

"To name a few."

"Which is it?"

"Everyone."

"That narrows it down."

Maitland sat down on the sleeping pallet and rested his head in his hands. "I wanted to be left alone. That's all. Just left alone."

Guy gazed at that scarred scalp and wondered why he felt no pity. Surely the man deserved at least a little pity. But at that instant, all Guy felt was irritation that Maitland was thinking only of himself. Willy had a right to a better father, he thought.

"Your daughter's already found you," he said. "You can't change that. You can't shove her back into the past."

"I don't want to. I'm glad she found me!"

"Yet you never bothered to tell her you were alive."

"I couldn't." Maitland looked up, his eyes full of pain. "There were lives at stake, people I had to protect. Lan, the children—"

"Who's going to hurt them?" Guy moved in, confronted him. "It's been twenty years, and you're still scared. Why? What kind of business were you in?"

"I was just a pawn—I flew the planes, that's all. I never gave a damn about the cargo!"

"What *was* the cargo? Drugs? Arms?"

"Sometimes."

"Which?"

"Both."

Guy's voice hardened. "And which side took delivery?"

Maitland sat up sharply. "I never did business with the enemy! I only followed orders!"

"What *were* your orders on that last flight?"

"To deliver a passenger."

"Interesting cargo. Who was he?"

"His name didn't show up on the manifest. I figured he was some Lao VIP. As it turned out, he was marked for death." He swallowed. "It wasn't the enemy fire that brought us down. A bomb went off in our hold. Planted by *our* side. We were meant to die."

"Why?"

There was a long silence. At last, Maitland rose and went to the doorway. There he stared out at the circle of huts. "I think it's time we talked to the elders."

"What can they tell me?"

Maitland turned and looked at him. "Everything."

Lan's baby was crying in a corner of the hut. She put it to her breast and rocked back and forth, cooing, yet all the time listening intently to the voices whispering in the shadows.

They were all listening—the children, the families. Willy couldn't understand what was being said, but she could tell the discussion held a frightening significance.

In the center of the hut sat three village elders—two men and a woman—their ancient faces veiled in a swirl of smoke from the joss sticks. The woman puffed on a cigarette as she muttered in Vietnamese. She gestured toward the sky, then to Maitland.

Guy whispered to Willy. "She's saying it wasn't your father's time to die. But the other two men, the American and the Lao, they died because that was the death they were fated all their lives to meet...." He fell silent, mesmerized by the old woman's voice. The sound seemed to drift like incense smoke, curling in the shadows.

One of the old men spoke, his voice so soft, it was almost lost in the shifting and whispers of the audience.

"He disagrees," said Guy. "He says it wasn't fate that killed the Lao."

The old woman vehemently shook her head. Now there was a general debate about why the Lao had really died. The dissenting old man at last rose and shuffled to a far corner of the hut. There he pulled aside the matting that covered the earthen floor, brushed aside a layer of dirt and withdrew a cloth-wrapped bundle. With shaking hands he pulled apart the ragged edges. Reverently, he held out the object within.

Even in the gloom of the hut, the sheen of gold was unmistakable.

"It's the medallion," whispered Willy. "The one Lassiter told us about."

"The Lao was wearing it," said her father.

The old man handed the bundle to Guy. Gingerly, Guy lifted the medallion from its bed of worn cloth. Though the surface was marred by slag from the explosion, the design was still discernable: a three-headed dragon, fangs bared, claws poised for battle.

The old man whispered words of awe and wonder.

"He saw a medallion just like it once before," said Maitland. "Years ago, in Laos. It was hanging around the neck of Prince Souvanna."

Guy took in a sharp breath. "It's the royal crest. That passenger—"

"Was the king's half brother," said Maitland. "Prince Lo Van."

An uneasy murmur rippled through the gathering.

"I don't understand," said Willy. "Why would the Company want him dead?"

"It doesn't make sense," said Guy. "Lo Van was a neutral, shifting to our side. And he was straight-arrow, a clean leader. With our backing, he could've carved us a foothold in Laos. That might have tipped the scales in our favor."

"That's what he was *meant* to do," said Maitland. "That crate of gold was his. To be dropped in Laos."

"To buy an army?" asked Willy.

"Exactly."

"Then why assassinate him? He was on our side, so—"

"But the guys who blew up the plane weren't," said Guy.

"You mean the Communists planted that bomb?"

"No, someone more dangerous. One of ours."

The elders had fallen silent. They were watching their guests, studying them the way a teacher watches a pupil struggle for answers.

Once again the old woman began to speak. Maitland translated.

"'During the war, some of us lived with the Pathet Lao, the Communists in Laos. There were few places to hide, so we slept in caves. But we had gardens and chickens and pigs, everything we needed to survive. Once, when I was new to the cave, I heard a plane. I thought it was the enemy, the Americans, and I took my rifle and went out to shoot it down. But my cell commander stopped me. I could not understand why he let the plane land. It had enemy markings, the American flag. Our cell commander ordered us to unload the plane. We carried off crates of guns and ammunition. Then we loaded the plane with opium, bags and bags of it. An exchange of goods, I thought. This must be a stolen plane. But then the pilot stepped out, and I saw his face. He was neither Lao nor Vietnamese. He was like you. An American.'"

"Friar Tuck," said Guy softly.

The woman looked at them, her eyes dark and unreadable.

"I've seen him, too," said Maitland. "I was being held in a camp just west of here when he landed to make an exchange. I tell you, the whole damn country was an opium factory, money being made left and right on both sides. All under cover of war. I think that's why Lo Van was killed. To keep the place in turmoil. There's nothing like a dirty war to hide your profits."

"Who else has seen the pilot's face?" Guy asked in Vietnamese, looking around the room. "Who else remembers what he looked like?"

A man and a woman, huddled in a corner, slowly raised their hands. Perhaps there were others, too timid to reveal themselves.

"There were four other POWs in that camp with me," said Maitland. "They saw the pilot's face. As far as I know, not a single one made it home alive."

The joss sticks had burned down to ashes, but the smoke still hung in the gloom. No one made a sound, not even the children.

That's why you're afraid, thought Willy, gazing at the circle of faces. *Even now, after all these years, the war casts its shadow over your lives.*

And mine.

"Come back with us, Maitland," said Guy. "Tell your story. It's the only way to put it behind you. To be free."

Maitland stood in the doorway of his hut, staring out at the children playing in the courtyard.

"Guy's right," said Willy. "You can't spend your life in hiding. It's time to end it."

Her father turned and looked at her. "What about Lan? The children? If I leave, how do I know the Vietnamese will ever let me back into the country?"

"It's a risk you have to take," said Guy.

"Be a hero—is that what you're telling me?" Maitland shook his head. "Let me tell *you* something, Barnard. The real heroes of this world aren't the guys who go out and take stupid risks. No, they're the ones who hang in where they're needed, where they belong. Maybe life gets a little dull. Maybe the wife and kids drive 'em crazy. But they hang in." He looked meaningfully at Willy, then back at Guy. "Believe me. I've made enough mistakes to know."

Maitland looked back at his daughter. "Tonight, you both go back to Hanoi. You've got to go home, get on with your own life, Willy."

"*If* she gets home," said Guy.

Maitland was silent.

"What do you think her chances are?" Guy pressed him mercilessly. "Think about it. You suppose they'll leave her alone knowing what she knows? You think they'll let her live?"

"So call me a coward!" Maitland blurted out. "Call me any damn name you please. It won't change things. I can't leave this time." He fled the hut.

Through the doorway, they saw him cross the courtyard to where Lan now sat beneath the trees. Lan smiled and handed their baby to her husband. For a long time he sat there, rocking his daughter, holding her tightly to his chest, as though he feared someone might wrench her from his grasp.

You have the world right there in your arms, Willy thought, watching him. *You'd be crazy to let it go.*

"We have to change his mind," said Guy. "We have to get him to come back with us."

At that instant Lan looked up, and her gaze met Willy's. "He's not coming back, Guy," Willy said. "He belongs here."

"You're his family, too," Guy protested.

"But not the one who needs him now." She leaned her head in the doorway. A leaf fluttered down from the trees and tumbled across the courtyard. A bare-bottomed baby toddled after it. "For twenty years I've hated that man...." She sighed. And then she smiled. "I guess it's time I finally grew up."

"Something's wrong. Andersen should've been back by now."

Maitland stood at the edge of the jungle and peered up the dirt road. From where the doctor's jeep had been parked, tire tracks led northward. The branches he'd used for camouflage lay scattered at the roadside. But there was no sign of a vehicle.

Willy and Guy wandered onto the road, where they stood puzzling over Andersen's delay.

"He knows you're waiting for him," said Maitland. "He's already an hour late."

Guy kicked a pebble and watched it skitter into the bushes. "Looks like we're not going back to Hanoi tonight. Not without a ride." He glanced up at the darkening sky. "It's almost sunset. I think it's time to head back to the village."

Maitland didn't move. He was still staring up the road.

"He might have a flat tire," said Willy. "Or he ran out of gas. Either way, Dad, it looks like you're stuck with us tonight." She reached out and threaded her arm in his. "Guy's right. It's time to go back."

"Not yet."

Willy smiled. "Are you that anxious to get rid of us?"

"What?" He glanced at his daughter. "No, no, of course not. It's just…" He gazed up the road again. "Something doesn't feel right."

Willy watched him, suddenly sharing his uneasiness. "You think there's trouble."

"And we're not ready for it," he said grimly.

"What do you mean?" said Guy, turning to look at him. "The village must have some sort of defenses."

"We have maybe one working pistol, a few old war relics that haven't been used in decades. Plus Andersen's rifle. He left it today."

"How many rounds?"

"Not enough to—" Maitland's chin suddenly snapped up. He spun around at the sound of an approaching car.

"Hit the deck!" Guy commanded.

Willy was already leaping for the cover of the nearest bush. At the same instant, Guy and Maitland sprang in the other direction, into the foliage across the road from her.

She barely made it to cover in time. Just as she landed in the dirt, a jeep rounded the bend. Through the tangle of underbrush, she saw that it was filled with soldiers. As it roared closer, she tunneled frantically under the branches, mindless of the thorns clawing her face, and curled up among the leaves to wait for the jeep to pass. Something scurried across her hand. Instinctively she flinched and saw a fat black beetle drop off and scuttle into the shadows. Only then, as her gaze followed the insect, did she notice the strange chattering in the branches and she saw that the earth itself seemed to shudder with movement.

Dear God, she was lying in a whole nest of them!

Choking back a scream, she jerked sideways.

And found herself staring at a human hand. It lay not six inches from her nose, the fingers chalk white and frozen into a beckoning claw.

Even if she'd wanted to scream, she couldn't have uttered a sound; her throat had clamped down beyond all hope of any cry. Slowly her gaze traveled along the arm, followed it to the torso, and then, inexorably, to the face.

Gunnel Andersen's lifeless eyes stared back at her.

Chapter 13

The soldiers' jeep roared past.

Willy muffled her cry with her fist, desperately fighting the shriek of horror that threatened to explode inside her. She fought it so hard her teeth drew blood from her knuckles. The instant the jeep had passed, her control shattered. She stumbled to her feet and staggered backward.

"He's dead!" she cried.

Guy and her father appeared at her side. She felt Guy's arm slip around her waist, anchoring her against him. "What are you talking about?"

"Andersen!" She pointed wildly at the bushes.

Her father dropped to the ground and shoved aside the branches. "Dear God," he whispered, staring at the body.

The trees seemed to wobble around her. Willy slid

to her knees. The whole jungle spun in a miserable kaleidoscope of green as she retched into the dirt.

She heard her father say, in a strangely flat voice, "His throat's been cut."

"Clean job. Very professional," Guy muttered. "Looks like he's been here for hours."

Willy managed to raise her head. "Why? Why did they kill him?"

Her father let the bushes slip back over the body. "To keep him from talking. To cut us off from—" He suddenly sprang to his feet. "The village! I've got to get back!"

"Dad! Wait—"

But her father had already dashed into the jungle.

Guy tugged her up by the arm. "We've gotta move. Come on."

She followed him, running and stumbling behind him on the footpath. The sun was already setting; through the branches, the sky glowed a frightening bloodred.

Just ahead, she heard her father shouting, "Lan! Lan!" As they emerged from the jungle, they saw a dozen villagers gathered, watching as Maitland pulled his wife into his arms and held her.

"These people have got to get out of here!" Guy yelled. "Maitland! Tell them, for God's sake! They've got to leave!"

Maitland released his wife and turned to Guy. "Where the hell are we supposed to go? The next village is twenty miles from here! We've got old people, babies." He pointed to a woman with a swollen belly. "Look at her! You think *she* can walk twenty miles?"

"She has to. We all have to."

Maitland turned away, but Guy pulled him around,

forcing him to listen. "Think about it! They've killed Andersen. You're next. So's everyone here, everyone who knows you're alive. There's got to be somewhere we can hide!"

Maitland turned to one of the village elders and rattled out a question in Vietnamese.

The old man frowned. Then he pointed northeast, toward the mountains.

"What did he say?" asked Willy.

"He says there's a place about five kilometers from here. An old cave in the hills. They've used it before, other times, other wars...." He glanced up at the sky. "Almost sunset. We have to leave now while there's still enough light to cross the river."

Already, the villagers had scattered to gather their belongings. Centuries of war had taught them survival meant haste.

Five minutes was all the time Maitland's family took to pack. Lan presided over the dismantling of her household, the gathering of essentials—blankets, food, the precious family cooking pot. She spared no time for words or tears. Only outside, when she allowed herself a last backward glance at the hut, did her eyes brim. She swiftly, matter-of-factly, wiped away the tears.

The last light of day glimmered through the branches as the ragged gathering headed into the jungle. Twenty-four adults, eleven children and three infants, Willy counted. *And all of us scared out of our wits.*

They moved noiselessly, even the children; it was unearthly how silent they were, like ghosts flitting among the trees. At the edge of a fast-flowing river, they halted. A waterwheel spun in the current, an elegant sculpture of bamboo tubes shuttling water into irrigation sluices.

The river was too deep for the little ones to ford, so the children were carried to the other bank. Soaked and muddy, they all slogged up the opposite bank and moved on toward the mountains.

Night fell. By the light of a full moon, they journeyed through a spectral land of wind and shadow where the very darkness seemed to tremble with companion spirits. By now the children were exhausted and stumbling. Still, no one had to coax them forward; the fear of pursuit was enough to keep them moving.

At last, at the base of the cliff, they halted. A giant wall of rock glowed silvery in the moonlight. The village elders conferred softly, debating which way to proceed next. It was the old woman who finally led the way. Moving unerringly through the darkness, she guided them to a set of stone steps carved into the mountain and led them up, along the cliff face to what appeared to be nothing more than a thicket of bushes.

There was a general murmur of dismay. Then one of the village men shoved aside the branches and held up a lit candle. Emptiness lay beyond. He thrust his arm into the void, into a darkness so vast, it seemed to swallow up the feeble light of the flame. They were at the mouth of a giant cavern.

The man crawled inside, only to scramble out as a flurry of wings whooshed past him. Nervous laughter rippled through the gathering.

Bats, Willy thought with a shudder.

The man took a deep breath and entered the cave. A moment later, he called for the others to follow.

Guy gave Willy a nudge. "Go on. Inside."

She swallowed, balking. "Do I have a choice?"

His answer was immediate. "None whatsoever."

* * *

The village was deserted.

Siang searched the huts one by one. He overturned pallets and flung aside mats, searching for the underground tunnels that were common to every village. In times of peace, those tunnels were used for storage; in times of war, they served as hiding places or escape routes. They were all empty.

In frustration, he grabbed an earthenware pot and smashed it on the ground. Then he stalked out to the courtyard where the men stood waiting in the moonlight, their faces blackened with camouflage paint.

There were fifteen of them, all crack professionals, rough-hewn Americans who towered above him. They had been flown in straight from Thailand at only an hour's notice. As expected, Laotian air defense had been a large-meshed sieve, unable to detect, much less shoot down, a lone plane flying in low through their airspace. It had taken a mere four hours to march here from their drop point just inside the Vietnamese border. The entire operation had been flawless.

Until now.

"It seems we've arrived too late," a voice said.

Siang turned to see his client emerge from the shadows, one more among this gathering of giants.

"They have had only a few hours' head start," said Siang. "Their evening meals were left uneaten."

"Then they haven't gone far. Not with women and children." The man turned to one of the soldiers. "What about the prisoner? Has he talked?"

"Not a word." The soldiers shoved a village man to the ground. They had captured the man ten miles up the road, running toward Ban Dan. Or, rather, the dogs had caught him. Useful animals those hounds, and absolutely essential in an operation where a single surviving eyewitness could prove disastrous. Against such animals, the villager hadn't stood a chance of escape. Now he knelt on the ground, his black hair silvered with moonlight.

"Make him talk."

"A waste of time," grunted Siang. "These northerners are stubborn. He will tell you nothing."

One of the soldiers gave the villager a kick. Even as the man lay writhing on the ground, he managed to gasp out a string of epithets.

"What? What did he say?" demanded the soldier.

Siang shifted uneasily. "He says that we are cursed. That we are dead men."

The soldier laughed. "Superstitious crap!"

Siang looked around at the darkness. "I'm sure they sent other messengers for help. By morning—"

"By morning we'll have the job done. We'll be out of here," said his client.

"If we can find them," Siang said.

"Find a whole village? No problem." The man turned and snapped out an order to one of the soldiers. "That's what the dogs are for."

A dozen candles flickered in the cavern. Outside, the wind was blowing hard; puffs of it shuddered the blanket hanging over the cave mouth. Through the dancing shadows floated murmuring voices, the frantic whispers of a village under siege. Children gathered stones or twisted vines into rope. Women whittled stalks of bamboo, sharpening them into punji stakes. Only the babies slept. In the darkness outside, men dug the same lethal traps that had defended their homeland through the centuries. It was an axiom of jungle warfare that battles were won not by strength or weaponry but by speed and cunning and desperation.

Most of all, desperation.

"The cylinder's frozen," muttered Guy, sighting down the barrel of an ancient pistol. "You could squeeze off a single shot, that's all."

"Only two bullets left anyway," said Maitland.

"Which makes it next to worthless." Guy handed the gun back to Maitland. "Except for suicide."

For a moment Maitland weighed the pistol in his hand, thinking. He turned to his wife and spoke to her gently in Vietnamese.

Lan stared at the gun, as though afraid to touch it. Then, reluctantly, she took it and slipped away into the shadows of the cave.

Guy reached for Andersen's assault rifle and gave it a quick inspection. "At least this baby's in working order."

"Yeah. Nothing like a good old AK-47," said Maitland. "I've seen one fished out of the mud and still go right on firing."

Guy laughed. "The other side really knew how to make 'em, didn't they?" He glanced around as Willy approached. "How're you holding up?"

She sank down wearily beside him in the dirt. "We've carved enough stakes to skewer a whole army."

"We'll need more," said her father. He glanced toward the cave entrance. "My turn to do some digging…."

"I was just out there," said Guy. "Pits are all dug."

"Then they'll need help with the other traps—"

"They know what they're doing. We just get in the way."

"It's hard to belive," said Willy.

"What is?"

"That we can hold off an army with vines and bamboo."

"It's been done before," said Maitland. "Against bigger armies. And we're not out to win a war. We just have to hold out until our runners get through."

"How long will that take?"

"It's twenty miles to the next village. If they have a radio, we might get help by midmorning."

Willy gazed around at the sleeping children who, one by one, had collapsed in exhaustion. Guy touched her arm. "You need some rest, too."

"I can't sleep."

"Then just lie down. Go on."

"What about you two?"

Guy snapped an ammunition clip into place. "We'll keep watch."

She frowned at him. "You don't really think they'd find us tonight?"

"We left an easy trail all the way."

"But they'll need daylight—"

"Not if they have a local informant," said her father. "Someone who knows these caves. We found our way in the dark. So could they." He grabbed the rifle and slung it over his shoulder. "Minh and I'll take the first watch, Guy. Get some sleep."

Guy nodded. "I'll relieve you in a few hours."

After her father left, Willy's gaze shifted back to the sleeping children, to her little half brothers, now curled up in a tangle of blankets. *What will happen to them?* she wondered. *To all of us?* In a far corner, two old women whittled bamboo stalks; the scrape of their blades against the wood made Willy shiver.

"I'm scared," she whispered.

Guy nodded. The candlelight threw harsh shadows on his face. "We're all scared. Every last one of us."

"It's my fault. I can't stop thinking that if I'd just left well enough alone…"

He touched her face. "I'm the one who should feel responsible."

"Why?"

"Because I used you. For all my denials, I planned to use you. And if something were to happen to you now…"

"Or to you," she said, her hand closing over his. "Don't you ever make me weep over your body, Guy Barnard. Because I couldn't stand it. So promise me."

He pressed her hand to his mouth. "I promise. And I want you to know that, after we get out of here, I…" He smiled. "I plan to see a lot more of you. If you'll let me."

She returned the smile. "I'll insist on it."

What stupid lies we're telling each other, she thought. *Our way of pretending we have a future.* In the face of death, promises mean everything.

"What if they find us?" she whispered.

"We do what we can to stay alive."

"Sticks and stones against automatics? It should be a very quick fight."

"We have a defensible position. Traps waiting in the path. And we have some of the smartest fighters in the world on our side. Men who've held off armies with not much more than their wits." He gazed up at the darkness hovering above the feeble glow of candlelight.

"This cave is said to be blessed. It's an ancient sanctuary, older than anyone can remember. Follow that tunnel back there, and you'll come out at the east base of the cliff. They're clever, these people. They never back themselves into a corner. They always leave an escape route." He looked at the families dozing in the shadows. "They've been fighting wars since the Stone Age. And they can do it in their bare feet, with only a handful of rice. When it comes to survival, *we're* the novices."

Outside, the wind howled; they could hear the trees groan, the bushes scrabbling against the cliff. One of the children cried out in his sleep, a sob of fear that was instantly stilled by his mother's embrace.

The little ones didn't understand, thought Willy. But they knew enough to be afraid.

Guy took her in his arms. Together, they sank to the ground, clinging to each other. There was no need for words; it was enough just to have him there, to feel their hearts beating together.

And in the shadows, the two old women went on whittling their stalks of bamboo.

Willy was asleep when Guy rose to stand his watch. It wasn't easy leaving her. In the few short hours they'd clung together on the hard ground, their bodies had somehow melted together in a way that could never be reversed. Even if he never saw her again, even if she was suddenly swept out of his life, she would always be part of him.

He covered her with a blanket and slipped out into the night.

The sky was a dazzling sea of stars. He found Maitland huddled on a ledge a short way up the cliff face. Guy settled down beside him on the rock shelf.

"Dead quiet," said Maitland. "So far."

They sat together beneath the stars, listening to the wind, to the bushes thrashing against the cliff. A rock clattered down the mountain. Guy glanced up and saw, on a higher ledge, one of the village men silhouetted against the night sky.

"Did you get some sleep?" asked Maitland.

Guy shook his head. "You know, I used to be able to sleep through anything. Chopper landings. Sniper fire. But not now. Not here. I tell you, this isn't my kind of fight."

Maitland handed the rifle to Guy. "Yeah. It's a whole different war when people you love are at stake, isn't it?" He rose to his feet and walked off into the darkness.

People you love? It filled Guy with a sense of wonder, the thought that he *was* in love. Though it shouldn't surprise him. On some level, he'd known it all along: he had fallen hard for Bill Maitland's daughter.

It was something he'd never planned on, something he'd certainly never wanted. He wasn't even sure *love* was the right word for what he felt. They'd just spent a week together in hell. *And in heaven,* he thought, remembering that night in the hut, under the mosquito net. He knew he couldn't stand the thought of her being hurt, that he'd do anything to keep her safe. Was *love* the name for that feeling?

Somewhere in the night, an animal screamed.

He tightened his grip on the rifle.

Four more hours until dawn.

At first light the attack came.

Guy had already handed the rifle to the next man on watch and was starting down the cliff face when a shot rang out. Sheer reflexes sent him diving for cover. As he scrambled behind a clump of bushes, he heard more automatic gunfire and a scream from the ledge above, and he knew his relief man had been hit. He peered up to see how badly the man was hurt. Through fingers of morning mist, he could make out the man's bloodied arm dangling lifelessly over the ledge. More gunfire erupted, spattering the cliff face. There was no return fire; the village's only rifle now lay in the hands of a dead man.

Guy glanced down and saw the other villagers scrambling for cover among the rocks. Unarmed, how long could they defend the cave? It was the booby traps they were counting on now, the trip wires and the pits and the stakes that would hold off the attackers.

Guy looked up at the ledge where the rifle lay. That precious AK-47 could make all the difference in the world between survival and slaughter.

He spotted a boulder a few yards up, with a few scraggly bushes as cover along the way. There was no other route, no other choice. He crouched, tensing for the dash to first base.

Willy was stirring a simmering pot of rice and broth when she heard the gunshots. Her first thought as she leapt to her feet was, *Guy. Dear God, has he been hurt?*

But before she could take two steps, her father grabbed her arm. "No, Willy!"

"He may need help—"

"You can't go out there!" He called for his wife. Somehow, Lan heard him through the bedlam and, taking her arm, pulled Willy toward the back of the cave. Already the other women were herding the children into the escape tunnel. Willy could only watch helplessly as the men grabbed what primitive weapons they had and scrambled outside.

More gunfire thundered in the distance, and rocks clattered down the mountainside.

Where's our return fire? she thought. *Why isn't anyone firing back?*

Outside, something skittered across the ground and popped. A finger of smoke wafted into the cave, its vapor so sickening it made Willy reel backward, gasping for air.

"Get back, get back!" her father yelled. "Into the tunnel, all of you!"

"What about Guy?"

"He can take care of himself! Go and get the kids out of here!" He gave her a brutal shove into the tunnel. *"Move!"*

There was no other choice. But as she turned to flee and heard the rattle of new gunfire, she felt she was abandoning a part of herself on the embattled cliff.

The children had already slipped into the tunnel. Just ahead, Willy could hear a baby crying. Following the sound, she plunged into pitch blackness.

A light suddenly flickered in the passage. It was a candle. By the flame's glow, she saw the leathery face of the old woman who'd guided them to the cave. She was now leading the frightened procession of women and children.

Willy, bringing up the rear, could barely keep track of the candle's glow. The old woman moved swiftly; obviously, she knew where she was going. Perhaps she'd fled this way before, in another battle, another war. It offered some small comfort to know they were following in the footsteps of a survivor.

The first step down was a surprise. For an instant, Willy's heel met nothingness, then it landed on slippery stone. How much farther? she wondered as she reached out to steady herself against the tunnel wall. Her fingers met clumps of dried wax, the drippings of ancient candles. How many others before her had felt their way down these steps, had stumbled in terror through these passages? The fear of all those countless other refugees seemed to permeate the darkness.

The tunnel took a sharp left and moved ever downward. She wondered how far they'd come; it began to seem like miles. The sound of gunfire had faded to a distant *tap-tap-tap.* She wouldn't let herself think about what was happening outside; she could only concentrate on that tiny pinpoint of light flickering far ahead.

Suddenly the light seemed to flare brighter, exploding into a dazzling luminescence. No, she realized with sudden wonder as she rounded the curve. It wasn't the candle. It was daylight!

Murmurs of joy echoed through the passageway. All at once, they were all scrambling forward, dashing toward the exit and into the blinding sunshine.

Outside, Willy stood blinking painfully at trees and sky and mountainside. They were on the other side of the cliff. Safe. For now.

Gunfire rattled in the distance.

The old woman ordered them forward, into the jungle. At first Willy didn't understand the urgency. Was there some new danger she hadn't recognized? Then she heard what was frightening the old woman: dogs.

Now the others heard the barking, too. Panic sent

them all dashing into the forest. Lan alone didn't move. Willy spotted her standing perfectly still. Lan appeared to be listening to the dogs, gauging their direction, their distance. Her two boys, alarmed by their mother's refusal to run, stood watching her in confusion.

Lan shoved her sons forward, commanding them to flee. The boys shook their heads; they wouldn't leave without their mother. Lan gave the baby to her eldest son, then gave both boys another push. The younger boy was crying now, shaking his head, clinging to her sleeve. But his mother's command could not be disobeyed. Sobbing, he was led away by his older brother to join the other children in flight.

"What are you doing?" Willy cried. Had the woman gone mad?

Calmly, Lan turned to face the sound of the dogs.

Willy glanced ahead at the forest, saw the children fleeing through the trees. They were so small, so helpless. How far would they get?

She looked back at Lan, who was now purposefully shuffling through the dirt, circling back toward the dogs. Suddenly Willy understood what Lan was doing. She was leaving her scent for the dogs. Trying to make them follow her, to draw them away from the children. By this action, this choice, the woman was offering herself as a sacrifice.

The barking grew louder. Every instinct Willy possessed told her to run. But she thought of Guy and her father, of how willingly, how automatically they had assumed the role of protectors, had offered themselves to the enemy. She saw the last of the children vanish into the jungle. They needed time, time no one else could give them.

She, too, began to stamp around in the dirt.

Lan glanced back in surprise and saw what Willy was doing. They didn't exchange a word; just that look, that sad and knowing smile between women, was enough.

Willy ripped a sleeve off her blouse and trampled the torn cloth into the dirt. The dogs would surely pick up the scent. Then she turned and headed south, back along the cliff base. Away from the children. Lan, too, headed away from the villagers' escape route.

Willy didn't hurry. After all, she was no longer running for *her* life. She wondered how long it would take for the dogs to catch up. And when they did, how long she could hold them off. A weapon was what she needed. A club, a stick. She snatched up a fallen branch, tore off the twigs and swung it a few times. It was good and heavy; it would make the dogs think twice. Prey she might be, but she'd damn well fight back.

The barking grew steadily closer, a demon sound, relentless and terrifying. But now it mingled with something else, a rhythmic, monotonous thumping that, as it grew louder, seemed to make the ground itself shudder. Not gunfire...

A helicopter!

Wild with hope, she glanced up at the sky and saw, in the distance, a pair of black specks against the vista of morning blue. Was it the rescue party they'd been waiting for?

She scrambled up on a mound of rocks and began waving her arms. It was their only chance—Guy's only chance—for survival.

All her attention focused on those two black pinpricks hovering in the morning sky, she didn't see the dogs moving in until it was too late.

A flash of brown shot across her peripheral vision. She jerked around as a pair of jaws lunged straight for her throat. Her response was purely reflex. She twisted away and a hundred pounds of fur and teeth slammed into her shoulder. Thrown to the ground, she could only cry out as powerful jaws clamped onto her arm.

Footsteps thudded close. A voice shouted, "Back off! I said back *off!*"

The dog released her and stood back, growling.

Slowly Willy raised her head and saw two men in camouflage garb towering above her. *Americans,* she thought in confusion. What were they doing here?

Rough hands hauled her to her feet. "Where are the others?" one of the men demanded.

"You're hurting me—"

"Where are the others?"

"There are no others!" she screamed.

His savage blow knocked her back to the ground. Too dazed to move, she sprawled helplessly at their feet and fought to clear her head.

"Finish her off."

No, she thought. *Please, no...*

But she knew that no amount of begging would change their minds. She lay there, hugging herself, waiting for the end.

Then the other soldier said, "Not yet. She might come in handy."

She was dragged back to her feet to stand, sick and swaying, before them.

An expressionless face, blackened with camouflage grease, stared down at her. "Let's see what the good Friar thinks."

Chapter 14

Made it to third base. Time to go for that home run.

Guy, sprawled behind a boulder, scouted out the next twenty yards to the gun. His only cover would be a few bushes and, midway, a pathetic excuse for a tree. He could see the AK-47's barrel extending over the rock ledge, so close, he could practically spit at it, but still beyond reach.

Slowly, he rose to a crouch and got ready for the final dash.

Gunfire splattered the cliff. Instantly, he flopped back to the dirt. *This is a crazy-ass idea, Barnard. The dumbest idea you've ever had.*

He glanced below and saw Maitland trying to signal him. What the hell was he trying to say? Guy couldn't be sure, but Maitland seemed to be telling him to wait, to hold on. But there was so little time left. Already, Guy potted men in camouflage fatigues moving through the brush toward the cliff base. Toward the first booby trap. *God, slow 'em down. Give us time.*

He heard, rather than saw, the first victim drop into the trap. A shriek echoed off the cliff face, the cry of a man who had just slid into a bed of stakes. Now there were other shouts, curses, the sounds of confusion as soldiers dragged their injured comrade to safety.

Just a taste, fellas, Guy thought with a grim sense of satisfaction. *Wait till you see what comes next.*

The attackers didn't delay long. A shouted order sent a half-dozen soldiers scrambling up the cliff path, closer and closer to the second trap: a trip wire poised to unleash a falling tree trunk. But now the attackers were warned; they knew that every step was a gamble, and they were searching for hazards, considering every rock, every bush with the practiced eyes of men well versed in jungle combat.

We're almost down to our last resort, thought Guy. *Prayer.*

Then he heard it. They all heard it. A familiar rumble that made them turn their gazes to the sky. Choppers.

That was the instant Guy ran, when everyone's eyes were focused on the heavens. His sudden dash took the soldiers by surprise, left them only a split second to respond. Then the maelstrom broke loose as bullets chewed the ground, throwing up a storm cloud of dust. By then he was halfway to his goal, scrambling through the last thicket. Time seemed to slow down. Each step took an eternity. He saw puffs of dirt explode near his feet, heard a far-off shriek and the thud of the poised tree trunk, the second trap, slamming onto the soldiers in the path.

He launched himself through the air and tumbled onto the ledge. Time leapt to fast forward. He yanked the AK-47 out of the dead man's grasp, took aim and began firing.

One soldier, standing exposed below, went down at once. The others beat a fast retreat into the jungle. Two lay dead on the path, victims of the latest booby trap.

Welcome to the Stone Age, Rambo.

Guy held his fire as the attackers slipped out of view and into the cover of trees. He watched, waiting for any flash of movement, any sign of a renewed attack. A standoff?

He turned his gaze to the sky and searched for the choppers. To his dismay, they were moving away; already they had faded to mere specks. In despair he watched them slip away into a field of relentless blue.

Then, from below, he heard shouts in Vietnamese and saw smoke spiral up the cliff face, the blackest, most glorious smoke he'd seen in his whole damn life. The villagers had set the mountainside on fire!

Quickly he scanned the heavens again, hoping, praying. Within seconds he spotted them, like two flies hovering just above the horizon. Was it only wishful thinking, or were they actually moving closer?

A new hint of movement at the bottom of the cliff drew his attention. He looked down to see two figures emerge from the forest and approach the cliff base. Automatically, he swung his gun barrel to the target and was about to squeeze off a round when he saw who it was standing below. His finger froze on the trigger.

A man stood clutching a human shield in front of him. Even from that distance, Guy recognized the prisoner's face, could see her blanched and helpless expression.

"Drop it, Barnard!" The command of an unseen man, hidden among the trees, echoed off the mountainside. The voice was disturbingly familiar.

Guy remained frozen in the pose of a marksman, his finger on the trigger, his cheek pressed against the rifle. Frantically he wracked his brain for a plan, for some way to pull Willy out of this alive. A trade? It was the only possibility: her life for his. Would they go for it?

"I said *drop it!*" the disembodied voice shouted.

Willy's captor raised a pistol barrel to her head.

"Or would you like to see what a bullet will do to that pretty face?"

"Wait!" Guy screamed. "We can trade—"

"No deals."

The barrel was pressed to Willy's temple.

"No!" Guy's voice, harsh with panic, reverberated off the cliff.

"Then drop the gun. *Now.*"

Guy let the AK-47 fall to the ground.

"Kick it away. Go on!"

Guy gave the gun a kick. It tumbled off the ledge and clattered to the rocks below.

"Out where I can see you. Come on, come on!"

Slowly, Guy rose to his full height, expecting an instantaneous hail of bullets.

"Now come down. Off the cliff. You, too, Maitland! I haven't got all day, so *move.*"

Guy made his way down the cliff path. By the time he reached bottom, Maitland was already waiting there, his arms hooked behind his head in surrender. Guy's first concern was Willy. He could see she'd been hurt;

her shirt was torn and bloodied, her face alarmingly white. But the look she gave him was one of heart-wrenching courage, a look that said, *Don't worry about me. I'm okay. And I love you.*

Her captor smiled and let the pistol barrel drop from her head. Guy instantly recognized his face: it was the same man he'd tackled on the terrace of the hotel in Bangkok. The Thai assassin—or was he Vietnamese?

"Hello, Guy," said a shockingly familiar voice.

A man strolled into the sunshine, a man whose powerful shoulders seemed to strain against the fabric of his camouflage fatigues.

Maitland took in a startled breath. "It's him," he murmured. "Friar Tuck."

"Toby?" said Guy.

"Both," said Tobias Wolff, smiling. He stood before them, his expression hovering somewhere between triumph and regret. "I didn't want to kill you, Guy. In fact, I've done everything I could to avoid it."

Guy let out a bitter laugh. "Why?"

"I owed you. Remember?"

Guy frowned at Toby's legs, noticing there were no braces, no crutches. "You can walk."

Toby shrugged. "You know how it is in army hospitals. The surgeons gave me the bad news, said there was nothing they could do and then they walked away. Shoved me into a corner and forgot about me. But I wasn't a lost cause, after all. First I got the feeling back in my toes. Then I could move them. Oh, I never bothered to tell Uncle Sam. It gave me the freedom to carry on with my business. That's the nice thing about being a paraplegic. No one suspects you of a damn thing." He grinned. "Plus, I get that monthly disability check."

"A real fortune."

"It's the principle of things. Uncle Sam owes me for all those years of loyal service." He glanced at Maitland. "He was the only detail that worried me. The last witness from Flight 5078. I'd heard he was alive. I just didn't know how to find him."

He squinted up at the sky as the rumble of the choppers drew closer. They were moving in, attracted by the smoke from the cliff fire. "Time's up," said Toby. Turning, he yelled to his men, "Move out!"

At once, the soldiers started into the woods in a calm but hasty retreat. Toby looked at the hit man and nodded. "Mr. Siang, you know what to do."

Siang shoved Willy forward. Guy caught her in his arms; together, they dropped to their knees. There was no time left for last words, for farewells. Guy wrapped himself around her in a futile attempt to shield her from the bullets.

"Finish it," said Toby.

Guy looked up at him. "I'll see you in hell."

Siang raised the pistol. The barrel was aimed squarely at Guy's head. Still cradling Willy, Guy waited for the explosion. The darkness.

The blast of the pistol made them both flinch.

In wonderment, Guy realized he was still kneeling, still breathing. *What the hell? Am I still alive? Are we both still alive?*

He looked up in time to see Siang, shirt bloodied, crumple to the ground.

"There! She's there!" Toby shouted, pointing at the trees.

In the shadow of the forest they saw her, clutching

the ancient pistol in both hands. Lan stood very still, as though shocked by what she'd just done.

One of the soldiers took aim at her.

"No!" screamed Maitland, flinging himself at the gunman.

The shot went wild; Maitland and the soldier thudded to the ground, locked in combat.

From the cliff above came shouts; Guy and Willy hit the dirt as arrows rained down. Toby cried out and fell. What remained of his army scattered in confusion.

In the melee, Guy and Willy managed to crawl to cover. But as they rolled behind a boulder, Willy suddenly realized her father hadn't followed them.

"Dad!" she screamed.

A dozen yards away, Maitland lay bloodied. Willy turned to go to him, but Guy dragged her back down.

"Are you nuts?" he yelled.

"I can't leave him there!"

"Wait till we're clear!"

"He's hurt!"

"There's nothing you can do!"

She was sobbing now, trying to wrench free, but her protests were drowned out by the *whomp-whomp* of the helicopters moving in. An army chopper hovered just above them. The pilot lowered the craft through a slot in the trees. Gently, the skids settled to the ground.

The instant it touched down, a half-dozen Vietnamese soldiers jumped out, followed by their commanding officer. He pointed at Maitland and barked out orders. Two soldiers hurried to the wounded man.

"Let me go," Willy said and she broke free of Guy's grasp.

He watched her run to her father's side. The soldiers had already opened their medical field kit, and a stretcher was on the way. Guy's gaze shifted back to the chopper as one last passenger stepped slowly to the ground. Head bowed beneath the spinning blades, the old man made his way toward Guy.

For a long time, they stood together, both of them silent as they regarded the rising cloud of smoke. The flames seemed to engulf the mountain itself as the last of the village men scrambled down the cliff path to safety.

"A most impressive signal fire," said Minister Tranh. He looked at Guy. "You are unhurt?"

Guy nodded. "We lost some people…up on the mountain. And the children—I don't know if they're all right. But I guess… I think…"

He turned and watched as Willy followed her father's stretcher toward the chopper. At the doorway, she stopped and looked back at Guy.

He started toward her, his arms aching to embrace her. He wanted to tell her all the things he'd been afraid to say, the things he'd never said to any woman. He had to tell her now, while he still had the chance, while she was still there for him to touch, to hold.

A soldier suddenly blocked Guy's way and commanded, "Stay back!"

Dust stung Guy's eyes as the chopper's rotor began to spin. Through the tornado-like wash of whirling leaves and branches, Guy saw a soldier in the chopper shout at Willy to climb aboard. With one last backward glance, she obeyed. Time had run out.

Through the open doorway, Guy could still see her face gazing out at him. With a sense of desolation, he watched the helicopter rise into the sky, taking with it the woman he loved. Long after the roar of the blades had faded to silence, he was staring up at that cloudless field of blue.

Sighing, he turned back to Minister Tranh. That's when he noticed that someone else, just as desolate, had watched the chopper's departure. At the forest edge stood Lan, her gaze turned to the sky. At least she, too, had survived.

"We are glad to find you alive," Minister Tranh said.

"How *did* you find us?" Guy asked.

"One of the men from the village reached Na Khoang early this morning. We'd been concerned about you. And when you vanished…" Minister Tranh shook his head. "You have a talent for making things difficult, Mr. Barnard. For us, at least."

"I had to. I didn't know who to trust." Guy looked at the other man. "I still don't know who to trust."

Minister Tranh considered this statement for a moment. Then he said quietly, "Do we ever really know?"

"A toast," said Dodge Hamilton, leaning against the hotel bar. "To the good fight!"

Guy stared down moodily at his whiskey glass and said, "There's no such thing as a good fight, Hamilton. There are only fights you can't avoid."

"Well—" grinning, Hamilton raised his drink "—then let's drink to the unavoidable."

That made Guy laugh, though it was the last thing he felt like doing. He supposed he *ought* to be celebrating. The ordeal was over, and for the first time in days, he felt human again. After a good night's sleep, a shower and a shave, he could once again stand the sight of his own face in the mirror. *For all the difference it makes,* he thought bleakly. *She's not here to notice.*

He was having a hell of a time adjusting to Willy's absence. Over and over he replayed that last image of her sad backward glance as she'd climbed into the chopper. No last words, no goodbyes, just that look. He wished he could erase the image from his memory.

No, no, that wasn't what he wanted.

What he wanted was another chance.

He set the whiskey glass down and forced a smile to his lips. "Anyway, Hamilton," he said, "looks like you got your story, after all."

"Not quite the one I expected."

"Think it's front-page material?"

"Indeed! It has everything. Old war ghosts come to life. Ex-enemies joining sides. *And* a happy ending! A story that ought to be heard. But…" He sighed. "It'll probably get shoved to the back page to make room for some juicy royal scandal. As if the fate of the world depends on who does what to whom in Buckingham."

Guy shook his head and chuckled. Some things, it seemed, never changed.

"He'll be all right, won't he? Maitland?"

Guy looked up. "I think so. Willy called me from Bangkok a few hours ago. Maitland's stable enough to be transferred."

"They're flying him to the States?"

"Tonight."

Hamilton cocked his head. "Aren't you joining them?"

"I don't know. I've got a job to wrap up, a few last minute details. And she'll be busy with other things…."

He looked down at his whiskey and thought of that last phone conversation. They'd had a lousy connection, lots of static on the line, and they'd both been forced to shout. She'd been standing at a hospital telephone; he'd been on his way out to meet Vietnamese officials. It had hardly been the time for romantic conversation. Yet he'd been ready to say anything, if only she'd given him some hint that she wanted to hear it. But there'd been only awkward how-are-yous and is-your-arm-all-right and yes-it's-fine-I'm-all-patched-up-now and then, in the end, a hasty goodbye.

When he'd hung up the receiver, he'd known she was gone. *Maybe it's for the best,* he thought. Every idiot knew wartime romances never lasted. When you were huddled together in the trenches and the bullets were whizzing overhead, it was easy to fall in love.

But now they were back in the real world. She didn't need him any longer, and he liked to think he didn't need *her* either. After all, he'd never needed anyone before.

He drained his whiskey glass. "Anyway, Hamilton," he said, "I guess I'll have a hell of a story to tell the guys back home. How I fought in Nam all over again—this time with the other side."

"No one'll believe you."

"Probably not." Guy looked off at a painting on the wall—Ho Chi Minh smiling like someone's merry uncle. "You know, I have a confession to make." He looked back at his drinking partner. "At one point, I was so paranoid that I thought *you* were the CIA."

Hamilton burst out laughing.

"Can you believe it?" Guy said, laughing as well. "You of all people!"

Hamilton, still grinning, set his glass down on the counter. "Actually," he said after a pause, "I am."

There was a long silence. "What?" said Guy.

Hamilton gazed back, his expression blandly pleasant and utterly unrevealing. "General Kistner sends his regards. He's happy to hear you're alive and well."

"Kistner sent you?"

"No, he sent *you*."

Guy stiffened. "You got it wrong. I don't work for those people. I was on my own the whole—"

"Were you, now?" Hamilton's smile was maddening. "Quite a stroke of luck, wouldn't you say, that meeting between you and Miss Maitland at Kistner's villa? Damned odd about her driver vanishing like that, just as you were heading back to town."

Guy looked down at his glass, swirled the whiskey. "I *was* set up," he muttered. "That mysterious appointment with Kistner—"

"Was to get you and Miss Maitland together. She was in dangerous waters, already floundering. We knew she'd need help. But it had to be someone completely unconnected with the Company, someone the Vietnamese wouldn't suspect. As it turned out, *you* were it."

Guy's fists tightened on the countertop. "I did your dirty work—"

"You did Uncle Sam a favor. We knew you were slated to go to Saigon. That you knew the country. A bit of the language. We also knew you had a…shall we say, *vulnerable* aspect to your past." He gave Guy a significant look.

They know, Guy thought. *They've probably always known.* Slowly, he said, "That visit from the Ariel Group…"

"Ah, yes. Ariel. Lovely ring to it, don't you think? It happens to be the name of General Kistner's youngest granddaughter." Hamilton smiled. "You needn't worry,

Guy. We can be discreet. Especially when we feel we've been well served."

"What if you'd been wrong about me? What if I was working for Toby Wolff? I could have killed her."

"You wouldn't."

"I had a 'vulnerable' aspect to my past, remember?"

"You're clean, Guy. Even with your past, you're cleaner than any flag-waving patriot in Washington."

"How would you know?"

Hamilton shrugged. "You'd be amazed at the things we know about you. About everyone."

"But you couldn't predict what I'd do! What Willy would do. What if she'd told me to go to hell?"

"It was a gamble. But she's an attractive woman. And you're a resourceful man. We took a chance on chemistry."

And it worked, thought Guy. *Damn you, Hamilton, the chemistry worked just fine.*

"At any rate," said Hamilton, sliding a few bills onto the bar, "you'll be rewarded with the silence you crave. I'm afraid the bounty's out of the question, though—budget deficit and all. But you'll have the distinct pleasure of knowing you served your country well."

That's when Guy burst into unstoppable laughter. He laughed so hard, tears came to his eyes; so loud, a dozen heads turned to look at him.

"Have I missed the joke?" Hamilton inquired politely.

"The joke," said Guy, "is on me."

He laughed all the way out the door.

Chapter 15

Her father, once again, was leaving.

Early on a rainy morning, Willy stood in the bedroom doorway and watched him pack his suitcase, the way she'd watched him pack it long ago. She'd had him home such a short time, only a few days since his release from the hospital. And he'd spent every moment pining for his family—his other family. Oh, he hadn't complained or been unkind, but she'd seen the sadness in his gaze, heard his sighs as he'd wandered about the house. She'd known it was inevitable: that he'd be walking out of her life again.

He took one last look in the closet, then turned to the dresser.

She glanced down at a pair of brand-new loafers that he'd set aside in the closet. "Dad, aren't you taking your shoes?" she asked.

"At home, I don't wear shoes."

"Oh." *This used to be your home,* she thought.

She wandered into the living room, sat down by the window and stared out at the rain. It seemed as if a lifetime of sorrow had been crammed into these past two weeks she'd been home. While her father had recuperated in a military hospital, in a civilian hospital a few miles away, her mother had lain dying. It had been wrenching to drive back and forth between them, to shift from seeing her father regain his strength to seeing her mother fade. Ann's death had come more quickly than the doctors had predicted; it was almost as if she'd held on just long enough to see her husband one last time, then had allowed herself to quietly slip away.

She'd forgiven him, of course.

Just as Willy had forgiven him.

Why was it always women who had to do the forgiving? she'd wondered.

"I'm all packed," her father said, carrying his suitcase into the living room. "I've called a cab."

"Are you sure you've got everything? The kids' toys? The books?"

"It's all in here. What a delivery! They're going to think I'm Santa Claus." He set the suitcase down and sat on the couch. They didn't speak for a moment.

"You won't be coming back, will you?" she said at last.

"It may not be easy."

"May I come see you?"

"Willy, you know you can! Both you and Guy. And next time, we'll make it a decent visit." He laughed. "Nice and quiet and dull. Guy'll appreciate that."

There was a long silence. Her father asked, "Have you spoken to him lately?"

She looked away. "It's been two weeks."

"That long?"

"He hasn't called."

"Why haven't you called him?"

"I've been busy. A lot of things to take care of. But you know that."

"He doesn't."

"Well, he *ought* to know." Suddenly agitated, she rose and paced the room, finally returning to the window. "I'm not really surprised he hasn't called. After all, we had our little adventure, and now it's back to life as usual." She glanced at her father. "Men hate that, don't they? Life as usual."

"Some men do. On the other hand, some of us change."

"Oh, Dad, I've been around the block. I can tell when things are over."

"Did Guy say that?"

She turned and gazed back out the window. "He didn't have to."

Her father didn't comment. After a while, she heard him go back into the bedroom, but she didn't move. She just kept staring out at the rain, thinking about Guy. Wondering for the first time if maybe *she* had done the running away.

No, it wasn't running. It was facing reality. Together they'd had the time of their lives, a crazy week of emotions gone wild, of terror and exhilaration, when every breath, every heartbeat had seemed like a gift from God.

Of course, it hadn't lasted.

But whose fault was that?

She felt herself drawn almost against her will to the telephone. Even as she dialed his number, she wondered what she'd say to him. *Hello, Guy. I know you don't want to hear this, but I love you.* Then she'd hang up and spare him the ordeal of admitting the feeling wasn't mutual. She let it ring twelve times, knowing it was 4:00 a.m. in Honolulu, knowing he *should* be home.

There were tears in her eyes when she finally hung up. She stood staring down at the phone, wondering how that inanimate collection of wires and plastic could leave her feeling so betrayed. *Damn you,* she thought. *You never even gave me the chance to make a fool of myself.*

The sound of tires splashing across wet streets made her look out the window. Through pouring rain she saw a cab pull up at the curb.

"Dad?" she called. She went to her father's bedroom. "Your taxi's here."

"Already?" He glanced around to see if he'd forgotten anything. "Okay. I guess this is it, then."

The doorbell rang. He threw on his raincoat and strode across the living room. Willy wasn't watching as he opened the door, but she heard him say, "I don't believe it." She turned.

"Hello, Maitland," said Guy.

The two men, both wearing raincoats, both holding suitcases, grinned at each other across the threshold.

Guy shook the raindrops from his hair. "Mind if I come in?"

"Gee, I don't know. I'd better ask the boss." Maitland turned to his daughter. "What do you think? Can the man come in?"

Willy was too stunned to say a word.

"I guess that's a yes," her father said, and he motioned for Guy to enter.

Guy stepped over the threshold and set his suitcase down. Then he just stood there, looking at her. Rain had plastered his hair to his forehead, lines of exhaustion mapped his face, but no man had ever looked so wonderful. She tried to remind herself of all the reasons she didn't want to see him, all the reasons she should throw him out into the rain. But she couldn't seem to find her voice. She could only stare at him in wonder and remember how it had felt to be in his arms.

Maitland shuffled uneasily. "I...uh... I think I forgot to pack something," he muttered, and he discreetly vanished into the bedroom.

For a moment, the only sound was the water dripping from Guy's raincoat onto the wood floor.

"How's your mother?" Guy asked.

"She died, five days ago."

He shook his head. "Willy, I'm sorry."

"I'm sorry, too."

"How are you? Are you okay?"

"I'm...fine." She looked away. *I love you,* she thought. *And yet here we are, two strangers engaging in small talk.* "Yeah, I'm fine," she repeated, as though to convince him—to convince herself—that the anguish of these past two weeks had been a minor ache not worth mentioning.

"You look pretty good, considering."

She shrugged. "You look terrible."

"Not too surprising. Didn't get any sleep on the plane. And there was this baby screaming in the next seat, all the way from Bangkok."

"Bangkok?" She frowned. "You were in Bangkok?"

He nodded and laughed. "It's this crazy business I'm in. Got home from Nam, and a week later, they asked me to fly back…for Sam Lassiter." He paused. "I admit I wasn't thrilled about getting on another plane, but I figured it was something I had to do." He paused and added quietly, "No soldier should have to come home alone."

She thought about Lassiter, about that evening in the river café, the love song scratching from the record player, the paper lanterns fluttering in the wind. She thought about his body drifting in the waters of the Mekong. And she thought about the dark-eyed woman who'd loved him. "You're right," she said. "No soldier should have to come home alone."

There was another pause. She felt him watching her, waiting.

"You could have called me," she said.

"I wanted to."

"But you never got the chance, right?"

"I had plenty of chances."

"But you didn't bother?" She looked up. All the hurt, all the rage suddenly rose to the surface. "Two weeks with no word from you! And here you have the gall to show up unannounced, walk in my door and drop your damn suitcase in my living—"

The last word never made it to her lips. But he did. She was dragged into a rain-drenched embrace, and everything she'd planned to say, all the hurt and angry words, were swept away by that one kiss. The only sound she could manage was a small murmur of astonishment, and then she was whirled up in a wild maelstrom of desire. She lost all sense of where she ended and he began. She only knew, in that instant, that he had never really left her, that as long as she lived, he'd be part of her. Even as he pulled back to look at her, she was still drunk with the taste of him.

"I *did* want to call you. But I didn't know what to say…"

"I kept waiting for you to call. All these days…"

"Maybe I was… I don't know. Scared."

"Of what?"

"Of hearing it was over. That you'd come to your senses and decided I wasn't worth the risk. But then, when I got to Bangkok, I stopped at the Oriental Hotel. Had a drink on the terrace for old time's sake. Saw the same sunset, the same boats on the river. But it just didn't feel the same without you." He sighed. "Hell, nothing feels the same without you."

"You never told me. You just dropped out of my life."

"It never seemed like…the right time."

"The right time for what?"

"You know."

"No, I don't."

He shook his head in irritation. "You never make it easy, do you?"

She stepped back and gave him a long, critical look. Then she smiled. "I never intended to."

"Oh, Willy." He threw his arms around her and pulled her tightly against his chest. "I can see you and I are going to have a lot of things to settle."

"Such as?"

"Such as…" He lowered his mouth to hers and whispered, "Such as who gets to sleep on the right side of the bed…."

"Oh," she murmured as their lips brushed. "You will."

"And who gets to name our firstborn…."

She settled warmly into his arms and sighed. "I will."

"And who'll be first to say 'I love you.'"

There was a pause. "That one," she said with a smile, "is open to negotiation."

"No, it's not," he said, tugging her face up to his.

They stared at each other, both longing to hear the words but stubbornly waiting for the other to give in first.

It was a simultaneous surrender.

"I love you," Willy heard him say, just as the same three words tumbled from her lips.

Their laughter was simultaneous, too, bright and joyous and ringing with hope.

The kiss that followed was warm, seeking, but all too brief; it left her aching for more.

"It gets even better with practice," he whispered.

"Saying 'I love you?'"

"No. Kissing."

"Oh," she murmured. She added in a small voice, "Then can we try it again?"

Outside, a horn honked, dragging them both back to reality. Through the window they saw another taxi waiting at the curb.

Reluctantly Willy pulled out of Guy's arms. "Dad?" she called.

"I'm coming, I'm coming." Her father emerged from the bedroom, pulling on his raincoat again. He paused and looked at her.

"Uh, why don't you two say goodbye," said Guy, diplomatically turning for the front door. "I'll take your suitcase out to the car."

Willy and her father were left standing alone in the room. They looked at each other, both knowing that this, like every goodbye, could be the last.

"Are things okay between you and Guy?" Maitland asked.

Willy nodded.

There was another silence. Then her father asked softly, "And between you and me?"

She smiled. "Things are okay there, too." She went to him then, and they held each other. "Yes," she murmured against his chest, "between you and me, things are definitely okay."

A little reluctantly, he turned to leave. In the doorway, he and Guy shook hands.

"Have a good trip back, Maitland."

"I will. Take care of things, will you? And, Guy—thanks a lot."

"For what?"

Maitland glanced back at Willy. It was a look of regret. And redemption. "For giving me back my daughter," he said.

As Wild Bill Maitland walked out the door, Guy walked in. He didn't say a thing. He just took Willy in his arms and hugged her.

As the taxi drove away, she thought, *My father has left me. Again.*

She looked up at Guy. *And what about you?*

He answered her unspoken question by taking her face in his hands and kissing her. Then he gave the door a little kick; with a thud of finality, it swung shut.

And she knew that this time, the man would be staying.

* * * * *

USA TODAY bestselling author **Barb Han** lives in north Texas with her very own hero-worthy husband, three beautiful children, a spunky golden retriever/standard poodle mix and too many books in her to-read pile. In her downtime, she plays video games and spends much of her time on or around a basketball court. She loves interacting with readers and is grateful for their support. You can reach her at barbhan.com.

Books by Barb Han

Harlequin Intrigue

An O'Connor Family Mystery

Texas Kidnapping
Texas Target

Rushing Creek Crime Spree

What She Did
What She Knew
What She Saw

Crisis: Cattle Barge

Kidnapped at Christmas
Murder and Mistletoe
Bulletproof Christmas

Cattlemen Crime Club

One Tough Texan
Texas-Sized Trouble
Texas Witness
Texas Showdown

Visit the Author Profile page at
Harlequin.com for more titles.

WITNESS PROTECTION

Barb Han

My deepest gratitude goes to the men
and women of the US Marshals Service for their
many sacrifices. A heartfelt thank-you to my editor,
Allison Lyons, and my agent, Jill Marsal, because
you make dreams come true. I'm still pinching
myself. Brandon, Jacob and Tori, you guys inspire
me every day. I love you with all my heart. To my
husband, John, you are the great love of my life.
And this is one heck of an adventure.

Chapter 1

A clink against the back door of the bakery sounded again. Sadie Brooks lost her grip on the twenty-five pound sack of flour she'd held. It struck the floor and a mushroom-shaped cloud of white powder formed over the bag's lip.

Creek Bend, Texas, was a far cry from Chicago, she reminded herself. No one from her past knew where she was. No one could hurt her. No one cared. And she was no longer Laura Kaye.

It was four-thirty in the morning in a town that rolled up the streets by eight. The noise was most likely a cat rummaging through trash. No big deal. Nothing scary.

"Only you and me are crazy enough to be up this early," she said to her two-year-old rescue dog, Boomer, while forcing air in and out of her lungs. He didn't so much as crack an eyelid. "And I think we both know I mean me."

Working when everyone else slept suited Sadie just fine. She'd had very little use for daylight or people ever since she'd been kidnapped two years ago.

Yes, she still flinched at every noise. Constantly checked over her shoulder at the slightest peep. But she was always ready. Always expecting the worst. Always on guard. And yet, the past year had been peaceful. There was no reason to believe anything would change save for the all-too-real feeling in the pit of her stomach screaming otherwise.

Being constantly on alert felt a lot like parking and then leaving her high beams on. Pretty soon her battery would run out.

Boomer whined in his sleep. Her protector? Now that was funny. She'd rescued a big dog for protection. She got the Scooby Doo of golden retrievers. All he wanted to do was eat, and he wouldn't scare away a cat. But he did make noise and his low-belly bark sounded fierce. Sadie figured it was good enough to make anyone think twice.

As she bent over to pick up the sack of white powder, another noise sent a chill skittering across her nerves. Boomer's head cocked at the unmistakable snick of a lock. Her heart drummed against her chest.

Using the lock was good, right? That meant someone with a key was most likely standing on the other side of the door. She thought of Claire, her very pregnant boss who was her only friend. With her baby due any day, she would be asleep right now.

Boomer, shackles raised, stalked toward the stockroom to investigate.

"It's okay, boy." She scoured the area looking for a weapon just in case. Was there anything she could use to defend herself? To protect Boomer? She moved toward the nearest counter.

A sparkle caught her attention. Light reflected from the blade of a knife. Her fingers shook as they curled around the black plastic handle.

Then everything went dark. No lights. It was too much of a coincidence to think the breaker could've been tripped. This blackout was on purpose.

Boomer's low throaty growl nearly stopped her heart. It was the same noise he made when a stranger approached the lake house. Boomer had found an intruder. And they weren't familiar.

His barks fired like a machine gun, rapid and ear-piercing.

Sadie's adrenaline kicked into high gear. Her fight, flight or freeze response jacked through the roof. Every instinct inside her screamed, "Run!"

But she couldn't.

She wouldn't leave Boomer defenseless. Could she signal to him without giving away her location? No.

What about help? Her cell? Good luck finding her purse in the pitch-black.

She crouched and felt her way behind a rack filled with pastries. A hand covered her mouth. Her fingers, which had been curled around the knife handle, flexed cold air. She had been disarmed with frightening ease.

"Shh. Don't say a word or they'll hear you. Be very still." A second ticked by before she recognized the voice as Nick Campbell's. Why in the hell would a radiologist show up at the bakery in the middle of the night?

The last time a man took her by surprise she ended

up spending two weeks in the ICU with facial lacerations and cracked ribs.

Determined to break free this time, she ignored the shivers running up her arms and bit Nick's hand.

"I said, 'be still,' and don't do that again," Nick said. His deep, quiet tone was different. Dark and dangerous. Experienced. And she knew instinctively not to push him.

With a total stranger somewhere in front of her and Nick's big frame behind her, she was trapped.

"I won't hurt you," he whispered.

What on earth was he doing here? And how had he gotten in without her noticing?

Boomer's barks mixed with growls and intensified.

Before she could wrap her brain around what was happening, Sadie felt herself being hauled toward the front door. The recollection of being snatched in daylight two years ago flooded her. His behavior brought up horrible memories. No way would Nick Campbell abduct her. Not a chance.

But what, besides a feeling that she could trust him, did she know about Nick? His brown eyes and black hair were almost always covered by a ball cap and shades. His shoulders hunkered forward, masking his true height. She hadn't fully realized his lethal potential until he stood behind her, his masculine chest flush with her back. She was five-foot-seven and he dwarfed her. He had to be more than six feet tall. Maybe six-one?

Neither his height nor his mannerisms had intimidated her before. She'd felt a sizzle of attraction, but then most of the women in Creek Bend seemed eager to get to know him better. With his forearm locked like a vise grip around her waist, she suddenly realized just how strong and buff he truly was.

"What do you think you're doing?" she whispered, choking down the anger rising inside her.

"No time to explain."

Hell if she'd wait. She wasn't about to be caught with no means of self-preservation again. She wasn't defenseless as she'd been before.

The first principle of judo was never to oppose strength to strength. Sadie shifted her weight enough to kick off the wall. She bucked, trying to throw him off balance while bracing herself to land on the painted concrete floor.

Didn't work.

Strong as an ox, he'd anticipated the move and counteracted by placing his feet in an athletic stance and tightening his grip. "I'll drag you out of here kicking and screaming if I have to, but we'll most likely both be killed."

"I can't leave my dog. Boomer's back there," she said, hating how her voice quivered and got all shaky with fear. She'd sworn no man would make her feel defenseless again. She realized, on some level, he was there to help, but she could walk for herself.

She kicked and wiggled. His grip was too tight.

It surprised her that a nerdy work-at-home radiologist knew how to counteract her martial arts moves. He also knew the back of the bakery well enough to navigate in the dark. She couldn't even do that without bumping into something and she'd worked there for a year.

Fighting was no use. She would bide her time and break free the second the opportunity presented.

"I'll go back for him. Once you're safe in the truck," he said. "Trust me."

She snorted. "Why? Because I know so much about you?"

"I can explain everything. Once you're out of danger."

Bright Christmas lights lit a cloudless sky. Once they were out of the building, she could see. Nick's expression was that of soldier on the front line.

He tucked her in the truck and then closed the door. The lock clicked. Trust him?

The door handle didn't work. She rammed the door. All that did was hurt her shoulder. Try again and there'd be a nasty bruise. There had to be another way. She banged on the window. "Hey!"

She tried to pop the lock. Nothing.

Spinning onto her back, she used a front kick to drive the heel of her foot into the door, praying she could find the sweet spot. No good.

She scrambled to the front seat. By the time she gripped the handle, she heard a horrific boom from the alley. The bakery caught fire. She couldn't catch her breath enough to scream.

The world closed in around her, and her stomach wrenched. Boomer!

Shattered glass littered the sidewalk. Thick black smoke bellowed from every opening.

What was left of the front door kicked open and out strode Nick, coughing, with her hundred-pound mutt in his arms.

As soon as she got a good look at him saving her dog, her heart squeezed and a voice inside her head warned, *Uh-oh.*

Out of the ashes and burning timber, he moved toward her, carrying her dog as if Boomer weighed nothing. Nick opened the back door of the truck and gently placed the dog on the seat.

"What's going on? Who are you really?"

There was something about his compassion with the animal, something nonthreatening about him that kept Sadie's nerves a notch below panic.

His face was stoic. His jaw set. Determination creased his forehead now dark with ash. "You're in serious trouble."

Icy tendrils closed around her chest. "What are you doing here showing up out of nowhere like that? Who was coming in the back door?"

He started the ignition.

"Start talking or I'm going to scream." She crossed her arms over her chest. "Or, better yet, take me home."

"No can do. And you needed help."

"Dammit, Nick, you're creeping me out. You have to give me something more."

His determination was written all over his squared jaw. He had obviously saved her life. He wasn't there to hurt her. She didn't know why he'd shown up. Nothing made sense. "At least tell me where you're taking me. I deserve to know what's happening."

He kept one eye trained on the rearview mirror as he reached in his pocket and pulled out a badge. "I'm a U.S. Marshal."

Her brain scrambled. Where was Charlie? He was her handler. And what did Nick mean he was a U.S. Marshal? All those times he'd stopped in the bakery and led her to believe he was flirting with her caused a red blush to crawl up her neck. A piece of her had enjoyed his attention, too. What an idiot. Was he monitoring her situation the whole time? She needed to call Charlie and find out what was going on. For now, it was best to ignore her embarrassment and play dumb. "You're a radiologist."

His lips parted in a dry crack of a smile. "You don't believe me."

"Why didn't you mention this before?"

"It would've blown my cover."

Anger flashed in Sadie's big green eyes as her gaze darted around the vehicle. Her phone was her only connection to her handler, and it was just as lost as she looked. She turned her attention to him, glaring as if this was all his fault.

"Sorry about your cell." He pulled a new one from the dash and handed it to her. The movement called attention to the bruise she'd put on the inside of his forearm when she'd tried to kick out of his grasp earlier. The memory of her slim figure and sweet bottom pressed against him stirred an inappropriate sexual reaction. Her flour-dotted pale pink V-neck sweater and jeans fit like a second skin over a toned, feminine body. Her fresh-baked-bread-and-lily scent filled the cab. "I didn't have time to retrieve your purse."

She looked at the phone as if it was a hot grenade. "Why should I trust you?"

Nick couldn't blame her. Her world was about to be turned upside down again, and he sensed she knew on some level. "You don't have a choice. I apologize for that."

She recoiled, most likely remembering being forced away from the only life she'd known in Chicago two years ago. His surveillance told him she'd made a home in Creek Bend and a friend in her new boss. The two had become close. Claire and her baby were a surrogate family to Sadie. He didn't like taking it all away again. He bit back frustration.

"Where are you taking me?" The fear in her voice was like a sucker punch to his solar plexus.

"Somewhere safe. Charlie's dead."

She gasped. Her shaky hand covered her mouth.

"How do you know? Did you...?"

"No. Of course not." She'd been taught not to believe anyone but Charlie. He had no idea how she would react now. He'd have to keep a close eye on her during the ride. "I know this is a lot to digest."

She sat there tight-lipped, looking as though she'd bolt if given the chance.

"This is real. You're in danger. I'm here to help."

Her angry glare trained on him. "Prove he's dead."

"Can't. Not tonight, anyway."

"Why? Shouldn't there be a news report? A U.S. Marshal dying should make the headlines."

"It's complicated."

"Then explain it to me slowly." She clenched her jaw muscles. Impatience and fear radiated from her narrow-eyed glare.

With her wavy brown hair pulled off her face in a ponytail, she could pass for a coed. Her lips were full, sexy. Not that they were his business. "He was found in his bed. A bullet through his brain. The agency is keeping his death under wraps."

"Oh, God. He was a nice man."

Nick bit out a derisive snort. "Good guys don't get in bed with the enemy."

"Are you saying what I think you are?" she asked incredulously.

"Yes, ma'am."

"I don't believe you. He brought me here. Set me up with this job. He would not help them."

He arched his brow. "Because he did a few nice things for you, he can't possibly turn into one of them?"

She stared at the road in front of them. If she bit down any harder on her bottom lip, she might chew right through it. "Don't twist my words. I know he was a family man. He cared about his work. I knew him better than you did. He wouldn't turn on me. Not now. Not after two years. Besides, what would he have to gain in hurting me?"

"Malcolm Grimes has been broken out of jail and someone on the inside helped. Your handler showed up at the prison two days before he escaped."

Her tight grip on her nerves shattered. Just like when a rubber band broke, Nick could almost see the pieces of rubber splintering in all directions. Her eyes closed. Her fingers pressed to her temples. Her body visibly shook. "He's out? Just like that?"

"I'm afraid so."

Her eyes snapped open and her gaze locked on to him. "How can you let that happen? Now he's free to come after me?" Her voice shook with terror.

"That's why I'm here."

"Let me get this straight. Grimes is out, and you automatically suspect Charlie? Wouldn't he be alive right now if he'd helped?"

"Not if he crossed Grimes. He was executed in his own bed. Someone was making a statement."

Weariness crept over her face as she gripped the

phone, closed her eyes again and rocked back in her seat. "The first thing Grimes does after killing Charlie is come after me? Why? Wouldn't he figure you'd be waiting for him?"

"Your file's missing from Charlie's place."

She drummed her index finger on the cell.

"I'm supposed to tell you 'Pandora.'"

The tension in her face eased slightly even though she didn't speak. Her movement smoothed, timed with her calmer breaths. She stopped tapping on the cell. The safe word resonated. "Any idea why my boss chose Pandora as your safe word?"

"Yeah."

"Care to fill me in?" It wasn't as if he was asking for her Social Security number.

"Not really." A solemn expression settled on her almond-shaped face. "The bakery. Did they blow it up because of me?"

"Most likely."

"That was all Claire had to support her baby and now it's gone. Why didn't they just shoot me straight out?"

He tightened his grip on the steering wheel. "Good question. My guess is they were trying to ensure there'd be no mistakes. Easier to just blow up a building with you in it. Also has the added benefit of looking like it was an accident. It's tidier. Leaves less of a trail."

"So, it's over. Just like that. I walk away from everything I know one more time because of these jerks. I'm on the move again?"

He nodded.

"I didn't do anything wrong," she said fiercely.

"I know."

"Is this what I can expect the rest of my life? Because some guys want to murder and maim me?" She drummed her hands on the dash. Her tension was on the rise again.

"It shouldn't happen to good people."

"Save the speech. I've heard it before. 'Nice folks deserve better than this, but we have to do what we can to protect you. It's not your fault. Sometimes the system doesn't work.'"

"It's true."

She pressed her lips together. "Yeah? Well, your system sucks."

He could appreciate her anger. When his youngest sister was kidnapped and beaten by a crazed ex-boyfriend, Nick had hunted the teen down and nearly ended up in prison himself. His mom intervened while his grandmother called 911 to stop him from meting out his own justice. Sadie's haunted expression reminded him of his kid sister.

Under the circumstances, Sadie was doing well. Damn that his own anger rose thinking about the past. He already felt a connection to Sadie. His protective instincts flew into high gear the moment someone breached the bakery. He shouldn't care this much about a witness. "It'll keep you alive if you let it."

A beat of silence sat between them.

He risked a glance in her direction. A ball of fury formed in his throat at the tears streaming down her pink cheeks. From what he'd observed in the few weeks he'd been in Creek Bend, she worked hard. She was always on time. By all accounts she did a great job. He already knew about her resilience and courage. She seemed decent and kind. She deserved so much more.

He might have to take away her home again, but he would keep her safe.

Rather than debate the quality of the WitSec program at the U.S. Marshals Service, he dropped his defenses. The experience of growing up with four women under the same roof had taught him a thing or two about the point at which he'd lost a battle. He didn't need any of his experience to see this one was long gone. He raised his hands in the universal sign of surrender then dropped them right back on the steering wheel. "I didn't say any of that to upset you."

She folded her arms. "It's fine. I guess you're right. The program probably helps a lot of people. Just not me. I get to be the exception. I might be the unluckiest person on the planet. Even a program meant to help people makes my life miserable."

"For what it's worth, I'm truly sorry."

She looked at him long and hard. Her green-eyed stare pierced him. "Your boss, Mr. Smith, said whatever I stepped into opened a Pandora's box because they started fighting to take over Grimes's territory."

"Sounds like something my boss would say." He clenched his back teeth. "It did. Violent crime shot through the roof after we put Grimes away."

"Doesn't seem like I helped by having him locked away."

"Testifying was still the right thing to do. You saved a lot of innocent lives."

"Did I? Not mine. And what about Claire? Now I've ruined the business of the one person who I could count on as a friend."

"She'll receive money. I guarantee it. Citizens are safer with these guys off the streets."

"But they aren't, are they?" she snapped. "I wasn't even the one Grimes wanted. They kidnapped me by mistake. The woman they were after moved away and disappeared. She was smart. Not me. I believed your boss. I testified. Look at me now. Shouldn't you check in with him or something?" She palmed the cell, scrolling through the names in the contact list with her thumb.

It didn't take long.

There were only two. Nick Campbell. William Smith.

They were the only two people in her world for now. Nick couldn't imagine being that alone.

"Nah. There's only one reason I want you to call that number. Anything happens to me, don't hesitate. Make contact. Smith will tell you where to go and what to do."

Her grip tightened on the cell phone. "But you're with me. Anything happens to you and we'll both be dead."

"Nothing's going to happen to either of us. I promise. I only gave you the number to ease your concerns."

"If one U.S. Marshal's already dead, our odds don't seem all that great." Her words came out raspy and small.

The back windshield shattered. The truck swerved as he slammed the brakes.

A truck rammed his left bumper, sending his vehicle into a dangerous spin. He grasped the steering wheel, turning into the skid.

Chapter 2

Cold blasted Sadie. "Boomer!"

He'd never been good at car rides. She glanced in the backseat. He was practically plastered to the floor mat. His fear might've just saved his life.

"Get down." Nick's tone changed to a dark rumbling presence of its own.

Rocks and dirt spewed from under the tires as he navigated the vehicle back onto the roadway.

Sadie curled into a ball on the floorboard. "That the same person who was trying to get through the door at the bakery?"

"No."

She flashed her gaze toward him. "How do you know?"

Oh. Right. He'd killed him. The soot on his face outlined the scratches he'd collected. Looking at this guy—this new Nick—she believed him capable of doing whatever was necessary to get the job done. The transformation from the old one still shocked her. The once almost nerdy-looking facade a stark contrast to the battle-weary expression of this warrior. If he drove as well as he hid his identity, she had no doubt he'd get them out of this.

The truck swerved and jolted her thoughts to the very real threat screaming toward the back bumper.

The image of Nick calm and collected despite the danger brought her panic levels down.

He aimed a revolver out the back and fired a round.

The squeal of tires, the crunch of metal against a tree, and she knew another bad guy was dead.

Nick floored the gas pedal. He had the wheel in one hand and his weapon in the other.

An invisible band tightened around her rib cage.

Nick looked at her, his expression serious and reassuring. "We're okay."

"I know."

With one hand on the wheel and his eyes on the road, he placed the gun on the seat between them and offered a hand up. She pulled herself up onto the bench seat.

He turned the heater on high and then shrugged out of his leather jacket. "This should help."

She realizing for the first time her teeth were chattering. Wrapping the coat around her shoulders, she was flooded with the masculine scent of leather.

"I'm not going to let anyone hurt you." He was sweet to make the promise even if they both knew he didn't have control over what happened to her.

Even so, her heart rate slowed a notch. "Th-thank you."

With the gun next to her, prickly heat flushed her

neck and face. An overwhelming fear pressed down on her body, making her limbs heavy.

Concern wrinkled his charred forehead. "What's wrong?" His gaze shifted from the firearm to her face then back to the road. "This? Does seeing my gun bother you?"

"It's okay. I have to get used to it, right? This is my life now." She heard how small her voice had become, hating that she'd lost her power by looking at the piece of cold metal.

"Not today." He slipped the weapon into an ankle holster and tugged his jeans over it.

She'd barely noticed his legs until that moment. Her gaze moved up to the line of his muscular thighs pressing against the denim material of his jeans. A black V-neck T-shirt highlighted a broad chest and arms as thick as tree trunks.

An electric current swirled inside her body. This strong man looked more than capable of protecting her. He seemed able to handle anything that came along. She realized why she'd never noticed how adept and strong he'd been before. There had been no reason to. He'd played the work-at-home radiologist to perfection. Most of the women in Creek Bend had noticed his seriously good looks and lucrative career, while she'd spent the past year trying to avoid everyone—especially men. She'd closed her eyes to anyone she'd dismissed as a nonthreat.

Odd as it sounded, she would miss seeing Nick come into the bakery right before her shift ended. Different didn't begin to describe the change in him. She'd already been introduced to his powerful chest and lean, muscled thighs when her body had been pressed against his earlier. Forget about his strong hands around her and the sensual current they had sent through her body.

This close, she could see his almost overwhelmingly attractive facial features. His brown eyes had cinnamon copperlike flecks in them. His jawline with two days' worth of stubble a sharp contrast to full, thick lips—lips she had to force her gaze away from. His dense, wavy hair was as black as his shirt. The combination made for one seriously hot package.

She thought about how fast the bakery had gone up in flames. Her boss and only friend who had become like family would have to start over. Claire had worked hard to build her business. The building would be burned to the ground by now. A little piece of her broke at the thought of never seeing Claire's baby. Her only real friend was out of her life forever.

Friend? Sadie almost laughed out loud. What kind of friend didn't even know her real name?

A sign that read Now Leaving Creek Bend filled the right corner of the window.

She thought about the town Christmas party she wouldn't attend. About the baby she would never meet. About the family of her own that was so out of reach. About all the things she would never have.

Burning tears rolled down her cheeks.

A feeling of loss anchored in her stomach.

Straightening her back, she clicked on her seat belt. Let those bastards get inside her head, and they won. "There are a few knickknacks back home I wish I had." She glanced at her taupe boots with teal outlay and sighed. "At least I get to keep these."

Nick's gaze intensified on the road. "I already sent someone for your things."

"Seriously? Isn't that against the rules or something?"

He shrugged. "We'll keep 'em somewhere locked away until it's safe to retrieve them."

"I don't know what to say. That was very kind of you. I was told everything had to be left behind when this happens."

"It's not the way I work." His gaze intensified on the stretch of road in front of him. "You deserve to have your clothes at least."

Appreciation washed over her. She knew not to trust it. "This is the second time I've thanked you since we've been in the truck."

Sadie forced herself to remember other positive things as she reached in the backseat to pet Boomer. Not losing everything was a huge blessing.

Besides, the alternative—giving up—was never an option. All she could gain there was depression. Feeling sorry for herself wouldn't change her circumstances. Alcohol? A drinking problem didn't sound like the worst demon to battle at the moment. But, no, she'd never really taken to the taste other than an occasional glass of wine.

She turned toward the stranger beside her as he pulled the truck off the main road. "Is Nick Campbell your real name?"

"Yes," he said with the voice that was like a caress on a cold winter's night. He arched his dark brow.

"Are you telling me the truth?"

"You deserve that much from me."

A traitorous shiver skittered across her nerves. It was chilly outside. Now that the window had shattered, there was nothing keeping out the frost. The shiver came from being cold, she told herself, and not the sexual appeal of the man next to her. "This can't be the work of Grimes alone, can it? Is he big enough to take out a U.S. Marshal?"

"It's stupid to come after you. The agency has been keeping a close eye on everything since his escape. Smith and I were hoping he'd leave you out of this. And, yes, there's more to this than we know as of now. But we'll figure the rest out."

"Doesn't sound good for me. Maybe he wants revenge badly enough to risk everything?"

"He didn't get where he is by being stupid."

"He's been out for a month? Timed with when you showed up?"

"We received intel something was brewing. My boss wanted to make sure our bases were covered. I came out a few days before he broke out."

The Christmas party invitation she'd received flashed in her mind. A small town holiday scene complete with four-foot-high snowdrifts piled on either side of the road. There were glowing street lamps. The scene reminded her very much of Creek Bend sans the snow. Sadie's boss had all but made her promise she'd show. "What would make him risk his safety to find me? He can't possibly want to go back to prison. I mean, why me? Why now?"

His jaw muscle ticked. "Revenge."

That one word packed more power than if she'd been struck with a fist. "I was upset before. I didn't mean to insult the agency. I honestly appreciate everything you guys have done to keep me alive so far."

"Our failures are putting your life at risk."

And keeping her on the run. Creek Bend would start

its day perfectly timed to the sunrise in another forty-five minutes. Life would go on without her.

Claire would have her baby. Sadie would never hold the little girl she'd anticipated for so long. Claire had become more than a friend, she'd become like family. And now everything was gone.

At least she still had Boomer. He was tucked safely in the backseat. "None of this has ever made sense to me. I didn't do anything wrong and yet I'm the one slinking out of town in the middle of the night."

Sadie's sadness was palpable. Worse yet, she put up a brave front.

One look into those haltingly green eyes, transparent like single perfect gemstones, and Nick might forget his real reason for being there. Protect his witness without getting overly involved. Not generally a problem for him. Discipline was more than his middle name. It was his life's creed.

Nothing and no one had threatened his ability to focus. Or could.

This was different. Her circumstance reminded him too much of his little sister's. The thought of another woman being targeted by a man hell-bent on revenge when she was innocent ate at his insides. Many of the people in the program he came across could use a fresh start. Giving them a new job and home also provided a new lease on life. Not Sadie. What had she done wrong? Nothing. By all accounts, she should've had a promising future with a business consultant in accounting. She'd be well on her way to two-point-five kids, a big house and a Suburban.

None of *this* had been invited into her life. A crazed criminal had sent her to the ICU.

People called her lucky for living.

Luck wasn't her gig. She'd had enough courage to defy the odds and enough spunk to fight when her future was bleak.

What she had was a hell of a lot better than chance.

And yet, seeing her now, she looked small and afraid. Chin up, she was determined not to give into it.

He'd give anything to ease her concern and put a smile on her face. Wanting to protect her and needing to were two different things.

Why was he already reminding himself of the fact?

He pulled the truck onto a narrow dirt road. "I have better transportation stashed here. Besides, we won't make it five miles without drawing attention with the condition of the truck."

Winding down the lane wasn't a problem. Turning off the lights and navigating in the dark was a different story. He'd memorized the area easy enough. But he hadn't had time to make a night run.

A thunk sounded at the same time they both pitched forward. The air bags deployed. Sadie gasped and Boomer yelped as he banged against the back of the driver's seat.

"Hold on, boy," she said.

Nick focused on Sadie first. "You okay?"

"Fine."

He hopped out of the truck and opened the door to the backseat of the cab. Running a hand over the frightened dog, Nick didn't feel anything out of the ordinary. He checked his hand for blood. Relief was like a flood to dry plains. "Shook him up a bit."

She struggled to work herself free from the airbag, and then climbed over the seat. "But he's fine, right?"

"Yep." Nick owed the big guy upstairs one for that.

What caused the wreck? Had he misjudged the road?

He circled to the front of the cab. His eyes were adjusting to the dark. The sight before him pumped his stress level fifty notches. A tree blocked the road.

He seriously doubted nature had caused the barrier. Had someone found his hiding spot?

A branch snapped to his right. Could be an animal evading, but he wouldn't take unnecessary chances with his cargo. He moved to the truck. "We can't drive through. We'll have to go on foot."

Sadie nodded, coaxing Boomer to follow.

Nick shouldered his backpack. They had enough supplies to last a couple of days. He hadn't expected to need them.

"Where're we going?" Sadie's eyes were wide and she blinked rapidly. Fear.

"There's a place about a day's hike from here. If we can make it by nightfall, we'll have safe shelter."

Her gaze locked on to the barrier behind them. "That wasn't an accident, was it?"

He shrugged his shoulders casually, not wanting her to panic. "I'd rather not take anything for granted."

The crack and crunch of tree limbs on the ground grew louder.

Boomer faced the woods on the opposite side of the truck. His shackles raised, and he growled low in his belly.

Nick reached for Sadie's hand, and then wound his fingers through hers.

"We have to go. *Now.*"

Chapter 3

Nick pulled Sadie into the woods at a dead run. Branches slapped her face and arms, stinging her skin.

Boomer quickened his stride, keeping pace by her side step for step.

They could've been banging drums for all the noise they made. No chance they'd slip through the brush unheard. Nick seemed more intent on moving fast. Another reason her pulse kicked up and her anxiety levels roared.

Her thighs hurt. Her lungs burned. She pushed forward, determined not to complain.

He stopped at the edge of a lake. She collapsed to the ground, gasping for air. Her ears were numb, frozen. Every other body part overheated.

Sunlight pushed through the trees, which meant they'd been on the go at least forty-five minutes. Her lungs felt as if they'd explode, whereas Nick hardly seemed affected. Of course he was in shape. His job— his *real* job—would demand excellent physical conditioning. She forced her gaze away from the way his muscles expanded against his jeans when he walked.

The rustle of leaves and bird whistles were the only noise. "Is it safe to take a break?"

He stood, listening. Then he scanned the area. "We can take a minute."

"What about the racket we made?"

"I made a few shortcuts that made it harder to track us." He opened his pack and handed her a bottle of water, taking one for himself. "Let me know when you think you can move again."

She could barely open the lid. Tired and dirty, her stamina waned. The cool liquid was a godsend to her parched mouth. "So what's the plan?"

"Shelter. But it's a ways ahead," he warned. "It isn't much, but it'll get us through the night."

"No. I mean ultimately. Where is all this hiding going? Surely no one expects me to keep this up forever."

"If you're tired we can stop."

"I don't mean now."

His face tensed. His glare intensified. His slack jaw became rigid.

"What? No answers?"

"You want the truth? We catch him, figure out who else is involved and why, and get your life back." He turned to face the lake.

"I doubt that," she huffed. "What good did it do me to testify? I never got my life back. His men kept searching for me. I've had two homes in two years. Now, he's out. Hunting me. I'm running for my life. Again. Your boss made promises he didn't keep."

Nick bent down and poured water on his palm, allowing Boomer a drink. When the dog was hydrated, Nick took a swig of water. "He shouldn't have done that."

"It was all well and good when people wanted me to help them." She pulled her knees into her chest. "I'm sure it didn't hurt his career to be able to put a man like Grimes away."

He whirled around on her. "What's that supposed to mean?"

"How much do you trust your boss?" Anger had her bating him into an argument.

"Smith is fine. You're tired."

"Is that right?"

"I hope so because if this is your personality, it's gonna be a long night."

"You think this is funny? Forgive me if I don't laugh along with you."

Nick cleared his throat. "I never said that. I'm not here to hurt you. In case you hadn't noticed, I'm trying to help."

"For how long? You can't watch me the rest of my life. Maybe I should go after him for a change." What she'd said was the emotional equivalent of raising a red blanket in front of a bull. She had two choices. Fight or cry. She'd rather fight.

"Now you're being crazy."

Tears welled, but she'd be damned if they were going to fall. "First I'm tired. Now I'm crazy. Which is it?"

"I get why you're…freaking out."

"Do you? You think you already know what's going

on inside my head? Why don't you tell me, then, because I'm confused." She shot daggers at him with her glare. Fear pushed away the cold air, replacing it with heat. Her body vibrated from anger, her defense mechanism for not losing it and crying.

She stood and took a step toward him. She expected to see anger or confusion. Instead, he faced her with his whole body. His hands were open at his sides. His relaxed gaze moved smoothly from her eyes to her mouth and back. His lips softened at the corners in a smile. She steeled her breath, but nothing prepared her for the warmth of his big hand on her shoulder.

The fight drained from her.

"We have a long walk ahead. You should save your energy."

Her chest deflated. She plopped onto the cold ground. Boomer nuzzled his cold wet nose on her neck.

"Give me a minute. I'll be fine."

The last thing Sadie looked was fine. If he'd learned one thing from having two sisters, the word *fine* didn't mean good things. He'd give her a minute to regroup even though he'd feel a lot better if they kept moving. They'd put some distance between them and whoever was following, but for how long? "For what it's worth, my sisters tell me I'm stubborn. If I were in your situation, I'd be crazy, too."

She rewarded him with a smile warmer than a campfire. "Smart women."

"Don't tell them that." He bent down on his knee, fighting the urge to provide more comfort than his words.

"Do I detect a case of sibling rivalry?" Her brow arched.

"No. But I do have two younger sisters to keep track of."

"You must be exhausted."

"Not really. They can take care of themselves mostly. Both work in law enforcement. They humor me, though."

She relaxed a little more. "Bet I could learn a thing or two from them."

"I doubt it. You're a survivor."

"How do you know?"

"You've made it this far."

"You never told me where we're going. Do you have a hunting cabin or something out here?" she asked.

"Guess I didn't adequately fill you in. I'd apologize but I'll just do it again. My sisters tell me I tend to get in a zone then information comes out on a need-to-know basis."

"Does that mean your brain can act and speak at the same time?"

He laughed. "It's possible. Words are empty, though." He could hear his grandmother's voice in the back of his head echoing the same sentiment. "Actions are better."

She'd also taught him to be grateful for what he had instead of sorrowful for what he'd lost. Some lessons were easier to catch on to than others.

Sadie's laugh had the same effect as the first spring flower opening. "You've been surrounded by a lot of smart women in your life, haven't you? You're lucky."

"Not sure if you would hold on to that thought if you spent more than five minutes with them."

Her gaze focused on the water and she absently

picked at a leaf. "I'm afraid I don't have a big family to draw experience from. It's just me. Has always been just me."

He nodded.

She glanced at him. "Right. You already knew that didn't you? You probably know everything about me, don't you?"

"The agency gave me your intel. For what it's worth—"

"Don't apologize. You'll just do it again when you need information about someone." She half smiled.

"True."

"I know you were doing your job. I'm not blaming you personally. It's just surreal to me that there's some file out there with my life history in it."

Silence sat between them.

"It's been me, alone, for so long, I can't remember what it's like to have a real family. It was just me and my parents growing up. I never had more than that. They were always working. I wouldn't know what to do with siblings who watch over me."

"A big family sounds like heaven in theory. In real life, not so much. Add my mom and grandmother into the mix and I've had four women constantly telling me what to do for most of my life." He chuckled.

"Sounds like the promised land to me right now."

"Mom had a lot of mouths to feed when my dad disappeared. She'd come home beat, but tried not to show it. I became a handful. My dad leaving didn't do good things to my head. But then I saw how much pain I added to my mom. She was already devastated. Being the oldest, I got a front-row seat to her pain."

"From the looks of it, you turned out okay."

"That's still up for debate."

"You're a U.S. Marshal. You change people's lives with your work. I'd be dead right now if not for you. I'm sure dozens of other people would say the same thing."

He tightened his grip on the water bottle as he screwed on the lid. "Think you can walk?"

"I'd like to hear more about your family." Her voice hitched on the word *family*. Was she thinking about his family, or the husband and kids she should already have with the accounting consultant in Chicago?

A twinge of jealousy heated his chest. He ignored it. "There isn't much else to tell. I have two brothers."

She rolled her eyes. "Are you focused again?"

He couldn't help but smile. "Not intentional. I'm thinking about getting us both through the night."

She straightened her back and glanced around. "Any chance they gave up and went home?"

"They've come this far. They won't stop looking."

"You said there's a place we can stay?"

He nodded.

"That the best idea? I mean, shouldn't we get out of here altogether? Maybe call for backup?"

"Afraid we're on our own this time." A warm sensation surged through him when he thought about the implication of being alone with her in the small cabin all night. One bed.

She turned and his gaze drifted down the curve of her back to her sweet bottom. Another time, different circumstances, he could think of dozens of things he'd like to do with her on that bed. This wasn't the time for inappropriate sexual fantasies.

"Why are we on our own?"

"Smith made the call. I agree. Can't risk anyone on

the inside knowing your status or whereabouts in case there's a leak. We have to consider the fact this might be bigger than Charlie."

"How many people in the agency know about me?"

"Now?"

She nodded.

"As far as we know, me and Smith. We'd like to keep it that way."

"Then what are you afraid of?"

"If Grimes found a way in with Charlie, I wonder what other connections he made. We think we're the only two with your intel, but we can't be sure. Your file was with Charlie. Now it's missing. Did he tell anyone else about you before he was killed? We have no clue. There's too much uncertainty."

"I know what they did to me, but what other crimes are they responsible for?"

"Grimes is well-connected. Has his hands in contract killings, loan sharking, gambling, bribery—to name a few. His channels run from South America to Canada, and straight through Chicago."

"Sounds big-time."

"Ever play the game Six Degrees of Separation?" He looked at her.

"Yeah. Sure. Why?"

"He's the Kevin Bacon of crime."

She shifted her weight and looked at him. "Or he was…"

"Until you put him away, which started a war. Now that he's out, we have no idea what to expect."

"Pandora's box?"

"Armageddon."

"Still doesn't explain what he wants with me. Except

good old-fashioned revenge, I guess." Sadie stood and wiped the dried leaves clinging to the back of her jeans.

"He's not exactly a nice guy. He's capable of doing a lot of damage on his own. We can't underestimate him or his connections."

"Lucky me."

Nick closed the water bottles, zipped the pack and shouldered it. The winds had picked up and the air had a cold bite. "We'll catch him. Or the marshals, or the feds will."

"You believe that, don't you?"

"It's my job. The system isn't perfect. Sometimes it fails. I see it succeed ninety-nine percent of the time."

She stared at him incredulously. "You don't need to tell me about the system. I'm living proof it doesn't work."

Nick didn't offer a defense. Sadie was the exception. He inclined his chin and powered forward.

The best thing he could do for her was give her a half-decent night of sleep in a comfortable bed. A hot shower and warm bowl of soup would defrost her and revive her energy.

"You good at what you do?"

"The best."

"Excellent. I wouldn't want to be stuck out here with an amateur." She turned and made kissing noises at Boomer, who dutifully followed.

Nick kept a brisk pace until they reached the small cabin before dark, only stopping long enough to eat a Power Bar for lunch. Sadie followed close behind; the crunch of tree branches under her boots and her labored breathing the only indication that she kept going.

The first thing he did when they got inside was to

fill a bowl of water for her dog. Boomer trotted over as though they'd become best friends. Maybe they had. They had a common bond. Protecting Sadie. Nick scratched the big red dog behind the ears.

"Shower in the bathroom works. Water's warm."

"Sounds like paradise."

"This place isn't much, but it'll get us through the night."

Her gaze moved around the one-room cabin, stopping on the twin bed. "Rustic, but has everything we need. Is it yours?"

"Belongs to a buddy of mine. Keeps it for when he wants to be alone. There's nothing and no one around for miles."

"He knows we're here?"

"Doesn't need to."

"How do you know he won't come walking through that door any minute? Or, worse, in the middle of the night, and scare us to death?"

"He's out of the country right now. We met in the military. He's career." He walked to the bathroom and back, delivering a dark green towel. "He'd look me up if he was on the continent."

"Fair enough."

"This place isn't exactly the Ritz-Carlton, but it serves our purpose for tonight."

She tugged the towel from his hand. Her green eyes sparked with her smile as she studied the gold shag carpeting, a relic from the '70s. "I had no idea the government paid so well. Maybe I should consider enlisting."

"They can be generous."

She glanced from the carpet to Nick. "No one can accuse this place of being boring. That's for sure."

"And we have the added benefit of being completely off the grid."

"Right. I almost forgot. The whole part about trying to keep me tucked away and alive." Her smile faded.

Instead of taking a shower, she sat on the edge of the bed. "So what happens next?"

"You clean up. Then, I'll take a turn." He knew what she was asking. Problem was he didn't have an answer.

"I'm serious."

"You want the honest truth?"

"Yes. Of course."

"I keep you alive tonight. Tomorrow, we'll figure out the rest. Find a good place to tuck you until this mess blows over and we fit all the puzzle pieces together." He ground his back teeth; didn't like this any more than she did, as evidenced by her frown.

"We? Does this mean you're staying with me?"

"I think it's best for now. With any luck, Smith will find Grimes, arrest him again. It'll turn out to be that simple, and you'll get a new home before sunrise."

She released a heavy breath. "I don't want a new home. Just a plain old home. I feel like I've been running so long I can hardly remember who I was before all this started." She stood and walked, pausing at the bathroom door. "I guess it's only been two years."

He could see the anguish darkening her green eyes, the frustration and loss causing her shoulders to sag. "Twenty-four months can feel like an eternity."

"I got too comfortable in Creek Bend. Started to think I might actually build a life there." She closed the door behind her.

Everyone deserved a stable home, a base. Speaking of a life, Nick had almost forgotten about his. His grandmother's birthday party was in a couple of days. He'd been so busy with work he'd forgotten. Not that his sisters would've allowed him to be late. He'd have to ask why they weren't riding him about what present he planned to bring. They generally started a month early. For reasons he couldn't explain, a very big part of him wanted to make sure Sadie spent time with a real family.

Could he take her home with him?

Being with his family definitely qualified as *special.* He just wasn't sure she was ready for the whole clan. Besides, he'd be breaking protocol.

He rubbed the scruff on his chin. No. There had to be another solution. He moved to the kitchenette and emptied his pack. He made two sandwiches and heated soup. They had a few more minutes before the sun completely disappeared. They couldn't risk using electric after dark.

Sadie walked into the kitchenette after her shower. She'd changed into the shorts and T-shirt he'd left in the bathroom. Did her long legs feel as soft and silky as they looked? She stopped so close he could smell her shampoo and notice the freckle on the inside of her thigh. He looked up and his gaze followed a water droplet rolling down her neck and then onto her shirt. Full breasts rose and fell as lust swirled through him, pulsing blood south, which couldn't be more inappropriate.

He forced his gaze away, handing her a cup of heated soup before she could see the effect she was having on him. Stray beads of water anywhere on or near Sadie's body weren't part of this assignment.

He wrapped a peanut butter sandwich in a napkin. "I made sandwiches. It's not much but should keep your stomach from growling."

She accepted the food, looking far more excited about it than he expected. "Good protein. I used to love PB&Js."

"This is just a PB. Hope it works."

She took a bite. The moan she released wasn't his business, either. But it still stirred a feeling. "I'll just grab a quick shower. I already fed your dog. He should be good until morning. Save mine for when I get out."

Boomer was already curled up on the bed.

"Will you leave me your gun?" Her voice rose and shook.

"I thought it scared you."

"It does. To death. Even so, I'd rather be prepared in case I need it."

An emotion that felt a lot like pride swelled in his chest. "Do you know how to use one?"

"I took a class. After…"

He set the weapon on the bed. "Anybody comes through that door, aim and shoot."

Chapter 4

Sadie stared at the gun. Her body trembled. Her hand shook as she held on to her sandwich. Boomer moved to her side. His gaze trained on her. His hackles raised. His sixth sense on high alert.

She didn't have enough saliva to manage a good spit. Every bite of bread and peanut butter was the equivalent of rubbing sandpaper in her mouth. She set down her PB sandwich and picked up her water bottle, taking a sip to ease the dryness in her throat. She picked up her sandwich and took another bite, ignoring her racing heart.

She could do this. She could sit near the gun. She could finish her meal.

Every instinct in her body screamed *run*.

But she'd learned long ago her body and mind couldn't always be trusted. They'd played tricks on her since her ordeal two years ago, making her afraid of little noises and shadows. Since then, it didn't take much to sound off her alert systems and kick her adrenaline into high gear.

Calming breaths generally did the trick to help her relax.

She took a few.

Another bite of sandwich and she'd be fine.

There were times when life called for taking one minute at a time. This minute, she could handle life. She could take another bite.

Another minute passed and she managed to keep it together.

She didn't know if she should thank her judo instructor or hug her yoga coach, but right now she appreciated them both.

A few more minutes ticked by and she heard the water in the shower stop.

Nick didn't take long to towel off.

He came out of the bathroom wearing jeans low on his hips. He tucked the gun in his waistband. The sight of him shirtless sent a warm flush up her neck.

With him in the room, she didn't have to remind herself to take slow breaths anymore. He brought her nerves down by the sight of him, capable and strong.

Her tense muscles relaxed as he moved to the kitchenette and picked up his PB sandwich.

A few freckles and a raised line with deep ridges curved below his left shoulder blade. A scar?

She shivered thinking about the ones she'd collected. "I've been thinking about something. Why didn't they just wait for us at the car? They could've surprised us. Why block the road?"

He shrugged, causing his muscles to stretch and thin,

his movement smooth and pantherlike. "Didn't think we should stick around long enough to find out. I stashed a backup vehicle not far from the site. There was only one way out. They must not've wanted us going anywhere in case we got past them."

Heavy pressure settled on her chest. "So, we're exactly where they want us?"

He took a bite of a sandwich, chewing as he turned. "I wouldn't say that. I doubt they figured we'd have another escape route. This cabin is too out of the way for them to know about. It's the reason we walked all day. I didn't want to be anywhere near where they'd expect us. That being said, we still have to be careful. No lights after dark."

Sadie shifted her position, stretching her sore legs. "I have proof of all the walking, too. Right here in my calves."

"Sorry. A good night's rest will help. A few stretches will do wonders, too."

Night would fall soon and everything would be black. The small space felt intimate. She pushed off the bed and walked into the kitchenette. "You did everything else. Kept us alive. The least I could do was walk to safety."

"We'll have a few more miles of hiking tomorrow. Part two of my backup plan."

"Any chance you have a horse or a four-wheeler stashed out there? I don't think my legs can take another round of Goldilocks tromping through the forest."

The corners of his lips curled. He took the last bite of sandwich. "Boomer here will keep the wolves away. Won't you, buddy?"

Boomer craned his neck and his ears perked up.

"I doubt that." She didn't see the need to explain her dog's deficiencies when it came to being badass.

"I can help with sore calves." Nick placed his hand on the small of her back, urging her to the bed before dropping down on one knee in front of her. He took her calf in his hand, rolling his thumbs along the muscles. An electric current shot up her leg.

She picked up the water bottle and squeezed, praying electricity wouldn't be conducted. The current ran hot enough to singe her fingers. His hands on her leg felt as if they belonged there.

"You know I'm going to find him, right?"

"Then what? Put him away and start the process of relocation all over?"

"Lock him away for good this time."

"And if he gets out again? What then?"

"We'll throw away the key this go-round. I know you don't trust the law. Hell, I can't blame you. But it works most of the time. And when it does, everyone is safer."

"You said this might be more complicated than you originally thought. What does that mean?"

"All we know for sure is that the case involves Grimes and your old handler. We don't know how the two are connected aside from you. Is he out for revenge? Or is it something more?"

"So you think this could be a lot bigger than Charlie and Grimes?"

"Yeah. I do. All I have to go on so far is gut instinct, a dead marshal and an escaped convict. You're the only link I have."

"Sounds like a mess. How on earth did you end up stuck with me?"

* * *

How did Nick explain he'd practically volunteered for the case?

"Smith asked my professional opinion about your case. He needed someone he could trust. He was leaning toward pulling you. I wanted to give you a chance to stay put." Those were the basic facts. All she needed to know. Besides, he couldn't explain to her what he didn't understand. From the moment he'd picked up her file and saw her picture a warning bell had fired and his heart stirred. He hadn't heard that sound or felt that feeling since the first time he saw his high school sweetheart, Rachael.

Hadn't heard it once since her death. Nick figured he was broken now and she'd taken that piece of him with her.

"Where do you even start looking for a man like Grimes? Someone with enough power to get to a U.S. Marshal?"

"He runs a tight operation. No one talks. We never would have convicted him without your testimony."

"At least I won't have to go through another trial. See him again, hear his voice…" Her entire body shuttered.

"No." He didn't want her to relive the experience, either. "His conviction still stands. If anything he's made appeal impossible. I'm sure his lawyers are frustrated. We'll get him and keep him locked up this time."

"You said he moves illegal stuff from South America to Canada. To do that, he must have connections in both. Maybe I'll get lucky and he'll leave the country."

He issued a grunt. "You don't trust me to catch him?"

She laughed. Her smile broke through the worry lines bracketing her mouth. "It's not you."

"Oh, we're going to have *that* conversation. It's *you* and not *me*." His attempt to lighten the mood was met with another smile.

His cell vibrated. He glanced at the screen. A text from Smith.

Deputy Jamison is missing.

Nick pinged back, asking if this was somehow connected to Sadie's case.

Smith responded that he couldn't be sure, but his contact had said he'd been spotted with one of Grimes's men several times in the past couple of weeks.

Nick could feel Sadie watching him as he absorbed the news that a supervisor in the U.S. Marshals Service might be involved in the case. Was Jamison in league with Grimes? With Charlie?

"What is it?"

"A supervisor inside the agency is being investigated." The reality staring at him from his three-by-four-inch screen startled him. Grimes's involvement with the agency could very well move up the chain. Sadie had never been more in danger.

"Whoever is doing this, I screwed with his livelihood. A man like that isn't going to forget, now is he?"

"Not likely."

"Then he'll keep coming at me until I'm dead." It wasn't a question.

"Not if I can get to him first."

"But there's more than just him involved."

He set his cell on the floor, and added pressure to the muscle in her silky calf. "When he was in jail, his business was the most vulnerable. His men were busy keeping rivals from taking over. Now, everything's changed. With him out running free, he can focus on what he wanted to get done. And, yes, his plans most likely involved leaving the country at some point. I'd almost hoped he was going to do that before because it meant he wouldn't be coming after you."

"I'm just unlucky, I guess." She clasped her hands. Subject closed.

He could see fear in her green eyes and it ate at his gut. He shouldn't want to be her comfort.

"I noticed a scar on your back. Mind if I ask how you got it?" She turned the tables.

"A stint in the army."

"Did you serve overseas?"

"One tour in Afghanistan was all it took to figure out military life wasn't for me. I got out when my number came up. Decided to fight the bad guys at home instead."

"We're lucky to have you here."

He cracked a smile, trying to break the tension. "*You* are not lucky."

"That's the understatement of the century." She rolled her eyes and almost smiled. "In a weird way, this is kind of…nice. I'm not used to being able to talk about being in the program. It's hard to hold everything in all the time. Pretend to be someone you're not."

He nodded.

"I kind of like not having to lie to you about my background or who I am. I feel like I'm deceiving nice people all the time. Worse yet, I'm always afraid I'll slip and introduce myself by my real name. I've always been a terrible liar. I walk around feeling like a fraud."

"I can imagine."

She looked straight at him. "What happened to the witness who disappeared? Do you know?"

He hesitated for a second. "We tracked her into Canada. There wasn't much we could do when she crossed the border with her husband and kids. They had dual citizenship, so they didn't come back. Not that it would've done any good. No one can be forced to testify unless they have something to lose."

"What happened? I mean, she was obviously ready to go to trial at one point. What changed her mind?"

He looked at her deadpan. "She heard about what happened to you."

"Can't say I blame her." Sadie's eyes grew wide as she stifled a yawn. "No offense to the U.S. Marshals office."

"None taken. I get to walk away from most cases feeling good about the job I did. Then there are those rare ones like this."

"Thank you."

"For what?"

"Not calling me lucky."

He smiled warmly but didn't say anything.

"I try to be grateful no matter what. But after everything I went through it's hard sometimes," she said.

"I have a superstitious grandma who drilled that whole gratitude bit in my head. I dreamed about catching bad guys when I was little. Hell, who am I kidding? After my father disappeared, I did my level best to become one of them. Life sucked. I wasn't grateful for much of anything."

"Were you angry?"

He nodded.

"Your family help you get through it?"

He nodded again. "Not sure where I'd be without them."

"Sounds like you have a lot to be grateful for."

That much was true. "Remind me of that the next time I want to pull my hair from them driving me nuts."

She laughed and he could feel her relax in his hands. He couldn't touch her much longer without giving away the effect. He needed to think about changing the oil in his car or caulking the tub when he got home. Anything besides the way her milky-soft skin felt pressed against his thumbs and how she flared his instincts to protect her that went way beyond the badge.

"Besides, you can decide for yourself if you like them when you see them."

Chapter 5

Sadie's jaw went slack. "You're taking me to *your* house?"

"Not exactly. We're going to my grandmother's ranch. I grew up there. I've given this a lot of thought and it's the only place I can guarantee your safety."

She shook her head fiercely. "Not a good idea."

Concerned wrinkles bracketed his full lips as he stood, then sat next to her. The mattress dipped under his weight. "Why not?"

"You seem nice. It sounds like you have a terrific family. So, don't take this the wrong way, but I'm not going." She folded her arms and turned her back so he wouldn't see the tears welling in her eyes. No way would she drag sweet, innocent people into her personal hell. Whoever killed Charlie and infiltrated the U.S. Marshals Service wasn't someone to take lightly.

She still had her doubts Charlie would turn on her but she couldn't ignore the evidence.

"I don't plan to give you a choice."

"I won't do it. You can't force me. I know my rights. I can walk out of the program anytime I want." She stood and then folded her arms.

"Talk to me. Tell me why this is a problem. It's my grandmother's birthday. There'll be lots of people around. You'll blend right in."

He came up behind her and brought his hand to rest on her shoulder. Her resolve almost melted under his touch.

She rounded on him, shooting daggers with her eyes. "Well, then, I'm really not going."

"Give me one good reason."

She didn't know how to be around a real family, that's why. "Because I don't want to go. I'd rather hide somewhere on my own while you do your family stuff. Maybe it's best if I strike out on my own, anyway. Especially if the Marshals Service has been compromised."

"You leave this program and you won't live an hour. I'm trying to do what's best for you."

His words nearly released the flood of tears threatening. He was right. She wasn't ready to relent. "Without including me in the decisions?"

"Of course you have a say. We can talk about options. I care about what you think, Sadie."

She rubbed her arms. Crying wouldn't change her mind. "It wouldn't be fair to put innocent people at risk because of me. That's why I don't think I should go to your family's place."

"All of my sisters and brothers work in law enforcement. You don't have to worry about them. They know how to handle themselves."

"Then I'm sure your wife has other plans for your family holiday than to hide me." Why did the word *wife* sit on her tongue so bitterly?

"I'm not married. And once you get there, you might change your mind about calling my brothers and sisters innocent." His steel voice warmed her as a wry grin settled over his dark features.

Being this close, she could see the depths of his brown eyes. The cinnamon copperlike flecks sparkled. He was attractive and fired off all her warning systems by being this close.

Her fight, flight or freeze response kicked in, escalating her pulse.

She didn't like danger. Danger caused her chest to squeeze. Danger had her waking up in the hospital in the ICU, and then on the run from everything familiar.

She focused on Boomer, who had moved to her side, and scratched him behind the ear.

Besides, she felt a little too relieved hearing the news Nick wasn't married. A man like him had to have someone waiting at home. If not a wife, then a girlfriend. Sadie needed to remind herself of that fact because when his dark gaze settled on her, places warmed that had been cold and neglected far too long. This close, he was almost too attractive. Nick was one seriously hot package. Why was she surprised by this admission?

Hadn't she been a little bit interested in him before?

An attraction now couldn't be more inappropriate. Her mind was grasping for a distraction, she reasoned, not wanting to admit Nick's true effect on her—her body.

She held up her hand, palm out. "I'm not agreeing

to anything. But if I do decide to go to the ranch, what will you tell your family about me?"

"My first thought is to tell them we're a couple."

"And they'd believe you? Just like that? I thought you guys were close."

"We are. Which is why that wouldn't work. They'd see right through it. Besides, I've never lied to my family and I have no plans to start now. Momentary lapse in judgment on my part."

The suggestion of her and Nick being a couple should repulse her. The thought of most men touching her sent her straight to nausea. Not him. What had changed?

Nick.

He was strong and capable and gorgeous. She also felt as though he was the first person who had her back in a very long time. Charlie had done a good job. But she had been part of his work, his job, no more or less. With Nick, it felt personal.

But could she trust him?

There were too many sleepless nights under her belt to convince her to let her guard down. The few private judo lessons she'd taken had helped ease the nightmares. She'd even convinced herself to keep a gun in the house, although the sight still made her chest hurt and the air become thick around her. There was something about having the wrong end of one pressed to her forehead that made her heart race every time she saw a sleek metal barrel. She couldn't even watch those popular cop shows on television.

Had she gotten comfortable recently? Become sloppy?

There was a good reason. Creek Bend had started to feel like home. She had a new life and a dog for company. There were even nosy neighbors to round out her small-town experience. She'd settled into a rustic cabin near the lake that, against all evidence to the contrary when she'd first arrived, had become her safe haven. She loved her job at the bakery, even the zany hours. And some day, maybe, she'd learn to trust men again.

Nick the radiologist had rented the lake house adjacent to hers, and had made a habit of coming by the bakery in the mornings as soon as it opened and her shift ended. She could hardly fathom the muscled man sharing the cabin was the same Nick. Then again, it was his job to go unnoticed when it served him best. So, why did she feel betrayed?

She hated all the lying. Could she continue this facade of a life? Lie to Nick's family? Deceive more people? "Can't we just be straight with them?"

"If I could tell them the truth, I would. I need to think about it first. They're law enforcement and Smith gave me strict orders not to risk exposing you."

"I already told you I'm a bad liar."

"The past couple of years have trained you better than you think. The whole time I watched you in Creek Bend, you didn't give yourself away. If I hadn't known in advance, I wouldn't have figured it out."

"My life depended on hiding my secret." She blew out a breath and then inhaled. The warmth of his body standing so close and the scent of citrus soap washed over her in a mix that was all virile and male. "Besides, I don't know if I could pull off pretending to be someone's girlfriend if I had to."

"Why not?" He seemed offended.

"I know you're here to help, but strange men still scare me."

"Maybe we should change that." He placed his hand behind her neck, leaned forward and pressed a kiss to her lips that made her body hum.

He pulled back first, leaving Sadie swirling with an emotion that felt an awful lot like need.

"We're not strangers anymore." He stretched out on the bed, clasped his hands behind his head and looked up at the ceiling. "We have all night to get to know each other better. Let the talking begin."

"What do you want to know first?" Nick had to repress the anger rising, burning a hole in his chest. He'd felt Sadie tremble when he'd touched her. His offer of comfort had had the opposite effect on her. Yet, it was something else that sizzled when they kissed.

When he'd put his hands on her calves, he'd felt her relax. He'd even felt a spark of something else. But he'd been on the floor in a less threatening position. When he sat beside her or stood next to her, he seemed to overwhelm her.

"Where'd you grow up?"

"Texas. In a small town outside Dallas on the ranch." He'd been grasping at straws when he offered to pretend she was his girlfriend. When he really thought about it, he'd never be able to convince his sisters she was his girlfriend. Not with his history. It was a desperate thought. His family would be very keen to figure out how Sadie had done what no other woman in seven years could. Make Nick fall in love again. He wouldn't bring a casual fling to the ranch.

"Did you have a lot of friends?"

"I had a lot of family. Not much time for anything else."

"Tell me about your brothers and sisters."

"You already know I have two brothers, Luke and Reed. My sisters' names are Meg and Lucy."

Sadie eased onto the edge of the bed. "And you're the oldest?"

"Correct. But that doesn't mean they listen to me." He chuckled. "I'm afraid they all have strong wills and minds of their own."

"And everyone works in law enforcement?"

"True. I guess we all felt the call to serve. Luke's FBI and Reed's Border Patrol."

"What about the girls?"

"Lucy works for the sheriff's office and Meg is a police officer in Plano. She's married to Riley and he works for the department, too."

"I take it they met through work."

He nodded. "You guessed right."

"What else should I know about you?"

"I can't think of much else." He'd always been there for his family, his mom. His other relationships were a bit more complex. After watching his mother's pain, seeing how much agony someone could go through when the one they loved walked out on them, a piece of Nick had closed off early on in life.

"What do you do when you're not working?"

"The usual guy stuff. Watch the Cowboys in football season. I like to work a good steak on the grill."

"Steak sounds like heaven about now." Her smile was the nearest thing to heaven he figured he'd get in this lifetime.

"I can't argue with that logic."

"What about school?" She turned on her side, facing him, and propped herself up on one elbow.

His eyes had adjusted to the dark and he could see her green eyes clearly. "Finished it as fast as I could and joined the military. I was the oldest, so I guess I felt the most responsibility for filling my dad's shoes. I tried to ease the financial burden for my mom best as I could. We were broke but we stuck together."

"Sounds like you made the best of a bad situation."

"We banded together. We joke around a lot, tease each other, but we're a close bunch. Mess with one of us, and you mess with us all."

She lay back and stretched out, absently running her finger along the top of the comforter. "Sounds like you gave each other a soft landing. What about the rest of your family? Did any of your brothers or sisters serve in the military?"

"Luke served before joining the FBI. War changed him. He lost his whole unit. Came back a mess. Ended up divorcing his wife. He doesn't talk about it much, but I know he hasn't gotten over it. He stopped our youngest brother from even thinking about enlisting."

"I'm so sorry. Sounds like you guys have had to overcome a lot."

"Doesn't everyone?"

She nodded solemnly. Her beautiful green eyes filled with sympathy.

His fingers itched to reach up and touch her face. To move her lips closer to his. To taste her sweetness…

He stopped himself right there.

His thoughts needed to stay clear to keep them both alive. He sighed harshly.

She had brought up an excellent point earlier. His family would see through a lie. They deserved to know the truth so they could understand the risks. He would have to be up-front with them. "On second thought, taking you home with me is riskier if I'm not honest with them."

"You mentioned your boss earlier. Didn't he tell you not to trust anyone?"

"No choice. Besides, they're law enforcement. They'll understand. Maybe even chip in their advice. The more minds we have on this, the better. Plus, they'll be able to keep you safe while I disappear to chase any leads we get on the case. The ranch is our best bet."

"Sounds like the best way to go."

Boomer faced the door and growled his low-belly growl. His hackles stood on end.

Nick jumped to his feet. He palmed his weapon and pressed his index finger to his lips.

Crouching low, he covered the distance to the door in a few strides. Anyone came in, they'd regret it. He turned and motioned for Sadie to follow.

She was already on the ground, comforting the dog. Good. Last thing Nick needed was for the men outside to hear barking. Someone had found them. Could be Grimes's men. Now the trick would be slipping out alive. It was dusk. He'd hoped to give Sadie a chance to rest. No luck. She'd have to make do on what she'd gotten so far.

Another thought crossed his mind. They'd have to leave what little supplies he'd brought with him. He shouldered his backpack. At least there was water inside.

The door handle jiggled.

He braced himself, waiting for the bang against the door or the cheap wood to splinter. Whoever was out there wouldn't wait long.

He glanced at Sadie. She sat there, fear and desperation in her eyes. Something inside him snapped.

"C'mon," he whispered, urging her to stay low and move toward him.

The sound of footsteps on the porch made his stomach muscles tighten.

"The door's locked. Want me to break it down?" A muffled voice came through the door. There had to be at least two guys out there, maybe more.

Boomer was quiet for now, but his ears were laid back and his body stiff. A low growl rose from his belly. He'd bark any second.

Nick ducked and rolled, keeping his profile low. "We have to go. I know you're scared. I won't let anything happen to you. Stick close by me." He pressed a reassuring kiss to the top of her head. "Don't think about them. Focus on me."

Nick's reassurance unleashed a flood of butterflies in Sadie's chest, and she breathed a notch below panic.

The voice outside was familiar. "I know him."

"Is it one of Grimes's men?"

"Y-y-yes." Her throat tried to close from panic. She refused to buckle and let them freak her out.

"I'm here. Nothing's going to hurt you this time." He slipped on his T-shirt and work boots, the motion pulled taut skin over thick ridges of pure hard muscle. His movements were fluid, almost graceful, as he found his way back to her and wound their fingers together.

Boomer growled his low-belly growl again. The rapid-fire barks bubbled just below the surface.

Nick's gaze moved from her dog to her. "You think he'll keep calm?"

"As long as my hand is on his back, he knows not to bark." At least she prayed he would. It had worked in training, but this was real-world. And nothing about this situation could be simulated in training mode. Besides, he wasn't some German shepherd or pit bull ready to lock jaws on an intruder the second they showed their face. This was Boomer, her sweet dog who was meant to be her companion.

"Then keep it there." Nick slid her boots on for her.

"It's okay, boy." She hated that her hand trembled on Boomer's back. Hated how helpless she'd felt when they'd abducted her the first time.

Not again.

Not now.

Not like this.

She was stronger now.

Besides, she had two very important assets this time that she didn't have the first go round… Boomer and Nick.

He released her other hand and moved stealthily along the windows, his weapon drawn, checking each one for sounds outside.

"I'm not sure how many others there are to contend with. We know there are at least two," he whispered.

"How did they find us?"

"That's the question of the day."

These guys were good. They knew how to track the movements of a U.S. Marshal. That couldn't be a good sign.

A foreboding feeling came over Sadie, eating away at her insides.

Grimes was important, smart…but this savvy?

He was also devious, and that scared her almost as much.

She watched as a shadow moved around the room. Thankfully, her eyes had adjusted to the dark a long time ago so she could see clearly.

A blast shattered the window near the bed, sending shards of glass splintering in all directions.

Chapter 6

The plywood door blasted open, smacking against the wall. An imposing man burst through. The tall, burly figure aimed a gun at Sadie.

Boomer fired rapid barks, holding his ground in a low stance between her and the intruder.

Sadie scanned the room for Nick, didn't see him.

The crunch of glass breaking sounded from behind. She spun around. A male figure framed the window, sealing the other exit. He had streaks of blond in his long hair and the build of an athlete on steroids. There was no place to run or hide.

Boomer surged, his collar slipped through Sadie's fingers. He lunged at the man coming from behind, startling him enough to back him off. The reprieve would be short-lived and Sadie knew it.

Nick lunged from a corner. He disarmed the burly

man breeching the door. Burly head-butted Nick, causing him to spit blood. A savage look narrowed Nick's dark eyes as he shoved Burly's face against the wall and twisted his arm behind his back. "I'm Marshal Campbell. And you're under arrest."

Burly twisted free at the same time a shot fired from the window area.

Sadie's heart lurched.

Had the bullet hit Boomer? Nick? Her?

Relief flooded her when she saw a red dot flowering on Burly's shoulder. The bullet meant for Nick had been a few inches wide. Boomer launched another attack toward the window. Steroids ducked.

Nick's gun lay on the floor in between her and Steroids. Could she dive for it in time before he popped up again and got off another round?

She tried to move but her limbs froze. Doubting herself for even a second gave Steroids the opportunity to fire another round. She resolved not to let that happen again. Her body had to move, fear or not.

The second bullet lodged in the bricks near Burly's head. He grunted and dropped to his knees. If Steroids had a second longer to aim, Nick would be dead. He cuffed Burly's hands behind his back.

In one swift motion, Nick dove and rolled, coming up with his gun and firing a round before Steroids could pull the trigger again. Nick's body was a shield between Sadie and the gunman. Nick took aim. Steroids disappeared under the window frame. Nick fired a warning shot and then motioned for Sadie to run.

She bolted toward the door.

Burly had managed to maneuver his hands in front of his body. He grabbed her foot before she reached outside. She twirled and kicked, but his grip was too strong to break away from by herself.

Boomer's shackles raised and he stalked toward Burly, barking wildly and focused on his target. He bit, clamping his jaws on Burly's forearm.

He grunted. "Get that mutt off me or I'll choke him."

Sadie pivoted. Burly released her boot and clasped Boomer's throat. His yelp cut through her.

Her shrill scream split the air.

She gripped the doorjamb with both hands and thrust her boot at Burly's face. The pointed tip connected with his jaw. A satisfying crunch, then blood spurted from his mouth.

Pivoting right, she stomped her foot on his face, her heel connecting with his nose. More blood spouted.

He grunted, "You bitch!"

Dismissing the nausea and pounding in her temples—the mother of all headaches raging at her heels—she stomped her foot another time.

Burly groaned and loosened his grip enough for Boomer to escape.

Sadie hopped out of reach, glancing back in time to see Nick firing his weapon. No doubt he was trying to keep Steroids from shooting again while she got away. She hesitated on the steps but Nick was already behind her, urging her toward the woods.

She made kissing noises at Boomer and he broke into a run beside her. Thank God he listened. Thank God he wasn't hurt. Thank God neither were they.

Running in boots cramped her feet and rubbed her blisters raw, but protected her legs from being cut by underbrush.

Boomer easily matched her stride, sticking beside her as Nick set a blistering pace.

They ran until her thighs burned and her lungs screamed for air.

Nick halted at the sound of crunching branches in front of them. He pressed his index fingers to his lips and scanned the woods. More broken stick noises came from behind. Rapidly. Push forward and they'd run into whoever was there. Going back wasn't an option, either.

"What do we do?" Sadie whispered.

"Follow me. We'll find a hiding spot and wait them out." Nick led them across a shallow five-foot-wide creek.

The sun had gone down, and the moon lit the evening sky filled with a thousand stars. A chilling breeze blew. There'd been no time to put on more clothing and the cold pierced through her T-shirt. Her teeth chattered.

"Wish I'd had time to bring something to keep you warm. I didn't have a chance to grab my jacket," he whispered, leading them farther east.

The memory of his smell mixed with leather assaulted her senses.

Another noise sounded ahead. More tree branches crunching under the weight of someone or something sizable. More people?

Nick stopped, listened. He looked as though he needed a minute to get his bearings. "This way."

She followed him as he zigzagged through the trees, branches slapping her in the face.

Faint voices grew louder. For all she knew they were running in circles. In the dark, it would be impossible for Nick to know which way they headed.

He stopped running and she took a moment to catch her breath.

The voices grew louder.

Nick searched around for something. But what? Where could they hide? At this rate, they might walk into a trap set by the men chasing them.

He stopped twenty feet away and waved her over.

"This ditch should hide us. Jump in," he whispered.

Boomer led the way into the four-foot-by-five-foot hole. Sadie hopped down and crouched low.

Nick disappeared, returning a moment later dragging several large tree branches. He used them to cover the opening. "This should buy us some time."

"Any chance you have matches or a lighter in that backpack to make a fire later?" Sadie gripped her cold knees, her chest heaving. She rubbed her hands together and blew on her fingers to bring the blood flow back. At this rate, she'd have frostbite before the sun came up again. Her eyes were adjusting to the blackness and she could see the outline of Nick's face.

Boomer's panting slowed as she stroked his back.

The only other sounds came from the men closing in on them and the insects surrounding them.

The sound of footsteps came closer.

The three of them stilled. Sadie kept her hand on Boomer's back to calm him.

One of the men muttered a curse. "When I find that bitch who kicked me, I'll kill her with my bare hands."

Burly? Hadn't he been shot? Must not have been enough of a wound to stop him. Should slow him down, though. Even if he found them, maybe she could out-run him?

Another man, most likely Steroids, made a shushing sound.

Their footsteps came closer.

Sadie's pulse raced. She bit her lip to keep from panicking. If Boomer so much as growled, he'd give away their position.

She squeezed her eyes shut, willing her teeth to stop chattering and him to stay quiet. Her hand didn't move from his back.

Nick's hand closed on her shoulder, radiating warmth and confidence she didn't own.

"Keep moving. They have to stop somewhere. When they do, we'll get 'em," Steroids said, disdain deepening his tone. He spit again. She presumed more blood.

A full minute of silence passed before Sadie exhaled the breath she'd been holding. Washed-out, weepy and running through a whole host of other emotions, she leaned back against the cold hard dirt, wishing for safety, a cup of hot tea and a warm bed.

"Here. Squeeze closer. You'll lose all your heat through the ground." He scooted behind her and pulled her onto his lap.

His powerful thighs pressed to the backs of hers, sending sensual shivers rippling through her. A powerful urge to melt into him and allow his body heat to keep her from freezing surged through her.

Or was it something more she craved?

His body pressed to hers reminded her just how long it had been since she'd been with a man. Arousal flushed her cheeks. She was relieved he couldn't see her face. Her physical response couldn't be any more inappropriate under the circumstances.

His arms encircled her waist. Impulses shot through

her. She pressed her back against his virile, muscular chest and all she could hear was a whoosh sound in her ears.

Boomer put his head on her leg. "You've been a good boy today," she said.

"He's special." Nick's words came out low and thick.

Sadie tried to focus on Boomer to distract herself from the sexual current rippling up her arms, her neck. On Nick's lap, she could feel his warm breath in her hair and it spread like wildfire down her back. Heat moved through her body, pooling between her thighs.

Sadie shifted in Nick's lap, her sweet bottom pressed against his crotch, and his tightly held control faltered. Why did he already have to remind himself this wasn't the time for rogue hormones?

Hell. It was as if he didn't already know that. He was a grown man, not a horny teenager who got an erection every time he was close enough to smell a girl's perfume. Sadie's hair hinted of flowers and citrus. He needed to ask Walter why he had flowery shampoo at his man retreat.

First, he needed to get a message to his buddy about the cabin.

Nick made a mental note to circle back to this subject when he had Sadie tucked away somewhere safe. He liked the idea of taking her to the ranch even more when he thought about how much reinforcement he'd have there. Between his siblings, someone could keep watch 24/7.

She shivered and he instinctively tightened his arms around her. He expected her to move away from him, but she didn't. Instead, she burrowed her back deeper against him. He didn't want to get inside his head about why that put a ridiculous smile on his face.

The last thing he wanted to think about was how two thin strips of cotton kept them from being skin-to-bare-naked-skin. At least her teeth had stopped chattering. He didn't care whether or not he was warm. He'd survive a few nights of cold. She wouldn't. Not in those cotton shorts he'd given her to sleep in.

He could see through the tops of the branches. The winds had picked up and the temperature had dropped a good ten degrees in the past fifteen minutes. The sky was blue-black. Exactly the way it looked when a cold front blew in.

They needed shelter and food. Neither of which were in his possession. Nor were the means to get any anytime soon.

Sadie shifted position, her curvy bottom grinding against him. He half expected her to push him away, but she didn't. Instead, her hands squeezed in between his. Her fingers were near frozen. He rubbed his hands over hers, warming them.

"Thank you. That's better already," she whispered.

She wouldn't thank him if she knew he mustered all the control he could to sit there with her and not slip his hands inside her shirt and caress those pert breasts the way his fingers itched to do. Needed to do? She wouldn't thank him if she knew how unholy his thoughts were about those taut hips. And she sure as hell wouldn't thank him if she knew how badly he wanted to spin her around in his lap and do things to her to remind her she was all woman and he was every bit a man.

He needed to redirect his thoughts. What other home projects needed addressing when he got back to the apartment? Wasn't there a small leak under the kitchen sink that needed attending to when he'd been called away last-minute for duty?

He was sure there were about a dozen other projects around the house that needed fixing, as well. And yet, his thoughts kept wandering back to how good Sadie felt in his arms. How he'd remember the scent of her— citrus and cleanliness—that was all hers long after this assignment was over. Didn't take a rocket scientist to see she affected him. He just hoped she wasn't offended by the growing erection he couldn't contain. She had to have felt it. Because blood pulsed south every time she moved, and so did his ability to think rationally.

He dismissed it as going too long without sex.

He'd fix that when this assignment was over. He'd have sex with the first beautiful and willing woman he could find. Hadn't there been a few? No woman from his past could erase the naked image of Sadie from his mind; the one where her legs were wrapped around his waist and he was buried inside her.

"Better now?" he practically grunted.

"Much. I can feel my fingers again."

The sweet purr in her voice had him wanting to stay exactly where he was. But he couldn't be sure they'd be alone for much longer. He couldn't risk sticking around. "We'd better head out. I slowed those two down, but there could be more."

"One of them was bleeding. He was shot in the shoulder. Won't he need to go to the hospital?"

"Depends on how deep the wound is and how prepared they are. His injury might slow him down or buy us a few hours. Unless they sent more than two men. We don't know how big the team is. Either way, they located us at the cabin, and that's bad. We're on foot and it's getting cold out. We have limited supplies. They'll expect us to camp nearby, which is why we have to keep moving. I disabled GPS on our phones for obvious reasons, so we need to keep moving until I see something familiar. If I can give our location to someone back home, they'll come pick us up."

"Okay."

She made a move to get up and it took a minute for him to send the message to his arms that he had to let go. She felt a little too right snuggled against his chest.

No woman, not since Rachael, had felt more right inside his arms.

Chapter 7

Sadie and Nick walked for hours before his brother messaged that he was close. Headlights were a welcome sight to her after walking in the cold black night in her boots.

Nick squeezed her hand. "I'll have you in a warm bed in two hours." He cleared his throat, seeming to catch how the last part sounded. "What I mean is—"

"It's okay," she said on a half laugh. "I know you didn't intend to say it like that." Remembering his powerful thighs and chest against her body had her thinking she might not mind waking up snuggled against a strong, warm body like his. Those brown eyes with cinnamon flecks and hair blacker than night made for a package most women would consider beyond hot. Sadie wouldn't argue.

That she was crushing on her handler also reminded her how ridiculous she was being.

When was the last time she'd allowed herself to notice a man? Or relax at all. There was no laughter in her life. No humor. No friends. No sex. Okay, where'd that last bit come from?

It was true, though. There hadn't been any sex in far too long. And nothing was funny anymore. She missed the simple pleasures of feeling warm skin against her back when she slept, or laughing at an inside joke.

If she was being brutally honest, she couldn't remember the last time she really laughed at anything. She could blame her hollow existence on this whole ordeal. Was that accurate?

Sure she'd had to lie and keep people at a safe distance in the past two years. What about before then? Her boyfriend, Tom, had wanted to get engaged. Start a family. And yet she'd kept putting off the conversation. Her skin had itched and the air had become thick at the thought of making the two of them more permanent. She'd had to abandon the notion before she could really consider it.

In the past two years, she could've been almost anyone or anything she wanted. What had she chosen?

A baker.

Someone who works in the middle of the night when everyone else slept.

Did a little part of her shrink at the idea of becoming close to anyone because of the pain of rejection she still felt with her aunt?

And yet with Nick, everything was different. She didn't have to lie. She didn't have to pretend she was someone else. She didn't have to fake a relationship. He was her new handler. It was his job to keep her safe. He was proving capable of the task. So much so, that she was starting to feel more like herself than she had in months.

But was letting her guard down a good thing?

Before she could get inside her head about what that meant, a dual cab pickup truck pulled up.

Nick braided their fingers. A slow smile spread across his almost too perfect lips. "Our salvation has arrived."

The passenger's-side window rolled down, revealing an attractive man in the driver's seat. Right away she could see the two were related. The driver had the same sturdy, muscular build. He was similar in size to Nick. He had the same nose and smile. Other than that, his hair was lighter and he had dimples when he smiled.

"This is my little brother Luke." He introduced the two, motioning toward the cab as he let go of her hand to open the door for her.

"Little?" Luke scoffed. He flashed perfectly straight, white teeth. "I'm second-youngest. And way better looking than this guy."

"Keep believing it, and maybe it'll be true someday," Nick grunted. "You're as modest as ever, I see."

"Beautiful dog," Luke said, as Nick coaxed Boomer into the backseat.

"Thanks," Sadie said. "He's been pretty brave today."

Nick pulled himself inside the warm cab after her. She was so cold she couldn't stop shivering.

"I can see my brother didn't prepare well enough for this trip. You're an icicle. What are you trying to do, freeze your witness into testifying?" He cranked up the heat and pulled a blanket from the backseat, spreading it across Sadie's lap for her. "This should help. Or you could scoot a little closer and I could put my arm around you. You know, body heat and all." Another show of perfect white teeth greeted her. Luke seemed to be greatly enjoying teasing his brother.

"She'll warm up fine without your paws on her," Nick said quickly, folding his arms.

"This is fantastic." Sadie pulled the blanket to her chin and leaned toward the vent. "Thank you."

"Where we headed?" Luke put the gearshift in Drive and handed a steaming foam cup to Sadie. "I brought hot chocolate for you."

"You've got to be kidding me. This is heaven." She gripped the drink with both hands and took a sip.

"Take us to the ranch," Nick said.

Luke cocked a dark brow, looking as though he needed a minute to rationalize the location before he spoke. "Darlin', do you want the radio on while I talk to my crazy brother?"

"No. I'm fine," she said. Besides, she wanted to see if sparks were about to fly.

"You just let me know if there's *anything* I can do for you, you hear?"

Sadie was certain she blushed. Good looks and charm must seriously run in this family. "I will."

"You didn't tell me the package I needed to pick up was this beautiful." Luke chewed on the piece of gum in his mouth.

Being so close to him, Sadie could smell the cinnamon.

Nick made a disgusted noise from his throat. "Don't you have a girlfriend somewhere?"

Luke didn't immediately speak. What flashed in his eyes? Hurt? Anger?

An expression crossed Nick's features that Sadie couldn't quite put her finger on. Was it regret? Did Nick wish he could take those words back?

She braced herself for more bantering. Instead, Luke's smile morphed to a serious expression, and he gripped the steering wheel tighter. "Nope. You're looking at a free man."

"Lucky for single women everywhere," Nick said, easing the tension.

She made a mental note to ask about that later.

"Aren't you on a case?" Nick glanced at Sadie when he said, "Luke works for the FBI."

"Coffee's for you, by the way." Luke held out a cup toward his brother.

Nick took it and held the cup to his lips for a few seconds before he took a sip. "Thanks, man."

"No problem. I'm around until after Gran's birthday. Do I need to be checking the rearview or did you ditch the son of a bitch who redecorated your face?" All the charm in his features returned full force.

"Just a couple of bumps and bruises. Nothing permanent, like a bullet hole. I think we walked far enough out of the way. No one should be able to track us."

Sadie leaned into Nick for warmth.

Luke's expression turned serious again, all cute playboy disappeared, when he asked, "What are we dealing with here exactly? I take it she's one of yours in the program."

Nick nodded. "Except she wasn't mine before. I inherited her when her handler was killed."

"And this guy being killed put her at risk?"

"She was relocated two years ago after testifying against Malcolm Grimes and assigned to a marshal by the name of Charlie."

Luke clenched his jaw muscle. "*The* Malcolm Grimes? One of the biggest crime figures in Chicago?"

"The very one."

"I read about that case, but I don't remember you being involved in that one."

"I wasn't," Nick said, taking another sip of coffee. He leaned his head back and closed his eyes for a moment. "That's good. Really good."

"Isn't that case old news?"

"It was until Grimes broke out of jail and her handler was found murdered."

"That's not good. Sounds like a mess. And an inside job. Does everyone at the U.S. Marshals Service check out?"

"Nope. This case has a stench so strong even my boss wants away from it just in case our channels of communication are dirty," Nick said. "A supervisor who was spotted with Grimes's men has now gone missing."

"Damn. Okay, so she testified and put the bad guy away. Why come after her now? They have to know the agency would be watching."

"You'd think. My predecessor relocated her after the trial twice, the last of which was to a small town where she should've been able to live out her life in peace."

"Until her man breaks out of jail and comes after her with reinforcements."

"Exactly," Nick agreed. "Possibly with her handler's help. And, worst-case, a supervisor's."

"That stinks to high heaven."

"Don't I know."

"And you think you can help her if…" Luke let his sentence die. He was silent for a minute, chewing on more than his gum. "Even so, taking her to the ranch?"

"I know what you're about to say."

"Then you know you can't break protocol. Not even to keep her safe. And you also know I mean this in the best possible way. God knows I invented doing things on my terms. But stashing her with us? Not a good idea." Luke turned to Sadie and said, "No offense."

"None taken. I agree with you," she said.

"True," Nick interjected. "Here's the thing. Everywhere I take her, these guys show up. They're barely a half step behind. The man power they have is staggering. I thought about staying on the run. And I can. But what do I do when I need to investigate a lead? Leave her exposed, alone in a hotel room? I don't have backup on this. And these guys are one step behind me out in the open like this."

"From the looks of your face, they've been catching you, too."

Nick pressed the heel of his right hand to his forehead. "It's been a problem."

"What about your boss?"

"He told me to go on Graco protocol, which basically means do whatever it takes as long as it's legal."

"I can see your problem. No one in the agency knows about the ranch."

"I've thought about every other possibility. The ranch is the only place I can keep her safe while I find Grimes. I can't leave her vulnerable in some random motel. I need backup I can trust, which means no one from my agency. I'm counting on you guys. I need everyone's help on this."

Luke didn't hesitate. "You know I have your back. I have a hot case but you have every other minute of my time."

"Chasing corporate spies again?"

"Nah. I got a serial killer on the loose in The Metroplex."

"The one in the media? Ravishing Rob?"

Luke rocked his head. "He's my guy."

"I appreciate your offer of help, little bro. I'll get back to you on that. Let's get through the next few days, and we'll see where we're at after Gran's party. You've got an important case of your own to work on."

"Nothing's too important for family. Besides, I'm a half hour outside The Metroplex on the ranch."

"Don't you mean forty minutes?"

"Not the way I drive."

The two bumped fists. Sadie's heart filled with warmth at the obvious affection these brothers had for each other. Their love came through even when they teased each other. And they were taking care of her, too. Not even Tom did that and she'd almost married him. Heck, when she'd caught a cold that turned into pneumonia, she'd asked if he could pick up her medication from the pharmacy and bring soup. He didn't show up for hours. When he finally came through the door, she was exhausted and in tears.

He'd asked what was wrong.

She'd said she was starving and had waited for him.

He'd given her a shocked look and had said, "You know I always play poker with the boys on Thursdays."

Where her relationship with Tom lacked in spark, he made up for in dependability—and he could be depended on as long as she didn't ask him to upset his normal routine. She'd also learned that depending on others was the fastest way to get her heart broken.

Sadie didn't let herself go there about how nice it would be to have a family supporting her. At least she had Boomer.

"You know I appreciate it," Nick said.

Luke glanced at Sadie. "Sounds like a mess. But don't worry, darlin'. I'll do what this guy can't. Keep you safe."

"I'd be dead already if it weren't for him." She wasn't sure why she felt the need to defend him against his brother's teasing. Or why her heart squeezed when Nick smiled his response.

Luke cocked an eyebrow. His gaze shifted from Sadie to Nick and back. He placed his wrist on top of the steering wheel and drove.

Sadie leaned her head back.

She woke with a start, and realized she was still in the pickup.

"Sorry about the bumps. Need to fill the potholes. Gran ran out of gravel, so more's on the way," Luke said.

Nick's eyes opened, and his hand came up to his forehead. Using the heels of his hands, he pressed against his eyelids. "Means we're home."

"I must've fallen asleep." She stretched and yawned. "It's been a long night."

She couldn't see much except for shrubs lining the winding path. "I'll be okay. Just need a boost of caffeine and then we can talk through our next steps."

"Your immediate future holds a hot shower and warm bed."

And leave her out of the important stuff? No way.

"You have to let me help. It's my life we're talking about here."

Nick started to protest, but she cut him off. "Look. I listened to the Marshals Service before and, with all due respect, I'm on the run again with no home and men chasing me with guns. I deserve to be included in any plans that involve me and my life. Clear?"

Nick emphatically shook his head.

Luke parked the truck and deadpanned his brother. "The lady has a point."

"Damn right," she said, grateful for the support. "And if you don't let me be part of the solution, then I'm out of here first thing in the morning. I'll figure out my own way. I can hide. I've gotten pretty good at it." She wasn't stupid enough to follow through on the threat. Her options were nil. She had no other leverage.

"Not a good idea. Promise me you won't disappear on me," Nick said. The worry in his tone almost shredded her resolve.

She had to be strong. Depend on him and she might as well roll up the tent because as soon as this assignment was over, he'd be gone. And she'd be left to pick up the pieces of her life again. Alone.

She glanced at Boomer.

Not completely alone. At least she had man's best friend as comfort. He'd shown himself to be not only a dedicated companion but a force to be taken seriously, as well. No more Scooby Doo nickname for this guy. His new moniker would be Cujo.

She folded her arms. "Fine. I'll agree to let you know when I decide to leave. And you owe me a promise, too."

"I'll include you. But you need to remember I'm the professional here. This is my job. I do this for a living and I'm trained. Not to mention I'm damn good at what I do."

"I've seen that already," she said. Then felt the need to point out, "We're alive but someone seems to anticipate our every move."

His downturned lips at the corners of his mouth told her everything she needed to know about how much she'd just insulted him. She wasn't trying to get into a fight. She wanted to be dead clear about her intention to be involved in her own future. She'd relied on the U.S. Marshals Service to keep her alive for the past two years. In that time, she'd also picked up a few survival tricks on her own. She wasn't as naive as when she'd first joined the program, wide-eyed, believing every word that came out of Charlie's and his supervisor's mouths.

Charlie.

Her heart still hurt at the thought he was killed most likely because of his involvement with her. If a criminal was powerful enough to get to a U.S. Marshal, what chance did she have? Even with Nick watching her back, there weren't any guarantees. He'd done an excellent job of keeping them safe so far, but the government wouldn't pay him to stay by her side 24/7. Surely he had other cases to work on.

Even if he was dedicated to her, how long before Grimes caught them? His men seemed to be one step behind so far, which blew her mind. Plus, life had already taught her that depending on others brought nothing but heartache.

"I understand you think my agency let you down. But from where I sit, they've also been the one thing that kept you alive."

"I won't argue that. I have a feeling if they'd sent any other deputy, I'd be dead right now and not here in this truck."

He ground his back teeth. Didn't argue.

Sadie knew she was right. "So, you won't mind if I take more of an interest in where I go and what I do next."

"What I say goes." Nick palmed the empty coffee cup. "You don't do anything to get yourself killed."

"I'll agree to consider your opinion but from now on I make decisions for myself. Whether you like it or not."

Nick crunched the cup in his hand.

She made kissing noises at Boomer and he lumbered out of the backseat. "I don't see the problem with sharing information with me."

"Can't tell you what I don't know." Was it frustration deepening his pitch?

He had a point. Admitting he had no idea where Grimes might strike next seemed to darken his bad mood. Everything was uncertain in her life. "When you do find out where he is and what he's doing, you have to promise to keep me informed. I get to know everything, including your plans for apprehending him."

"As long as you agree not to do anything stupid that could jeopardize your safety or mine," he whispered, toeing off his shoe at the doorstep.

"Why would I do that?" she snarled, angry at the accusation. She deserved to be in the loop. It wasn't like she was asking to be sworn in or anything.

"Just making sure we're clear."

"I'm not confused. Are you?"

He blew out a sharp breath. "You don't leave without

telling me first. I don't make a move without informing you. Sound about right?"

"Yes. Break your promise and all bets are off."

"Got it."

Even with the lights off, she could tell she was being led into a ranch-style home.

Despite the bickering, Nick twined their fingers. He led her down a dark hallway with Boomer on her heels. Her faithful companion. He'd done well today.

When the chips were down, he'd stood his ground and growled.

Precisely what she planned to do from here on out.

Chapter 8

By the time Sadie cracked her eyes open again, she could tell by the amount of light streaming in through the window that noon had come and gone. When was the last time she'd slept that well? Her queen-size bed, shaker-style, with a matching chest of drawers next to it made the room feel cozy.

The decor was simple. The white sheets were soft. The bed had four thick, plush pillows. A handmade quilt with alternating patterns of deep oranges and browns had warmed her through the otherwise chilly night.

Boomer lay snoring at her side. He didn't budge when she sat up.

Poor baby. He must be exhausted after all the walking they'd done in the past two days.

"You did good, buddy," she said in a low voice.

He didn't budge.

There was clothing folded on top of the five-drawer chest. She slipped out of the covers quietly, so as not to disturb her hundred-pound hero who was now growling and panting in his sleep. No doubt, he was reliving the ordeal from last night.

Sadie placed her hand on his side and soothed him until his breath evened out and he snored peacefully again. She moved to the dresser and examined the clothes. Jeans and a T-shirt suited her just fine. Her pink silk bra and panties had been washed and folded neatly in the pile. Red heat crawled up her neck at the thought of Nick handling her undergarments. Warmth flushed her thighs. Because it wasn't so awful to think of him touching her personal things…and she knew instantly she was confusing her feelings for him.

Feelings was a strong word.

She appreciated his help. He was her knight in shining armor, ripping her out of the hands of killers. Who wouldn't be wowed by that? What she experienced was gratitude. Nothing more. So why did she feel the need to remind herself of the fact?

One thing she knew for certain was that she'd been so tired last night she scarcely remembered taking a shower or changing into bedclothes. Nick had brought them in while she was showering, saying he'd borrowed them from one of his sisters. She didn't even want to think of the current running through her at the realization she was completely naked behind the shower curtain not five feet from him.

How long had it been since she'd been held by a man? Two years.

The last time she and Tom were together they'd had their usual Friday night movie at his place. He'd ordered deep-dish pizza from their favorite restaurant on the corner just as they had every week for the entire year and a half they'd been dating. If anything, Tom was consistent. Boring?

Where did that come from?

To be fair, her ex was a little too predictable, but he was also decent. There were no surprises when it came to Tom, and Sadie appreciated him for it. Wasn't knowing she could count on someone a good thing?

Why did it suddenly feel as though she'd been settling?

Her aunt had been unpredictable, and look how their relationship had ended. Sadie had felt no need to visit the woman one last time before she'd left Chicago.

The time she'd stopped by after her first semester of community college, her aunt had practically blocked the door. Sadie's excitement at having made good grades shriveled inside her at her aunt's reaction to seeing her. She'd expected a warm greeting, and chided herself for being foolish when she didn't receive one.

When she pressed to come inside so she could pick up a few of her things, her aunt had turned on the tears. She'd complained of not having space or enough money for rent before delivering a crushing blow. She'd sold all of Sadie's belongings.

Her heart broke that day.

She'd left many of her prized possessions behind until she got settled in her new place. Between work, class and study, she hadn't had time to stop by and retrieve them once the semester hit full stride.

Gone was her mother's wedding ring. Gone was the baby blanket her mother had crocheted for her when she was born. Gone was her father's revered vintage coin collection.

Everything from her parents had been sold, stripped away from her.

She'd stood in the doorway, feeling raw, exposed and orphaned all over again.

Her stomach twisted, the pain so very real. Even now.

Tom could be unyielding, but he would never have done that to her.

Did he make her pulse race the way being around Nick did? No. She and Nick ran from bullets and murderers. Of course her blood would be pumping and her adrenaline surging. And he did so much more to her on the inside. Her heart fluttered when he was close. Electricity pulsed between them. Her thighs warmed.

The comparison to Tom was apples and oranges. She loved Tom. Didn't she?

Not the same thing, a little voice told her. She ignored it. When this blew over, she would still end up alone with a new identity, a new lie. *If she survived.* Grimes seemed intent on making sure she never had to hide again. Or breathe.

She pushed aside those heavy unproductive thoughts and slipped on the jeans. They fit well enough. She cinched her waist with the belt and pulled on the T-shirt.

After dressing, she moved down the hall toward the sounds of voices, her heartbeat climbing with each step closer. There had to be at least six or seven people in the room. She followed the chatter, stopping at the door to the kitchen where a handful of people sat around the table. Her nerves stringing tighter with each forward step.

Nick stood at the kitchen sink, looking out the window.

The oldest woman, the one who had to be Gran, sat with a large pair of scissors and a stack of cloth. She met eyes with Sadie first. "C'mon on in, dear. Take a seat. Nick will get you a cup of coffee."

Nick had already begun pouring.

When attention turned toward Sadie, she wished she had the power to shrink. She knew all of two people in the Campbell family. Nick and Luke. And Luke wasn't in the room. She tentatively stepped inside, her back plastered against the door frame. Her heart pounded her chest and her breath came out in short bursts. She almost turned back and retreated to her room, offering an excuse about needing to go to the bathroom. Families were scary.

"Go ahead and sit, dear. We're a loud bunch, but we don't bite." Gran motioned toward the chair next to hers. She looked younger than her years. Her white hair was in a tight bun positioned on the crown of her head. She wore jeans with a blouse, and a turquoise necklace with matching earrings.

Sadie eased onto the edge of the chair, wishing she could crawl out of her skin and disappear for all the eyes on her, staring. "Good morning. Uh, I'm sorry to sleep so late. We got in pretty late last night."

"I'm glad you're here. Feel free to call me Gran just like the others. And don't worry about what time you get up around here. I bet you're starving."

"I'm on it," Nick said, handing her a cup of fresh coffee. "How'd you sleep?"

"Fine. Better than fine actually. I almost forgot who I was."

He gave a knowing glance before diverting his gaze to the hallway. "How's Boomer? Still asleep?"

"He didn't even budge when I got out of bed."

"I can feed him as soon as he wakes," Nick said.

Then tension lines bracketing his mouth told her he hadn't forgotten about their discussion last night.

She needed to soften the message, set things right with him, but she already felt as out of place as celery in cherry-flavored yogurt.

Although, looking around, everyone seemed so at ease with each other. The vibe in the room was comforting.

Nick returned a moment later with cream. "Pass the sugar, Meg." He turned to Sadie. "This is my sister Meg, by the way."

"Nice to meet you."

"Pleasure. I'd stand, but…" Meg, with a cute round face framed by cropped brown hair, leaned back from the table far enough for Sadie to see a round pregnant belly. "I'm due soon."

Sadie's heart squeezed. Her thoughts snapped to Claire and the baby she would never see. "When?"

"Any day now." A tall, blond, attractive man with a runner's build moved beside Meg and planted a kiss on the top of her head. His affection toward his wife could melt a glacier. "How's your back today?"

Meg's cheeks turned a darker shade of red. "It's better."

"What can I get you? Another pillow?" he asked.

"Nothing. I have everything I need right here." She smiled back up at him and patted her big belly.

Sadie had to tear her gaze away. The tenderness and love between them brought a flood of tears threatening. She sniffed back her emotions and took a sip of the hot coffee as a pang of self-pity assaulted her. Had Claire gone into labor? Was her little girl swaddled in her arms? Did the sweet baby have her mother's honest blue eyes? Her father's dimples?

The tall man interrupted her moment of melancholy, introducing himself as Meg's husband, Riley.

Sadie took his outstretched hand, praying he didn't feel hers shake. She wished Nick was closer. He was the only thing familiar to her in the room. He stood at the stove over a pan of eggs.

A figure cut off Sadie's line of sight. She stared at the hand being stuck out toward her. "I'm Lucy."

"Nice to meet you." Sadie shook the hand being offered, surprised at the strength coming from someone who couldn't be more than five-foot-four-inches tall. The term "cute as a bug in a rug" had to have been invented for Lucy. She had curly brown waves that fell past her shoulders, big brown eyes and Luke's dimples.

Luke came through the back door. A six-foot-two version of the Campbell men followed. "I see you've met the clan. Except for my brother Reed." Luke motioned toward his younger brother. "Our mother will be here tomorrow."

Reed tipped his black cowboy hat and smiled. His cheeks were dimpled, too. "Ma'am."

Sadie smiled, trying not to show her nerves, and turned to Gran. "You have quite a beautiful family." Her voice hitched on the last word. Truth was, she had no idea how to interact with a family. It had only been she and her parents when she was a child but they both had worked long hours in the small trinket store they'd owned. She was lucky if she saw them for more than a half hour before bed every evening.

"We're blessed." Gran beamed.

Nick delivered a plate of food, and the earlier chatter

resumed. Sadie was thankful the spotlight wasn't on her anymore. As it was a rash had crawled up her neck. A few deep breaths and she might be able to stop it from reaching her face. She focused on the food. The eggs were scrambled with chopped red pepper and onion. A couple of homemade biscuits smothered in sausage gravy steamed. This was heaven on a stick.

Sadie wasted no time devouring her meal.

Nick had taken the seat across from her. "Guess you were hungry. I have more." He made a move to stand.

"No. Don't get up. I'm fine." Sadie's cheeks heated when she realized he must've been watching her eat the whole time.

The satisfied smile curving his lips warmed her heart more than she should allow. She couldn't risk getting too comfortable. She wondered just how much everyone knew about her aside from Luke. He knew enough.

"Meg's on leave until the baby's born. She and her husband work for Plano P.D. And Lucy works in the Victim Advocate Unit for the sheriff's office."

Was he reassuring her everything would be okay? Maybe he'd misread her tension.

Luke and Reed stood at the kitchen sink, eating fresh cut watermelon.

Gran's gaze narrowed on the outline of weapons in their waistbands. "I hope I don't have to remind either of you about the 'nothing that fires is allowed in the house' rule."

Luke shot a concerned look toward Nick. After picking them up last night and hearing the threat, Luke seemed more comfortable keeping his weapon as close as possible. He seemed to be waiting for acknowledgment from Nick that it was okay to leave his gun outside.

Nick barely nodded.

"Go on. Don't make me repeat myself." Gran shooed them toward the door.

"Sorry, Gran." Luke glanced back in time to see Nick smoothing his hand down his ankle.

His slight nod said he understood. Nick was telling him where to hide his weapon.

A boulder would've felt lighter on Sadie's chest at the reminder of just how much danger she was still in. To be in a room full of law enforcement out on a country road, and still need to have weapons within reach at all times didn't say good things for her situation. Plus, being in a room full of well-intentioned strangers shot her blood pressure up. At this rate, she'd have hives before she finished her coffee.

"I should check on Boomer." She made a move to stand, but Nick held his hand up to stop her.

"I got this." He picked up her plate and set it on the counter before disappearing down the hallway.

Lucy looked at her intently. "So, how'd you get my brother to come back home?"

"Now, Lucy, that's none of our business, right?" Gran shooed her away, winking at Sadie.

Apparently, not everyone knew the real reason she was there.

Nick returned a minute later with her hundred-pound rescue trailing behind. Boomer's ears perked up as soon as he saw Sadie and he trotted over to her side, tail wagging.

"Sweet boy. Did you get some rest?" Sadie asked, grateful she had something familiar to focus on besides Nick in this room full of strangers.

Nick's hand grazed hers as they scratched Boomer's

ears and her skin practically sizzled where he made contact. An electric current raced up her arm.

She stood. "He probably needs to go out." She practically ran through the opened screen door to find a place where she could think straight.

Boomer's nose immediately scanned the ground. He stopped at a tree and hiked his leg.

The screen door creaked and Nick bounded down the porch stairs holding a plate. "Don't have any kibble, but I figure he won't object to biscuits and gravy." He set the meal down on the ground.

Sadie rubbed her arms to stave off a chill even though the thermometer displayed a number in the high seventies. "Darnedest thing about living in Texas. Never know what the temperature's going to be this time of year." She turned her back to Nick and looked out on to the wide-open sky.

"Supposed to be a storm blowing in tonight. It should be plenty cold later. Remind me to give you an extra blanket."

She turned to face him, unsure of the right words to tell him she needed to go. She rubbed her arms to tamp down the goose bumps—the chill she felt from deep within encasing her heart. "Thanks. For all this. But I think we both know I don't belong here."

"Sure you do." He moved closer, took off the shirt he was wearing and wrapped it around her shoulders. Even through his undershirt, his broad, muscled chest rippled when he took in a breath. "What makes you say that?"

"I just don't. This is your family." She gripped the top of the fence, turning her face away from him, not wanting him to see how much it hurt to say those words. "And I'm grateful for everything you're doing for me.

But I'd rather stay at a motel where I'd be out of the way."

"We're just normal people. There's nothing special about us."

She looked out across the landscape. The way they loved each other seemed pretty special to her. "You have a gran and sister with a baby on the way. This is a family moment and I don't feel right intruding."

"Did anyone say anything to you? Lucy? She can be quick to judge, but she means well."

"No. No one had to. I can see with my own eyes. This is a special celebration. Your gran is sweet. She deserves to have all the attention."

"You don't know Gran. Don't get me wrong, she loves for us all to be together. But she doesn't need to be the center of attention. She's content right here with all of us running in and out. If she had her way, not one of us would've moved out. We'd all still be here, tripping over each other."

Sadie glanced around at the yard that seemed as if it went on forever with the low shrubs and mesquite trees, then toward the blue skies with white puffy clouds. "I can think of worse places to be. It's beautiful here. This where you grew up?" She leaned her hip against the fence.

"Yeah."

"Where do you live now?" she asked.

Boomer loped over, sniffing around as though he tried to get his bearings. This was a far cry from his home at the lake house. Was he as lost as she felt?

"Dallas. I have an apartment in The Village. But, I'm never there. I guess it doesn't really feel like home."

"Why'd your sister say you don't come around here anymore?"

"Who? Lucy?" He paused. "Must've been her. Everyone else has been briefed." The muscle in Nick's jaw pulsed. "Sorry about that. I'll fill her in."

Why did he dodge the question? There was more to the story and her curiosity was piqued. She told herself it was because it would be nice to know one thing about him that didn't have to do with how well he did his job. "So you get to know everything about me and I don't get to return the favor. Is that it?"

"Afraid so. Besides, some subjects are out-of-bounds."

"Oh, that's great." What was the big deal? Did she hit a nerve?

"Tell me about the accountant."

"Who?" She had to search her memory for a second. "Tom?" She'd almost forgotten about him, being this close to Nick. Even so, what right did he have to ask about Tom? Indignation squared her shoulders. "He's none of your business."

"All indicators show you two should be married by now, planning for your kids' college funds."

Anger simmered. He didn't have a right to judge her life, past or present. Besides, none of those normal things were in her outlook anymore.

"Kids? Me?" She laughed out loud. It came out as a choked cough. "That's about the most ridiculous thing I've ever heard. How exactly am I supposed to have time to push around a stroller while I'm being chased by a man who won't stop until I'm dead? How selfish do you think I am?"

He stood there as though words wouldn't form. Did he regret his tone?

It didn't matter. Tears had already boiled over and spilled down her cheeks. A family had never been more out of the question for Sadie. And when could she ever stop running? What was her future going to be like? Relocate every six months? No friends? No roots? No home?

Sadie couldn't stop the sob that racked her shoulders. Or the flood of tears that followed. Before she could fight, Nick pulled her into his chest where she met steel wrapped in silk muscles. His strong arms wrapped around her and he spoke quietly into her hair. "It's going to be okay. You're going to be all right."

"You don't know that." She needed to get tight and stop feeling sorry for herself. She'd been strong so far. This was not the time to unravel.

"I'll find Grimes and anyone else trying to hurt you, and lock them up. I have help here. We don't have to do this on our own anymore."

"You already said this is your job. And I'm glad you're good at what you do. But this is my life. And it sucks. I never get to be me again. I always have to play the part of someone else. Those bastards took it all away. Everything." Tears fell freely now. Sadie had no power to stop them. It had been two long years of being strong. Twenty-four months of lonely nights, freaking out every time a creak sounded, and a lifetime on the run to look forward to. She could never stop or slow down for fear one of Grime's gang members would be right behind her, lurking, waiting.

And Tom?

Did Nick really want to know the truth about Tom?

Did he need to hear that Tom was stable and that was about it? He provided all the things she'd been missing in her childhood? His life was about order, routine and ties that matched his suits. Where he lacked in excitement, he made up for in stability. He was the kind of guy who would stay the course, no matter what. And she'd almost agreed to marry him for it.

And yet, she now realized that with him she'd be living a different lie. Because she never felt *this* good in Tom's arms. Never wanted so desperately to feel his bare skin against hers. Never wanted any man this much. Nick was a safe haven in a storm.

A temporary shelter, a little voice said.

Nick stood there, holding Sadie, and for a split second in this mixed-up crazy world everything felt right.

He ignored the danger bells sounding off in his head. The ones that threatened to end his career. "We'll figure this out."

His cell buzzed. He fished it from his pocket. "Smith."

He answered the call and put it on speaker. "What's the word?"

"My source has been able to identify a dozen real estate holdings. There's a couple you'll be the most interested in that were bought by a dummy corporation. One of which has had a lot of activity."

"Let me guess, this company is licensed out of the Caymans," Nick practically grunted.

"You guessed it. Word has it that Jamison could've been in business with Grimes all along."

"If Jamison was involved with a known criminal, he'd have a lot to lose if someone could identify him."

"This might explain why they've come at Ms. Brooks so hard. It could be more than revenge. He might need to make her disappear to bury his involvement."

Nick focused on the floor intently as his free hand fisted. "They can't be thrilled I'm alive, either."

A sigh came across the line. "I agree, which is why it's more important than ever to keep you off the radar. I'd initially thought we were dealing with one rogue deputy. Charlie. But, this? A supervisor? To be honest, it scares the hell out of me that one of our own could be in on this."

"I agree. It also explains how they keep anticipating my moves."

"They must've narrowed down her location. It doesn't appear that they have Charlie's file, but anything's possible. And, now, I believe you're a target." His solemn tone sent a shiver down Sadie's spine.

"Explains why they seemed so eager to run me off the road before," Nick agreed. "They would have known we were watching her."

"Another thing bothers me and makes me believe what I'm hearing about Jamison could be true. They didn't seem particularly bothered that a U.S. Marshal was involved," Smith said.

"No, they didn't." Nick paused. "If he's involved, it explains how they knew where to look for us."

"It does make their job easier."

"What did you say a minute ago about those holdings?"

"I've narrowed down two locations as possibilities. One in Houston and one in Dallas. We can't find any information on these. I can't send anyone else to check them out. Can't risk word getting to Jamison."

Nick took out a small notebook and pen from his back pocket. "I'll do it. Give me the addresses."

"1495 Oliver Street in Houston and 2626 Brenner Drive in Dallas," Smith said.

The Dallas address wasn't far. He'd look it up on Google and pinpoint the exact location. "Got it."

"Report back as soon as you know what's in there."

"Will do, Chief."

He ended the call and turned to Sadie. Big green eyes stared back at him. The hurt, loneliness and disbelief he saw there was a knife to his chest. He wanted to take it all away. Make her world safe again.

The only way to do that was to make sure Malcolm Grimes didn't hurt her again.

Protecting Sadie just became his number one priority.

Chapter 9

Evening had fallen quickly. Now, after everyone had said their good-nights and the house was dark, everything was quiet, save for the crickets chirping outside Sadie's window in the middle of the night. The stillness reminded her of the lake house. The place had been eerie when she'd first moved from the city. There was no hustle and bustle. No horns honking. No sounds of the L train running. Everything about living in Creek Bend had felt foreign because of her Chicago upbringing.

And yet, she'd felt an almost instant connection to the place. To the people. To the slower pace.

Sadie rolled onto her left side and glanced at the alarm clock again. A whopping three minutes had passed since the last time she'd checked.

She didn't even bother to close her eyes again. Wouldn't do any good. They'd just bounce open again, anyway. The winds had kicked up and there was a storm brewing outside.

It was four in the morning. Normally she'd be leaving the house for work at this time. An ache pressed into her chest. The small bakery had become her second home. She missed everything about it. The smell of dough leavening. The first sip of coffee she took once inside the quiet shop. All the little tasks that added up to a productive day.

Working in the bakery made her feel as though she contributed something positive to the world. There was something primal and satisfying about feeding people.

And having a routine. She missed the comfort of a schedule.

The wind outside howled. A gust slammed into the window. Her gasp made Boomer stir. *It's only the wind.*

Her morning coffee ritual would have already started. Wouldn't she kill for a double shot latte with extra foam about now?

She missed the feel of dough in her hands. The weight of it. The warmth.

She always started by mixing and weighing it. Baguettes were first, and then the sourdoughs since they took the longest to ferment. As Claire neared her due date, there had been only one specialty bread on the menu. A mini cranberry panettone.

Another blast of wind rocketed and a dark shadow crossed her window. *A tree branch. It's only a tree branch.*

While dough mixed, she'd hand-laminated croissants for the day, rolled out tart shells and mixed muffins and cookies. Some breads needed to be knocked back as much as three times before being left to ferment until just right for scaling. Each loaf had to weigh an equal amount, or they wouldn't bake at the same rate.

Tap, tap, tap on the window. *Raindrops finally fell.*

The timer had become her new best friend. She'd learned that small batch bread-baking was so much about timing. Ten minutes early or twenty minutes late made a huge difference in the quality of what came out of the oven. *So much in life was about timing.*

By now, Sadie would have been preheating the ovens. Helping wake the town with handmade treats after it had been so good to her felt right. After all, there were no strangers in Creek Bend, or so they'd said. At first, she'd thought it was their way of being nosy. She soon realized, they'd meant it. Neighbors popped in to check on her and see if she needed anything. When she'd brought Boomer home, it wasn't long before baskets of treats with cards started showing up on her doorstep.

Her heart ached for the friendly faces she'd never see again.

Time to move on.

On her agenda?

A new town. A new job. A new start.

If—and it was a big if—Grimes was found and locked up, how long before he got out again? He seemed to have connections in high places. Would he ever stop looking for her? Would his men ever move on?

She doubted it.

Another boom of wind blasted against the window, causing her to jump. Could someone be out there? Lurking? Using the storm as cover?

She slid out of bed and moved to the side of the window, trying to gather enough courage to peek outside. She thought about the guns in the shed. How easy would it be for someone to locate them? Her throat suddenly felt dry, and her heart hammered her ribs. She quieted her thoughts and listened intently.

Had she heard something? No. Couldn't be. No one was awake. Her imagination was playing tricks on her. No one dangerous knew where Nick's family lived. And they were all asleep.

She peered through the window. Nothing.

The sound of a board creaking outside her door sent her heart into her throat. Had someone slipped inside the house? Were they sneaking down the hallway? Her pulse kicked up another notch even as she knew her imagination was most likely running wild. What she needed to do was chill out.

If anyone was up, they were probably making a night run to the bathroom, she reasoned. With a pregnant woman in the house, middle-of-the-night bathroom trips weren't out of the question.

The weather had Sadie skittish, looking for things hiding in dark shadows.

She couldn't think of pregnancy without picturing Claire. Her belly had been so round the last time Sadie saw her friend. She'd wobbled when she'd walked and said her ankles were lead weights. Was Claire awake feeding her little angel? Changing her diaper? Crying over the loss of her bakery? She probably thought Sadie had died in the fire.

Oh, no.

Claire would be told Sadie was dead. Her heart squeezed thinking Claire would be mourning when she should be celebrating. Was there any way to get word to her friend?

Not without putting her in danger.

Now she really couldn't go back to bed and close her eyes because she'd picture a sad-faced Claire.

Sadie's heart ached. Dwelling on it was only making the pain worse. Claire, her baby and the bakery were all part of the past now. Time to pick up and move on. And what about Tom? What did it say that he barely crossed her mind anymore?

When she missed a man's arms around her, she thought about Nick.

Startled at the realization, Sadie eased out of bed. She needed to get to the kitchen to get a glass of water.

Questions raced through her mind. What was her next move? How long would it take before Grimes found them at the ranch?

They couldn't stay long. She wouldn't put his sweet family in danger, no matter how much he insisted. Whether Nick liked it or not, she would move on soon. She'd need to change her appearance again. Maybe she wouldn't look too bad as a blonde?

And her name.

She would need a new name. Maybe she could pick her own this time? What about Elise? Or Brittany? Or Ann?

She hadn't taken two steps into the kitchen before Luke poked his head in.

"Everything okay?" he whispered.

"You mean aside from the small heart attack I just had?"

He chuckled before glancing down the hall, and waving someone away. "Doesn't pay to walk around at night in a house full of law enforcement officers."

"I'm sorry. Who was that?"

"Reed, Riley, Lucy and, of course, Nick."

"Oh, great. Now I've gone and forced the whole house out of bed. I'm sorry. I was thirsty." She pulled a glass from the cupboard.

"No trouble. I'll let everyone know." He disappeared down the hall before she could thank him.

She poured water and took a sip, not ready to go back to bed. She hadn't meant to interrupt everyone's much-needed rest, even if relief washed over her knowing an intruder wouldn't get through those doors unnoticed.

She didn't realize she'd pulled out a mixing bowl and located a bag of flour until she looked down. A lamp-post streamed light through the kitchen window. It was enough to see what she was doing. Her actions at the bakery had become so routine she could do them in the dark if she needed to. She mixed yeast into the flour, then added butter and water. When she'd beaten them thoroughly, she dumped the contents onto the counter. Pressing her palms into the mix, folding it over, kneading it, brought a sense of sanity and calm over her.

Luckily, the bedrooms were on opposite sides of the house. She could only hope to work quietly enough so as not to disturb anyone again, and least of all Boomer. If he started barking, the whole house would be up faster than she could say *quiet*.

Sadie pressed her palms into the dough, rolled and repeated until her shoulders burned.

Doing something familiar had her almost forgetting about the scary men chasing her and their ability to find her almost everywhere she went.

She turned on the oven and left the dough to set on the counter.

The feeling of eyes on her gave her a start. She turned to the doorway and caught a glimpse of a male figure filling the door frame. She knew exactly who it was. "Nick? I'm sorry if I woke you."

"You didn't. I couldn't sleep." He stood there all shirtless man and muscle, his jeans hung low on narrow hips, one arm cocked in the doorjamb and a grin on his face that made him even more handsome if that were possible. "What are you making?"

His words traveled across the room as soft as feather strokes.

"I got bored. Thought I would do something useful and bake a loaf of bread." She motioned toward the counter. "That should do it. Needs to sit for a while."

"Can't wait," he said, pulling up a stool and taking a seat. "You're used to being up all night, aren't you?"

"Yeah," she said on a sigh. She thought about how different he was now. Women had lined up in Creek Bend to talk to him. But they'd had no idea what was really underneath the ball cap and sunglasses he'd worn. He'd always stood to the side, awkward. If he hadn't been so shy she feared he would've asked her out on a date. Feared or hoped? The question had to be asked.

She'd almost convinced herself that she didn't need anyone. Her past certainly had taught her the same lesson. It would be a long time before she'd be ready to spend her Saturday nights with a stranger. And yet, didn't he awaken a tiny piece of her that she'd tried to ignore far too long?

It would be easy to lie to herself now and say she hadn't given him a second thought before. But what good would it do? Sure she'd been interested. She knew then as much as she knew now that she would never allow herself to get caught up in feelings for a man. She wasn't ready.

There'd been a time when she thought she had it all figured out. She'd been dating someone nice, decent and reliable. She and Tom were on track to walk down the aisle. He'd hinted about making the relationship more permanent. She'd made it clear she wasn't ready. Yet. Plus, she'd figured he was working up the nerve to ask her officially.

A case of mistaken identity had changed everything about her life.

She'd escaped with her life and nothing from her past. Her testimony had put Malcolm Grimes away for what was supposed to be a very long time.

Nick moved behind her and encircled her waist with his arms, covering her hands with his, entwining their fingers.

"You sure I can't help with anything else?"

She shouldn't allow him to get this close to her, but her body screamed *yes*.

Bad idea. She ducked out of his hold and moved to the sink, filling a glass with water.

"After Gran's celebration tomorrow afternoon, we'll dig deeper into the case again."

The mention of family caused the muscles in her shoulders to bunch. Her skin felt as though a thousand tiny ants were biting her. She straightened her back. "Your gran is very sweet, so don't take this the wrong way. There any chance I can sleep through the festivities?"

Nick watched Sadie's movements intently as she folded her arms and hugged them into her chest. "I can tell she likes you if that's what you're worried about. Everyone does."

"Not everyone. Did you see the way your sister Lucy looked at me earlier? What was that about?"

"She's protective." He stopped himself before he explained that they were all most likely shocked beyond hades he'd brought a woman into the house again. Even if it was for professional reasons. "Don't pay any attention to her. She doesn't mean anything."

Sadie looked ready to crawl out of her skin. "I'm sure. But I think I'd be more comfortable leaving you to your family celebration while I take a walk outside with Boomer or something."

Her cold shoulder made the room feel as if the temperature had dropped twenty degrees in the past second. He thought about her past. How overwhelming a big family can be for anyone and especially someone who'd lost theirs. He needed to ease her into his. "We can figure out something. I didn't mean to make you uncomfortable—"

"It's fine. Don't worry about it. Really." She checked a timer and put the ball of dough on a baking sheet. She slid it into the oven, put a pan of water underneath and closed the door. Then she turned off the heat so the dough would rise faster. "What do we do next? We can't stay here forever. It probably isn't safe to stay here past tomorrow."

"I thought about that. Smith sent a text on my throwaway. He believes Grimes is still somewhere in Texas. The locations of the warehouses are perfect for moving merchandise from the Gulf all the way to Canada."

Sadie covered her mouth.

"Reports are saying he wants to stay close to the Mexican border so he can escape quickly if need be.

It'd be easy for him to slip across the border and get lost if he feels the heat. Except we can't trust intelligence."

"There any other possible reason for him to be here other than me?"

"Smith isn't sure. The Dallas warehouse is leased to his company. He might be using it to move...product."

"What does that mean?"

"Guns, money, illegals. Whatever he needs to move through the country. These guys adapt their business quickly, keeping pace with what's selling."

"So we start looking for him at the warehouse?"

"I agreed to keep you informed. I didn't say you could come with me to follow a lead. I plan to leave tomorrow night after midnight." He actually planned to leave at eight o'clock, but he had no plans to share that information with her. He figured he'd find her sitting on the hood of his truck if she knew the real time.

"Fine."

"There's a dangerous word coming from a woman."

"What do you want me to say? Do you need me to beg? I will." Her green eyes were pleading. "I want to go. I want to be included. I want to be part of this 'sting' or whatever you call it."

If he wasn't so frustrated, he'd laugh. "There's no sting. I'm just going on a fishing expedition."

"You need someone to watch your back."

"True."

She folded her arms and tapped her foot. "Okay, tell me. Who else is going with you?"

Perceptive. "Luke. As you can see, I have all the backup I can handle."

"You said you're leaving at eleven, right?"

Was she testing him? He drew his brows together.

"I'm pretty sure I said midnight. And I'm even more sure you heard me the first time."

"My mistake." She turned on her heel. Before she left the room, she said, "Throw the bread into a loaf pan and turn on the oven when it's ready."

Sadie's brain was way too active to sleep. She needed a little space to be able to think clearly and that was increasingly difficult to do with Nick around. It was all too easy to get lost when he was near. With him close, she started thinking about a future that might involve children and a husband. She knew herself better than that. Sadie would never knowingly put someone else in her situation.

She curled on her side, trying to ignore the sounds outside her bedroom window. Her imagination could go wild with every snap of a tree branch.

Closing her eyes did no good. All she saw were the faces of her abductors. The sounds of their voices would haunt her forever.

She curled on her side and counted sheep. On the tenth round of that joy, she surrendered.

What was the use?

By six o'clock, she was ready to crawl up the walls.

She didn't want to go in the other room, but boredom got the best of her and she was getting hungry, too. The scent of her fresh loaf filled the air. Someone had finished the job for her.

After getting dressed, she followed the noise coming from the kitchen hoping she'd find Nick there so she could ask him what their next steps were. She froze when she saw Lucy sitting at the table.

In fact, no one was in the kitchen but Lucy. Well, this just got awkward.

If Sadie turned around like she wanted to, Lucy might catch her sneaking away and that would just be embarrassing. So, she didn't. Better face down the raging bull. Besides, she'd be out of there soon and Lucy would never have to set eyes on her again. Her heart squeezed. She would be long gone and into a new life— a life without Nick.

"Morning."

"Hey."

Great. Didn't seem as though Lucy wanted to talk to her any more than she wanted to talk to Lucy. "That coffee I smell?"

"Yep. Cups are in that cabinet." She pointed next to the sink.

Sadie gripped a mug and shot a weak smile. "I'll just grab a cup and get out of your way."

"No. Stay. We should talk."

Oh, glory. Sadie filled her mug and took a sip. At least she had coffee. "What's up?"

"Sit." Lucy motioned to the table.

Sadie took the seat opposite her. "Are you an officer?"

"Yeah. It's in the blood, I guess."

Could a second tick by any slower?

Lucy leaned her weight to one side and tucked her foot underneath her. "My brother's had it rough."

Should Sadie know what Lucy meant by that? She shrugged. "I'm afraid I don't know much about him."

"He didn't tell you about his past?"

"Afraid not." Sadie sipped the steaming brew, welcoming the burn on her lips. "Why would he?"

Lucy's eyes widened in surprise. "I just thought…"

Sadie leaned back in her chair, trying not to look as if she was hanging on Lucy's every word. The truth was she would like to know more about Nick. He already knew so much about her. She felt at a complete disadvantage.

"Did he at least tell you why he went into law enforcement?"

"Nope."

"Wow. I overestimated the situation, then." Lucy looked even more surprised by this revelation.

"All I know about your brother is that he works for the U.S. Marshals Service. He is my handler while I'm on the run from men who want to see me dead. But you already know that, right?" It was more statement than question.

Lucy nodded.

"So, if there's something you want to tell me, I'm all ears. But I don't like playing games." Sadie was being bold, and she knew it. But Lucy would not intimidate her, dammit.

Lucy's jaw went slack. A beat passed. She sat up stiffly and said, "I knew there was something about you I liked."

The pair burst into laughter, shattering the tension that had been between them.

Sadie spoke first. "If there's something you think I should know about Nick, tell me now."

Chapter 10

Lucy shifted in her seat. Her expression darkened and her gaze focused out the window. Sadness overcame her once-bright features. "I can be protective of my brothers, but especially Nick. I owe him my life."

Sadie leaned forward and gripped her mug with both hands. "He said you two were especially close. I can see the bond your family has. It's sweet."

Lucy's eyes brimmed with tears, but she didn't immediately speak.

Sadie took a sip and waited. She knew what it was like to try to recall a painful experience.

"I don't normally bare my soul to strangers, but my brother told me a little bit about what happened to you. I think you of all people will understand."

Thinking about what Grimes and his men had done to her still elicited a physical response. Her heart rate increased, and she found it hard to swallow. Sadie forced herself to stay calm. "I was in the ICU for a couple of weeks after what those jerks did to me."

"It takes a strong person to survive something like that. You're really brave. I know firsthand what it takes to keep going after someone hurts you."

"That why you work at the sheriff's office as a victim's advocate?" Sadie asked, realizing her initial assessment of Lucy had been all wrong.

Lucy nodded. "When I was young, my ex-boyfriend became obsessed with me. Didn't think much about it at first. I was dumb enough to think it was cute. That it showed how much he cared. So I didn't tell anyone right away. Let it go on way too long. Then, it got weird. For weeks he'd show up unexpectedly. We'd already broken up. Time to move on for me. He had other ideas."

"The people you care about shouldn't want to hurt you."

Lucy nodded in agreement. "Tell that to a young girl. They don't always listen." She took a sip of coffee. "It got worse. He started threatening my guy friends and stalking me."

"I can't see your brothers putting up with that."

"Which is exactly the reason I didn't tell them. They'd outright hurt him, and I thought I could handle my own problems. Figured this was my fault somehow. It was on me to finish it. I had no idea what was he was truly capable of." Tears streamed down her cheek. "Sorry. It's been years. And, yet, it still gets to me when I think about it."

Sadie patted Lucy's hand. "I can see it's still hard to talk about it. We don't have to keep going if you don't want."

"It's okay. Just especially emotional lately for some reason," Lucy said quickly. "Guess we have a lot going on in the family right now. Anyway, the experience made it hard for me to open up to anyone and especially men."

Anger burned Sadie's chest. No woman deserved to be intimated by a man, but especially not a young girl. "How old were you when this all happened?"

"Sixteen. He was my first love. I was so dumb."

"You were young," Sadie corrected.

"And stupid."

"Naive, maybe. But you're not capable of being stupid."

Lucy half smiled, kept her gaze trained out the window. "He kidnapped me. Planned to rape me and then kill me. Said he didn't want another boy touching me. That I belonged to him."

"Sounds like he was a very sick boy."

"I can't believe I didn't see it before. He was a little jealous at first. I thought it was cute. When I wanted breathing space, he got worse."

"You couldn't have known. Grown women get themselves in worse situations. I hope you don't blame yourself. You didn't ask for any of this." Sadie noticed a small scar above Lucy's eye. Did that bastard do that to her?

"I tell people the same thing all the time. Strange how hard it is to believe for yourself." She paused a beat. "My family didn't like him to begin with. I was being defiant, sneaking around dating him behind their backs. I should've listened in the first place. I could've saved myself a lot of heartache. He wasn't even my type. I guess his bad-boy image hooked me. I figured he was good underneath. Learned the hard way not every person is."

"We all do things as teenagers we regret later. No one's perfect. We learn. It's part of growing up."

Lucy shifted her gaze to Sadie, turning the tables. "I just want you to know I understand your fears. What you went through was hell. And my brother told me it was all a mistake. You weren't involved in any criminal activity. They grabbed the wrong woman."

If Lucy was trying to make Sadie feel better, she was succeeding. "Crappy things happen sometimes. We don't always get to control everything."

Lucy's ringtone sounded. She held up a finger and answered the call, lowering her voice.

Sadie tried to block out the conversation, focusing instead out the window and on the beautiful yard.

Lucy ended the call with, "I love you, too." She stuffed her phone back in her pocket, turning her attention to Sadie again. "He's the reason I finally decided to go to therapy. I don't want to lose him."

"Sounds like a good guy. You better hang on to him."

"Yeah, he is. His name is Stephen, by the way." Lucy sipped her coffee. She grinned. "I don't know where you come from, but there's no shortage of good men around here. If it weren't for Nick…"

"Don't get any crazy ideas about me and your brother. I'm his work, remember?"

Lucy held her hands up in surrender.

"Good." Why did her heart race at the mention of Nick?

Seeing the warmth and love Lucy had for her brother, for all her family, hit Sadie in a deeply emotional place.

She had no doubt if one Campbell was in trouble, the rest would step up. Her heart opened a little more.

Sadie pushed aside her heavier thoughts, allowing the sun to shine through the opening in her chest. "Can I be honest with you?"

Lucy nodded.

"I didn't think you liked me at all."

"It's not you. I was thrown off when my brother brought another woman home. He hasn't since his girlfriend died."

He didn't say anything about that. "What happened?"

"It was a long time ago, but to look at the way he's still suffering you'd think it was yesterday. He doesn't talk about it."

"What happened?"

"She didn't see her twenty-second birthday."

"Oh, no." Sadie pressed her hand to her chest to stop her heart from hurting for him.

"They hadn't actually made their relationship official…" She cast her gaze around the room and fidgeted. "He always gets a little down this time of year because of it."

Talking almost seemed irreverent. Sadie let the words hang in the air.

"She was killed by a drunk driver," Lucy said.

"I had no idea." Is that why he sounded so bitter at the mention of her fiancé? Or having a family? Sadie couldn't imagine losing the one person in the world she loved. Her heart ached for Nick. To lose his one true love. She couldn't fathom it. And yet, hadn't she lost hers? What she and Tom shared was different. Was it earth-shattering, world-ending love? No. Their relationship was more mature, she lied.

Had she been sad when she'd walked away from Tom?

Of course.

Heartbroken?

No.

This explained a lot about Nick's reactions. Was it also the reason he broke protocol to collect her things in Creek Bend? He understood loss.

Nick obviously held his emotions inside. Had he learned to do that when he was a kid, watching his mom suffer?

"I'm so sorry."

"He was a mess for a while. Got out of the military when his time was up, and eventually got his head screwed on straight again. Started dating. He's been out with lots of women since then. No one seems to measure up to her. I haven't heard about him seeing anyone in the past year. I was afraid he'd given up. Even though she died years ago, he's never been the same—"

The sounds of feet landing on the tile floor stopped Lucy midsentence. She stood and half smiled. "I'll catch up with you later."

"Morning." Nick grunted the word as he passed Lucy on his way to the coffeepot. Boomer trailed behind, wagging his tail as if he were home.

Nick's black hair was tousled and he wasn't wearing a shirt.

Sadie's heart squeezed. She stood and walked to

the back door, making kissing noises at her dog as she opened it. "C'mon, Boomer. You need to go outside."

He trotted past her unceremoniously.

She followed him. Not because she had to stand over him while he did his business, but because she needed air. Her heart ached for Nick, for his tragic loss. Maybe he did understand the feeling of losing everything.

She breathed in the crisp air, inviting it into her soul.

The grass glistened, still wet from the storm. The birds chirped their morning songs. The sun, a warm glow, rose just above the trees. Everything about the ranch was perfection. How could a place she'd never been before feel so much like home?

This must be what heaven is like.

Or maybe it was the love she felt from the moment she saw the Campbells together. Even though Luke teased Nick that first night in the truck, she felt an unspoken, unbreakable bond between the brothers. She imagined they could get away with teasing each other, but let someone else try. No doubt they'd rally for one serious fight.

A little piece of her heart opened.

Being on a ranch seemed to suit Boomer, too. He ran toward the fence and then cut a hard left a second before crashing into it.

The place wasn't extravagant. The barn needed a good coat of paint. And yet, it was a beautiful, serene place.

This would have been a great place to grow up.

Boomer returned to her side with a stick clenched in his teeth.

He dropped it at her feet. She picked it up, red paint dotting her fingers. No. Not red paint. She examined the stains closer, fanning out her fingers…blood. She released her grip on the stick, sending it tumbling to the ground.

Boomer lurched toward it.

"Leave it." The command came out harsher than she'd planned.

He froze.

She kicked the stick, launching it into the air while distracting Boomer with kissing noises.

She scanned the tree line, the barn, the fence. Her heart jackhammered her ribs with painful stabs.

Where'd the blood come from? Boomer's mouth? Maybe the stick had jabbed his gums and caused them to bleed. She bent down to get a better look in his mouth and opened his jaw flaps. "You okay, boy?"

She examined her fingers. His saliva mixed with blood. "Did you cut your gums with that stick?"

Her warning bells sounded. She stood and glanced around one more time, ignoring the chill racing up her spine. Could someone be out there? Waiting for the right moment to strike?

The explanation was right in front of her, on her hand. The sight of blood still goose bumped her flesh.

She opened the door to see Nick standing near the coffeemaker. Seeing him there had a similar effect to feeling morning sunshine on her face.

The door creaked closed behind her and she turned long enough to lock it.

"Everything okay?" Nick asked, studying her expression.

"Yeah. Fine." She didn't want to tell him every shadow made her jump. Being cautious was one thing. Letting her fear get the best of her was something totally different. She washed her hands and poured a bowl of water for Boomer before setting it on the floor. "I need to pick up dog food. Anything around here he can eat until I can get to a store?"

"I can make a trip into town later. I'll find something for him in the meantime." He turned and searched the pantry. A minute later, he poked his head out. "The bread turned out to be pretty amazing. I had to fight my brothers to save a piece for you." He pointed to the counter by the stove. "I missed waking up to that smell first thing in the morning."

A chunk had been neatly wrapped for her and placed on the kitchen island.

Sadie peeled open the Saran wrap and took a bite after pouring a fresh cup of coffee. "You finished it?"

"We make a good team." Nick stepped out of the pantry. "Nothing in there for our boy to eat."

She liked the sound of the words *our boy*.

Luke strolled in, rubbing his eyes. "I'm going in this morning for supplies. What do you need?"

"Food for Boomer," Sadie said then frowned.

"What's wrong?" Luke asked.

"I just realized that I don't have any way to pay for food or anything else. I lost my wallet along with my purse when the bakery caught fire."

"You don't need money." Nick bent down and scratched Boomer's head. "You hungry, boy? I got something around here for you." He moved to the fridge and pulled out enough meat to fill a small pan. "I'll cook up something for him. He'll like this better, anyway."

A look passed between Nick and Luke.

"What's going on?" Sadie asked.

Neither spoke.

"I deserve to know." She stood her ground.

Nick stood and folded his arms. "I don't want my brother in town buying dog food all of a sudden. We can't break with routine. Otherwise we'll alert people to our presence. I can't have anyone stopping by unexpectedly or asking too many questions."

"He's right," Luke interjected, watching Sadie as a wall of emotion descended on her with more force than a rogue wave. "I'm surprised he let you keep the dog this long."

Panic crawled through her veins and she forced back the urge to cry. "I'm not going anywhere without Boomer. He needs me."

"I understand, but you have to think of it from our perspective. He's a liability," Luke said apologetically.

"He saved our lives," she said. Her gaze flew to Nick.

He nodded agreement. "He's a good boy, don't get me wrong. It's just the other team already knows about him. He might give us away at a critical moment."

On some level, she knew he was right. Yet, the thought of being without her constant companion was almost too much to handle. "I hear what you're saying, but no. I can't do this without him. You have to let me keep him. Please."

"I didn't say you had to get rid of him, did I? I just don't want to wave a flag in town that we're here." He patted Boomer's head.

Luke disappeared down the hall.

She couldn't pinpoint the emotion darkening Nick's features. She'd seen it before in the truck moments before he'd said he sent someone to pick up her personal things from the lake house. A shared sense of loss? A kindred spirit? A person who truly understood her dog was the only family she had left? She didn't care. He was agreeing to let her keep the one thing she loved the most. She took a step forward and wrapped her arms around his neck. "Thank you."

She could feel his heartbeat against her chest, his rapid rhythm matching hers. His arms encircled her waist. His body, flush with hers, caused sensual heat to pulse through her.

She wouldn't argue that she felt drawn to Nick from the start, even when she thought he was a nerdy radiologist. Getting to know him better was only deepening the attraction.

"Don't mention it," he said, his low baritone vibrating over her already sensitized skin.

Sadie took a step back, trying to get her bearings and erase his warm body and citrus soap scent from her thoughts. He was masculinity personified. Her mind tried to wrap around the fact the air could be charged with so much chemistry and heat in such a short time.

She suddenly remembered Luke could walk in any second. Embarrassment crawled up her neck in a rash as she glanced around.

She focused on Boomer. "He did good yesterday."

Nick cleared his throat. "Sure did. He's not the only one. He'd make a good officer, wouldn't you, boy? We'll figure out a way to keep him."

Sadie should feel relief. She was getting what she wanted. Or was she?

The past few minutes had her suddenly wanting more…she wanted the whole package. Would she ever have a house with the white picket fence and the perfect man to go along with the dog? Was Nick that perfect man?

Whoa. She was seriously getting ahead of herself.

There was an undeniable sexual current running between them. But real feelings? Wasn't it way too early to tell?

A short, well-kept curly-haired woman who looked to be in her late fifties walked in the back door. "Boys, come help me get bags from the car."

Luke didn't make eye contact with Sadie or Nick as he walked by, and out the door. He'd already said his piece about Nick breaking protocol to bring her to the ranch. Now she was practically throwing herself at him in front of his brother.

Nick introduced Sadie to his mother—she had the same thick black hair as him. Hers curled around her ears. She couldn't have been more than five foot four. Her arms were filled with grocery bags. Her wide brown eyes took Sadie in for a minute before she spoke. "You must be Sadie." His mom looked her up and down with a smile.

"Nice to meet you," Sadie said. "Let me help with those."

"The pleasure is mine, sweetheart. I'm looking forward to getting to know you better." Her gaze honed in on Nick. "I brought the supplies. Grab your other brother and help unload the truck so we can give Gran the celebration she deserves."

Nick relieved his mother of the bags she held. As soon as her arms were free, she wrapped them around Sadie in firm hug. "It sure is nice to meet you. Call me Melba."

"It really is nice to meet you, Melba." Sadie didn't shrink at the older woman's contact. Instead, she had an unexplainable feeling of being right where she belonged. It was a temporary feeling at best. Sadie hadn't felt as though she belonged anywhere in her entire life. Even when her parents were alive, they'd never made her feel this safe.

The memory of when she was twelve flooded her. She'd had to stay after school for choir practice. She lived too far away to walk home. Her parents had had to work but promised to be there to pick her up by six o'clock.

Choir practice ended and she went outside with the other kids.

The carpool line was long.

She watched each car go past, smiling parents picking up their children.

The choir teacher gave her an annoyed look.

She'd told them her parents would be there any minute. She prayed they hadn't forgotten like they did her school play.

They were so wrapped up in their business, their own lives, Sadie wondered if they'd cared about her at all.

She never knew what to expect from them.

The choir teacher marched her inside after waiting forty minutes at the curb and told her to call her parents. He took that moment to remind her they'd had to sign a slip at the beginning of the school year saying they understood the commitment they were making.

They didn't pick up the phone.

Sadie lied, saying she suddenly remembered they'd wanted her to walk home.

The teacher reluctantly agreed, saying they were supposed to send a note if other arrangements were needed.

She'd sworn to him they'd be fine with her walking.

He let her go.

Anger and humiliation had her stalking toward home. Then she realized she'd have to walk through a dicey part of town to get there.

Fear assailed her when she heard music thumping from a boom box. Cars with missing parts were parked on front lawns.

Sofas were used as porch furniture.

Midway up the street, several men stood around the cars, downing forty-ounce cans of beer.

The anger that had brought her there turned to apprehension. When one of the men catcalled her, apprehension gave way to fear.

Her heart thumped so loudly she was certain people could hear it from a block away.

She kept her head down and crossed the street.

One of the men, the one who whistled at her, followed.

In that moment, Sadie realized what true fear was. And how someone could instill it in her in five seconds flat.

The other men goaded him on.

Sadie broke into a run.

A voice from behind her, nearing, called to someone in front of her. A man four houses down stepped onto the sidewalk. The look on his face, the grin, was still etched in her memory.

Her twelve-year-old self picked that moment to scream.

"No one can hear you," the man behind her said, his hand on her shoulder. To this day, just the thought of his touch gave her the willies.

She slapped it off.

"Someone's feisty."

The man in front of her closed in.

"This one's spunky."

Fear and anger and abandonment welled inside her. Where were her parents when she needed them?

Yes, it had been stupid to think she could walk.

Anger had her doing that when she shouldn't.

This was too much to handle.

She had no means of escape and one of the men touched her ponytail. His hands were dirty.

Sadie shivered, glancing around wildly.

She was trapped.

"You better think twice before you touch that little girl again." An unfamiliar man's voice to her left said.

She hadn't noticed the couple standing on their porch until just then.

"I push one more button on this phone, and the police'll be here before you can count to three. I doubt your parole officer would be real impressed, Sean." The woman held up a phone.

The man they addressed as Sean, the one who'd touched her, hesitated before holding his hands up in the universal sign for surrender. "No harm here. We was just having a little fun, wasn't we?"

His gaze flicked to his buddy before settling on the couple again.

The woman had handed the phone to her husband and moved to Sadie's side. The older woman's arms around Sadie marked the first time she'd felt safe. "You best keep your fun on your side of the street if you don't want to serve the rest of your time in prison."

Melba's arms around Sadie gave her that same fleeting feeling of comfort as the strangers' had. They'd asked her if her mother knew she was alone in the neighborhood and, embarrassed, she'd said no.

Sadie searched her memory for a time when she'd felt protected by her parents and came up empty.

They'd been frantic when they'd found out what had happened.

Were they a perfect family?

No.

She didn't question their love for her. Work always came first. They'd always told her the best way they could secure a future for her was to make sure she had enough food in her mouth.

Even so, she couldn't help but wonder if they'd notice if she was gone.

Nick's mom patted Sadie's back before letting go.

She gave a quick smile and then clapped her hands together once. "You boys ready to get started? I've got a new bread pudding recipe I've been dying to try out. I've been looking up recipes for the last week."

"All we need are a few good steaks for the grill," Nick said, smiling.

The warmth on his face at his mother's reaction to Sadie put a wide smile on his face.

Luke walked in the back door, bags hanging from his arms, and winked. "You better run while you can get away, Sadie. Or she'll put you to work, too."

"Sadie's quite a talented baker. She might teach us a thing or two if we let her loose in the kitchen," Nick chimed in.

Was he beaming when he said that?

Nah. Couldn't be.

Sadie had to be seeing things.

She'd seen Nick Campbell survive bullets, lead her

through underbrush and trees to safety, and outsmart dangerous men. He was most definitely not the type to beam.

Boomer, tail wagging, walked circles in front of Melba.

"And who is this baby?" Melba acknowledged, as Gran and the others filed into the kitchen.

"He's mine." Sadie smiled, despite feeling like the odd man out in the room. And yet, everyone in Nick's family had made her feel welcome in some way.

Maybe, someday, when all this was behind her and she had a normal life again, she'd live on a ranch like this one.

The image of children running outside, drinking Kool-Aid on a hot summer's day, pierced her thoughts.

What did she think about having children?

For so long, she thought she'd marry Tom, and they'd start a family two years after the wedding. He'd wanted to give them a chance to adjust to being husband and wife before they added to their family.

Part of her thought planning everything out was a good idea. Another side to her railed against the notion. She, of all people, knew how life had a way of charting its own course for people, and especially her.

In her life, if she planned an outdoor vacation, it was sure to rain.

She'd learned years ago not to fight it. Things tended to work out best for her if she found a way to relax and go with the flow.

Tom had been order and plans and spreadsheets.

Miraculously, his plans seemed to work out. The sun even knew when to cue for him if he'd planned their getaway. She had no idea how he'd managed it, but it had worked out.

He'd wanted to graduate from college before he got a job. He did.

He'd planned to work for a company that was willing to pay for his advanced degree so he could save for a wedding. Check.

His last year of graduate school, he expected to date the woman he planned to marry. They'd met Valentine's Day of that year.

He planned to get engaged after dating for two years. He'd already started laying hints.

The marriage part? Well, that didn't work out quite so well for him.

Sadie glanced around at people milling around the room.

She only hoped she could survive the next couple of hours surrounded by all the people Nick loved.

Chapter 11

The special occasion plates had been washed and put away in the china cabinet. Everyone had settled into the family room to watch a movie. The sun was beginning its descent. Nick figured he could zip out relatively quietly.

He borrowed Luke's keys and slipped out back.

Most people confused Nick for his brother at a distance, anyway. The safest way to slip out of town unnoticed was to be mistaken for Luke.

Sadie wasn't expecting him to leave until midnight, so he should be good there. She'd excused herself to go lay down after supper, no doubt her body was still on bakery time. Adjusting to being awake in the daytime would take a few weeks.

Dallas was a good forty-minute drive. What was Grimes doing with a warehouse downtown? The obvious answers? Funneling weapons. Human trafficking. Or using it to store product.

As he opened the door and then slid into the driver's seat, his internal warning bells sounded. He drew his weapon, turned around and yanked the blanket from the floorboard.

"Dammit, Sadie. What do you think you're doing?"

She didn't respond.

"You didn't answer my question," he said, immediately withdrawing his weapon and tucking it in the back of his jeans.

"Um, I guess there's no point pretending it's not me." She gave the universal sign of surrender and smiled.

She was kidding around? Trying to make light of the situation? He didn't think so.

"I don't appreciate this at all. What kind of relationship will we have if I can't trust you?" He immediately realized just how hypocritical he sounded.

She gave him a "go to Hades" look that could set ice on fire. "My thoughts exactly."

"Point taken," he conceded, offering a hand up. "How'd you know I was leaving early?"

"I wasn't sure. I guessed. Why? What does it matter? I'm here. That's the most important thing." She hopped over the seat and eased onto the passenger's side.

"No. It isn't." He deadpanned her. "You're not coming."

"Yes, I am. Please. I promise to stay in the truck." Her green eyes pleaded, and his heart stuttered.

"No, you won't." He let out a suppressed laugh. Not a good idea to let her affect his decisions. He'd crossed a line with her physically. Couldn't say he was especially sorry for holding her in the kitchen. But that's where it had to end. When it came to his investigation, there was no give-and-take. She might jeopardize his information-gathering mission.

"I will. Just let me come with you. I'll do whatever you say."

He could think of a few interesting suggestions with their bodies this close. None of them involved work. "Give me one good reason not to haul you out of this truck."

"Because I'm scared something will happen to you if you go alone and you said Luke was coming. Because my conscious wouldn't be able to handle knowing you'd gone alone. Because maybe I can help."

She was concerned about his safety? "That's three."

"I'm scared."

In a split second, she scooted next to him. Before he could argue, her lips found his. All rational thought as to why he shouldn't allow this to happen flew out his brain when he tasted her sweet lips.

With her mouth moving against his, wasn't as if he could stop himself. He took hold of her neck and positioned her head exactly where he wanted her. Desire was a current running through him, seeking an outlet. This close, the scent of her flooded him. His body so in tune with hers, he was already getting excited. Blood pulsed thickly to the erection growing in his jeans.

He laid her back against the seat, his heft covering her. Her tongue battled with his in the best war he'd ever waged. She tasted sweet, and he wanted more. Now. Not a good idea.

With great effort, he disengaged. "You sure this is what you want?"

Her hands slipped inside his shirt, feeling their way up his chest in answer.

She tasted better than the fresh-baked-bread-and-lily scent he'd first been attracted to. He hadn't forgotten the brief kiss they'd shared at the cabin. He'd had to break apart too soon for his liking.

He cupped her full breast and groaned when her nipple beaded in his palm. A little voice in the back of his head said he shouldn't be doing this. He should take a step back. Analyze the situation. *Like that was about to happen.*

He'd wanted, no needed, to feel her milky skin against him. It had been too long since he'd had sex, and he was already growing hard as her fingers outlined the muscles in his chest. Her hands came up to his shoulders, pressing deep.

His body ached to feel her naked and positioned right where he wanted her underneath him. Then again, he wouldn't complain if she decided to take charge and climb on top, either. She wrapped her legs around his hips, denim on denim, and he thrust his hips deeper inside the V of her legs.

His tongue slicked across her lips and he swallowed her moan.

Much more and he wouldn't be able to quit.

To hell with that. Another second and his control would be shattered.

Every bit of his body battled against his logical mind. He pulled on all the restraint he could muster to break away from her. "You make one hell of an argument, but if you don't stop this right now, I won't be able to. Your lips are the sweetest things I've ever tasted."

"Then what's stopping you?"

"I don't want you to regret anything you do with me, for one."

The sun was an orange glow in the distance.

She looked up at him, all big green eyes and full pink lips. "Then don't stop. I want you to make love to me right here. And then I want to go with you."

The first part? No problem.

The second presented the hiccup. He had no plans to take her with him. And yet, all he had to do was give her a quick nod, and he'd be in paradise in the time it took them to strip.

He had no doubt it'd be the best sex of his life.

But then what?

Their physical connection would be built on a lie. Not exactly the way he'd planned to start their relationship.

Relationship?

Whatever this was. No good could come of deceit.

She looked up at him, desire darkening those incredible green eyes. Didn't seem as though she planned to make this easy. Did she have any idea how easy it would be to rip open the condom in his wallet and show her how sexy and desirable she was right then and there? He wanted nothing more than to thrust himself deeper inside the V of her legs without all that denim getting in the way...to allow her to wrap those naked silky legs around him.

The heat had been building between them since he'd broken into the bakery to save her.

If he was being honest, there'd been sparks from the second their eyes met the month before. That spark had grown into a raging fire. He wanted her more than he wanted air.

But he couldn't let her make a mistake she'd regret.

"I'm not trying to punish you by keeping you at the ranch. I'm trying to keep you safe."

"The only way you can guarantee that is to keep me with you. Besides, you've waited too long to kiss me. Is there something wrong with me? Don't you find me attractive?"

She shifted her weight underneath him, and his erection throbbed.

If she wasn't going to stop this, he should. He wanted to make love to her. Just not on the bench seat of a pickup truck. He wanted to take his time and kiss that freckle on the inside of her thigh until she moaned.

"Finding you desirable is not the problem. You sure you want to make love with me?"

She nodded.

His resolve fractured. "You just gave me an even better reason to march your butt in the house. But I guarantee we wouldn't leave anytime soon. I plan to take my time. And I need to follow up on this lead. Make sure those men can't hurt you anymore."

Her smile made him want things he shouldn't. Threatened to open old wounds, too. More alarm bells sounded, but these had to do with a totally different danger. His heart. He ignored them, dipping his head one more time to taste her sweetness.

With every bit of his strength, he pushed himself up on his arms. "So, you have to go inside."

"We have an agreement. Remember? You don't make decisions without me."

"I didn't violate—"

"No. You didn't. And I don't plan to, either. But take me back in there and I'll be gone before you get back."

He searched her eyes to see if the threat was hollow.

He'd suspected it was when she'd made it earlier after they'd first arrived at the ranch. Where would she go? Just run off into the night? She had to realize she didn't have a bargaining chip in this poker game. She wasn't stupid. On the other hand, her back was against the wall. Would she be desperate enough to follow through with her threat? She was smart, sexy and stubborn.

She watched him intently as he processed the information. The minute she figured out she had him, she smiled.

He had no choice but to let her come with him. He didn't want to risk her leaving, even though somewhere inside he knew she was bluffing. Calling her on it would take away what little power she had left. He didn't have it in him to do that. He could make this work. Stash her in the truck and keep her a safe distance from the warehouse. That way, even if she did try to find him, she wouldn't be able to.

"Are you considering taking me?" Her smile melted what was left of his resolves.

"Yes."

She rewarded him with another sweet kiss that was gently pressed to his lips, which almost had him thinking bedding her right then wasn't such a bad idea.

"That kiss is to be continued later. And, sweetheart, I don't plan to be in a hurry when I peel off your clothes and kiss every inch of the silky skin on the inside of your thigh." He pressed his hand to the inside of her leg. "Or your stomach." He ran his finger along the waistband of her jeans, barely touching the sweet skin there. "Or your neck." He dipped his head and skimmed her breastbone with his lips.

She let out a sexy little moan through ragged breaths.

Her jewel-toned eyes glittered with need. "I sure hope you're a man of your word."

A big piece of him cursed the timing of the drive to Dallas. He'd be a lot happier if he were back at the ranch. With her. In bed.

The thought sobered him as he took the driver's seat. He patted a spot next to him. "Buckle up."

She scooted over and leaned her head on his shoulder. "You know, if you'd asked me out on a date back in Creek Bend, I most likely would've gone."

"I couldn't. Against the rules. There were times when you looked like you could barely stand to be in the same room with me. Thought for sure I'd scared you off more than once."

"Everyone freaked me out but you. There was something about you that put me at ease. I guess it's all your training. It worked."

His gaze moved to hers and intensified. "Darlin', flirting with you was the only time I wasn't acting in Creek Bend."

He put the truck in Reverse and backed out of the lot. He maneuvered onto the highway with the all-too-real notion his feelings toward Sadie were growing. She'd put a chink in the armor surrounding his heart. This wasn't part of the plan.

What he needed to do was focus on the job ahead.

Grimes was out for revenge. They had no idea where he was but believed him to be somewhere in Texas. He'd partnered with her handler, and quite possibly given up his supervisor. Grimes wouldn't let up until he erased the woman Nick was falling for.

Hold on there.

Was he admitting she'd become so much more than

a witness to him? The sexual chemistry between them could light a fresh-cut log on fire. But his heart? Not on the table.

His cell buzzed. He fished it from his pocket and handed it to Sadie, instructing her to put the call on speaker when he saw the name Smith on the screen. "You're on speaker with me and Sadie. What's the word?"

"I have good news for you, Sadie. Evidence points toward Charlie's innocence. Looks like your handler was clean. And there's a pretty good chance he hid your file before he was murdered."

A mix of relief and sadness played across her features.

"Thank you for telling me," she said.

"I figured you'd want to know that first."

Nick kept his gaze trained on the yellow stripes in front of him, leading the way to Dallas. His headlights slashed through the darkness descending around them. This turned his theory upside down. "What else did you find out?"

"I have it on good authority Jamison is the one who set Charlie up. He threw Charlie under the bus to appease them, since Jamison wasn't having luck finding information on Sadie's whereabouts."

Nick muttered a curse.

"Worse yet, Jamison wasn't their lackey. He was their partner. My source discovered—"

"Don't tell me. Let me guess. Money in a Swiss bank account." Nick grunted the words.

"Close. Jamison had a weakness for the Cayman islands."

"So, Jamison was on the take? The greedy bastard got a good agent killed to pad his own retirement fund?"

Smith coughed. "My sources say it's worse than that. Two hours ago, a list of all Texas deputies and their personal information surfaced."

The words hit Nick like a sucker punch.

His mind snapped into focus. He knew exactly what that meant. The ranch was no longer safe. He had to get word to Luke. His brothers would know how to handle any threat. It wouldn't be safe for Sadie to return, either. He hated to think of her reaction when he told her she couldn't go back for Boomer. They couldn't go back to the ranch now.

He glanced at her. She held up the phone. Didn't say a word. He could almost hear the wheels cranking in her mind.

"Nick."

"Yeah." He was still trying to get his head around this last bit of information.

"I won't stop until I find him." His voice was nothing but steel resolve.

"Any chance Charlie stashed her folder somewhere safe?" He gripped the wheel. "Never mind that question. They wouldn't have found her."

"I'm going to send some pictures. Sadie, I need you to look at them. If you can identify him, I'll be able to get a warrant to search his house."

Sadie sucked in a breath. She must've realized the implication. "One of the guys who abducted me might be a U.S. Marshal."

There was dead silence.

"It would certainly explain why they're coming at you so hard," Smith said. "You said in your statement that you'd seen their faces."

They'd been relentless so far. It also made sense why

they seemed to understand how Nick would work. How they anticipated his moves or had had someone on his heels at every turn. A man with the same training would have a better idea where to look.

Nick took the next exit. "Send the photos."

He ended the call and located an abandoned lot. He parked and flipped on the cab light.

Sadie's grip on the phone had turned her knuckles white. Her hand shook and her skin had gone pale.

Nick gently pulled the cell out of her hand and kissed the tips of her fingers. "I need to warn Luke."

His brother picked up on the first ring.

"Bad news."

A yawn came through the line. "You didn't wreck my truck, did you?"

"Nope. Much worse. We've confirmed our suspicions. This case involves some of my own."

The line went dead quiet.

"That's not good."

"My involvement in the case has most likely caused them to target me," Nick said, his gaze on Sadie the whole time. She was afraid but brave.

"That's really not good."

"No, it isn't."

"Any chance they know about the ranch?" Luke asked.

"A list just turned up with Texas deputies' personal information on it."

Luke let out a string of curse words.

"So far, I know one supervisor was involved. He got a deputy killed to protect his healthy bank account on the islands," Nick said.

"Hard to believe someone would turn on their own for a few bucks, but to each his own, I guess."

"He's a jerk."

"One I'd like to be alone with in a room for ten minutes."

"Agreed. Problem is, because of him a good deputy was killed and many more are at risk."

Luke grunted.

"My boss is sending over pictures for Sadie to look at, so I can't stay on long. We're certain all the deputies in Texas have been identified for Grimes and his men."

"Bastard."

"Agreed. Get everyone off the ranch, just in case."

"Will do. I'll have Reed take them to Galveston. Everyone except Meg and Riley. They'll have to stick around to be close to her doctor. I'll stay at my place in Dallas. Can't get too far from The Metroplex while I'm working on my case."

"Sounds like a plan. Make Meg and Riley promise to have their place watched. Better yet, do Riley's parents live in Fort Worth?"

"I believe so."

"Any chance you can get them to agree to stay there? I don't want to take any risks with her so close to her due date."

"I'm on it," Luke said. "I'll get the others out by tonight. Don't worry. And I'll make sure Sadie's dog is taken care of, too."

"Boomer," Sadie said in almost a whisper.

"I'll take care of him while you're on the go. You got a safe house, man?" Luke asked.

"Yeah. I'm heading to Richardson after a little trip

downtown. I might need a favor while Reed's down south."

"Yeah?'

"Grimes has a real estate holding in Houston. I need someone to check it out for me. Dig around. See what they can find."

"Wish I could go myself." The telltale adrenaline that hit before a big assignment deepened Luke's tone.

"I wish we could go together. I like my odds better if I have someone I can trust backing me up."

"I'll tell Reed. Text the address."

"Will do."

"When this is over, you should come on over to our side. FBI needs more good people they can trust," Luke said, using his sense of humor to lighten the mood.

"Believe me, after this assignment, I'd almost consider it."

"If we were smart, we'd leave our day jobs and work for ourselves."

"Another tempting idea. Have Reed give me a call as soon as he gets to that warehouse."

"Can I give him a heads-up on what he might expect to find?"

"Wish I could help."

"That close to the border, Grimes might be moving product in through Galveston," Luke said.

"Yeah. I have no idea what to expect. All I know is he has a straight line up to Canada."

"You've found the right man for the job if they're hauling stuff through the Gulf," Luke agreed.

"His department might find something interesting. He'll need a reason to search the place officially."

"Reed can be damn inventive when he needs to be." Luke paused. "Keep me in the loop."

Nick agreed and ended the call. He had eight text messages waiting. He opened the first and showed the picture to Sadie.

She shook her head.

The second received the same response.

The third, fourth and fifth had the same affect.

When he opened the sixth and glanced up, he saw recognition stamped all over Sadie's features. Her pupils dilated and her breath came out in a gasp.

"That's him."

Chapter 12

"This guy looks familiar?" Nick asked. Anger rose inside him as he watched a tremor rock her body.

Her chin came up, and she locked gazes. "Yes."

He fired off a confirmation text to Smith.

"He was one of the guys who abducted me," she said, her body shaking. "I'd been grocery shopping. I was putting the bags in my car when all of a sudden this van pulled up behind me, blocking my car. I didn't think much about it. I mean, I lived in a relatively safe suburb. I actually thought the driver was about to ask for directions when this man came out of nowhere from behind the van. He put some kind of cloth over my mouth. I couldn't scream. I couldn't fight. I couldn't believe this was happening to me in broad daylight. The smell of whatever was in that cloth burned my nose and eyes."

Nick's fists clenched and released. He was more

determined than ever to stop whoever was after the woman he was falling for. Forcing Sadie to remember such a heinous experience went against every fiber of his being. He'd buried his own bad memories so deep hell itself could rise up and not find them. Except remembering might just save her life.

Causing her more pain ate at his gut. Everything she'd been through was totally bogus.

She was in trouble. So was he. His feelings ran deeper than he should allow. He still wasn't sure what the hell to do with them. No one since Rachael had touched his heart so deeply or threatened to crack his tough veneer and he still hadn't figured out why he'd kept her ring in his pocket for a year. He figured something inside him didn't work right after watching his mom's pain and deciding love was about the cruelest thing that could happen to a person. He assumed that part of his heart had been closed off forever. "The whole scenario had to be scary as hell."

"Yeah, panic didn't cover it. I felt so helpless. Next thing I knew I woke up in the back of the van, and that guy was staring at me."

Nick didn't say the agent must've expected to kill her if he let her see his face. "You're safe now. That's the important thing."

A car pulled into the lot.

Nick checked his rearview mirror, started the engine and drove away, spewing gravel from the back tires.

He didn't want to press Sadie to talk but if she remembered something, anything, they might be able to pinpoint a location. He'd talk to her about it more when they arrived at the safe house later. Right now, he had a warehouse to investigate.

They'd been driving a good twenty minutes before either spoke again.

"Where are we going? Sadie asked.

"Brenner and Harry Hines. Near Love Field."

"How convenient to have a warehouse so close to an airport."

He exited Stemmons Freeway onto Walnut Hill and then turned right onto Shady Trail. "It's regional. But, yeah, it would be handy. If they needed to go farther, DFW's twenty minutes away depending on traffic."

He parked the truck in a small lot next to Old Letot Cemetery. The cemetery was the size of a half-decent backyard encased in a four-foot-high chain-link fence. Getting to Brenner would be an easy walk from there.

Leaving a beautiful woman like Sadie in the truck in a bad neighborhood—even locked—was riskier than taking her with him. Besides, he doubted she'd stay put, anyway. He could keep a better eye on her if she went with him.

"We'll need to keep quiet."

She seemed to catch the word *we* quickly, and perked up at the realization she was coming. "Not a problem."

"Anything happens to me and you'll need a way to protect yourself." He pulled his .38 caliber from his ankle holster.

Her hand shook as she reached for it.

"You okay?"

To her credit, she nodded and gripped the gun.

"Stick close behind me. I stop too fast, I want to feel you run into my back. Got it?"

She nodded again.

"Then, let's do this."

She scooted out his door, exiting the truck right behind him. Apparently, she had every intention of taking his request to heart. Good. He wanted her so close he could hear her breathe.

He hopped the fence and helped Sadie over. They cut across the small cemetery so he could investigate the warehouse from the back first. He crouched low behind the Dumpster in the back parking lot and watched.

There was no activity in the row of warehouses. A handful of vehicles were parked in the small lot—two vans and a couple of flatbed trucks. Everything was quiet. He didn't hear any traffic. He located the numbers 2626 on top of the metal sliding door.

They'd wait and see if there was any activity. He needed to ensure no one came or went before he and Sadie made a move to get closer.

So much of this job was about patience.

Twenty minutes passed and nothing moved except for a raccoon in the trash bin that almost made Sadie jump out of her skin. She'd kept her cool.

"Stay right here while I check out the vehicles."

Her eyes were wide, but she nodded.

Nick kept a low profile as he moved across the small lot, squat walking, just in case someone was waiting in one of the trucks. He'd learned to expect anything in these situations. Someone could be there asleep. At least he was sure no one was getting lucky in the backseat. He hadn't seen the telltale fog of the windows. Near Harry Hines, anything was possible. In his years with the agency, he'd pretty much seen it all.

He touched the hood of each vehicle. Cold.

None of them had been driven lately.

One by one, he checked the cabs.

Clear.

Good.

He returned to Sadie. "Ready to move to the front?"

She nodded again. She was either scared to the point of being mute or a good listener. He hoped for the second. He could work with that.

"Let's move."

He was almost surprised when she followed him. Meant she was coherent. Another good sign.

The strip of warehouses was encased by wrought-iron fences out front. He hoped none of them were hot. He could scale the six-foot barrier easily with one hand on the top rail, but Sadie wouldn't be able to. He picked up a rock and tossed it at the fence.

No telltale crackle of electricity.

The sounds of tires turning on pavement caught his attention. Two dots appeared down the street. The headlights were moving toward them.

He grabbed Sadie by the hand and climbed over the fence. She dropped to her hands and knees and crawled behind him.

The headlights moved closer.

Adrenaline thumped through his veins. He couldn't guarantee Sadie's safety. Didn't especially like the feeling gripping him that he'd compromised her security by bringing her along.

Wouldn't do any good to second-guess himself.

She was there.

He was there.

He'd make sure they both made it out alive.

Brakes squeaked the car to a stop two buildings

down. Nick made out an older model Lincoln. There was a driver and a passenger. The passenger moved over to the driver's side and the seat flew back. Both of them disappeared.

Nick watched carefully for the overhead light to come on in case someone was exiting the vehicle. An experienced criminal would know to turn it off before slipping out. Neither Grimes nor the U.S. Marshals searching for them were amateurs.

Nick waited another five minutes, his gaze intent on the dark sedan.

"I'm moving closer to check it out. You stay right here," he whispered when enough time had passed. He had to crawl across the empty parking lot to get close enough to see what was going on. No one had left the vehicle as far as he could tell.

A light came on in the third building as he neared the halfway mark across the lot. The warehouse was right next to him. He froze, making himself as small as possible.

Nothing but stillness surrounded him.

He inched closer to the Lincoln. Made it to the corner where his lot and the one for building number two met. The car wasn't a hundred yards away. He was close enough to see the windows fogging up and hear the shocks creaking. Lovers? Not likely. Not at this time of night on this road. But they were having sex.

Nick had a problem on his hands. He could flash his badge and get rid of the prostitute and John, but possibly call attention to himself and Sadie. Or he could wait it out. His back already hurt like hell.

The light flipped off on building number three.

He had to assume whoever was there had gotten what

they came for. They must've used the back entrance, which made the most sense if they were loading supplies. He didn't have time to care why a person would be here at this late hour.

Even though he knew exactly what was going on in the car, he had to make sure. Getting close enough to get a visual would be right up there with his least favorite task of the night.

On closer assessment, the pair was doing exactly what he suspected.

Nick crawled across the lot. Relief flooded him that Sadie was exactly where he left her. Not having his eyes on her for even a second did all kinds of crazy things to his insides, to his heart. This didn't seem like an appropriate time to get inside his head about what that meant.

She leaned so close he could feel her breath on him. "What could they possibly be doing over there? I freaked when they pulled up, thinking the worst, but no one's getting out of the car."

He couldn't wipe the ridiculous grin off his face. This wasn't the time to be charmed by her innocence. "You don't want to know."

"What does that… Oh." With the dim glow of a street lamp, he could see her cheeks flush with embarrassment. "What do we do now?"

"Wait."

Fifteen minutes passed before the passenger's door opened and a tall skinny girl crawled out.

Sadie reached out to Nick, placing her hand in his. Hers seemed small by comparison. And soft.

He squeezed her fingers for reassurance. A few more minutes and they'd get what they came for.

The door slammed shut and the Lincoln pulled away, squealing its tires.

Skinny tucked something, presumably cash, in her bra and stumbled away, either drunk or high, or both.

Nick didn't like the idea of her or anyone else being around or the possibility they could be seen. Her presence also most likely meant there were others like her wandering around, searching for their next twenty dollars or fix.

His warning system flared up that anyone else could see them or identify them at the scene. Especially since he had no idea what this warehouse was being used for.

He had to prepare himself for any possibility.

Damn that anyone could signal inside or send up a red flag, alerting Grimes's men to their presence if anyone was there.

"Stick close by me."

Sadie nodded.

He had to make sure Skinny was far enough away, and there was no pimp nearby working this end of the street.

Nick kept to the shadows, with Sadie right behind him every step of the way.

He followed Skinny back to Harry Hines, where she met up with a few similarly dressed women.

Relief flooded him as he backtracked the couple of blocks to the warehouse.

Instinct told him they needed to get the information they came for and get the hell out of there.

Chapter 13

As expected, the front and back doors were locked. Sadie hadn't expected a man like Grimes to leave his inventory, or whatever he kept in there, unprotected.

"We can't break one of the windows up front, can we?" she asked.

"I don't want to raise suspicion we were here." Nick moved to the dock door, bent down and examined the lock. He fished a small Swiss army knife out of his pocket and went to work with his flashlight and small pick-looking tool. "I can manage this one easily enough."

"Can you do this?" Sadie asked, shocked. Surely he wasn't planning on breaking and entering. Wasn't that a felony offense? He'd lose his job. Possibly even go to jail.

He deadpanned her. "Not legally. Anything we find won't be admissible in court. But they've involved my family. I'll do what's necessary to protect them."

The way he clenched his jaw left no doubt he meant every word.

She tamped down the emotion tugging at her heart. The air stirred around them. With the way he watched over the people he loved, Nick would make an amazing father someday. He was exactly the kind of man she'd want to father her children someday.

The shock of her realization she wanted kids was only dwarfed by the one that said she wanted to be with Nick.

"What do you think we'll find in there?" she asked.

"Could be anything from guns to illegals. It's dark and quiet inside. Whoever takes care of the shipments has gone home."

Images of poor, hungry people packed inside trucks without air-conditioning popped into Sadie's mind. Since she'd been in Texas, she hadn't gone a month without seeing something in the news about human trafficker raids or inhumane conditions.

A snick sounded, and she knew he'd cracked the lock. He closed the tool and stuffed it in his pocket.

He rolled up the door enough for them to squat down and slip inside. "I'll go first and make sure it's clear."

"Okay."

A few seconds later, he told her it was fine.

She ducked down and crawled into the opening.

Nick pulled the metal door closed, drew his weapon and picked up the flashlight he'd set down.

The thin beam skimmed the large room, exposing a line of twin mattresses on the floor spanning two walls. Some had pillows and blankets, others had nothing but a towel on them. Looked as if they could pack fifty illegals in there at one time. The place smelled like sweat and fear.

Other than that, the place was empty save for shipping evidence like boxes, tape and a small forklift.

Every indicator pointed toward this place being used for moving illegals through the country, and God only knew what else. "Can you call the police? Have them arrested? It's obvious criminal activity is going on in here."

"Not without proof."

"What about those beds?" She pointed before she remembered he couldn't see her in the dark.

"Circumstantial. Plus, I can't use evidence gathered without a proper search warrant."

Seriously? "Isn't it obvious what they're doing?"

"Yes. But courts, judges and juries want indisputable evidence and an appropriate paper trail before they send people to jail. A good lawyer would shred this case to pieces."

"Seems like a pretty screwed-up system if you ask me."

"From where I stand right now, I wouldn't argue. But that's the structure. It isn't perfect, but it does keep innocent people out of prison."

"It shouldn't be so hard to get guilty people off the streets."

"Agreed." Nick ran the stream of light up a stairwell to what looked like a second-story office.

Hope bubbled. "Maybe there will be something in there we can use."

She followed him up the narrow steps.

The wood door was locked. She had no doubts that Nick could pop the door open with one good bump of his shoulder, but he wouldn't.

Instead, he pulled out his tool and jimmied the lock.

This one took even less time to crack.

The flashlight beam skimmed over the room. There was a solid mahogany desk with a leather executive chair tucked into it.

Nick moved to it. The top was clean. He tried to open the drawers of the desk. They didn't budge.

"Whatever they're doing must pay well," Sadie said, taking in the expensive-looking leather sofa against one wall, and the opulent chairs positioned across from the desk.

"Tells me something else. The big boss works from here."

"How do you know that?"

"They wouldn't approve spending this much money on furniture for a captain. And Dallas is a great place to locate his headquarters. We have the worst jury pulls. Even if we gather enough evidence to arrest them, it's harder to get a conviction here. Criminals know it. Grimes knows it. Everyone in the agency would, too."

"Grimes. Here?" She glanced around. A band of tension tightened around Sadie's chest.

"Yes." Nick moved to a filing cabinet positioned against the wall behind the desk. "Might find something useful in here."

He opened drawer after drawer while Sadie helped flip through folders.

She pulled one out. "What is this?"

Nick focused the beam on the piece of paper she held. "An invoice for silk scarves."

Sadie hauled out another one and held it under the light. "And this is for Chinese footwear."

The rest of the contents of the drawer yielded similar results.

Her heart stopped at the sound of a car pulling into the front parking lot. "What do we do now?"

Nick turned off the flashlight and held her hand. "We wait."

She had to remind herself to breath.

Was this another paid late-night tryst with the prostitute they'd seen earlier or one of her friends? Sadie couldn't allow herself to consider anything worse. Like Grimes returning. If he found her this time, would she and Nick be dead?

Minutes ticked by.

A siren blast followed by squad car lights split the darkness.

Sadie thought she could hear her heart pounding in her chest as they waited for the cop to pull away.

Five minutes later, everything was dark out front.

Nick flicked on the flashlight.

Sadie held up another useless invoice. This one was for bracelets. "We aren't going to find anything, are we?"

"Don't give up yet." He pulled the file cabinet away from the wall.

"What are you doing?"

"I learned this trick a long time ago." He felt along the back of the wood then produced a manila folder. "Taped to the back."

"Oh, my gosh." He'd found something.

They moved to the desk. Nick opened the envelope. He dumped the contents out. There were a few documents, pictures and, holy cow, Sadie's personal information. They had the name of the bakery where she worked, which she already knew they'd discovered, and a picture of her lake house.

She gasped at the picture of her and Nick in the truck,

escaping from the bakery. Whoever took it must've been with the person who'd followed them.

Her pulse quickened with every new picture. Luke. Reed. Meg. Riley. Lucy. One by one, each of Nick's family members appeared.

Nick fanned out the photos from the deck and grunted a foul word.

She'd been thinking the exact same one.

The message was clear. No way did they plan to leave his family alone.

Nick splayed the pictures and documents from the envelope across the desk after making the call to his safe house contact. He pulled out his camera and took photos then texted the new information to Luke. "I'll forward this to Smith once we get to the safe house. We can examine these more closely there, as well."

Nick figured it would be easy to hide Sadie in Richardson's Chinatown among the strip malls.

He pulled onto Greenville Avenue, located Dim Sum, the restaurant, and parked in the dark behind it. Paul Huang's new Japanese import was parked under the street lamp.

Nick flashed his headlights and Paul zipped past him and out of the lot, slowing down enough for Nick to follow. His contact was about as far away from the U.S. Marshals Service as he could be. No one knew about Paul.

A cold front was due, and Nick would at least give Sadie a solid roof over her head tonight.

Winding into a neighborhood behind the shopping mall, Paul pulled in front of a house and jumped out of his car, motioning Nick to park on the pad in front of the house.

"My man, Nick," the Asian said, twin plumes of smoke rising from his nostrils.

They shook hands and bumped shoulders in a man greeting.

"It's been a long time. How's your mom?" Nick asked.

"Ah, you know her. She slaves away in the kitchen. I finally have enough money to give her a decent retirement. I don't need the help. She can relax. What does she do? Work. She's so stubborn."

"Probably wants to feel useful," Nick offered.

"That's true. She worries about getting too old."

"You have any more trouble at the restaurant?" Nick had intervened on several occasions on Paul's behalf when gangs tried to move in on his block and force him to pay protection fees or risk having his livelihood burned to the ground.

"No. Thanks to you. They didn't come back." Paul stood staring at Sadie, waiting for an introduction.

Nick shook his head. "Better if you don't know anything on this one."

Paul, a middle-aged Asian with white hair dotting his temples, nodded his understanding. He popped the butt of his cigarette in his mouth and puffed on it while he stuck the key in the lock. He opened the door. "It's not a big place but it's clean. You hungry?"

"Nah. We're okay for the night."

"You need anything, you take it. I stocked the fridge as soon as you called." He tossed a key onto the counter next to the one he'd used to open the door a moment ago. "The restaurant is behind you. This yard backs up to it. Hop the wall and you're there. If you don't find what you need here, go there."

"I appreciate you letting us use your relatives' place for a few days. We won't be here too long."

"Nothing's too much to ask from you, my friend. You saved my life. My aunt and uncle are out of the country, anyway. Went back to China. I don't know why. I told them there's nothing back there I forgot." He laughed at his own joke and shook his head. "They don't need to use this place right now. It's no trouble at all. I put fresh sheets on the bed for you." His gaze moved from Nick to Sadie. "If not for this guy, I'd have nothing. Those thugs almost ran me out of business. Out of town. But this guy. He stopped them." He gave Nick a friendly tap on the shoulder. "You didn't let them push around the little guy."

Nick smiled. "Glad to help."

"He's a good guy," Paul said, winking at Sadie. "He'll take care of you."

Sadie stood by the door as Nick thanked Paul again.

The place was tight, but had everything they needed. From the front door, she could see the living and dining rooms, as well as the kitchen. There was a flat-screen TV on one wall and a hunter-green recliner sofa positioned in front. Pictures of family covered most of the white space on the walls.

She excused herself to the bathroom and starting filling the tub while she undressed. A warm bath sounded like heaven. Besides, she needed a minute to process what they'd brought from the warehouse.

A soft knock at the door startled her.

"Come in. I'm covered." She sat on the side of the tub with a bath towel wrapped around her.

The door barely opened, and she could see a sliver of Nick's face. "I don't want to bother you. Just wanted to give you an update. Smith has the information."

"It's fine. I was just sitting here thinking. If there's a U.S. Marshal involved, then no one's safe, are they?"

"You are. I am. My family is on their way to Galveston right now. No one knows about our place there. They sure as hell won't get to us here." He opened the door a little more and leaned against the jamb. "I just spoke to Reed, by the way. Boomer's doing fine. It's probably best for him to be with them right now."

She nodded, ignoring the ache in her chest. "I do realize that. I wouldn't want to do anything that would put his life at risk. And especially not just so I can have him with me. He has to come first."

"He's lucky to have you."

"He's in good hands with your family."

"Gran might fight you for him later." He smiled, and it brightened his whole face. He held out two beers. The label read Tsingtao. "I found these in the fridge. They're actually pretty good. Best of all, they're cold. Want one?"

"Do I? Yes. I would very much like a cold drink."

He opened the bottle of beer and handed it to her.

"Don't worry. We'll figure this out. We're getting closer to uncovering the truth. Knowing who's involved is a huge plus for our side. Now we have to gather enough evidence to put the jerk away."

His words provided a small measure of comfort. There was something about his presence that calmed her rattled nerves. He was just this amazingly calming man. She could get used to this, to him.

"I'll be in the other room if you need anything else. I promise not to peek, but do you mind if I leave this cracked?"

"Not at all. In fact, I'd feel better knowing you could hear me."

He disappeared and she set her beer down, slipped off the towel and eased into the warm water. The tension from a long day evaporated, similar to boiling water turning into steam.

She picked up her drink. Beads of water dripped down the longneck bottle as she curled her fingers around the base. The light taste and cool liquid refreshed as it slid down her throat.

Seeing her abductor's face again had brought up painful memories. She was exhausted. Her mind was spent, her body drained. She calculated how long it had been since she'd slept. Her body screamed *too long*.

Sadie leaned her head back and closed her eyes.

After a good soak in the tub, she washed herself before stepping out and hand-washing her clothes in the sink. The shower rod was as good a place as any to hang her garments to dry, so she did.

There was toothpaste on the counter. She squeezed some from the tube and finger-brushed her teeth. It was better than nothing. She tightened the towel around her, and moved into the hall, closing the door to the bathroom behind her.

Nick sat on the couch, flipping through TV channels. He did a double take when she stepped into the room wearing only a towel.

She stopped in the living room, completely aware of how naked she was underneath the towel. His reaction had set off a small fire inside her.

"You, uh, want to sit down?"

If she wasn't so tired, she would've experienced a thrill that her femininity seemed to rob his ability to speak clearly. "Okay."

She curled up on the other end of the sofa.

"You want the remote?" He held it out toward her, but his gaze didn't leave hers. He pushed off the sofa and disappeared into the bedroom, returning a minute later holding a comforter. "This should keep you warm."

The blanket was thick, warm and soft. She pulled it up to her neck and thanked him. "This is perfect."

He stood there for a long moment and raked his fingers through his black-as-night curls. "I, uh, should probably go get cleaned up."

Sensual heat vibrated between them. "I found a towel for you and folded it on the counter."

He double-checked the locks on the window in the living room and kitchen. "You want this?" He held out his weapon.

The sight of a gun sent her body into a full-on shiver. "Yeah. I should be prepared. Just in case."

"No one will find us here. I trust Paul. No one in the agency knows about him." He hesitated outside the bathroom door. "I won't be long. You need anything, yell. I'll be here in a snap."

The image of him naked, wet, muscled, lit another small fire. Combine the two and the blaze could get out of control quickly.

True to his word, he wasn't ten minutes in the shower. He strolled into the living room with a towel secured around his hips. Beads of water trailed down his muscular chest.

Now it was Sadie's turn to flush.

"Found these." He held up toothbrushes still in their wrappers.

She turned off the cooking show she'd been watching and joined him next to the sink in the bathroom.

He handed one over, and she opened it immediately,

put toothpaste on it and scrubbed her teeth. "This is heaven."

They hovered over the sink, their heads so close they almost touched as they took turns under the faucet.

"I can throw your clothes in the wash with mine." He picked up his jeans and shirt.

"You found a washer?"

"In the hallway leading to the bedrooms."

"Wouldn't hurt to run them through a cycle." She made her way back to the sofa as he turned on the washer. Was there anything sexier than a half-naked man who knew how to take care of himself and everyone around him? She didn't think so. She couldn't imagine Tom washing his own clothes. Everything had to be sorted by color, placed in the correct bins and dropped off at the cleaners who knew exactly how he liked his things washed and pressed. She was almost embarrassed to remember that he had his summer shorts ironed. He had good qualities, she reminded herself. Manly? Not so much.

Nick, who was nothing but all-man and muscle and smart, walked into the room. Her gaze dipped to his towel and the line of hair from his navel to…the trail ended at his towel. His raw sensual appeal lit another little fire.

"You can change the channel if you want. There wasn't much on earlier excerpt for crime shows."

"I don't mind watching whatever." He settled next to her. His thigh touched hers and the power of that one touch ignited little blazes all down her leg.

She pulled the blanket over her and turned the cooking show back on.

"Want to share?"

His gaze intensified on the screen. "I'm, uh, okay."

Did he feel it, too?

He must have. He'd never had so much trouble putting together a string of words before. Another trill of excitement rushed through her at the thought she had the power to affect such a beautiful man. His body was perfection on a stick. He didn't seem to realize or care, and that just made him even sexier.

He put his arm around her, and she settled into the hollow of his neck. His body radiated warmth.

It would be a mistake to get too comfortable in his arms. The reasons were clipped onto the waistband of his jeans most of the time. His gun. His badge.

Two excellent reasons to keep her emotions under control and not fall into the trap of thinking this could be any more than what it was right then.

Nick was her handler.

It was his job to protect her.

Making her feel safe was part of his assignment. Making her feel sexy wasn't. He stirred another part of her she shouldn't allow.

Sadie didn't want to think about that tonight.

The cooking host sliced an onion in half, running the blade through each side again and again until it was chopped.

The sounds from the TV in the background couldn't drown out the beating of Nick's heart.

She burrowed deeper into the crook of his arm and closed her eyes.

Chapter 14

Sadie woke to the smell of fresh coffee. She sat up and realized she must've dozed off on the couch last night. Naked save for a towel wrapped around her. Embarrassment sent a rash crawling up her neck. She immediately checked to make sure all her body parts were covered.

The blanket still covered her.

Nick sat at a desk that was tucked into the corner of the small dining room. His back was to her, his face toward the screen. She glimpsed cold metal from the waistband of his jeans—a constant reminder he lived in a violent world—one she might never get used to. His job was dangerous.

She pushed the thought aside, preferring not to think about many reasons they would never be able to be a couple. Even though there wasn't exactly an offer of a relationship on the table. The draw she felt to him was unexplainable. Then again, he was one seriously hot guy who was strong to boot. Who wouldn't be attracted to that?

"That coffee I smell?"

He held up a foam cup. She hadn't even heard him get up or go out.

"It is. And good morning to you."

"You didn't happen to buy two of those, did you?"

He turned to face her, and her heart stuttered. His black hair disheveled, stubble on his chin, only made him more irresistible. Damn that he was gorgeous in the morning. In the afternoon. In the evening. Hell, he looked good all the time.

He was also a man with a gun and badge.

"As a matter of fact, I did." He grabbed a small paper bag from the desk and removed another cup. "And I picked up food. Breakfast tacos. I got one with bacon and one with sausage. I wasn't sure which you liked."

Scrambled eggs with cheese, bacon and salsa rolled in a warm tortilla. A Tex-Mex treat she'd grown to love since living in Texas. "That smells amazing. I'm all about the bacon. Definitely bacon. On second thought, this is too good to be true. You're probably just a hallucination, a figment of my overtired imagination. Am I even awake yet?" She blinked, taking the treasures from him. "If I am, I should get dressed."

"It's real." He bent down and kissed her forehead. "I'm real. I happened to like what you're wearing. But if you don't stop looking so damn adorable, you're going to find out just how very real I am."

"Oh."

"So you better distract me by telling me how well you slept last night." He smiled and stroked her cheek.

"Best night of sleep I've had in a long time." The

fire he'd lit last night blazed to attention again. She half remembered his body curled behind hers, and the feeling of everything being right in the world while she was nestled against him. She'd never felt like that in another man's arms.

There was something special about Nick.

Did she just blush again? "How about you? Did you get any sleep or did you stay awake all night at that computer?"

"And miss out on feeling your body against mine? Hell, no. I was right there all night." He pointed to the space behind her. "And I slept like a rock."

She took a sip of coffee, welcoming the burn. "Let me guess, job hazard?"

"Yeah. It'd be dangerous for me to let my guard down." His smile tightened. His gaze focused on a square on the carpet.

Based on the change in his expression, she had the very real sense they were about to talk about a heavy subject.

They hadn't finished their conversation from yesterday. He would most likely want to know more about the man in the picture. And what he'd done to her. Her body shuddered, thinking about it. She didn't want to relive the past. She'd much rather stay in the present, the here and now. A primal urge had her wanting to trace the muscles of his back with her finger, follow the patch of hair from his navel down to where his blood pulsed.

First, she'd enjoy her meal. "Have you heard from your family this morning?"

"Luke called first thing. Everyone agreed to check in every few hours until this is over and he's heard from everyone but Lucy. Said she's probably tied up on a case. He says Reed took Boomer out for a run this morning."

"I bet he loved it. I used to take him out back and

throw the ball. Half the time he'd end up splashing in the lake. What was supposed to be a quick outing turned into an ordeal. Muddy paws. The smell of lake water. I'd have to give him a bath before I could bring him back inside." She took a bite of her taco, washing it down with a sip of coffee. The warmth felt good on her throat.

"I'm sure he misses you. I know I would."

The statement made tears prick her eyes. Not being with Nick? Her stomach lurched at the thought. Yet, there would come a time when this case was over and they'd go their separate ways. Her heart squeezed and she couldn't deal with thinking about it right now. "What about the others?"

"Meg and Riley are in Fort Worth with his parents, so they're good. She's started contractions."

"Oh, how exciting for them. They must be thrilled." Thoughts of having a baby tugged at her heart. Would she be around to meet the little one? She hoped so. If not, maybe there could be a special arrangement worked out. "I'm so happy for them both. That's going to be one lucky little kid."

"Yeah, they'll be great parents."

"They sure will. This little one will also be surrounded by an amazing family. I can imagine spending summers out on the ranch with Gran. The place would burst with people on the weekends with cousins, aunts and uncles. And there'd be food everywhere." It was exactly the environment she'd want for her child, if she ever had one.

"I like the sound of that."

His smile warmed her heart.

"For now, they sounded nervous as hell. And my little tough Meg in the background sounded like she was in pain." He chuckled.

"She'll do great. It'll all be worth it when she holds that baby in her arms."

"Doc says a first labor can go on for days before the baby comes." He shrugged. "I'll make sure and check in with Meg later. Almost forgot. Luke said the last time he spoke to Lucy she said there's some big news about her and Stephen but they won't say what it is until we're all under the same roof and can celebrate together."

"Are you thinking what I'm thinking?" She took another sip of coffee anticipation lightening her heavy heart.

"I'm guessing they're announcing an engagement."

Sadie was genuinely happy for Lucy. "I hope so. He did say it was good news, right?"

Luke's smile reached his eyes that time. "Yeah. They also said it was scary. Marriage can seem that way. So I've heard."

His brown eyes sparkled. He got that glittery look of pride every time he talked about his family. His love for them was written all over the sappy smile on his face and the pride in his eyes. His smile might be sentimental, but the way those lips curled at the corners was sexy, too.

She didn't want to ruin his mood, or make him think about the past but curiosity was getting the best of her. "What about you? Ever have any plans to take the leap with anyone?"

Nick couldn't exactly pinpoint why he wanted to tell Sadie about his past, but he did. Whatever the hell it was, it must be the same driving force making him want to share details about his family. Something he rarely ever did with anyone. "Yeah. There was someone once. It was a long time ago."

"Do you mind if I ask what happened?" She offered him her coffee.

"No. Ask me anything." He paused long enough to take a sip and hand her cup back to her. "I was young. Thought I had life all figured out. What did I know? She and I had been going together for years already."

"Was she your high-school sweetheart?"

"How'd you know that?"

"I hope you don't mind. Lucy told me a little bit about her."

"Lucy is the most protective of me. I'm surprised she told you anything. She's the quiet one in the family."

"I sensed you two were close. She told me about what happened to her."

A set of surprised eyes stared at her. "That she told you anything about me is shocking. I have no words for her telling you about what happened to her. I can tell you this, though—when that bastard hurt her, I nearly lost my mind. I wanted to kill him with my bare hands."

"If I'm being honest, I'm surprised you didn't. Your family stopped you?"

Tension had him grinding his back teeth. "Thankfully. When he went to trial, I sat in the courtroom and listened to his testimony. All I could do was sit there, helpless, trying to figure out how many punches I could get in before the bailiff could pull me off him."

"But you didn't."

"Not with Gran sitting next to me, holding on to my arm. She knew exactly what I was thinking."

"I've said it before and I'll say it again. Smart woman."

"It almost killed me to let the courts handle him. I

was young and angry. The world pissed me off, and I was ready to take out my frustration."

"What happened?"

"I signed up for the military, ready and willing to fight just about anyone. Rachael didn't want me to go to war. She wanted me to go away to school with her."

"But you didn't."

He intensely focused on the patch of carpet at his feet. "Nothing like nonstop fighting for four years to screw your head back on straight. Before my tour was up, I'd planned to ask her to marry me. I'd sent money home to help Mom and Gran take care of the others. I had a little tucked away for college. Rachael wasn't thrilled I didn't listen to her before, but I thought we had it worked out. She had no idea I was about to surprise her with a ring."

"And then…"

"We argued about where the relationship was going. She decided to party with her friends on New Year's Eve instead of spending it with me. A drunk driver crossed the median and hit her car head-on."

"I'm so sorry."

"The crazy thing was I'd had that ring in my pocket for a year. For some reason, I didn't ask. I held on to it. Even though she'd made it clear she wanted me to. Guess I thought I had plenty of time. Or maybe I had my doubts about taking the plunge. Marriage seemed so permanent. When I finally realized I wanted to ask, I wanted everything to be perfect. Maybe make up for not asking before. I had it all planned out. I was going to ask first thing New Year's Day…"

He heard Sadie mumble a few words meant to comfort him, like *I'm sorry,* and *Life can be so unfair.*

This was the first time he'd spoken about Rachael

with anyone outside of his family. Hell, he didn't say much to his family about the topic.

God, it felt good to finally talk about it. To get it off his chest. He'd been holding everything in for so long, erecting an impenetrable barrier around his heart.

Sadie got up, stood in front of him, her arms around him. He leaned forward, resting his forehead on her stomach, holding on to her around her waist.

"I can't help thinking if I'd asked her sooner, somehow things would have turned out differently."

"You don't have a crystal ball."

He still felt the burden of wishing he could go back and change the past. "My timing sucked."

"You couldn't have known what would happen."

"Maybe if I'd asked her the night before, she would've been with my family celebrating instead of going out with her friends."

"That might not have changed the outcome."

He clenched his fists. "Yeah, well I'll never know now. I could've been the one to run into her for how responsible I felt after."

"It wasn't your fault."

Those four words were more effective than a bullet, piercing the Kevlar encasing his heart.

He sat up, keeping his gaze on hers the entire time, waiting, expecting her to tell him to stop or give him a signal this couldn't happen.

Instead, her tongue slicked across her lips and he couldn't tear his gaze away from the silky trail.

"Do that again and I won't be able to stop myself from doing things I'm not convinced you're ready for."

He could see her heartbeat at the base of her throat. It took everything in him not to lean forward and press his lips there.

"You didn't try to kiss me last night. I thought you'd changed your mind about making love to me."

Damn, she was sexy with her big green glittery eyes staring at him. "I don't flip-flop. I just wanted you to be sure you're ready for this—this changes things between us."

"Are you telling me you've never had sex for sex's sake before?"

"Sure, when I was young and stupid. I'm a grown man now, and I like to know I'll be welcome back before I go down that road. I don't do one night."

"I like the sound of that."

"Then make sure you're good and awake because I want full awareness for what I plan to do to you."

She sucked in a little burst of air. "Hold that thought."

She disappeared down the hallway, and he could hear the sink water running in the bathroom and the swish of her toothbrush.

He clasped his hands together and rested his elbows on his knees. The debate about whether or not this was a good idea was a lost argument at this point.

Nick wanted Sadie more than he needed air.

His pulse hummed when he saw Sadie standing there. Her wavy brown hair layered around her shoulders, wearing nothing but a towel wrapped around her and tied at the top.

"You want me, Nick?"

His chest hurt for how bad he needed to be inside her. His erection was already painfully stiff. "I think you already know the answer to that question."

"Then I'm all yours." She untied the knot in one quick motion, and the towel pooled at her feet.

Chapter 15

The pure beauty of her body, her sensuous curves, kept him rooted to his spot as she walked toward him. Her gaze never left his as she walked him to the couch and nudged him to sit down.

She stood in front of him then gripped his shoulders and pushed until he pressed against the backrest. "Dammit, Sadie. Are you determined to finish this before it gets started?"

She grinned, looking as if she understood and enjoyed the effect she had on him. "Something wrong?"

"Abso-freakin-lutely-not. Everything in my view couldn't be more perfect. But I do want this to last and you're making that very difficult for me."

She straddled him. "How about now?"

"Heaven." He gripped her waist as she rocked back and forth, fighting the urge to drive himself inside her.

He needed to remove his jeans, but she felt so damn incredible, he didn't want to move. Plus, truth be told, he liked allowing her to set the pace.

She leaned forward, her bare breasts skimming his chest, and he breathed in her floral soap scent.

The image of her in those boots, wearing jeans and her pale pink sweater, broke through his thoughts. He'd been wanting, no needing to touch her ever since that moment in his truck. Hell, if he was being honest, ever since that first day he'd met her at the bakery.

He smoothed his palm over her flat stomach, and then wrapped it around her sweet bottom. Electric impulse drilled through him. The need to be inside her caused an ache in his chest.

Patience.

"You're an amazing woman, Sadie," he whispered, "and incredibly beautiful."

A pink flush rose to her cheeks. Her green eyes darkened. Desire. "Then make love to me."

Better-sounding words had never crossed those pink lips in the time he'd known her.

He pressed a kiss to the hollow of her neck. Then, he lowered his head to her breastbone and feathered kisses there, making his way down to her pert breasts.

Kissing the tip of her breast, he slid his tongue up to her neck. He feathered a kiss on the small mole on her cheek. He found her mouth and groaned when she teased his tongue into her mouth. She nipped his bottom lip.

Little did she know, it was her turn to squirm. He slid his tongue in her mouth. He palmed her breast. With his other hand, he drew circles on her sex.

She moaned.

He pulled and tugged at her pointed peak.

Her eyes opened and the power of that one look almost knocked him back. She didn't need words to tell him she wanted him inside her. Right then.

"Patience."

Her cheeks were flush as he gripped the dimpled spot above her sweet bottom.

With her naked and warm body pressed up against him, he realized just how perfectly she fit him.

The feel of her bare, clean skin was enough to drive him to the brink even with his jeans on.

But he would force himself to wait, to savor every second of this until passion couldn't be held at bay anymore.

He thrust his tongue deep in her mouth, needing to taste every inch of her. She returned the intensity of his kiss.

With one arm wrapped around her waist, he pulled her body in tight against his until her heat pressed against his stomach. His hands wandered over every inch of her stomach until they rose to her full breasts. Her skin was soft.

Her wet heat was so close to his erection, his body hummed.

Patience.

He pushed up enough to sit, picked her up and carried her into the next room, where he placed her on the bed and dipped down to kiss her. She gripped his neck and pulled him on top of her.

He trailed kisses down her neck until his mouth found her breasts, roaming, as the tip of his tongue flicked the crest of her nipple before taking it in his mouth.

She moaned and gripped his shoulders.

"Just a minute," he said. His hands went to the button on his jeans, but her hands were already there, hungry, tearing button by button. Damn, he got so caught up in the moment, he almost forgot something. "Hold that thought."

He retrieved a condom from the wallet in his back pocket, then let his jeans drop to the floor.

"This is insane. I've never been with a more beautiful woman." With both knees on the bed, he leaned forward and his lips crushed down on hers.

He broke free long enough to rip open the condom package. Her hands were already around his shaft as he rolled the condom over his tip and moaned as she stroked him.

"I want you. Now."

"Then take me," she said. Her hands were on him again. Her fingers traced his jawline, down his chin, along his Adam's apple. "I have never wanted a man like I want you right now."

He eased her onto the bed. Before he could make another move, her legs wrapped around his midsection. He tensed as she guided him inside her.

He thrust, her body taking him in, and his control nearly shattered. He plunged deep inside her again and again, slowing his pace every time he neared the edge.

She greedily clutched at his back, pulling him deeper into her as their bodies molded together.

He thrust. Surged.

When her muscles clenched, released, exploded around him, he pumped harder as she bucked her hips and said his name over and over until he detonated.

He collapsed on top of her, careful not to overwhelm

her with his weight, needing to stay inside her, with her, in this moment, for as long as he could.

Nick's body still glistened with beads of water when he returned from the shower with nothing but a towel wrapped around his waist.

His cell buzzed. He located his jeans and retrieved it from his front pocket. "It's Meg."

"You better take the call." She patted the seat next to her, reaching out for his free hand.

He twined their fingers and took a seat.

"How's she doing?" He asked into the phone. His gaze locked on to Sadie's. "It's Riley."

She nodded.

"How far apart?"

"Fifteen minutes," Riley said.

He heard Meg in the background groaning and clamped his back teeth. "And the doctor doesn't think she should go to the hospital yet?"

"We're leaving my parents' house now. I don't care what the doctor says. Fort Worth is a long drive from Plano."

"Which hospital?"

"Presby."

Nick glanced at his watch. This time of morning traffic shouldn't be too bad. "I can be there in twenty minutes."

"I'll meet you there."

"Okay, man. Meg is saying she doesn't want you to come."

"Did I say I was planning on asking permission? Besides, what she doesn't know won't hurt her."

"Feel free to take your life in your own hands." Riley chuckled. "I'll call you as soon as we get there."

"Hell, I'll be waiting at the front door."

Sadie squeezed his hand before disappearing into the other room.

He presumed to get dressed. He could think of a few things he would've liked to have done while she was still almost naked on the couch. His hormones were overriding rational thought again.

When it came to Sadie, he had little control over either.

He ended the call with his brother-in-law.

Could he and Sadie have a future when this was all over? The very real notion she had a U.S. Marshal whose career, hell, life, depended on her not being alive to identify him pressed down on Nick.

Sadie stepped across the hall and he could see that she'd put clothes on and left the bathroom door open as she brushed her teeth.

If Nick could protect her, he might just be able to think about having a relationship with her. Or could he? She was scared to death of his constant companion, his Glock, and he wore a badge. The very badge he loved also prevented him from getting involved personally with her.

And yet, she'd broken through the shield protecting his heart. She'd cracked the armor…and he couldn't say he was especially sorry.

Chapter 16

"Change of plans today. I picked up a few supplies when I was out. Put these on." Nick held out a sweatshirt, wig and sunglasses. "Meg and Riley are on their way to the hospital."

"That's so exciting." Sadie tried on the black cropped hair, tugging at the sides until it felt right. "How do I look?"

He grinned, wrapped his arms around her waist and kissed the hollow of her neck. "Not bad."

He thrust his hips forward and she could feel his arousal.

Need welled deep inside her.

"I don't think you should start something you can't finish," she teased, enjoying the feel of his lips on her skin.

"You're probably right, but I wouldn't mind trying." His sexy smile tore at her heart. And her better judgment. Memories of those lips taunting and teasing other places on her body warmed her. And the feel of his arms around her. She could get used to him. Dangerous thinking for a woman who wanted a peaceful life in the country. No guns. No scary men. No hiding. And yet, he made her think having kids and a husband might not be such a bad idea someday. Maybe she could get another dog to keep Boomer company, too?

The life that everyone else took for granted made her heart ache for how badly she wanted it. Kids, a husband…a stable life were a world away.

A painful stab, like a bullet piercing bone, slammed into her ribs.

Seriously? Hadn't she learned to protect her heart any better than that? If her own family constantly disappointed her, wouldn't Nick do the same? She thought she'd gotten pretty darn good at keeping everyone at a safe distance. But here she was falling hard for Nick. The icing on the cake was that he wore a gun for a living.

Didn't she have any more sense than to fall in love with a man whose job would ensure many late nights of her wide awake worrying about him? A lifetime of fear?

And, yet, looking into those cinnamon, copperlike eyes melted her reserves every time.

They'd had incredibly hot sex. She couldn't argue that. Clearly, the bedroom would not be a problem for them.

But most of life was lived outside the sheets.

The big question would be did they have what it takes to make a relationship work with their clothes on? Or would two very important pieces of equipment get in the way? A badge and a gun.

She already knew the answer. Her body shook every time she was near either one.

What if he left the Marshals Service and got another job? a little voice inside her head asked.

And take away everything that was Nick?

No way would she ask. He was too good at what he did to think about him in another line of work. He saved innocent people. She would never be so selfish as to ask him to change.

She straightened her wig. "Ready?"

He groaned, nuzzling his face in her neck. "Just give me another minute."

"Okay, but you might miss the birth of one very important little person."

"You're beautiful when you're right." He skimmed his lips across her collarbone. "And you're sexy when you're thinking about others." He feathered kisses where her heart beat at the base of her throat. "And especially when you're looking out for me." His lips found hers, and he pressed a sweet kiss to her mouth.

She wanted to dissolve in his arms.

Bad idea.

He'd regret not being there for Meg.

"Keep this up and we won't get out of here," she said.

He grumbled, mumbled a curse word and pulled back. "We'll get back to this later."

"I'm planning to hold you to your word." She returned his smile.

"You, a couple of steaks on the grill, a cold beer and I might never want to leave." He finished getting dressed. He dipped his head under the running faucet to wet his hair then finger-combed it. He put on a ball cap and shades.

Her heart stuttered.

This was the Nick she remembered from the bakery. The one who'd first piqued her interest.

"Heard from Lucy yet?"

"No. I left her a voice mail. I'll check in with Luke once we get to the hospital."

Sadie slid her feet into her boots. She should hate them by now. Her heels might never recover from the blisters. But the hard leather was beginning to give. She was starting to wear them in and, heck, they were too awesome not to adore. They fit her to a T. Once the leather was worn in, the blisters would go away, too. She could definitely see herself becoming a Texan when this whole ordeal was behind her. Okay, she'd learned "real" Texans were Texas-born, but she could be a transplant. One of those people who may not have been born in Texas but got there as fast as they could.

Nick put on his shoes, twined their fingers and led her outside to the truck parked on the pad out front.

Sadie glanced down the street, her usual habit, checking for anything or anyone that looked out of place. Would there ever come a time when she didn't instinctively do this?

Two years of training had her watching shadows, checking cars and searching strangers' faces.

At a house four doors down there looked to be someone in the driver's seat of a small blue sport-utility. Could be nothing. A friend waiting outside for someone to run inside their house and grab something they'd forgotten.

Being snatched from the grocery store parking lot two years ago had taught Sadie to fear what was out in the open more than anything in the dark.

She squeezed Nick's hand and inclined her head toward the parked vehicle. "Think we need to be worried?"

"I saw that. We'll keep an eye on him," he reassured.

Traffic on Interstate 75 was almost at a crawl, but picked up once they merged onto President George Bush Turnpike, heading west. Nick took the Dallas North Tollway exit, heading north to Parker Road. Once he exited there, he made a left. A small white building came up quickly on the left. To the right was a strip mall. Beyond those, the three towers that made up Texas Health Presbyterian Hospital of Plano stood on the left.

"Did they say which tower?"

"The second, I believe."

He pulled into the parking garage and found a parking spot on the third floor.

"Doesn't seem like we had any company on the way." Thankfully, no blue sport-utility had followed them.

"Nope."

And, yet, Sadie had an uneasy feeling.

"You don't look relieved."

Most likely her alert system was set to high beam again. "It's probably nothing."

"Gut instinct has kept me alive more than once." Nick scanned the parking garage as they walked toward the white building.

An ambulance, sirens blazing, roared toward the emergency entrance.

Sadie's nerves were already stretched to their limits. The blare of the sirens caused her muscles to pull tighter with each step toward the elevator.

She caught herself judging every person who passed by, evaluating their threat. Being outside in daylight had her feeling vulnerable even though she wore a disguise.

Nick squeezed her hand reassuringly as they walked inside the building and to the elevators. He seemed to second-guess himself when he glanced at a metal door with a sign over it that read Stairs. "Let's take those instead."

"What floor are they on?"

"The third." He pulled out his phone and thumbed through his texts as the metal door *cu-clunked* behind them. He stalled on the first step. "She's in room three-fifteen."

They'd climbed one set of stairs when Nick's cell buzzed, indicating a text. He checked the screen. "It's from Riley."

Sadie's pulse increased. "What did he say?"

His eyes stayed on the screen for a long moment as though he needed a second for the words to sink in. He muttered a curse. "Men are in the room asking questions about me and he doesn't like it."

"What? How can that be?"

"Riley's telling us to get out of here." His jaw clenched.

"Wait a minute. Isn't this the break we need? Shouldn't we call the police? Have them arrested? Or at least hauled in for questioning?"

"For what?" He paused. "Asking questions in a hospital? If these guys are flashing badges, then local police aren't going to touch them."

"What about the envelope we found in the warehouse last night?"

"Inadmissible in court. We could go to jail for breaking and entering."

"Oh, right. I forgot."

"I need to check in with Smith. Let him know what's happening. And he damn well better be prepared to send extra resources to make sure nothing happens to my family."

He'd already turned around and started back down the stairwell when the door to the first floor flew open. He froze and ended the call before Smith could answer, biting out another curse word under his breath—the exact one Sadie was thinking.

Sadie followed Nick up the stairs as quietly as she could, fearing the people below would hear her heartbeat for how loud it hammered against her ribs.

She heard the unmistakable click of a bullet being loaded in a chamber. She bit down a gasp, staying as close to Nick as she could manage as he ascended the stairs.

Feet shuffled below, climbing closer. By the sounds of it, someone was in a hurry.

She and Nick had two floors on whoever was chasing them, but they were gaining ground fast.

Nick popped out on the seventh floor and immediately pressed the elevator button.

Hurry.

The elevator dinged and a set of doors opened. Nick rushed inside. "Get against the wall."

She pressed her back against the glass, saying a silent protection prayer.

The stairwell door flung open.

"This where they ditched?" a familiar-sounding voice asked. Did it belong to Burly?

Nick jammed his thumb on the L button a few more times.

Come on.

"I don't think so. I don't see anyone. Maybe one up?" another voice replied. Steroids?

The elevator door closed at the same time as the one leading to the stairs.

"You know who that was, don't you?" she asked.

"I do. They sure have come a long way from the cabin to find us," he said, staring at the screen on his phone intently.

"My thinking exactly. Is it possibly they work for the agency?"

"No. I'd know if they did. Those guys are hired."

She gasped. "You mean professional killers?"

He nodded. "We need to get to my truck and I need to get ahold of Smith. But I want to see who else comes out of the front door before we leave."

The elevator stopped at the second floor. Sadie's heart lurched to her throat.

Nick drew his weapon, and hid it behind his leg. Sadie went shoulder-to-shoulder with him, frighteningly aware of how close the gun was to her own leg, in order to shield the weapon from view. Her body started to shake.

Four or five people pushed in before the elevator doors closed again. A man in scrubs, two nurses and an older couple squeezed inside, making the small space cramped.

The lobby was a welcomed sight.

Nick walked quickly the few steps away from the elevator then broke into a run, not stopping until he was out the front door. He walked across the pathway to an uncovered parking lot and phoned Smith.

"Meg's in the hospital getting ready to have her baby. She had visitors. I need people on her, Smith. My life is one thing, but keep my sister safe."

Sadie only heard one side of the conversation, mostly

Nick stressing the need to provide adequate protection for his family.

He asked his boss to hold then checked a text message. "My brother-in-law says the men who stopped by gave names. They also claimed to be coworkers of mine."

By the time he closed the call, he'd relayed the message whoever visited Meg claimed to work with him said their names were Young and Turner.

Based on Nick's reaction, those identities didn't sit well with his boss.

"What did he say?" she asked as soon as Nick looked at her.

"It's impossible for Young and Turner to be here because they're on assignment in Virginia."

"He's sure they're there? I mean couldn't they say they were in one place but actually hop a plane and be here in a few hours?"

"Yeah." His gaze constantly shifted, scanning for possible threats. "But they didn't."

"What makes him so certain? I mean it's not as if someone follows you guys around checking out your every move."

"He knew because he'd just left them at breakfast. They had a meeting about the case they were working on. No way could they eat with him then make it here in an hour."

"Then clearly someone is getting away with impersonating marshals. How can that happen?"

"Jamison would have access to everyone's personnel records. All he'd have to do is find men who looked similar and then have their credentials faked."

"And his association with Grimes would give him access to a variety of known criminals and channels.

Men who would be good at pretending to be someone else when they needed to. Men who could fake government documents skillfully."

"Men who wouldn't be afraid to kill someone to get what they wanted." He finished for her.

Shock wasn't the word for what Sadie experienced. "Isn't it pretty brazen of them to come to the hospital like this? I mean they have to know Meg and Riley are cops."

"Why not? They've already gone to prison and fooled guards. Killed a U.S. Marshal. They're good at this and clearly comfortable with what they're doing."

"What did Riley say to them?"

"He told them I was driving in from Houston, and that I'd be there in two hours. He also asked them to stick around. He said they couldn't get out of there fast enough. He had no reason to detain them, so he had to let them go."

"Not to mention his wife's in labor, and he has no backup." Sadie pointed out.

"Even so, he would've done anything necessary to keep her safe. Even if that meant placing them under arrest."

"What was Smith's reaction to the news?"

"He has extra security coming. I'd like to stick around in case Riley needs me until they arrive." Stress gave way to a long face.

"I hate that you can't be there for Meg while she's in labor."

"Me, too. At least she has Riley with her. He said she probably wouldn't let me come inside, anyway. Something about not wanting to scare me off ever having children." His smile didn't look forced, but faded quickly.

"Who are we looking for?"

"For one, I'd like to know more about the two men who seem to be behind us every step of the way." He checked his messages. "Then there's the pair of men wearing dark suits. Riley said they should stick out."

Sadie studied each person as they came out of the turnstiles.

Five minutes passed before anyone fitting the description came out of the revolving doors of the main building.

"Looks like we have them." Nick switched his phone to camera mode and snapped a couple of pictures. "I'll send these to Smith, and we'll hope for a positive ID."

"You think they might be deputies?"

"Could be. If Jamison sent them and they're following his orders then it's possible they might not even know what he's really after. If they're known criminals, they'll show up in the database, and we'll get a hit." He sent the photos to his boss with a couple of clicks.

"We haven't seen Burly and Steroids. Where could they have possibly gone?"

"It's a big building with multiple exits. They could've gone out somewhere else, and we'd never know. Or they could be in the building. I should warn Riley." He fired off a text to his brother-in-law.

"Can't he detain those guys?"

"He needs to have probable cause." He studied the screen intently.

"Any word from Smith?"

"Not yet. It could take a while to get a match."

"Should we wait here for backup?"

"Let's see where these guys go first. We might want to follow them. At least get a good look at the license plate."

The men walked to a white sedan.

Nick repositioned. "Damn. I can't get a good look at the plate. Too many cars in the way."

He crouched low and moved behind another car, trying to get a better position.

Sadie saw a man in white shirt and black pants heading toward them. "Security's coming."

The radio squawked.

"Keep an eye on him." He moved up another couple of cars.

"He's heading right this way, Nick."

He dropped to his knees and fanned his hands out on the ground, feeling around. "Can you see them, babe?"

"Looking for something, sir?" the guard looked concerned.

"My keys." He felt around underneath a different car. "Dropped them."

The security officer bent down, placing his hands on his knees for support. He had to be close to fifty, and his belly prevented him from bending too far.

Sadie pointed toward the key Nick had dropped moments before. "That it?"

"Where?" He played the part perfectly.

"There. Near the grass by the front tire."

"Look at that. Sure is."

The officer stood to his full height, which looked to be five-foot-ten, as Nick rose to his and offered to shake hands.

"I'd be lost without her."

The officer smiled and nodded, shaking his head and walking toward the building. "I wouldn't be caught dead admitting that to mine. She'd never let me hear the end of it. But it's true."

Sadie turned in time to see the white sedan turn the corner onto Communications Parkway and disappear.

Nick muttered a curse. "You didn't happen to get that number, did you?"

"Nope. I didn't. And we wouldn't be able to catch them at this point, either, would we?"

He grumbled while he shook his head. "Not even if we ran to the truck. Besides, being in a hurry might cause us to make a mistake and be seen. Burly and Steroids might still be in the building."

It was most likely her danger radar overreacting again, but she didn't like the thought of those men being anywhere near Nick's pregnant sister.

This situation couldn't get more frustrating to Nick. If they went inside, where he wanted to be to watch over his sister, they risked Burly and Steroids seeing him. Jamison's camp had been led to believe Nick was nowhere around. His henchmen would be expecting him and Sadie to be on Interstate 45 heading north. They would most likely put some resources there.

Riley's knee-jerk reaction to throw them off the trail had been brilliant. Jamison wouldn't be happy waiting around for Nick to show up at the hospital. He'd send resources to cut him off and dispose of him long before he had a chance to make it to Plano. Jamison's life depended on getting rid of Nick and Sadie.

Spreading out Jamison's men improved Nick's odds greatly.

He pulled his cell from his pocket and informed Smith, so he could put resources on I-45. In exchange, he learned support should be arriving at the hospital any second.

Glancing at Sadie, he could see how stressed this situation had been on her. He wanted to reach out to her, to be her comfort, to take all her fear and anxiety away.

He hated that he couldn't.

Another part of him wanted to find Burly and Steroids, if only to force them to talk. He had a few other ideas of things he'd like to do to them, but jail sounded like a good enough option.

Leaving Sadie alone so he could track them was a bad idea.

Bringing her along wasn't an option.

He had no doubt if he was alone he would find them if they were still in the building. Two people would be harder to hide.

Sitting and waiting was a bitter cup of tea for Nick.

Yet, that was what he had to do.

Once he knew Meg, Riley and baby were safe, he could leave. Stashing Sadie at the safe house was his best bet until he heard back from Smith. His men were zeroing in on Jamison, and it wouldn't be long before they had a location.

Until then, Nick would be better off in hiding, too.

The last thing he wanted to do was lead Jamison to Sadie. She was the only one who could identify him as one of her abductors. They needed her statement against Jamison to be able to make an arrest. He had another more personal reason for keeping Sadie safe, but this was not the time to get inside his head about what that meant.

Without proof, Jamison would most likely get off scot-free if Nick and Sadie were killed. She was the only person who could identify him and put him away.

It was bad enough they had to deal with an out-of-control marshal, but Grimes was another story. He had a vested interest in seeing Sadie dead, too. He also seemed hell-bent on making sure she was erased for good. Dead would do it.

Nick's cell buzzed. Smith's name popped up on the screen. He showed it to Sadie before answering. "What's the word, Chief?"

"My men have arrived. It's safe for you and 'the battery' to leave." The boss must've realized Nick wouldn't leave the grounds until he knew his sister was out of danger.

"I appreciate this. You'll keep someone here until she checks out in a couple of days?"

"I'll send someone home with them if it means you won't worry. They'll have twenty-four-hour security. You have enough on your plate right now without wondering if your family's safe."

"What next?"

"I'm in the process of trying to attain a search warrant for Jamison's house. Sadie's word and the bank account might just be enough."

"Jamison lives in Dallas, I presume."

"Right."

Nick would like to be part of the guys serving that warrant, but he suspected the place would be empty. "He's smart enough to know better than to hide evidence at his house."

"I suspect you're right."

"Doesn't hurt to take a look, anyway," Nick conceded. "Keep me in the loop."

"You know I will."

Nick ended the call. "Back to the safe house."

Waiting made him want to go insane. He also wasn't thrilled by the fact he hadn't heard from Lucy.

He could see fear in Sadie's eyes when she looked at him and nodded. His muscles tensed. She shouldn't have to hide for the rest of her life. Just thinking about how afraid she'd been—how afraid she'd most likely be forever—stirred anger that pierced another hole in his armor.

Grimes needed to be behind bars. Jamison especially needed to be in a cell. And there were a few things he wanted to do to the both of them first that he was sure the agency wouldn't approve. And, yet, if he got his bare hands near them, he'd make sure they knew he'd been there.

He needed to tuck Sadie away until they found Jamison and made sure he couldn't hurt anyone again.

Sadie was quiet on the drive back to the safe house. Nick could feel fear radiating from her. He occasionally reached over to squeeze her hand, to reassure her.

He told her everything would be okay and that they'd find them first.

What he refused to tell her was that this had just become a high stakes game of hide-and-seek…and both of their lives depended on not being found first.

Chapter 17

Nick pulled onto the parking pad with the ever-present feeling of eyes watching him. His instincts didn't normally lead him down the wrong path, so he didn't ignore them.

Yet, scanning the houses, yards and vehicles parked on the street didn't reveal anything out of the ordinary. Kids were still in school, so the streets were quiet.

The winds had kicked up, typical late-November weather. It was noon but the clouds rolling in covered the sun, making it feel more like nightfall. In six hours, the sky would already be dark this time of year.

"Think it's going to rain?"

He shrugged as he exited the cab. "Never can be sure with Texas weather."

"One minute the sun's shining, the next it can be raining. I'd heard about the storms that come this time of year and how the wide skies open up and pour rain. The thunder that cracks right in your ear."

"I never minded a big storm. We can always use the rain." He caught a glimpse of something moving out of the corner of his eyes. He quickly moved next to Sadie, and realized, for the first time, she was trembling. Anger hit him faster than a bolt of lightning.

He put his body between her and whatever had moved. Might be nothing, but he knew better than to take chances.

Unlocking the front door, he urged Sadie inside. If someone knew where the safe house was, they could be waiting inside. He thought about the blue sport-utility that had been parked a few doors down earlier. He glanced over his shoulder in the general direction where it had been parked. The vehicle was gone.

Was it a coincidence?

Instinct told him not to take anything for granted.

Once inside, he hauled Sadie behind him and drew his gun. He leveled his weapon in front of him.

The lights were off. Without sunlight filtering in through the windows, the place was dark.

He had to take into account the possibility that Paul's relatives had come home early. The scenario was unlikely but had to be considered. "This is Marshal Campbell."

No one responded.

If someone was in the house, they didn't want to be found. Not yet.

Sadie's body shook from fear and probably cold, since the temperature had dropped twenty degrees in the past hour, and they didn't have coats.

With her pressed against his back, he felt every rigid muscle in her body. Everything in him wanted to take away that feeling for her. Make it go away forever.

From his vantage point at the front door, he could see the living room, kitchen and dining room. He swept the area. No surprises there.

The bathroom and pair of bedrooms yielded similar results. The laundry room in the hallway was clear.

Now to assess any threat outside.

He could leave Sadie inside where he was relatively sure she'd be safe. Or risk taking her outside with him. Leaving her alone could be exactly what Jamison or Grimes would want. Could someone be setting a trap?

On balance, bringing Sadie was a risk he had to take.

Nick moved to the big window in the living room, leaving the lights off.

He peered outside and waited. *Patience.*

A text came through. Everyone had checked in but Lucy.

Movement around the back of Luke's truck caught his attention.

This was no coincidence.

"Stay behind me. Don't move unless I do."

Her eyes were wide, but she nodded.

He moved to the door leading to the small backyard. There was enough of a glow from the lamps across the alley for him to see lines for clothes and winter melon plantings that led from the house to the back fence. The gate was on the opposite side of the house as the parking pad. Nick slid outside with Sadie practically glued to his back.

Gusts of winds blasted, sending leaves thrashing through the air. Tree branches bent and snapped. A big storm was brewing.

Nick dropped down on all fours and crawled toward the front of the house, his shoulder scraping against the building as he moved, urging Sadie to follow along. He stopped at the corner, checking the building next to them, across the street and then behind them.

Rain pelted his face and made it hard to see clearly.

Wind whipped sideways, and a cracking noise split the air. Thunder.

Nick needed to get a visual of the front of the building and see what was going on. With his weapon drawn, he peeked around the building. He was greeted with a spray of bullets.

He planted on his chest, dropping flat on his stomach with Sadie on his heels. He fired a shot toward the figure moving behind the truck as the guy backed away, using the building as cover. His bullet went a little wide and to the right. Between the darkness and the wind, he'd have a difficult time getting off a good shot. *Patience.*

The rustle of someone running toward them came from the yard behind. Stay put and they'd be trapped.

"Listen to me carefully. We're going to have to make a run for it."

Sadie's mouth moved to speak but no words came out. She had been freezing just walking in the house. She had to be in bad shape by now. She'd warm up when she got her blood pumping again. He needed her to move when he gave the signal.

He also knew exactly what she was thinking. "I want you to go first so I can cover you. Once you pop up and get your footing, don't stop running. Got it?"

"Run where?" Panic brought her voice up an octave. To her credit, she fixed her gaze in the direction he pointed.

"Away from the sound of fire."

She nodded.

"On my count. One. Two. Three."

By the time he said the last number, she was to her feet and sprinting across the neighbor's yard.

He covered her, firing a warning shot directly toward the location where bullets had come from.

A figure moved behind the truck, firing one shot after the other. He had to be using a Glock or Beretta or a Sig—there were lots of choices for an automatic—as he dashed toward the tree in the front yard, ducking and rolling to avoid Nick's shot. The guy knew what he was doing. Could it be Jamison?

If so, maybe Nick could end this right there. Arrest him. Put the bastard in jail where he belonged.

Not a chance, a little voice in the back of his head said. Jamison was in too deep. He wouldn't go out willingly. Not after coming this far or going to these lengths to protect his investments. If the supervisor was around, he was there for one purpose. Erase Nick and Sadie.

Nick discharged his weapon again.

The male form used the tree in the front yard as cover. He wasn't running away from anyone, so much as he was running toward Sadie.

Nick heard voices in the backyard. Two, maybe three men were coming from behind. There were too many for Nick to fight off for long, even with his second clip. He was in over his head. He needed to send out a distress call.

Nick fished his phone out of his pocket to call for backup at the same time he heard a shot. Shock overwhelmed him. Was he hit?

He glanced down and saw blood. He made a move to stand, but everything went blurry.

Someone yelled, "Got him!"

Sirens blared.

Could he hide? He belly-crawled toward the vegetable bin he'd spotted earlier. His limbs were weak. His head spun. Where was Sadie? She'd disappeared after she turned the corner around the neighbor's house. Was someone there? Waiting?

No. Couldn't be. She would have screamed. She didn't. And that meant she'd made it to the shops. She could hide there until Nick could find her.

He hauled his heavy frame inside the bin, closing the lid as he heard footsteps nearing. Another flash of light followed by a crack of thunder sounded overhead.

It was only a matter of time before they would find Nick. He'd left a trail of blood, leading to the bin.

"I saw her turn this way," one of the bastards said. He couldn't be more than five feet from Nick.

His muscles tensed, ready for a fight, then everything went black.

Sadie ran. Her thighs burned and her lungs clawed for air, but she dragged in another deep breath and pushed forward.

Footsteps were close, closing in, and she had no way to defend herself if the attacker caught up.

Every gunshot blast sent her pulse rocketing into the stratosphere.

"Please, God, let it be Nick behind me." She knew he wasn't there but repeated the prayer, anyway.

There were too many men for Nick to take on by himself.

Thunder cracked, and Sadie let out a yelp before she could squash it.

If someone was behind her, chasing her, wouldn't that mean they'd stopped Nick?

Her mind screamed, *"No!"*

She expected fear to grip her, to paralyze her. Instead, white-hot anger roared through her veins.

If they did anything to Nick, hurt him because they were looking for her…

She wanted to scream.

Maybe she could make it to the strip mall, ditch them and circle back to Nick. The possibility of him lying on the sidewalk, alone, in a pool of his own blood sent anger licking through her veins. If she could get to him—get help—surely paramedics could save him. *Cling to positive thoughts,* she reminded herself. Nick was good at his job. He knew how to handle men like these. He would survive.

She dashed behind one of the houses that backed up to the lot and scrambled up the brick wall separating the neighborhood from retailers.

Nothing bad could happen to Nick. She couldn't allow herself to go there mentally…he would be fine, and they would be together.

If she could get inside one of the stores, she could hide. She still had her cell phone. She could get a message to Smith. He'd send reinforcements. *Stay alive, Nick.*

The reality of him staying back there, alone, to give her a chance to escape pressed down on her chest, making breathing even more difficult. His act of valiance was commendable. Except she couldn't face losing the only man she'd ever loved. Love?

Yeah. Love.

No man had ever made her feel the way he did.

She pushed on.

Rounding the corner to the strip mall, she glanced

back in time to see a large man hopping over the brick wall. Not a good sign that he'd gotten past Nick.

Did that mean...?

No.

She refused to think negative thoughts or let fear overtake her. She needed a clear head.

Sadie kept her feet moving forward even though her heart wanted to turn around and find him. He'd said run. He'd told her not to look back. He'd saved her life.

She wouldn't repay him by getting caught if she had anything to say about it.

Turning the last bend to the storefronts, she glanced across the parking lot. The terra-cotta warriors standing sentinel had men ducking behind them.

She checked behind her. Another minute and the man chasing her would catch up.

Sadie couldn't allow that to happen.

In a sea of black-haired people, she was grateful for the wig. The fact she was a few inches taller than almost everyone else made her easy to spot...not so good.

Luckily, there were lots of shoppers. She pushed through them, keeping as low a profile as she could. When she'd made it past a barbershop and a restaurant, she spotted a supermarket. Perfect.

It was in the middle of the shopping center, but if she could make it there, she could disappear in the aisles. Maybe even slip out the back door, which would lead to the loading dock. She could circle her way back to Nick. He was alive. She refused to think otherwise. He had to be worried about her by now.

Nick was fine. She would find him. They'd get through this.

She'd testify again in a heartbeat if it meant she

and Nick could live out the rest of their lives in peace. Maybe even together?

A chest pain so strong it nearly brought her to her knees pierced her.

For a split second, she almost thought she'd been hit by a bullet.

The agony in her chest, she realized, came from knowing deep down that something had happened to Nick.

Otherwise he would be coming for her.

She had to know what happened. What if he lay there, bleeding, and she could help him? Could she get to him in time?

Sirens wailed and her heart stuttered as she made it to the grocery store.

She pulled the cell Nick had given her in Creek Bend from her back pocket. The one she was only supposed to use if he wasn't there—the one she wasn't supposed to need—and hit the only other name in the contacts as she bolted toward the stockroom.

Smith's phone ran into voice mail. "This is Sadie Brooks. We're in trouble…"

A few more steps and she would be able to hide among the boxes of food waiting to be stocked.

A few more steps and she had options.

A few more steps and she could make it to freedom.

Sadie pushed her legs, full force, ignoring the cramp in her calf.

The set of double doors was in reach.

They both flew open at exactly the same time.

There stood Burly.

Chapter 18

Instinct kicked in the moment Burly clamped her in his meaty grip. Sadie wheeled around, trying to break free.

He grinned and tightened his hold on her, forcing her to face him.

She grabbed two fists full of his shirt at chest level, screamed and pivoted her body, sticking her leg out to trip him using his own body weight against him.

He broke into a laugh as he widened his stance. "You think a little thing like you can take me down?"

The leg wheel technique had failed against his two-hundred-plus pounds.

"Help me, somebody," she pleaded.

The small crowd of Asian onlookers dispersed quickly, diverting their gazes away from Sadie.

No one would make eye contact.

Burly hauled her into the stockroom before she could

get her mental bearings again. Fists like pit bull jaws locked around her upper arms.

She bent as low as she could, fisted her hands and in one quick motion burst toward the ceiling, breaking free from his hold.

Before he could snatch her again, Sadie wheeled around and exploded toward the metal doors, toward freedom.

Certain she could outrun Burly, hope ballooned in her chest. If she could escape, she could find Nick.

Just shy of reaching the doors, they sprang open.

Steroids.

Sadie screamed a curse as her forward momentum forced her to run smack into his chest. Hopelessness clawed at her. *Not happening. Not again.*

They'd taken away her life before. She'd had to separate from Boomer because of them. They may have killed Nick. She would not go down without a fight.

Rage, not fear, burned hot through her veins.

"In a hurry?" Steroids coughed, closing his arms around her as she kicked and screamed.

This time, she would fight back.

Burly must've drawn his gun. Cold metal pressed to the side of her head, and her arms went limp at the memory of what had happened before.

Give up and they win.

Those bastards wouldn't get the satisfaction. She leaned forward and bit Steroids in the chest as hard as she could.

"Bitch!" He pushed her back a step until she slammed into Burly, whirled her around and tied her hands behind her back.

Sirens grew louder. Thank God, someone had called the police.

Maybe she could stall long enough for the cops to save her?

They dragged her a few steps toward the back door. She made her body go limp.

A blow below her left cheek made her eye feel as if it might pop out of its socket. She spit blood.

Tires squealed out back.

The cops?

No. Couldn't be. There'd be sirens.

Realization crashed down on her, squeezing her lungs. Her heart sank.

The getaway vehicle had just arrived.

Let them take her out of that market, and she may as well be dead.

Sadie kicked and screamed, but they hauled her hands tighter and kept dragging her.

Steroids stuffed a piece of cloth in her mouth, muffling her cries.

Tears burned down her cheeks as fury detonated inside her.

Another ten feet and they could take her anywhere they wanted, do anything they wanted to her. The ICU would be a gift this time. She knew with everything inside her if they got her out the door this time, she'd end up in the morgue.

Her body railed against the bindings on her wrists.

Instead of feeling fear, she felt...resolve.

They could take away her body. They could do anything they wanted to her physically. They could end her life and erase her existence. But while she had breath in her lungs, they would not control her mind.

She felt herself being hauled up and tossed into the back of the sport-utility. Burly got in on one side, Steroids the other. There were two men in the front. The one on the passenger's side was bleeding, losing a fair amount of blood. He held a blood-soaked T-shirt to his left-arm triceps.

She memorized every detail of their faces before the two in the backseat forced her onto the floorboard.

If, no *when,* she escaped, she would testify against the whole lot of them. She would ensure these men were locked away forever. They would not hurt another soul.

Moving her jaw back and forth, she was able to get her tongue behind the cloth to force it out of her mouth.

She remembered sticking her cell phone in her right front pocket. Could she get to it without them noticing?

With her hands tied behind her back, it would be challenging. Could she stretch far enough?

Think. Think. Think.

Lying on her left, facing toward the back, pretty much ensured they'd see her trying to reach into her pocket. Maybe she could distract them somehow? Or bait them into rolling her over to her other side.

"You're a bunch of idiots if you think you'll get away with this. A U.S. Marshal is right behind me. He knows who you are. He knows who your boss is. And he'll find me. When he does, you're all going to jail where you belong."

"I don't think so," Burly said.

A glance passed between them that parked a boulder on Sadie's chest. *Oh. God. No.*

Nothing could happen to Nick.

And, yet, she knew he'd have to be shot or dead not to have come after her already. He hadn't made an attempt to reach her. Her cell hadn't vibrated. No one had called her name or ambushed the men who'd abducted her.

Her heart lurched, threatening to lock up and stop beating.

And let those bastards win? She didn't think so.

She had to reach out to someone.

If she was able to palm her cell—and that was a pretty big if—she'd have access to Smith. For a brief moment, she wondered if Smith had put a tracer on her phone. Maybe he was tracking her right now?

A little voice inside her head reminded her that wouldn't happen. Smith would have given them an untraceable phone. He'd been specific about not wanting to know where they were. It was a safeguard. He'd do it to protect them.

She kicked up at Burly, connecting with his shin.

"Dammit," he grumbled. He tied her ankles together, making it impossible to kick again.

She fought back, not because she thought she'd win, but in order to sell switching positions so she could roll on the other side and access her phone.

By the time they finished, she was facing the opposite direction. On her right side, she could hide the fact she was slipping her phone out of her pocket.

Tears pricked the backs of her eyes.

Despair was an ache in her chest. Sorrow for Nick threatened to suck her under like a riptide and spit her out into the deep.

Before she could say another word, the cloth was being jammed into her mouth again. This time, they tied a strip of material around her head to secure her gag.

Sadie couldn't afford tears.

She had to keep herself calm and force herself to believe that Nick was out there, somewhere, making his way back to her.

Every movement hurt. The bindings around her wrists tightened as she tried to angle her hands toward her right front pocket.

With two fingers, she managed to grasp the corner of her cell well enough to slide it free. She scooted forward, managing to block it with her hip. The phone was already set to vibrate mode. She switched to mute, touched the second name on her contact list, Smith, and covered the speaker with her finger, just in case.

"Where are you taking me?" Her words were muffled by the gag. She knew full well these guys wouldn't hand over the answer easily.

"Someplace no one will hear you when you scream," Burly said.

Nick blinked his blurry eyes open. Darkness surrounded him. He couldn't quite put his finger on why he had the urge to run. And what the hell was up with the hammering between his temples?

His body ached. His knees jammed into his face. There were hard walls all around him.

Where was he?

He felt around on his head for bumps, located a couple.

Memories flooded him, coming back all at one time, as if someone had unlocked the gates and sprung open both doors.

"Sadie."

He tried to kick. Only managed to thump his lip with his knee when he moved. He was inside some kind of compartment. No signs of light either meant it was nighttime, or the storm still hadn't passed. The place was airtight.

Rocking back and forth, he tried to free his arms.

Thoughts of the gun battle broke through his mind. He'd told Sadie to run. He'd known they were outnumbered, but he'd tried to get the attention on him and allow her to escape.

He knew they were both in trouble when he saw the shooter immediately give chase.

The vegetable bin. He'd made it. Must've hid him long enough for the police to arrive and scare off Jamison and his men.

Nick felt around. He'd wedged himself inside in a position that was impossible to get out of.

There was no escape.

He heard a familiar voice.

Paul?

Shouting to his friend was a risk. Nick couldn't be sure how long he'd been in that box. Could be minutes or hours. The cops could've come and gone, and so could Grimes or Jamison.

Nick listened intently through the pounding in his temples, straining to hear if there were other voices.

A neighbor must've phoned the police after hearing gunfire.

When he was reasonably certain Paul was alone, he shouted.

"Paul," Nick repeated, louder this time. Shouting made everything hurt, and his head feel as if it might explode. He ignored the pain. Sadie was in trouble. He had to get out of this box and find her.

"Paul!"

Nick heard sounds outside.

"Who is that? Who's here?" Paul's voice trembled.

"It's me. Nick. I need your help to get me out of here."

"Nick?" came the trepid response.

"Open the door, Paul. It's me."

Light split what was left of Nick's head. Yet, it was welcomed.

"What the heck happened to you? How'd you end up in my aunt's vegetable bin?"

"What time is it?" Nick asked, trying to muscle his way out of the container.

"Here. Let me help you."

Where was Sadie? "The woman I was with earlier. Where is she?"

"I don't know. She's not here," Paul said, offering a hand up.

Nick took it and, with a push, broke out of the small container he'd forced himself in. He scanned the area.

"The police are out front. They're asking a lot of questions. I told them I don't know what happened. My neighbor called me when he heard the guns. The old guy kind of freaked out. Called the police, too."

"Did they arrest anyone?" If the police were still there, then Sadie couldn't be too far.

"No one here. My neighbor said he saw everybody run. I didn't expect you to be here, either. I jumped when I heard your voice. That's for sure."

"Which way did they go?" He remembered telling Sadie to run, some of his thoughts were still jumbled, and he'd already lost precious time. He didn't want to risk going off in the wrong direction while his brain was still scrambled.

"The old guy said she went this way." Paul inclined his head toward the left.

"Good. Now do me a favor, and go get the police." Nick needed as many hands on this case as he could get. He checked his pockets for his cell.

His legs cramped.

He tried to walk, but they gave.

Paul grabbed Nick's arm in time to keep him from losing balance and landing on the ground.

"You wait right here, my friend. I'll get the police."

"I lost my cell. It might be on the side of your house." He was grateful to be alive, but what about Sadie?

With him out of the picture, they could do whatever they wanted to her.

Maybe she'd escaped?

Not likely. There were too many men. Jamison must've brought everyone to this fight.

Damn, Nick needed his cell. He needed to make contact with Smith.

The thought of anyone hurting Sadie was like an acid burn on his skin.

A uniformed officer approached. "I need to see some ID, sir."

Nick produced his badge and gave a statement.

"Nick," Paul shouted from the other side of the fence. He burst through. "I found it. These belong to you?"

He held out a cell and a gun.

"Looks like mine." His Glock felt right in his hand. He checked his cell. A dozen missed calls from Smith. "I need to check in with my boss."

The officer nodded.

Smith answered immediately.

"Is she alive?" Nick asked.

"Someone activated her cell phone and used it to call me. I believe it was her."

"Any idea where she is?"

"No. I can tell she's in some type of vehicle. She asked the question of where she was being taken and a man replied they were taking her where no one would hear her scream. It was tough to make out her words. Sounded like something was covering her mouth." He paused. "They could be taking her to a field out in the middle of nowhere for all we know. Without GPS on that phone, I can't track her."

Nick's brain immediately kicked into gear. "There's a place I can think of that no one would hear her scream. The warehouse."

The sounds of fingers flying across a keyboard came through Nick's line. "My closest man is a half hour away."

"I can be there in fifteen minutes."

"Nick," Smith said. Nick didn't like the sound of his voice when he said it. "They've sent word through one of my informants that they've got Lucy."

Nick ground out a curse. "Can you confirm?"

"I spoke to your brother Luke and she hasn't checked in or answered her phone. Doesn't mean they have her. I just can't confirm one way or the other. They're threatening to drop her body off below the Ferris wheel ride in Fair Park."

Nick's knees buckled. The officer held him steady. "I go to Fair Park, and they'll kill me and Sadie. I go to Sadie and they'll kill Lucy."

"If they have her."

Was it a risk he was willing to take? Jamison clearly knew how much Nick loved and protected his family.

"I can send people to either place, or both. It's your call," Smith said quietly.

Could Sadie already be dead? No. They'd use her to bring Nick out. As soon as they got to him, they'd kill her.

His mind clicked through other possibilities. If he went to Lucy, they'd be ready for him. As soon as they got him, they'd kill Sadie.

He had one advantage. "They don't know that I know about the warehouse. That's where they'd take Sadie. I go to Lucy, and we're all dead."

His stomach lining braided. Make the wrong call and two of the people he loved more than anything in the world would be dead.

"Send your people to Fair Park, but have them wait for my word."

"Got it."

Ending the call, Nick locked gazes with the officer. "I need a ride."

The man in uniform was already bolting toward his squad car.

Running sent a wave of nausea rippling through Nick. He ignored it and pressed on. The thought of anyone hurting Sadie or Lucy sent him to a dark mental place.

He forced all thoughts out of his head that he might be too late.

En route, he bandaged his gunshot wound using supplies from the officer's first-aid kit. They'd split his shoulder with a bullet. He packed gauze on it to stem the bleeding, and secured it with tape.

"No chance you'll let me investigate this lead after I drop you off at the hospital?"

"None whatsoever."

"Then I'll have an ambulance waiting a block away."

"No sirens. I don't want to give these scumbags any warning," Nick said.

The officer nodded before calling it in.

With lights blazing, the cop beat the time by two minutes. He'd cut the lights a block away. "I'll take the front entrance."

"You already know this, but these men are armed, and they're not afraid to shoot an officer. Be careful." Nick hopped out of the car before it came to a complete stop.

He moved to the back of the building, fighting the pain and nausea threatening to buckle his knees. There was a beige sport-utility parked in the back of the building.

Crouching low, he made it to the rear of the vehicle. His gun drawn, he raised high enough to see through the dark window. The vehicle was empty. He moved to the side.

Whoever sat on the passenger's side sure lost a lot of blood. The thought this could be Sadie's blood cut through him. He bit back a curse.

Could belong to anyone. Nick had fired quite a few shots at the jerks, he reminded himself.

A thought nearly leveled him.

Was she even here?

He canceled the thought. This was the most logical place to take her. She had to be inside. He would find her and give her life back to her. A life with him? The thought of opening himself up to that kind of potential pain usually almost flattened Nick.

Not when it came to Sadie. She was different.

Yet, no matter how strong Nick's feelings were, he couldn't ask her to spend the rest of her life waiting up nights and wondering if he'd be coming home. She deserved so much more. Could he give her everything?

A piece of him wished he could.

He loved her. And because he did, he planned to give her something she could only have without him. Peace.

The bay door was half-closed, providing an opportunity to slip into the back of the warehouse.

Breeching the building was easy.

Too easy?

Nick might be walking into a trap.

The main floor of the warehouse was empty.

He glanced up a small flight of stairs into the office.

Several men were there.

His heart raced when he saw her. Sadie. She was there. In the upstairs office.

There were too many men for him to take on, even with the officer who was making his way through the front of the building as backup.

Two against five. Grimes was there. As was Jamison. There were three others in the office.

Nick heard a door open to his left. He pressed his back against the wall and eased toward the sound. A bathroom?

Two against six. He liked those odds even less.

Burly walked out, zipping his pants, his gun holstered.

Nick hit him in the back of the head so hard, he knocked Burly unconscious, catching him on the way down.

The move took almost all of Nick's strength.

He leaned against the wall and took a deep breath.

Glancing up, Nick saw the officer moving toward him. The officer inclined his chin, moving silently.

When he approached them, he pulled out handcuffs. Nick hesitated, almost unsure who those were meant for. But the officer went right to work on Burly.

Five to two increased the odds. Sadie was a fighter. Maybe he should count her as a third.

The officer grabbed the scruff of Burly's neck and hauled him outside.

He returned a moment later. "He's not waking up anytime soon," he whispered. "And if he does, he's not going anywhere."

"Good job. And thanks."

"What do you want to do next?"

The correct answer would be to wait for backup. As long as the men in that room gave him time, Nick would take it. They make a move toward Sadie, and game on. "Keep an eye on them until more men arrive."

He motioned the officer to follow him.

They made it up the stairwell without giving away their position.

The sight of a gun aimed at Sadie's head forced Nick's hand.

He burst into the room, hoping like hell they would believe Burly was returning from the restroom. "I'm Marshal Campbell. You're all under arrest."

Catching them off guard gave him the advantage. Grimes redirected his weapon toward Nick, but he'd already leveled his and fired.

The officer came in behind Nick, weapon raised.

Steroids put his hands in the air, as did the other pair of men in the room.

"You think you can arrest me?" Jamison aimed his weapon at Sadie.

If Nick fired, Jamison might pull the trigger out of reflex.

Sadie would be dead.

She looked up at Nick, and he expected to see fear in her big green eyes, and he did. But he also saw anger and determination. Good. He could work with that.

If she could distract Jamison, Nick could make a move. Could he signal her somehow?

Her gaze was intent on him. He glanced from her to Jamison's knees.

She gave a slight nod. Bent over on all fours, with Jamison standing over her, she dove into his legs.

He buckled. Nick surged toward Jamison, knocking him a couple of steps backward and away from Sadie.

Gunfire split the air as Nick landed on top of his target and wrestled for control of the weapon. Jamison threw a jackhammer of a punch, connecting with Nick's nose. Blood spurted.

Nick counterpunched, his fist slamming into Jamison's jaw.

Jamison bucked and rolled, causing Nick to lose his grip on Jamison's wrist. Nick adjusted, popping to his knees. He squeezed powerful thighs to hold Jamison, facedown, in place.

Blood poured down Nick's shirt as he cuffed the snake.

Shock overtook Nick as he realized the blood was his.

Once Jamison was secure, Nick folded over to the sounds of officers rushing downstairs. The one who'd breeched the building with him stood over Jamison, his gun aimed at his temple, as Nick rolled over onto his side, fighting the nausea and fatigue gripping him.

Damn.

He was shot? He immediately thought of Sadie. She was safe now.

The next thing he knew, she was over him, tears streaming down her beautiful cheeks.

"Stay with me, Nick," she begged. The desperation in her voice was palpable. Almost enough to force him to come back to her.

She was safe.

What about Lucy?

As the scene in front of him played out in slow motion, he watched officers handcuff the dirtbags. One of them moved to Nick's side and held his cell phone to his ear. "Someone wants to speak to you."

"Nick? It's Lucy. I'm okay."

Relief flooded him. Sadie was safe. Lucy was okay. Nothing else mattered.

All he wanted to do was close his eyes and go to sleep.

Sadie's voice became distant. Her pleas for him to stay awake faded.

Nick closed his eyes and allowed darkness to claim him.

Nick woke with a start.

He glanced around the stark white room. His vision was blurry. Where was he?

He tried to push up, unwilling to admit the fear creeping through his system, its icy tendrils closing around his heart.

The case was closed, and he'd most likely never see

Sadie again. The thought caused worse pain than the bullet hole in his shoulder. A few stitches, a little physical therapy, and he'd eventually heal from that. Being without Sadie for the rest of his life put a hollow ache in his chest he'd never recover from.

"Nick?" the voice sounded uncertain and afraid.

Sadie?

He forced his eyes to stay open through the burn and glanced around the room. She was already to the side of the bed before his eyes could focus properly.

"How do you feel?" she asked, reaching out to touch his face.

The sight of her quieted his worst fear—the fear he'd never look into those beautiful eyes again and tell her just how much she meant to him.

"Dizzy. Nauseous." *Relieved.*

"You lost a lot of blood when you were shot," she said. "You must be in pain. Let me call the nurse."

Of course, he just realized, he was in the hospital. But he didn't want the nurse. He had everything he needed right next to him. Sadie.

He covered her hand with his, preventing her from pushing the call button. The whole scenario came back to him in a flood. The warehouse. Grimes. Jamison. "How long have I been out?"

"Two days."

"You've been here the whole time?"

Her cheeks flushed as she nodded. "Luke sneaks Boomer in every chance he gets."

"Tell me what happened."

"Grimes is dead. Jamison shot you. They arrested him, and he's going away for a very long time. So are the others in the warehouse. A few more of his men were arrested at Fair Park."

"And Lucy?"

"She's fine. Calls every hour to check on you, though." Her smile warmed his insides.

"And Meg?"

"She had a little boy."

He couldn't stop himself from reaching out and touching her beautiful face. "You've been keeping track of everyone?"

"I knew you'd want to know as soon as you woke up."

"How's Boomer?"

"He's keeping Gran company at the ranch. She texts me pictures of him every hour." She laughed.

"I remember what you did in the warehouse. I'm proud of you." His chest filled with an emotion that felt a hell of a lot like pride.

She leaned into his palm, and then kissed his hand.

"You been here the whole time?"

She nodded. "There's nowhere else I want to be."

He couldn't believe the love of his life was sitting right there. It would be better if they were somewhere else besides the hospital for what he needed to say. He wished they were somewhere romantic. He needed to ask her something, and he wanted everything to be perfect.

He canceled the thought.

Fact was there would never be a better time than now. "I need you to know that I've fallen hard for you."

He was rewarded with a bright smile. She leaned over and pressed a kiss to his lips. He kept her close when he whispered, "I love you."

She kissed him again, with more enthusiasm this time.

"I love you, Nick Campbell."

This time, he wouldn't be stupid enough to let Sadie walk out that door without knowing exactly what she meant to him. He had no intention of repeating his past mistakes.

He knew what he wanted for the rest of his life, and he wanted Sadie.

"I'd prefer to do this on one knee, but I'm guessing that would cause a whole host of people to come rushing through that door…"

She gasped, tears streaming down her cheeks.

"I don't have a ring to offer you right now. But I sincerely pray my heart and the promise of forever will be enough. Sadie Brooks, will you marry me?"

The minute she took to answer felt like an eternity.

She nodded through her tears. "Yes. I will marry you, Nick Campbell. I want very much to be your wife."

"And I want to be your protector for the rest of our days."

* * * * *

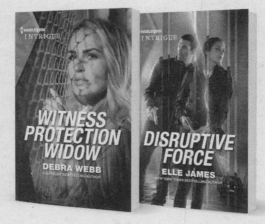